ELDERMYST SERIES

Court of Emerald Dreams

H. WULF

Author's Note

Hello Readers,

Diving into the pages of this enchanting book feels like stepping into a world of magic and fae - a realm I wish I could journey to for a while. A world that I truly loved writing about. Despite the haunting themes of past death and mental health struggles, the characters' resilience shines through, reminding us of the strength within us. Let this story be a beacon of hope, a reminder that even in the darkest of times we will get through. I truly hope you fall into a magical world and love these characters just as much as I do!

With lots of love and magic,

H. Wulf

To my amazing husband. You have been so supportive of all my crazy endeavors. I would never have had the courage to write this book if it were not for you.

To all my readers. You are amazing and I'm honored to have the love and support from you all! Thank you so much!

Contents

"The whispers of the wind and the songs of the forest guide my soul."

Ancient Emerald saying

Glossary

People:

- Adilyn – (ad-i-lyn)

- **Iridessa** - (ir-i-des-sa) radiant, colorful, ethereal

- Corian – (Kor-ee-an) – stone

- **Elouan** - (EH-luw-en) light

- Keijo (KAY-yo) Fae, elf

- Zara (Zar-ah) radiance

Places:

- **Etheria** - (ethe-ria) – town

- Solonia (So-low-nee-a) – Court

- Numaria (new-mari-a) – Country

Things:

- **Arion** - (are-i-on) the better one, the braver one (He probably thinks he is by far the greatest one)

- Aoife – (EE-fa) beauty (creature)

- Pterippi – (te-rip-eye) winged horse

- Keasi (ki-a-see) (monster)

Prologue

Tonight is a chilly night. Winter is starting to settle in the quaint town of Claywood. The cool breeze seeps into my bones, causing me to shiver. I need to be as quiet as possible and as quick as possible. I don't want to wake the sleeping bundle in my arms, nor do I want her to get a cold.

Everything has happened so fast. The war has turned our lives upside down in a matter of days, and I feel so lost and full of grief. My best friend is gone. She is gone. They ripped her from my life in a way that I don't think I will ever recover from. Memories flood into my mind from that fatal day. Iridessa told me this outcome was possible, but I didn't want to listen. I didn't want to accept that my best friend might not make it. She was so brilliant, ensuring she had a plan for every possibility. I shudder at the thought of her. A silent tear runs down my cheek—cold, biting at my skin where the drop leaves its path. Now was not the time to contemplate the what-ifs and the what could be. I must be strong. I must do this for her. I know my duty and will fulfill it, no matter what.

I creep through the town unseen, clutching the tiny being close to me. I could see my destination up ahead. I quickly make my way to where I had been instructed to go. I approach the house and sneak up the stairs as quietly as possible, trying not to bring attention to myself. I must get this mission done. So much is riding on me and this mission right now.

I look down at the little bundle sleeping in my arms.

"My dear, you will be reunited with your people and land someday. But until then, they bid you a farewell," I whisper, kissing the baby's forehead. I set her down in front of the door, bundled tightly. I stroke her face one last time, inhaling sharply as I straighten. I ring the bell, then hurry down the stairs to hide behind a tree on the front lawn so no one can see me. I hold my breath. Part of me is screaming to run back, grab her, and take her with me, but the other part knows that Iridessa wanted this for a reason, even if I don't understand.

I crouch down, making sure that I can't be seen. There would be too many questions that I can't answer if I'm spotted. Leaving her here is how it's supposed to be; for now, this is the plan I was instructed to follow, even if it breaks my heart.

I send a silent prayer to whoever will listen that someone is home and will hear the doorbell. I peek towards the door behind the tree, the darkness covering me. I see lights turning on inside the house. That is a good sign. The front door slowly creaks open. A man pops his head out, looking around for the culprit of the doorbell ringing. He must not have seen what he expected because he opens the door and steps outside. His foot brushes the swaddled baby, and his head immediately snaps down.

"Until we meet again, my dear Alona," I whisper into the darkness and sneak into the night.

Chapter One

Normal Life

ADILYN

Mondays drag on for what seems like an eternity, especially this Monday. I sit at my desk, resting my face in my hand, watching the clock. Tick.

Tock.

Tick.

Tock.

I have one week left of my senior year of high school, and the time seems to drag on. Do I want high school to be over, though? When high school ends, I will be closer to my 18th birthday. There's only one week left of high school and two weeks until I turn 18. I don't know how I feel about it: excitement, terror, dread, freedom. I don't know.

"Adilyn, did you hear me, or are you not listening again?" Miss Lianca bemoans, crossing her arms.

"I'm sorry, what was the question?" Color flushing my cheeks.

"I asked if you have your art piece ready for the exhibit tomorrow?" Miss Lianca asks with annoyance in her tone, really emphasizing 'tomorrow'.

"Oh! Yes, ma'am, I do. I will bring it in tomorrow," I say quickly as I feel my cheeks beginning to warm. How embarrassing. I'm at the top of my class and usually stick to myself. Unfortunately, with my recent streak of daydreaming in class, I've been called on more than I prefer. I don't like to be the center of attention. I have never really fit in, so I would rather stay unnoticed. It's been quite hard to concentrate with the impending graduation and birthday. I don't know why I'm allowing it to eat at me so much, but it is.

Miss Lianca drones on about the exhibit, reviewing what will happen and how exciting it will be. The exhibit presents the artwork of the top student artists in the school. This will be where one can honestly get noticed as an artist, making or shattering dreams. The exhibit is held in Clay's Art House, the local art gallery. People from all over the country come to see the artwork in search of the next great artist. In the past, some great artists got their big breaks at this event. It's the one thing that this small town is known for.

Miss Lianca swears I will become the next prominent artist. I think she wants me to be found so she gets the credit for helping me "grow into my art abilities." I paint things I see in my head, not things you would see around this town or any city. I see images of mountains, forests, meadows, and flowers that are so surreal, but I can't shake the feeling of being in those places before. Maybe these inspirations are why I'm not a bad artist. I have a strong imagination, vision, and the talent to put them on canvas. However, becoming an artist will mean that I will be in the spotlight. That is something that I want to avoid. I love painting so much, but for a more personal reason. I paint to get a release, but I struggle with the idea that it could get me noticed. I don't think I would ever want to paint as a career.

The bell rings, and I jump at the sound, zapping me out of my daydreaming. School is finally over, and we are one day closer to the last day of school. I must rush to work and then go home to work on that art project. I know, I know. I told Miss Lianca I had my piece done already, but I haven't even started on it yet. I groan as I rise from my desk, wishing I had slept more last night. I was caught up reading and couldn't put my book down. I barely even left bed on time to make it to school. I'm exhausted, and my day is only part of the way over. I still have so much to do, and that thought makes me want to call in sick to work and crawl back into bed to get a few hours of sleep. To hell with my art piece. I don't feel it today. I begin to collect my drawing book and pencils, carefully placing them into my bag. Unfortunately, life doesn't stop just because I didn't get enough sleep last night. The show must continue.

I trod down the stairs and out the door. I'm hit with a thick film as I walk out the door. The humidity clings to my skin like a wet paper towel.

"Ugh," I mutter. I feel sweat rolling down my temples in seconds. "I will look like a hot, humid mess by the time I get to work." I don't have the same luxuries that most kids my age do. Most have cars of their own so they can go wherever, whenever. All I have are my two feet. With this humidity, I'm a little jealous of them, but what will I do? Complain and not go to work? I chuckle, knowing that won't happen. So, off I go, walking to work. It's springtime here, yet some days feel horribly like summer; this is one of those days.

After a short walk down the road, I go to the usual path to work: the forest. I love being surrounded by nature and so many aged trees. It fills me with peace and a connection to nature. I always seem more at ease in the forest, more centered and aware, than I ever do being surrounded by buildings. I step into the line of trees along the dirt road and weave through the trees, meandering deeper into the forest. I brush my hand along the mossy-covered trunks as I walk by. The crunching of twigs beneath my feet adds to the beautiful song the birds sing above me. I soak everything into my senses: the sound, the smell, the feel. These trees have been here for so long and survived it all. The awe I feel while weaving between them, gazing up at the knotted arms of the trees, it looks like they are reaching for the heavens. The scent of aged wood and soft blooms fills my nose. I breathe it in, letting it fill me, allowing myself to release all the anxiety and stress of my situation for just a moment. I roll my shoulders as the weight lifts off me, releasing all the built-up tension.

Being here in the forest, surrounded by all these trees, brings me to the place I frequently visit in my dreams. A vast forest of vibrant trees, rich in colors of deep emeralds and browns, floral blooms of colors unimaginable popping up from the ground. These dreams feel so real to me. I would wake up and still feel the soft touch of the moss on my hand and the rich smell of the majestic trees and blooms hanging in the air. I walk purposefully since I'm in a time crunch and work calls. I head straight for a giant oak in the middle of the forest, one I have visited for many years. I stumbled upon this forest one day while exploring when I was younger. I felt almost like something was pulling me towards it, and I followed. The tugging brought me to the forest, and I came upon this giant oak, which somehow became my oak. Since then, whenever I need time alone or to talk, I come here, sit against this tree, and speak to it as if it were my friend. I reach the oak and lay my hand on its weathered trunk.

"Hello, my dear friend. I don't have time today but just wanted to stop by and say hi." I lean my forehead to its' trunk, closing my eyes.

Peace settles upon me as all tension is released. I inhale deeply and stay there for a moment. I step back, and my eyes follow the oak's trunk to its canopy, reaching the sky. In a far-off magical land, somewhere I read, nature and humans were friends. They could speak to each other and lived in harmony.

"If only it were real..." I sigh to myself, laying my hand on the oak once more. "You would be my best friend then." A soft breeze caresses my face as if the tree is responding, and I smile. As I turn, my hand drops to my side, returning to the road slowly dragging my feet.

"The whispers of the wind and the songs of the forest guide my soul," I pause and say softly, turning back to see the trees. A saying that I have been saying my whole life. I don't know where I got it from, but I always whisper it while I'm in the forest, hoping the trees one day will understand what I'm saying. Sometimes, I almost think the trees wave back at me. The moment I step out onto the dirt road, a hole rips open inside of my chest. I can't quite explain it, but nature is missing in my heart. I start in the direction of the coffee shop. I must hurry, or I will be late. Thankfully, I don't have far to go until I make it. Even so, my feet feel like they have lead weighing them to the ground. I'm just so exhausted; I'm not even sure how I will be able to walk home later tonight when I get off.

"Only a little bit longer left. I will make it," I whimper. I continue to put one foot in front of the other, inching my way towards the coffee shop. Some days, like today, when I'm running on little sleep, I don't particularly desire to work. Not only did I get almost no sleep, but the humid air has now turned me into a wet cat. I have worked at Stella's Coffee Shop for three years now. It's the only coffee shop in Claywood. Most people from town come to drink coffee and read books. Sometimes, they just come in to talk to Dani and feed off the life that she brings to everyone. The shop is a cute, homey little spot that offers the locals a steady, chill hangout place. It's remarkable, for sure.

Nestled between two large oak trees, Stella's was constructed out of old, weathered oak logs flanked with bright-colored curtains on the windows, giving it a rustic look with a pop of color. The coffee shop reminds me of a quaint cottage from a fairytale with a happy ending. It has this undeniable peace, a charm that makes it glow and stand out. The rest of the town is pretty much cookie-cutter or a run-down version of cookie-cutter. Almost everything in this town looks the same: the homes, the buildings, everything. Even the run-down places look like everything else, with a little more moss and a few more stones out of place. There is only a slight color variance as all the buildings were white, cream, or beige. But not Stella's. It was vibrant, with its orange curtains flanking the red door.

CHAPTER TWO

Cafe

ADILYN

I make it to the cafe, huffing and puffing, but I make it. I trudge through the front door, and the smell of roasted coffee beans with a hint of vanilla hangs in the air permanently. I take a deep breath, filling my senses and savoring the scent. A warm feeling blankets me, possibly from the heat radiating from all the lattes made in this place. However, there is something almost supernatural about the feeling, something I can't place my finger on. I take just one moment to soak it all in, and then I'm back to reality as I hurry to the bathroom to wash my face and freshen up a little before I start my shift.

"Hey, Dani!" I shout as I run by the kitchen, glancing inside the kitchen. Dani is back there with an apron covered in flour. What is she up to now? I smile.

"Hey, Adilyn," she shouts back with a wide grin on her freckled face; mischief glistens in her eyes. Dani is the owner of this coffee shop. She is a middle-aged, curvy lady who loves coffee and loves talking even more.

She makes everyone who steps into the cafe feel noticed and cared for. That is one of the reasons why I love her so much! Everyone loves her; I can't think of a single person who has a bad word to say about her. I look up to her; she is the most formidable yet gentle person I have ever known. Dani has no family, or at least not that she ever mentioned. I find it peculiar, but I never wanted to pry too much about it. The few times I brought up her family, she seemed uneasy, and her answers were short, so I left it alone. Since I don't have a family, I consider myself her family.

After quickly refreshing myself in the bathroom, I drop off my bag in the back office and make my way to the front of the cafe. I weave through the small tables towards the front. As I make my way, I take inventory of all the books left by customers, hoping to find something new that piques my interest in the stacks. As I glance over to the tables in the middle of the shop, I spot one that looks new in a stack on a table right at the center. I make a mental note to come back later and snatch it up.

Here at Stella's, people bring in books to exchange. Books are scattered around the shop in stacks on the tables and tucked into any shelf or space in the shop. One can come in and take a book at no cost. The only thing Dani asks is that you bring a book in exchange if you have one. Dani has always been big on reading. She says reading can take you to a world you would have never imagined in your wildest dreams, and it can bring you new life. She always encourages everyone who comes in to pick up a book and read, even if it is for a while. This is another reason I love this place, as it has provided me and all the guests with a great way to find new books and a temporary escape. Stella's has all the feelings of a cafe but the benefits of a library.

I nod at customers as I walk by, "Good afternoon." The customers look up at me and nod back with a grin. Two people are sitting at the far table, huddling together. It makes me think that this must be their first date. I have seen giggling and huddling together, mainly with new couples. Most of the town are regulars at Stella's. I've spent my time while working here learning how to analyze people. Now, I feel like I know the signs of a new couple, an old couple, or a secret couple. This job has taught me so much in my three years here. It has been so beneficial.

I stride behind the counter to grab a rag to clean tables. Dani beams at me from the kitchen as I walk by. I raise the rag in the air so Dani can see I will wipe down tables. I wander from table to table, wiping them down and straightening the books. As I approach the table in the center of the shop, I glance at the front door as a group of girls from my school walk in.

"Oh joy," I mutter sarcastically. I do fine with clients I don't attend school with, but I feel awkward when my classmates come to the cafe. I have always managed to be the outsider in this town. I often overhear my classmates' whispering obscenities and indecencies about me as I pass by. They call me the "weird kid" or the "fake kid". Everyone believes that my eye color is not my actual color. They claim I use colored contacts and that I dye silver strands in my hair because "there is no way it's natural." I get it; I'm different in many ways, but what they claim isn't true. I stand up, straightening my apron, square my shoulders, and walk over to the counter.

"Good afternoon, everyone. How can I help you?" I say with a fake smile. The two girls I know look at me, then at each other, and giggle. The third girl stands beside them, staring at them with disdain written all over her face.

"We want to order coffee," Cindy says, stepping forward. If I could roll my eyes without making anyone mad, I would in moments like this.

"Okay. What kind of coffee would you like?" I ask, forcing a cheerful tone.

Cindy says in a valley girl voice, "I would like a caramel latte with soy milk."

The second girl, Stacy, adds, "I would like a... um... vanilla iced latte".

The third girl kindly requests, "I would like a latte with soy milk, like Cindy, but no flavor, please," gesturing towards Cindy. She stands out from the other two girls she is with, not conforming to the typical 'popular girl' persona. She is kind, and there's something familiar about her, something I cannot quite put my finger on. She is beautiful, with fair skin and long, wavy, brown hair. Her eyes are captivating; they draw me in and make me not want to look away.

"Alright!" I enter the order into the register. "It will be $15.97," I say, looking up from the register towards the girls.

Cindy looks over at her friends and reaches into her purse. "I will use my dad's credit card," smirking as she swipes her card in the reader.

"Aw, thank you! You are the best!" Stacy shrieks. The third girl smiles and nods her head.

"Give me just a moment to make your coffee." I turn and walk towards the espresso machine. Girls like that, who feel like they are entitled because their parents have money, make my skin itch. They do nothing to help anyone and flaunt their parents' wealth in the faces of others as if they were better than everyone because of money. Cindy and Stacy have been the popular girls in this town since always. Cindy's dad is the mayor, and Stacy's dad owns the local newspaper. They are what everyone considers "important people." I think differently, however. Their dads do what is best for them and don't think about those who are lesser.

"Thank you!" The third girl leans over the counter and says with a gentle smile. A warmth builds in my chest at her kindness.

"Stephanie, why are you so nice to that freak?" Cindy scoffs.

"Why would I not be?" Stephanie steps over to the girls, annoyance in her tone.

"She is different. She doesn't belong here. She tries acting cool by dying her hair, adding in streaks of silver, claiming that it is natural. She even goes as far as using colored contacts so that people notice her. She is not only a freak but a teacher's pet, too. It's gross how much the teachers like her." Cindy looks at me and laughs mockingly.

"Yeah, she's a little strange, but I think she's harmless," Stacy whispers. Stacy has always been the nicest one out of the two. On the other hand, Cindy is always cruel towards me and makes sure that I know she doesn't like me. "Stephanie, your eyes are similar to hers, not the same, but not different either. That's interesting." Stacy says, trying to change the subject. She looks between Stephanie and me, placing a finger on her chin.

I glance over at the girl, Stephanie. I don't look at the color of my eyes often, but hers don't fall into what one would consider the norm. Her eyes are similar to mine, though not the same as Stacy said, but they are indeed close. Cindy snaps her gaze to mine and rolls her eyes. I avert my gaze back to the espresso machine.

"Ugh." Cindy sighs.

"What? Does that make me a freak, too?" Stephanie places her hands on her hips, tilts her head, and looks at Cindy.

Cindy rolls her eyes. "No, you're not a freak. You're not like her... You're more like us." She gestures to herself and Stacy. The annoyance rolling off of Cindy is thick in the air; I can almost cut it with a butter knife. Cindy links her arms with Stephanie and Stacy and waltzes over to a table to sit.

I shake my head in defeat because I will never win against her. She will never be nice to me, no matter what. If someone is not like her, they're not good enough for her, or at least that's how it seems. I sigh and clear my mind of Cindy, deciding not to allow her to ruin my day. I grind the coffee beans and press the coffee grinds into the portafilter quickly. Making coffee is easy for me now, almost second nature, since I have had years of practice, just like painting. I finish making their coffee, carefully place the mugs on a tray, and bring it out to them.

"Here you ladies go!" setting the coffee down at the table where they are seated.

"Thank you!" Stephanie says and smiles genuinely. I smile at her and nod my head. She is much nicer than the other two, especially considering the others didn't even acknowledge when I brought their coffee. I feel guilty because I didn't introduce myself when she first moved here. She moved to this town only a month ago, and the popular girls quickly latched onto her, so I never had a chance to get to know her. I turn around and go back to clean the espresso machine.

Dani strolls out of the kitchen, her arms swinging at her sides. Even though she is a small woman, her presence fills any room she enters. She looks over to me and winks, then makes her rounds. She chats with the couple in the corner, then moves on to the three girls. I watch as she chats with them. Lost in conversation, she throws her head back with a deep laugh bubbling to the surface, her fiery red hair glistening in the sunlight. The room fills with joy, and it hits me. I smile, knowing Dani's laughter will always make me feel a thousand times better, no matter how mad or irritated I can be.

"What's new girls? How is high school treating you?" I overhear Dani asking them. They talk about what's new in their lives, and she intently listens. Everyone wants to talk to her and tell her all about their life. She is so personable; I wish I were more like that, like her. She finishes talking with the girls and makes her way towards me with a smile beaming on her face.

"Hey! How was school?" she asks with sparkling eyes.

"It was okay, I guess. I was called on again in front of the whole class." I say, shrugging my shoulders.

"Daydreaming again?" She raises an eyebrow at me.

I nod and look down.

Dani leans in, cupping the side of her mouth to whisper in my ear as if what she said was top secret. "Don't be embarrassed about it. You're almost an adult, and between you and me, adults can daydream, so you are allowed to do so as well." She straightens and smiles. "I hate how people make adults into these boring monsters with no dreams. Everyone deserves to dream; it gives them something to aspire for. Just like reading, dreaming can transport you to a place that your everyday mind may never have thought of. Some of the greatest things people have done have come from dreams. So, dream, and don't be ashamed if you don't have every puzzle piece of life in place just yet. That's fine. It took me some time to get my life figured out." she says, smiling, her hands resting on her hips.

This relieves some of my embarrassment because talking with Dani is easy and comforting. I never sense judgment from her or feel the need to conceal anything from her. I know she's right. I love reading and being whisked away to other realms, even for a moment. I believe that's the reason for my best paintings—dreaming. I understand I shouldn't feel as embarrassed as I do, yet the anxiety of a life with scattered pieces occasionally overwhelms me.

"Thank you. I know that sometimes I may be a little too hard on myself. Sometimes, I feel like with this impending adulthood, I shouldn't allow myself to get so distracted. I should be more focused and know my plan. Yet sometimes it's like I'm drowning and unsure of what direction to swim in." I say softly, crossing my arms over my chest, embracing myself, not wanting anyone to overhear the anxiety I feel. "You didn't have your life all figured out when you were my age?"

"My life was far from figured out when I was your age. I was a raging mess of emotions, wanting to rebel against my parents and live my own life without rules and constantly being told what to do. I was tough on my mother, and I wish I had done things differently, but it's life. It took me years to realize what I wanted to do with my life." Sorrow fills her eyes, and a soft smile blooms as she recalls a bittersweet memory. "My mother was there the entire time, withstanding how mean I was to her. She knew all along I would find my love for cooking. Never figured out how she knew I would, but she did." A silent tear escapes her cheek, and she quickly reaches to brush it away.

"That must have been tough." I'm at a loss for words. I feel her sadness deep in my bones, but I'm too afraid to ask what happened to her mother and possibly bring up more painful memories for her.

"I know you will figure life out when the time is right. Your life will fall right into your lap, and then you will know what direction to swim in. I'm going back to the kitchen to finish baking my cookies." She pats my shoulder as she walks by me.

"Are you saving some for me?" I ask, praying to the gods that she says yes because everyone in this town knows Dani can bake!

"You bet, hon!" she says, smiling, then returns to the kitchen humming. She has hummed this song on many occasions. I asked what she was humming, and she always said it was a lullaby from her hometown. She won't talk about her hometown other than that. I wish I knew the words to her lullaby, but I can hum with her. I have heard it so many times. My spirits perk up, knowing that I have cookies reserved for later.

I turn back, humming the lullaby, and begin cleaning.

"Everett, come back here!" a woman shouts.

I quickly turn at the sudden impact on my legs. I look down, and a laugh spills from me. Everett Grover has his tiny arms wrapped around my legs in a big embrace. I lean down, wrapping my arms around him, and smile. He slowly releases his grasp on me, and I crouch to meet his eyes.

"Hey, buddy! How are you? Did you come to see me or did you come to see Dani?" I grin at the little boy, and he grins back at me.

"I came to see both of you!" My heart melts at his tiny, cheerful voice.

The woman rushes up to us, "I'm sorry, Adilyn. I hope he didn't hurt you." She slowly pulls the boy towards her.

"Oh, Deborah, no worries! He surprised me, but I love surprises, especially ones like this." I caress the boy's face, the face of an angel.

Dani's head pops out of the kitchen, "Is that Everett I hear?"

"Yes, it is, Deborah and Everett," I respond.

"Dani said she wanted us to come by because she was baking cookies for Everett," Deborah says shyly, cheeks blushing. She has always been shy but sweet. Her son, Everett, is the light of the Grovers' life. He brings so much happiness into our lives as well. He is such a special kid. When Everett was born, some health complications caused him to be in and out of the hospital for the first two years of his life. He was born autistic and had severe issues with his heart. His heart complications mostly have been corrected with surgery, but the doctors still monitor that there is no regression in his heart condition. Yet, he is still here, fighting and bringing light to the world daily.

A delicious smell floats through the air right to us. Everett's eyes light up as the smell of freshly baked cookies reaches his nose. Dani makes the best cookies in the world.

"Cookies!" Everett jumps up and down, clapping his hands.

I grab Everett's hand, "Hey Everett, I will get you some cookies from Dani. Is that okay?"

His grin melts my heart; he is missing his two front teeth, and there's nothing more adorable than him. He nods furiously, and I smile back at him. I stand slowly so I don't spook him.

"I will be right back," I tell Deborah, quietly rustling my hand through Everett's strawberry-blonde hair.

"Thank you, Adilyn," She smiles, grabbing Everett's hand and leading him toward a table.

I stroll into the kitchen and see flour on the counter and the mixing bowls soaking in the sink. She is wearing an apron covered in flour. This is Dani's happy place; you can feel that when you enter. Strangely, a place can feel so magical and happy, but this kitchen sure does.

"Everett is here for some cookies," Dani beams, carefully placing cookies in a Tupperware for the Grovers to take home.

"Oh, how we all love when you bake!" I grin.

Dani looks over at me, and for a moment, her face looks different, almost otherworldly. I rub my eyes and look at her again, but everything is normal. Hmm. I must be tired. I could have sworn, though, that her appearance was different.

"Are you okay?"

"Yes, I am. I think I'm just tired, that's all," I shrug it off. "You better hurry. You know how Everett gets." I chuckle at the thought of the little boy's excitement. Dani turns to the cookie tray and places several more cookies into the Tupperware. She places the lid on top and walks my way.

"Let's get these cookies to him then!" We walk out together and spot Everett and Deborah sitting at a table close to the window. Everett looks out the window and then back down at the paper in front of him, with a pencil in hand. Art is something that he has a love for, similar to me.

Memories flood my mind of the days I sat with him here in this cafe, just drawing. We would sit there for what felt like forever, happy in our little art bubble. I offered to watch Everett as much as possible to give Deborah and Carl a break so they could have some time to relax. Their life is complex, with little relaxation. The Grovers are a small family that have lived in this town their entire lives. They have always been kind, striving to give the best life to their son. I know they have struggled significantly in many ways over the years. Deborah had a very rough pregnancy with Everett, and they both almost lost their lives. Carl works several jobs trying to make ends meet so that Deborah can stay at home with Everett, and so they can afford all of the medical bills. They are genuinely good individuals who have been dealt a challenging hand.

"Everett, I promised you cookies and here they are," Dani exclaims. He turns to face us, dropping his pencil on the table, and his eyes light up, seeing the container filled with cookies.

"Can I have one right now?" He jumps out of his chair, reaching out a hand towards Dani. Dani glances at Deborah, and Deborah nods with permission. Her eyes look weary. I can feel the anxiety rolling off of her, yet she does well at pretending everything is alright. Dani opens the container, and the scent of freshly baked cookies blasts out of the container. Everett jumps feverously in excitement. The joy on his face is priceless. I wish I was a kid again and felt that same kind of excitement. He nibbles on the cookie.

He plops the last bite of his cookie into his mouth and gives me a toothless grin. He grabs my hand and guides me to the table where his drawing is. He points towards his drawing, so I bend to examine it. He

has drawn the giant oak that shades the cafe. I admire his determination
to capture the world that he sees in his drawings.

"If you need to run an errand or two, you can leave the little guy here
with me. It is now slow at the cafe and I would love to sit and draw with
him." I cross my fingers behind my back, hoping she will say yes. Everett's
toothless grin makes it impossible for Deborah to say no.

"Um...I guess I can do my grocery shopping and then return for him.
If that works?" She turns towards Everett, placing her hand on his head.

I nod my head and look down at Everett.

Deborah crouches down and looks at Everett, a soft smile gracing her
features. Not many things can make this woman smile, but Everett sure
does.

"Will you be alright with Miss Adilyn for a little while?"

"Yes, mommy!" He gleams.

"Okay, sweetie! You be good now, you hear me?"

He smiles widely and nods his head. She stands up, leaning over, giving
him a quick kiss on the top of his head, then walks towards the door. He
turns to me, and I raise my hand to give him a high-five.

"Since it's slow, would it be okay with you if I take a break?" I glance
over to Dani.

"Darling, when it comes to him, anything is okay." Dani ruffles his
hair. "I need to go wash those dishes. Holler if you need anything." She
opens the Tupperware and quickly hands another cookie to Everett. His
eyes lighten up, and he snatches the cookie. Dani winks at him and then
turns to walk back towards the kitchen. I turn to see Everett inhaling this
cookie. I chuckle and pull over the chair to sit next to him, and he hands
me a piece of paper and a pencil. I look over at him and see his brows
furrowed as he draws. I let my pencil glide across the page, in a trance
almost, looking up every so often at Everett. I place my pencil on the

table and pick up my page when I'm done. I drew a dragon with butterfly wings. I have seen this in my dreams before, dreams I have several times a year for as long as I can remember. I tilt my head and think about this creature. This is nothing that I have ever read about in books or seen in movies. Dragons don't have butterfly wings.

He shakes his page, getting my attention, and brings me out of my daze, "Look at my drawing!" he squeals. I grab his paper. He has drawn an adorable picture of his mother, father, himself, and two people. He reaches over and points at the page, "This is you, and that is Dani." Tears form in my eyes, and my heart skips a beat. I reach over and ruffle his hair.

"I love it!" I choke out.

CHAPTER THREE

Intriguing Book

ADILYN

Work is finally over. Dragging my feet to the back, I throw my apron in the washer and grab my bag from the office. "I'm out of here," I shout to the back.

"Wait just one moment, Adilyn. I want to talk to you," Dani shouts. I can hear her in the kitchen finishing up the last few dishes left from today.

"Alright, I'll wait. Please don't take too long. I have to go home to finish my project, then get some sleep," I say, pausing in the middle of the cafe.

"Don't worry, hon, I won't be long. I know I can't mess with your beauty sleep," she laughs.

I groan, shaking my head at her comment. She tends to make comments about my appearance often. It's in her nature to always attempt to say something nice. I half think it's because so many people comment about how much of a freak I am because of my looks. She must know that it gets to me every once in a while. No one else in this town is tall, with long ash-blonde hair, natural silver strands woven through it, deep emerald eyes, pale skin, and sharp features. Being so different from everyone else has always made me feel somewhat uncomfortable. Everyone in the town teeters on more of an average height, sun-kissed skin, brown or blonde hair, but not as light as mine. I wish I knew where I came from.

"All this thinking gives me a migraine," I mumble to myself, rubbing my temples to ease the throbbing pain growing in my head. Thinking of these things tends to drag me into a dark place. It gives me a sense of hopelessness, a sense of being lost. I want to know something. Anything about where I came from. I wish I knew who my family was. If only I knew, then maybe it would all make sense. Unfortunately, I have no clue. I don't even know what my real name is. I had nothing attached to me when I was left at the doorstep of Claywood's fire chief. He gave me my name so I would at least have one.

The fire chief and his wife were my first foster parents. However, when they stumbled upon me that night, they were not the youngest people in the town. I stayed with them for six years and then went to the Himwalds. I was with the Himwalds for nine years. They, too, were not young when I went to stay with them, so after nine years, they could no longer care for someone, especially a teenager. Mr. Himwald's health tumbled downhill, so Mrs. Himwald had to care for him full-time. Despite their age and health, they gave me a great life while I was with them. After that, I came to stay with Hillary and Tim (Toxic Tim, as I call him). They are in their 30s and have no kids. I'm unsure how long they have been married, at least ten years. They are an interesting couple, complete opposites, but not in a good way; from what I have seen while at the house, Tim seems controlling and unkind to Hillary.

I sigh and glance at the table in the middle of the cafe. Upon the table is a stack of books, one of those books is the one that had caught my attention earlier. Sometimes the people in this town are boring with the genres that they read. There are a lot of memoirs of the rich and famous, recipe books, the latest diet trends, travel, and non-fiction read in this town. I want adventure; I want magic! I snatch up the fantasy books when they come through the cafe. I love fiction books, especially fantasy, being carried away to a faraway land where magic lives and life is exhilarating. Fantasy books take me to a world I wish I was in, which only exists in my imagination. I continue to walk to the table and sit down in the chair with a deep sigh. Finally, off my feet! I pull the book I had seen earlier from the stack, "The Fae Princess." Turning it over, I begin to read the blurb on the back.

Laura leads an ordinary life, finding solace in the mundane things. On her twenty-first birthday, her life changed. She discovers a long-kept secret. Laura is from a distant land. Also, her parents are the King and Queen of Numaria.

Intriguing, I have to read this book. The strange thing about this book is that it looks brand new, as if no one has even opened it. All the books around here have been read, and there are never any new books. I look around, skimming the stacks on the other tables. I can see all the worn spines of all the other books. Curiosity rattles through me. I know this book was not here yesterday. I wonder who brought it, maybe someone accidentally bought it and then realized it wasn't what they were looking for.

"I'm glad you are still here," Dani says, strolling towards me from the kitchen and pausing by the counter.

She pulls me from my trail of thoughts, "You said you wanted to talk to me, so here I am." I raise my hands.

"I did, indeed. You want some tea, hon?"

"Yes, that would be amazing." Dani makes a fantastic tea. One that I drink quite often because of how good it is. She has never told me what is in it that makes it so delicious. She says it is a secret blend of herbs and flowers. Dani nods her head at me and moves behind the counter. She busies herself making the tea, so I return to the book in my hands.

"Hey, Dani," I call out to her. "I'm going to take this book if that is okay with you. I can bring one in tomorrow in exchange."

"Which book is that?" she asks, looking over where I am sitting. I lift the book so that she can see the cover. "You don't need to bring a book in exchange for that one. You can have it. You have worked so hard these past few years here. You deserve a book or two every once in a while, for all your efforts," she winks.

"Thank you!" I smile at her answer. I constantly doubt myself and wonder if I am doing well enough. So, it is nice to know I am not doing a terrible job every so often.

"Now, that doesn't mean you can read all night. You hear me?"

"Yes, I hear you. I promise I won't," I laugh. Oh, how she knows me so well. I can't count how many nights I have stayed up late or skipped sleeping just to read.

Dani returns to the table where I sit with a tray of tea and cookies she baked earlier. It is incredible watching how she floats on her feet. I have never seen her spill anything or bump into anything. She sets the tray down, and I lean in and inhale the aroma of the tea.

"How I love your tea! It is always so good." I say as I grab a cup. I hold it between my two hands, examining the contents inside and letting the warmth of the tea flow into me. I inhale the smell of it, trying to place what is in it, yet I can never quite figure it out. I blow on it, attempting to cool it down some, then take a small sip, allowing the warm fuzziness to slowly trickle down my body. I close my eyes and bask in this feeling of warmth and peace that begins to consume me. Every time I drink this tea, I relax afterward. I take a deep breath in and then exhale. I open my eyes and turn towards Dani.

"So, what was it that you wanted to talk about?" I set down my cup of tea and pick up a cookie.

"Right, I wanted to talk to you about your life and what you will do. I know we briefly talked about the topic earlier, but I wanted to sit down and have a heart-to-heart with you about it," she says, with something in her voice that I cannot quite place. Was it hesitation, curiosity, or fear?

"What do you mean?" I ask right before taking a bite of the delicious cookie in my hand. I silently moan at the first bite, closing my eyes momentarily.

"Well, what do you plan on doing once you graduate and turn 18? Are you planning on staying here, or are you planning on running as far away from this place as you can?"

I pause to think about my response.

"Honestly, I don't know." I shrug and quickly glance at her then down at my tea. I feel flush staining my cheeks, embarrassed yet again that I have not figured my life out yet.

"You don't know, and that is okay. As I said earlier, not everyone knows exactly what they want to do immediately. I just don't want you thinking that you have no one to talk to or at least to bounce ideas off of." she says.

"I have thought about it a lot lately, about what I want to do. Part of me wants to run as far away from this small town as soon as possible. Yet another part of me feels like I need to stay. But honestly, if I stay, what is there for me here? I'm the town freak with almost no friends. I want nothing more than to have at least one friend besides you," I sigh.

Speaking that out loud somehow makes it even more real. Dani looks at me, trying to collect what she will say.

"Adilyn, you are not a freak; you are special, and you know that. You are meant for greatness. You are meant for so much greater than Claywood," she says with a hint of sadness.

"I sure don't feel special." I laugh nervously. That is the truth; I don't feel special at all. "What do you think I should do?" I ask, peering over at her.

"Well, you shouldn't make any irrational decision just yet. I think you should give it some time and then you may see if something falls into your lap one day." She smiles softly, her eyes sparkling.

"I guess. But I have to move out when I turn 18. Toxic Tim was very clear about that. So how is it possible to take my time? I will be 18 in two weeks. What am I supposed to do then? Live on the streets?" A mixture of emotions begins to flutter through my chest, tightening it, and I start to fidget with my fingers. I'm at a crossroads with many paths I can take and no real direction.

Dani chuckles; she has always found my nickname for him humorous, "No, hon, you won't live on the streets. I will not let that happen. You can stay with me until you figure life out. I know I don't have a mansion, but I have a room you can have, a roof over your head, and a homemade meal every evening. Anyways, I have been with you your entire life; why would that change now?" She winks.

"I like the sound of that. I may take you up on your offer. And yes, you have been with me pretty much my whole life. You have watched me bounce from foster to foster." I grin. Dani may not share the same blood as me, but she is closest to my family. She has always been there my entire life, one way or another, helping me. I can't imagine what my life would be like without her. "I don't know what I would do without you, Dani," I say, reaching out to grab her hand and squeeze it.

"Well, hon, you would be boring without me. Now finish up your tea, and off you go." She squeezes my hand and lets it go. "This old lady needs to go dry the dishes and get myself up to bed. I have an order for a birthday cake tomorrow that I will be waking up early to start making." She rises from the chair and slowly makes her way to the kitchen.

I watch her as she returns to the kitchen, shaking my head at the fact that she calls herself old. It doesn't surprise me that she would wake up early to bake. The woman loves being in the kitchen. I pick up my tea and breathe in the smell of it. Lost in a haze, I imagine what life would be like to stay in Claywood and work in this coffee shop for the rest of my life. I suppose it would be a peaceful life, nothing overly exciting, just peaceful and straightforward. However, Miss Lianca wants me to become a great artist. She swears that is what I am made for, but I feel that's not where I should go. Due to that feeling of discomfort, I hesitate to dream of something like that. I guess I prefer going unnoticed. I don't like being asked who I am and where I come from. I would much rather just blend in.

Such decisions. The worry runs through me like wildfire. What if I don't make the right choice? What if I hate my life? I take another sip of my tea, trying to allow the worry to wash away, and I feel the warmth spread through me. I'll stay here for now in Claywood and see where life takes me. Maybe one day, I'll know where I truly fit in and belong.

I sit for a few more minutes, sipping tea and munching the cookies Dani had left on the tray. I know it is time to go, yet I dread how much is left to do.

"I have to go before it gets too late! Thank you for the talk, cookies, tea, and the book! You're the best!" I yell back to her as I stuff the book in my bag.

"Be safe, Ad!" she yells back.

"I always am. Good night."

"Good night". Then, I make my way towards the door. I have a mile to walk to get home. I throw my bag over my shoulder and push the door open.

The sun is setting, and the shadows are slipping up the trees, drowning the world in darkness. A cool breeze passes, kissing my face and sweeping my hair into my eyes. It is peaceful and quiet. Claywood is a small town, and life tends to settle once the sun sets.

I start walking in the direction of my home, debating to myself what I will paint. I told Miss Lianca I had done my painting, but I have yet to start it. I feel this unsettling feeling as I walk along, trying to imagine something in my head. A chill runs down my spine. Something is not correct. I look around, but nothing is there. There is no one outside, no one that I can see, yet I have a strange feeling as if I am being watched. The hair on my arms rises as my heart begins pounding in my chest. Beads of sweat start surfacing on my forehead, and I can feel my anxiety beginning to climb. I can't see whatever it was that was making me feel this way, and I have no clue if there is something there or if I am hallucinating it all. I wrap my arms around my stomach and pick up my speed, deciding to power walk the rest of the way home. I glance around every few steps because the feeling will not go away.

"Am I going crazy?" I say to myself, trying to make light of the situation.

Then I swear there is a faint echo of voices. Voices speak in a language that I have never heard before. I halt. My eyes dart all around, trying to find the source of the voices, but nothing.

"Are you kidding me?" I say with frustration. Frustration with myself and with the whole situation. "I must be losing my mind; absolutely nothing is out there." Shaking my head, I try some of the breathing techniques I had learned about to try to calm my nerves. I am losing my mind and hearing things, that is all. My mind is playing games with me. I need to get more sleep. I start walking again towards my house, and within a few paces, the feeling disappears instantly. The hair on my arms settles back down, and everything is normal.

"I guess I need to breathe more." I chuckle in annoyance, knowing that no matter how much I tell myself everything is fine, something is off. I scan around once more before setting off again, seeing nothing.

Relief washes over me as I finally see the house up ahead. "I made it in one piece," I say quietly. I never really liked coming to my foster home, but tonight, I sure did. There is usually a tension hanging in the air when Tim is home, making things uncomfortable, but tonight, I didn't care. I walk up the stairs and sneak into the front door. I tiptoe through the house, up the stairs, and to my room. Tim prefers me to be quiet. He is the type that would complain when a neighbor makes a big commotion. Hillary is not the same way, and she isn't mean like Tim. She is quiet. Part of me thinks that is because of Tim. I'm sure I could have worse foster parents.

So I tiptoe upstairs to my room. I enter my room and close the door behind me, leaning against the door and letting out a sigh of relief. I am so thankful to be in my space finally. This room is my space where I can be myself and nothing else. I set my bag down next to my desk, slumping into my chair. Blowing out a breath. What a day, and yet it was not over yet. I close my eyes and take several deep breaths, breathing in and out, trying to center and calm my nerves. I'm still a little rustled over what had just happened. The feeling of being watched is still searing into my skin. I take another deep breath, open my eyes, and sit in my chair. "Time to work on my painting," I mumble to myself. I glance over at my Monstera plant sitting on my desk. "Hey, buddy! I hope you had a lovely day." I stroke the leaves, examining the new foliage growing from the stem.

I stare at the Monstera, imagining what it would be like if plants could hear me and understand what I was saying. What if they could answer back? What a fantastic world that would be! I snap back into reality, leaning over to grab a canvas to begin my painting. Setting the canvas on the desk, I rummage through the drawers. I pull my brushes and paint out. I set them all up and lay my hands on my lap. Before I paint, I always close my eyes and try to allow my imagination to flow. My imagination has always brought amazing scenes to my mind. Beautiful colors and plants. Happiness. Visions from faraway lands that did not exist. Lands that I wish did exist.

I close my eyes and take a deep breath, allowing my mind to calm and roam—another deep breath in and then out. A warm fuzzy feeling creeps upon me—a sense of belonging and home. Images start to flow into my mind. I'm in a forest surrounded by ancient wise trees. The colors are vibrant, deep emerald greens that seem to be dancing. The trees hum as if they were alive. I tilt my head back to see the ancient trees stretching higher than I can see. I breathe in the moist air, and the scent of cedarwood, wildflowers, and flowing rivers fills me. I can feel the wet ground beneath my feet, crunching the leaves between my toes. I can hear the birds whistling through the trees above me and the forest animals chatting around. I feel grounded and calm. This is a place where I genuinely feel at home. This is what I will paint: this place, these trees, these flowers. I want to try to paint the comfort I felt here. I slowly open my eyes, take a deep breath, and grab my paintbrush. I begin painting.

When I paint, I go into almost a trance until I finish the painting. I paint what I see and what I feel. I want nothing more than for this place to become a reality. In my imagination, this place is the one place I think is where I'm the most at home. The strokes of my brush came so naturally to me. An hour passes by, and I finally set down my paintbrush. I stand my painting up, leaning it against the wall. I stand up and take a step back. I look at the painting, examining the colors and brush strokes. The vivid colors have a warm feel to them. The soft brush strokes blend, making the painting look so realistic. Yet the image I painted was not quite what I had envisioned. The colors weren't vibrant enough. I could not capture the humming of the trees.

"Every brushstroke tells a story, and every petal holds a secret," I whisper. Another one of those sayings I don't know where it came from, but I always whisper after painting, like a ritual. I close my eyes for a moment and take a deep breath. I let it out slowly, and I open my eyes. I glance again at the painting. "If only I could jump into the painting or my imagination..." I chuckle to myself. Much more of a desire than I let myself think about. I am covered in paint, and my hair is in an unkempt bun atop my head. "I need to shower and get to bed." I turn and grab some pajamas from my dresser. Then, walk to the bathroom to shower.

As I leave the bathroom, I glance up at my plant and notice something hiding underneath a leaf. I slowly lift the monstera leaf and spot a small flower almost identical to the one I had just painted. What the heck is going on? How did that get here? I do not remember planting anything in the pot with the Monstera.

My head turns at the soft knock on my door. The door creaks open slowly.

"I just want to say good night." Hillary peeks in.

"Good night!" I smile at her. She is a peculiar woman. I know she tries hard, but she has her struggles that I think prevent her a lot of the time. In my time here, she has slowly come out of her shell. Without Toxic Tim dragging her down, I can't wait to see who she is.

She quietly closes the door. I refocus on the flower in my pot. This has happened before, flowers popping up where they were never planted. At this point, I'm sure Dani or Hillary is trying to mess with me or both. I have no desire to investigate the truth behind the flowers right now.

I grab the book that I got from the coffee shop earlier. I want to skim through it before I go to bed. I look at the cover, trying to imagine what lies inside its pages—the Fae Princess. "I wonder what it would be like to be a fae princess.... It must be a much better life than I have now." I mumble to myself. I daydream often of living in that kind of world, a world of fae and magic, one much different than my world. I stride to my bed, snuggling myself under the covers. I crack open the book and begin to read.

CHAPTER FOUR

Dragging

ADILYN

The alarm insistently beeps, stirring me from my sleep. I moan and swing my hand to hit the top of the alarm, shutting it off. "Alright, alright, I'm awake," I grumble. The book lies on my chest. I must have fallen asleep reading.

"I made it to page 3," I laugh, picking the book up off my chest and closing it. I sit up and set the book on my nightstand beside my alarm clock. I glance at the clock and see that it is 6:00 a.m. I look over and see the sunlight beginning to trickle in through my window. Since today is Tuesday, only four more days of school are left. I raise my arms high and give a big yawn, stretching to prepare for the day. I glance again towards the dancing sunlight in my window and know it's time to get up and ready. I have school, work, and the art exhibit today. I swing my legs off the bed, rubbing my eyes, trying to wake myself up fully.

I have this feeling of dread for today, for the art exhibit. I don't want to be a part of it. I don't want to be in the spotlight in any way, shape, or form. However, I'm not too fond of letting someone down and having them disappointed in me. If I do not show up with a painting, I will disappoint Miss Lianca. Miss Lianca has always believed in my abilities and has been kind. I can't say that about many others in this town. Now, whether the kindness of Miss Lianca is because she is genuine or out of hope, I will become something I don't know. Yet, I still do not want to disappoint her by not going. That will for sure let her down. So I get up and go to my desk where the painting stands, leaning against the wall. I wrap my painting in kraft paper to make sure nothing happens to it on the way to school. All set, one thing down, now to get ready. I head towards my closet, trying to figure out what I will wear tonight.

The art exhibit is at 7 p.m. I will drop off my painting at the gallery before going to the cafe and then head to the exhibit after work. So I need to bring clothes to change into for the event. I have never gone to formal events or anything that required elegant attire. I mainly wear T-shirts and jeans. I will wear a plain mid-length black dress. That will have to work. It hugs my shape just right, not so tight that I will feel self-conscious yet not so loose to make it hang off of me. I fold the dress and then place it in my bag. I retrieve some decent-looking black slip-on shoes to accompany my black dress, putting them in my bag as well. I return to the closet to grab a tee and jeans for the day. Then, head to get changed and ready. After changing, I momentarily stare at my reflection, reminiscing who I am and who my family possibly could have been. The physical differences I have compared to everyone else in Claywood are noticeable. I stand out like a sore thumb. Maybe my family came from Anaria, a country across the sea. The people there have fair complexions like me. Who knows. I can't sit here all day and dwell on things I don't know. Life was not going to pause for me to wonder for a bit.

I turn towards the bathroom door to return to my room, pausing at the doorway and looking back at my reflection one last time. I wish I knew where I belonged. A sigh escapes from my lips. I grab my phone from the nightstand and walk to my desk to grab my bag and canvas. I tuck the canvas under my left arm, assuring I have a good grip on it so nothing will happen along the way. I creep into the hallway and silently walk down the stairs. It is early, and I don't know if Tim and Hillary are still sleeping. I don't want to disturb them. Once on the first floor, I stroll quietly towards the kitchen to grab an apple for breakfast. Rounding the corner to the kitchen, I notice Hillary is standing there stirring creamer into her coffee.

"Oh, good morning." She jumps at the sight of me. I must have startled her.

"Hi! I didn't mean to scare you! Just grabbing an apple for breakfast." I nod towards the apples on the counter next to her. She turns and looks at the apples, slowly reaching to grab one.

She turns back towards me and looks from the apple to me.

"This is all you're eating for breakfast?" Concern fills her features.

"Yeah, that's all I need." I smile softly. I feel the overwhelming emotion emanating from her. I don't want her to worry about me. I know she already has so much on her plate.

"Are you sure?" Her eyes lock with mine.

I nod my head and reach my hand out for the apple. She looks down at my hand and places the apple in it.

"I'm sorry, Adilyn. I know you deserve better." Tears beginning to puddle in the bottom of her lids.

"Don't be sorry! Everyone is in a different boat at different times, and you are doing your best." I honestly do know that she is trying. If it were up to just Tim, there would be nothing in this house except for the basics.

A forced smile crosses her face. "I'm not this emotional, I promise."

"I have my days, too, where my emotions get the best of me. So, I completely understand." I do understand. I know that sometimes emotions override all other senses, and we can be emotional trainwrecks.

"Thank you." She whispers, slowly stepping towards me and giving me a quick embrace. "Now off you go so you won't be late."

I chuckle and nod, dropping my hands down to my sides. I turn and walk to the front door.

I step out the front door, and the morning breeze greets me, caressing my face. The smell of freshly cut grass and new floral blooms drift through the cool breeze. Spring has always been my favorite season, and sunrise and sunset are my two favorite times. It is as if the world holds its breath when the sun rises and sets and the beauty dances across the sky. I look out and see the colorful flowers popping up all over and the trees coming to life with green leaves. It fills me with an unexplainable peace. I stand on the porch for a moment, taking in my surroundings. The colors dancing, the earthy smell floating around me, the soft buzzing of the town coming to life, the rustling of the little animals, trees swaying in the breeze, and dogs barking off in the distance. The sun creeps up the horizon, casting its light onto the world. I close my eyes, basking in the sun and envisioning the forest I always run to in my imagination. The one place that truly feels like home. Opening my eyes, I take a deep breath in and then out.

I can feel Hillary is changing. The wheels in her mind must slowly be creaking into movement. She is making more of an effort to be around. Yes, she may be a little emotional sometimes, but I wonder why that is the case. I half think she wishes to be a mother, and seeing me brings up emotions of longing. From the fights I have heard between her and Tim, Tim has never wanted to be a father and thinks things are fine just as they are. Hillary was the one who volunteered to foster me, not Tim, and he was very against the idea. I think the only reason why he even allowed me to stay in their home was because I was older and didn't require much attention.

I survive the first half of my day at school. Nothing of great importance or excitement happens at school, as usual. I walk from one class to another, silently listening to all the gossip as I walk through the hallway.

"Can you believe that she tried to hit on Cindy's boyfriend?" one girl snickered.

"I know! How cringe of her, seriously. What was she thinking?" the other girl shrieked.

I roll my eyes and keep walking down the hallway. This is the usual drama that goes around this school. Someone accusing another of doing something they probably did not even do. I always ensure I never partake in any of that, spreading gossip. That is not who I am. I hate talking poorly about someone else, especially if it is not valid, and most of the gossip whispered in the hallways is only rumors spread to start drama. This town doesn't have much excitement, so the high school students like to stir the pot.

I'm almost to Miss Lianca's class, the last class of the day for me. I'm so ready to get to art class. I can present her with my painting and relinquish the burden of carrying it around any longer.

"She thinks she is better than us," Cindy snaps.

"She is a loser. She has no friends," Trent mockingly says, staring in my direction.

"Right? Her only friend is that old lady from the cafe. Who wants to be friends with someone who lies about the changes they make in their appearance? Let's be real; her hair and eyes aren't natural. She has to do something to get those colors." Cindy snickers. They both laugh and saunter off.

Wow, she thinks I have a holier-than-thou mentality? If she had only gotten to know me, she would have discovered that I didn't think I was better than anyone else. On top of that, she says that no one will want to be my friend because of the "changes" I make to my appearance. She has brown hair with highlights! Isn't that a change to her appearance? I blow out a long breath, trying to suppress my anger and sadness. Usually, the mean comments don't affect me because I have learned to ignore them. I don't allow them the satisfaction of their mean comments dragging me down. However, Cindy's comment hit me like a steamroller crushing everything. I have wanted nothing more than to belong and feel cared for and accepted. Unfortunately, I have never felt either of those things here. Is there something wrong with me?

Most people did not even try to get to know me. I'm different, and I stand out in a crowd. Maybe they are scared of me because of my looks, or maybe it is something else. It is not like I haven't tried to make friends. This high school, well, this town actually, has always been very cliquey. I have never really been accepted into any group. In all reality, there is no group that I truly belong to. I don't fit into the intelligent kids group because I am too artistic for them. I don't fit into the artsy clique because I am a straight-A student; they call me "too smart." I'm not great at sports, and I'm not good in the drama club, pretending to be something I'm not, let alone in the spotlight. I just do not quite fit into any one category.

I try to shake off the pain of her comment and make my way into Miss Lianca's class.

School is finally over. I have survived yet another day in this place. Today hit me harder than it usually did. The longing to belong was so much more intense than usual. I needed to unwind before I got to work.

I inch down the stairs, and head towards the one place I know will help me collect myself. Walking up the road, I see the trees peeking over the hill. I'm almost there, almost to the forest—the one place where I feel at home, at peace.

I skip up the remaining incline of the hill. Joy fills my insides. I pause for just a moment at the border of the trees. I place my hand on the large oak that towers over the road. Closing my eyes, I inhale, sucking in a deep breath. I hold it just for a moment. I let the peace of the tree wash over me. I release the air in my lungs and open my eyes.

I wander into the forest. I slowly walk, extending my hands to touch each tree I walk by. I weave through the tree, going to one of the giant oak trees deep in the forest. No one can see me here from the road; they seldom come into the forest. I spot the massive oak tree, standing prouder than the surrounding trees. Its vibrant green leaves swaying in the cool breeze. I stand before the peaceful giant and look at it. The moss that covers most of its trunk, the branches that reach sky high, and the leaves slowly swaying. I can hear the birds flying in the canopy of the trees, singing their beautiful melody.

I sit down and lean against the oak, resting my head against its trunk. The earthy scent fills my senses, calming my body and my soul. If only I could live out here surrounded by such beauty all the time.

I know that really is not possible, but how I wish otherwise. I see two squirrels scampering across the forest floor, jumping upon fallen branches. I smile at their playful banter. They pause on a broken branch and look at me. It's as if time is frozen, looking at each other. I nod my head towards them, and they nod back. Interesting... I didn't think an animal would understand the gesture of a nod. They scamper off deeper into the forest, and my gaze trails after them. Once I can no longer see them, I turn in the other direction. Only about an arm's length away is a small patch of Bloodroot flowers, yet on the verge of flourishing. The flowers will decorate the ground with color and life in another day or two.

I lean my head back onto the trunk and close my eyes. I sit there, allowing my mind to wander, taking me to a place far away from here, and breathing in and out—slow, deep breaths. I let nature wash over me, the ancient oaks standing tall, the tiny blooms that let off a sweet perfume, the small creatures that bring so much life to this place. True peace. I envision what the flowers look like, opening in full bloom. A warm fuzzy feeling spreads inside my chest, passing down my arms. I let it wash over me as I began to doze off.

A bird chirping in a branch directly above me jolts me awake. It is time for me to go. I have to be at work soon. I open my eyes and glance around, imprinting it into my memory. As I begin to stand up, I look over to the Bloodroots. They are fully opened. There are more of them than I last saw only minutes ago. Before, there was a small patch of about ten. Now, there are at least twenty-five Bloodroots.

"That can't be possible! They still had another day left until they bloomed, and there weren't this many," I say, puzzled. I rub my eyes in hopes of bringing my vision back to reality. I know flowers, and they still had time left until they were in full bloom and fully opened. Something is wrong. This cannot be possible. I must have seen them wrong earlier, but this doesn't seem right. That warm sensation slowly fades from my body, and a feeling of discomfort replaces it. There is something strange here, and I don't know how to explain it. I grab my bag from the ground and look at my watch.

"Crap, I have to be at work in ten minutes! I dozed for a little too long!" I pull my bag on my shoulder and jog towards the cafe. I don't have time to figure out what happened with the flowers. Otherwise, I will be late.

I arrived at the cafe on time. There is no one inside. No one is sipping from their hot tea or coffee, getting updates on the recent gossip or reading. I'm thankful for that because I am huffing and puffing as I come through the front door. I jogged the entire way here and feel like I could collapse on the floor.

"Hey, Dani!" Out of breath, I yell back towards the kitchen and drag myself to the office to set my bag down.

" Hey! Tonight is your big night! I am sure you will blow all the other artists out of the water!" she exclaims as she comes from the kitchen. I would not dare roll my eyes at her while she was looking right at me. I don't want to be scolded by her. She's like a mother to me, and I don't want to anger her.

"Will you be coming tonight to the art exhibit?" I ask, hoping she will say yes.

"Of course, honey. I would not miss that for the world. I will get my little old self over there after I have everything closed up for the night," she says, beaming at me. Her words mean so much to me. They warm my heart. I never really get actual words of affirmation from anyone except her.

Chapter Five

Hillary

My head is throbbing because I didn't get much sleep last night. Tim was up late, drunk again, complaining that he was still upset with Adilyn living in the house. I don't know why he has the right to be angry over anything about her. She is out of the house a lot and is typically quiet when she is home. Since she got a job, she has left money around to help pay for things. I have tried to tell her there is no need, but she worries about being a burden. Anyway, I don't get why he moans about it so often, considering he has been unemployed for quite some time, and there is no sign of him getting another job. Tim needs something to whine about, so she is his target.

Many of our fights are because he is dead set on her moving out as soon as she turns 18. I'm tired of fighting with him, especially when he has been drinking. It's mentally exhausting. After 16 years married to him, I thought things would get easier, but it hasn't. He was my high school sweetheart; he was perfect for me at the time. We got married as soon as we turned 18. Boy, did I think life would become amazing after marriage, but it only got worse. The nasty remarks escalated with each passing year. Sometimes, I wonder why I am still putting up with him. Why am I still allowing this? Unfortunately, I don't think I deserve better.

I quietly sneak down to the kitchen to make some coffee. The joy of technology today is that I can work from home. Now, I create a curriculum for schools, especially elementary schools. I loved the fun of teaching little ones, the singing, and the dancing. The excitement of the students when they see you. I used to be a kindergarten teacher, but there were flaws in the curriculum, and I wanted to help improve it. However, these past years, I feel like maybe my dreams have changed. I don't know. I used to love teaching and doing what I was doing. However, I no longer find it as exciting as before. I feel like there is something more for me out there, but I don't know what that is.

I was lost in thought when Adilyn entered the kitchen. It startled me for a moment. I hadn't heard her footsteps, so I didn't realize she was awake. It wasn't surprising, though, because she has always been quiet. She is such a remarkable teenager. I knew she would be.

All those years ago, when the Himwalds could no longer care for her and were searching for someone to take her in, I had a dream. Recalling it is still a little hazy, but I remember in that dream, I walked with her into a place that was alive; it was magical. In this dream, a voice whispered to me that Adilyn would be very important in my life. I woke up and felt I had to open my doors to her. I made the phone call as soon as I could. Tim was so angry, but I thought I had to do this. Here we are now.

I watch Adilyn outside from the window. Things have to change. I feel this urgency that they have to change. It terrifies me not knowing what this feeling of urgency is for or how life-altering things will be. I do know that a change will be for the best. I may not deserve the best in the world, but I don't know how long I can handle Tim.

"Hill, hurry up and bring me breakfast and something for my migraine!" Tim yells from upstairs.

I roll my eyes. "Get it yourself," I whisper to myself out of fear of him hearing.

"Hurry the hell up!" He demands.

Ugh, he woke up in a foul mood, as usual. I was hoping to have a few more moments to myself before hell snatched me again. I turn, walking to the fridge to grab the milk. He will have to eat cereal for now. I have work I need to go and do. If he wants anything more, he can come and get it himself.

CHAPTER SIX

Art Exhibit

ADILYN

I leave the cafe and go to the art gallery along the road. The sun is setting, and the night is creeping up, leaving me to walk in the dark. Walking hidden in the shadows, unnoticed by the world, is oddly soothing. The night air is cool on my skin. There isn't a strong breeze sweeping through, thankfully, otherwise my hair would become a mess. I'm content that it has been a slow day at work, allowing me to finish most of my things early. This gave me just enough time to get ready. Everyone in town has been discussing attending the event tonight, so few people came into the cafe this afternoon. Nothing big happens in this town except for this event once a year. I know that quite a few people will be attending tonight.

The walk from the cafe to the art gallery is not very long, only about 15 minutes. I use this time to take deep breaths, attempting to wrangle in my nerves. The thought of me possibly winning this exhibit starts creeping into my mind, causing my anxiety to spike. What am I going to do? I mindlessly walk to the gallery, trying to focus solely on my breathing so that I don't have a panic attack before arriving. Deep breath in, slow breath out. I pause for a moment, closing my eyes, soaking in the stillness of my surroundings, grounding myself. I open my eyes and look out around me, seeing small flowers that look to have just bloomed scattering along the road edge.

"Hmmm. I don't remember seeing them there a moment ago." I shrug it off. I must have missed them, distracted by my anxiety. That's so strange, but this wouldn't be the first time something precisely like this has happened.

I can see the gallery only a short distance up ahead of me. "This is it... almost," I say, laughing, trying to make light of the situation that is about to unfold in my lap. I walk up to the main door of the gallery and place my hand on the handle. I stop for a moment and take a deep breath in. I am breathing in all of the confident and courageous vibes that I can muster up—exhaling all the nerves and negativity I feel. "I got this," I whisper, desperately trying to convince myself. I give myself a quick shake, then push the door open and walk in.

The room's warmth immediately hits me as I walk in, causing me to feel uncomfortable. I pull around the neck of my dress. The room is buzzing with people and excitement. I can hear the soft jazz music play-ing in the background. There are a lot of people, all dressed formally and sipping from their champagne glasses. People walk from one painting to the next, tilting their heads from one side to the other, discussing the art piece before them. There are reporters from local newspapers and radio stations, as well as from the big cities nearby. People are here to find the next prominent artist. I spot the mayor of Claywood and the sheriff over by the appetizer table, and I chuckle. That is where I usually see them at events.

I wander around the gallery, looking at all the art pieces hanging, trying to keep to myself. Some paintings around the room are abstract, and others are landscapes, portraits, etc. The talent is awe-inspiring. I can see why this event is so popular. My nerves are starting to bite at my insides. I fidget with my fingers to try to distract myself. I can do this, I can do this, I can do this, becomes the mantra in my head. I begin to feel lightheaded by all the excitement in the room. The winners will be announced soon. I walk to the refreshment table to grab some water and a quick bite to eat, hoping to stabilize my composure. As I drink my water, Ms. Lianca calls out to me, waving her hand and signaling for me to come over to her and a group of reporters she's standing beside.

"Ugh, this is what I wanted to avoid," I mumble. I toss my cup in the trash, suck in a deep breath, and graciously make my way over to the group, willing all of my charms to the surface.

"Good evening, Ms. Lianca! Good evening, everyone!" I say with a shy smile.

"Adilyn, my darling, I want to introduce you to some of my friends!" she exclaims. I'm sure they are your friends, Ms. Lianca, more like your fifteen seconds to fame.

"This is Darren Loster from CW News, Thomas Fisher from Claywood Chronicle, and Stewart Freman from Ivybrook Tribute."

"Hello, Adilyn," the three say in unison.

" I saw your art piece and am very impressed! Such detail and precision in your painting! Where do you get your inspiration from?" Thomas asks.

"Thank you, Mr. Fisher, that is so kind of you. My inspiration comes from within." Placing a finger on my temple. I shift on my feet because these three men in front of me are big names. My nerves start chewing faster on my insides.

"From within?" Thomas asks curiously, eyebrows shooting up to the middle of his forehead.

"Yes, sir, from within. All of my paintings are things I have dreamed of at some point, places that come to life in my head. These are places that I have traveled to in my imagination, and it has felt almost just as real to me as this place we are standing in now does," I respond, opening my hands and signaling around us to the gallery, then put my hands behind my back immediately. My hands are shaking, and they can't see that. The three reporters are all furiously writing away on their little notepads. I shift on my feet, trying to center myself and push past the nerves. I will not make a fool of myself in front of these men.

Darren looks up at me, "That's amazing! I can tell that is what has made your art so astonishing! You are very talented, Adilyn." The other two nod in agreement.

"Thank you for your kind words, sir. They mean so much to me," I smile and nod towards Darren, feeling the reddening in my cheeks. "Are there any other questions I may be able to answer for you?" I ask, crossing my fingers behind me, hoping their answer will be no.

"If we think of anything, we won't hesitate to ask. But for now, continue to enjoy your evening," Darren says with a smile.

I nod, thanking the reporters and then Ms. Lianca. I retreat quickly without making my desire to flee too obvious. Wiping away the sweat from my forehead, I make my way to the farthest wall from the front door. I continue browsing the paintings, glancing every so often towards the door. Dani should be here any moment. I hope she can make it soon because I can only walk around this place so often alone. I continue walking around the gallery slowly, admiring the hanging art. I study each one, trying to understand the minds and imaginations of the artists to whom these pieces belong. There are genuinely some incredible paintings here. I turn, ready to explore the art on the other side of the gallery, when something catches my attention: someone standing in front of my painting. He's not someone I have ever seen before. He seems out of place here, kind of like me. There is a rugged and commanding presence about him. I smile at the thought that he is out of place here, just like me. A warm tingle passes through my body like wildfire, just under my skin at the sight of this man. My heart is picking up its pace. It feels like it will jump right out of my chest onto the floor. What the hell is wrong with me?

He's tall and looks like he threw spears for a living with those broad shoulders. The muscles in his arms and back were well-defined. He's wearing all black, sleeves rolled halfway up. I can't see his face. His dark hair falls in untamed waves, covering my view. He's facing my painting, captivated by it, unmoved by the crowd around him. My curiosity spikes, or is it the tingling sensation that flows through my body? I feel a pull towards him. I want to know who he is and talk to him. I decide to wander over to him and find out just that. I make my way, winding through all the people ooh-ing and ahh-ing the paintings, nodding at those who look my way. I am honing my focus on this man until I hear voices starting to rise. I turn, looking away from the stranger for just a moment to see what's going on. There is a girl about 22 years old. I recognize her. She works at a local diner as a waitress. She has had one too many drinks and is arguing with her boyfriend.

"I'm fine. I'm not drunk!" she yells, sloshing her words. My mouth closes; it sure does seem like you are, honey.

"Please let me get you home before you embarrass yourself or me," he says calmly, trying to de-escalate the situation before it gets too out of hand. From what little I know about the two, she has always been loud and wild. He, on the other hand, is quiet and pretty reserved. I always thought they were a funny match since they were complete opposites like Hillary and Tim. I shake my head at the scene that is unfolding right here in the art gallery. I don't envy him at all. I would never want to be like that, drunk in public. Drinking to that point has never been a desire of mine. I turn back to where the mystery man was, redirecting my focus to him. However, he's no longer there. He's gone. I stand in the middle of the art gallery, dumbfounded and looking all around. I can't see him anywhere in the gallery, as if he disappeared into thin air. How is that even possible? I know I didn't turn away for that long, only a few seconds.

He was just there. Ugh, I shake my head. He must be a figment of my imagination. I guess I let it run a little too wild at times. A void fills my chest, and disappointment runs through me. I shrug it off. I shouldn't be fussing over a man I don't know, let alone a man that probably doesn't even exist. A moment later, I spot Dani walking through the door.

"Oh, thank god," I mutter, feeling relief that she has arrived. I wave to her and stroll in her direction, trying not to look too eager. Her presence here tonight means so much to me.

The winner is about to be announced. The judges decided to announce two winners this year since so many paintings were submitted. The owner of Clay's Art House, Calla Ortega, stands in front of the crowd with a broad grin. Tension fills the room as everyone notices Calla in the front. The crowd begins to quiet down, and only a few murmurs of "Who do you think the winner is?" are spoken around the room. I stand in the back of the room with Dani behind everyone else. The front door is only feet away.

It's the perfect spot to be for the ideal escape.

"We have just enough time to run out the front door! No one will notice that we are missing." I grab Dani's arm, tugging it softly.

"No, Adilyn. We are staying long enough for them to march you right up to the front as a winner. I believe in you and know you are more talented than anyone else in this town." Her eyes are gentle and filled with understanding.

"Dani, please, the door is so close though.... You know this kind of thing makes me uncomfortable." I beg, feeling my palms start to sweat.

"I know... I know it makes you uncomfortable. However, it would be best if you stepped up. Your life will be filled with many greater and more challenging things than this. So you must push yourself and learn to adapt because you'll have to, sooner than you think." Her eyes lock with mine. Something simmering behind her irises makes me think there is something she knows that I don't. She reaches over, gives me a quick hug, and rubs my back to try to soothe the anxiety roaring inside of me.

I know that she is right. Dani has always given me sound advice, even if I don't follow it. But how is she so confident that my life will be filled with more extraordinary and more challenging situations? My nerves going haywire throughout my entire body. I must put on my big girl panties and bite the bullet. In a little more than a week, my life will be changing. I'll go from a teenager to an adult and have to figure life out.

"Okay. You are right. I need to push past my fears. I can do this because you believe in me," I say, straightening my back, squaring my shoulders, and holding my chin up high. This one event will not tear me down or make me feel less. This event will teach me and mold me into something more significant.

Calla hushs everyone. "Welcome, everyone! Welcome artists of Claywood. I am so pleased to see all of your wonderful faces here tonight. I could not be happier! I know that everyone here is so excited about this exhibit. This can be a life-changing event. We have all gathered to see who our next big artists are."

Cheers rise through the crowd. Calla grins, raising her hand in the air to calm everyone. "As I said, we are all here to see who will be the next star. However, since we have received so many entries this year, the judges and I have decided to choose two winners!" More cheers break out through the crowd. The air is filled with excitement, yet an undertone of tension. So many artists here hope and pray they will be this year's winner. So many want this and rely on it to take them far away from Claywood.

The pressure grows in my chest, and my head starts to swim. My heart is pounding. Beads of sweat begin to form on my forehead. I have to remind myself to breathe. I won't allow myself to panic or get sick in front of all these people. I will not let myself be embarrassed. I rock myself on my heels, trying to distract myself from the crowd.

"Is everyone ready to hear who the winners are?" Calla voices. Hushes echo through the gallery. Everyone goes silent. I can cut through the silence and the tension with a knife. I glance around to see all of the nervous faces of the artists. "Drum roll, please!" Everyone begins patting their bodies in anticipation. Calla made the theatrics of slowly opening the envelope with the winners' names. She is the type of person that thrives off of the spotlight. She has never been a great artist, although her husband was when he was alive. The gallery belonged to him before he passed. She inherited it from him and has been living the life she always wanted.

"Our winners are...." She pauses to read the paper. "Henry and Adilyn!" she exclaims. The crowd claps and cheers Henry's name. "Come on up, you two!"

Dani nudges me to go forward. I give her a look that I am sure looks like death has just passed over me. She smiles and nods, pushing me towards the front. I can't get my feet to move, as if they are glued to the floor. Everyone is staring at me, waiting for what I will do. My lungs begin to close, and I'm taking in short breaths, struggling to get any air. I glance at the doorway, checking how many obstacles are in my way.

"I can't believe she won." Stacy rolls her eyes.

"Right? What a disappointment." Cindy snickers at me.

"Shut up, both of you!" Stephanie snickers and then turns to me.

Stephanie is standing next to them. She looks at me, and a grin spreads across her face. She gives me a thumbs-up and winks. That small gesture from someone I don't know eased some pressure in my chest.

I can do this. I will not cower, nor will I back down. I think to myself, mustering up all my strength to put one foot in front of the other. I walk forward with my chin held high. I paste a smile as I near Calla in the front. Henry is already in the front, standing beside Calla, cheering and waving his hands. Once I reach the front, I move to stand on the other side of Calla. I broadened my smile, knowing the reporters would snap pictures for the news story. I think the last thing that I want is a photo of me with some stupid face on the front page news.

Calla hushes everyone in the room once again. "Henry, you painted a very intriguing and beautiful abstract painting. Would you like to tell us something about the piece?"

"Sure, Calla, I would love to!" Henry affirms. He's very charming and can quickly grasp the attention of a crowd. "The human mind inspired this painting. Our minds are very complex things. Sometimes they can be messy and not clear. So I wanted to bring that to my canvas."

The crowd applauds and chants Henry's name. "That is truly inspiring, Henry. Where do you see yourself in a few years? Will this opportunity lead you to become the next Pollock?" Calla says.

"Yes, ma'am. I will become the next Pollock. I will be even bigger than him!"

"I am sure you will!" Calla says and then turns to me. "Adilyn, darling, you had a very stunning piece. Your painting was of the woods at night time. The judges and I were all very impressed with your technique and precision. You truly made your painting come to life," Calla praises.

Henry rolls his eyes at Calla's comment. I swallow hard, my hands start to clam up. Everyone is staring at me. Calla is expecting me to respond. Everyone is waiting for me too. Please say something, anything, for goodness' sake. I feel like I just might be sick. I scan the crowd, and my eyes lock on Dani's. Her reassuring smile and nod comfort me. They give me strength. I inhale sharply and turn to Calla.

"Why, thank you, Calla. I am so pleased to hear you all loved it." I say with the biggest smile I can plaster to my face. Fake it until you make it, as Ms. Lianca always told me in school. So here I am, going to fake it until I can make it.

"Yes, dear, we did. Now, where did you get your inspiration? The painting is of the woods, yet they are not woods that you would see anywhere around here. There is something more to them. Please explain to us. We are all dying to hear." Calla claps her hands together.

I smile because this answer is easy for me, "Well, my inspiration comes from my imagination. I paint what I have seen in my dreams. The woods are something I hold dear to me, so I am not surprised that I dream of them often enough. However, in my dream, they are different. Much more vibrant than the woods we find here in our lovely town."

"Astonishing, Adilyn, just astonishing, being able to remember your dreams so vividly to be able to paint them. I envy you, my darling," she exclaims.

"Well, nature is my canvas, and I am but a humble artist," I nod.

"Of course! Now, where do you see yourself in a few years?"

"If I can be honest, I don't know. Don't get me wrong, I love painting, but not necessarily to always share with the world."

"Understandable!" Calla's grin disappears with my response, and she turns towards the crowd. "Alright then, everyone here, you have them! You're Claywood's winners of our 23rd annual festival!" The crowd cheers, everyone lifting their glass in salute of Henry and myself. I can see Dani in the back, gleaming with joy. Seeing Dani's face makes it easier to be up in front of people in the spotlight. I take a deep breath, lift my chin high, and truly smile this time.

The event has come to an end, finally. I feel like I can finally breathe. Dani left moments ago because, as she said, she had baking to do. That woman is always baking; however, that is her love language. I shake my head and then look up at the night sky. How beautiful nighttime is here. All the stars sparkling in the night sky since there aren't many street lights in this town to drown them out. I can feel the cool breeze drying the beads of sweat on the back of my neck and forehead.

"Hey, you! I am glad I caught you before you left." Stephanie steps outside of the gallery.

"Uh... hey." blinking several times to double-check that she is talking to me.

"I wanted to let you know that your painting is amazing, absolutely stunning!" her smile is kind.

"Thank you," I glance down, hiding my rosy cheeks.

"If you ever want to teach art, please let me know! I would love to take some classes from you!"

"Oh, um, yeah I will have to think about that. I will get back to you on that, though."

"Totally! I understand. Maybe since you love painting, I believe, as much as I love self-defense, we can trade. Class for class?"

Is this conversation really happening? I look around for people hiding in the bushes with cameras, but there's no one there. It is just her and I outside.

"Self-defense? I can say that I have never taken a self-defense class before, but it's not a bad idea!"

"Awesome! I will let you go; I'm sure you have had a long day and are ready to get home. When you decide on that class trade, let me know," she winks at me.

"Okay, will do! Thank you!"

"Oh, my name is Stephanie, by the way," she reaches out with her hand.

"My name is Adilyn," I look down at her hand and then reach mine out to grab hers. Her hand is warm, giving me a feeling of home hits me.

She drops my hand and then walks into the shadows of the night, leaving me standing there staring after her. She feels like home, and I cannot shake that feeling.

CHAPTER SEVEN

Asher

C laywood is undoubtedly a strange place. Everything here looks the same. There's nothing special in this town. Things here are much different than where I'm from. I have been to Claywood only a few times before tonight in the past few months.

I walk up to the Clay's Art House. Tonight, from my understanding, an art event is going on. So, the gallery will be busy. I walk into the gallery, scanning the room, not seeing what I'm here for. The gallery is crawling with so many humans walking around, drinking, and laughing. Many of them analyze the paintings hanging in front of them. Some of them are there to get noticed by people of power, or so it seems. I stroll around the gallery, looking from painting to painting.

"These colors are muted," I mumble to myself. I continue to analyze the paintings hanging on the walls. I finish looking at all the paintings on this side of the art gallery. Many paintings I just saw have no depicted image to them, more of an abstract. I turn my head, seeing the paintings on the other side look like portraits and landscapes. I walk to the refreshment table towards the back, scanning the room for that one person. Still not here. I roll my neck, trying to ease the tension. I grab a glass of water and lean against the back wall, observing the crowd. One girl in the middle of the room is guzzling down drinks. The man next to her is pleading for her to stop. I shake my head at the girl's response, and she brushes him off. That cannot turn out very well if it continues. I continue looking around.

My eyes lock with someone I recognize, with emerald green eyes and long, wavy brown hair. I nod at her, and she nods back in acknowledgment. This sitting and waiting is beginning to test my patience. I push myself off of the wall. What time will she be here? Irritation is starting to rise in my core. Dani said she will be attending. I don't particularly appreciate standing around and doing mundane things when there are more significant issues. I roll my shoulders, trying to relieve some of the built-up tension in my muscles. This job is becoming tiring, just sitting around, watching, and waiting. However, I know the wait is necessary. Iridessa always said that everything has its perfect time. I can hear her voice as clearly as day as if she were still here.

I turn and wander to the other side of the gallery to continue viewing the paintings. Then, it catches the corner of my eye: a painting hanging on the other side of the room to the left. It was in the far corner along the wall, and I had yet to browse. I know that place; it looks muted, but I know that place. I toss my cup in the trash and beeline for the painting. I stand in front of it, analyzing the colors, the brushstrokes, the trees, the details—the trees in the distance and the never-ending meadows full of flowers.

"Every brushstroke tells a story, and every petal holds a secret," I mutter an ancient saying that those back in my homeland said. This painting is filled with trees and flowers contrasting the beautiful night sky. The stars glistened brightly. The beauty in this painting is almost as comparable to the beauty back home. As I admire the painting, I feel it: an itch roams through my body and under my skin. I feel her eyes gazing upon me. She's here. I turn my head slightly to the right to catch a glimpse of her from the corner of my eye. She is staring at me, trying to figure out who I am. The side of my mouth curves up. She has no clue who I am. Time seems to freeze for a moment before she starts to make her way towards me. I can see her weaving through the crowd so gracefully. She politely nods at people as she walks by them; however, she focuses on me, as if I'm her prey and she's the huntress.

A slurred yell causes Adilyn to turn her head in the other direction of the room. Someone doesn't sound very happy. I glance towards the commotion and see the couple from earlier. The woman must have had too many drinks and lost control of herself. The commotion is my perfect ticket out. At that exact moment, I slip out of the gallery. Tonight is not the night, not just yet. I have to wait just a little longer. I just wanted to see her for a moment.

CHAPTER EIGHT

Life Choices

ADILYN

I wake up to the sound of my foster parents fighting downstairs. I sit up straight in my bed, trying to listen to the argument to ensure it doesn't turn out for the worst. I rarely see them, and I manage to be scarce during their waking hours with school, work, and painting. Well, at least I managed to stay out of Tim's way as much as possible. Hillary isn't bad, but I can't say the same for Tim.

Once my previous foster parents could no longer care for me because of their old age and health, the Stents were the only other foster family in Claywood that volunteered to take care of me. If I must be honest, I don't think they ever expected to foster a child, then I came along! I always left notes for Hillary so she knew my plans and where I would be since I did not have a phone. I also would leave her money every time I got paid because I did not want to inconvenience or burden them. I'm sure if I didn't help, Tim would have a cow over it. He seems to be the one against me staying here, but Hillary is the one who wants me here.

I don't see her much between her work schedule and Tim's dramatics. I wish I could see her more. I may not see them much, but I hear them often. Arguments between them were pretty ordinary.

"Are you kidding me, Hillary?" Tim shouts.

"No, I'm not kidding, Tim. How is it my problem that you can't seem to hear anything I say? I asked you to pay it by today, Wednesday, and you drank yourself silly last night with the money." She shouts back. This was not an unusual topic for their argument. I don't think Tim ever really pays attention to anything Hillary says. Hillary is a quiet and kind person. She doesn't like fighting or drama, but I know that it bothers her that Tim doesn't listen. Tim is as stubborn as a mule, loud, overbearing, and downright mean. Tim is one of those annoying people that you never want in your face. I don't understand how they have made it this far, but they have.

I flop back on my bed and cover my ears with my pillow. Wednesday mornings were the days I would sleep in a little since school starts later; however, it looks like this will not be one of those days. "Just one more hour of sleep, please; that's all I'm asking for," I whine into my pillow. I hear the loud stomps as one climbs the stairs and storms down the hallway, slamming the bedroom door, followed by the thud of the front door. The walls shake at the force of both slamming doors. Well, that is the end of that argument for now. One stormed to their room, and the other took off to god knows where. I lay in bed for a bit longer before I realize I won't be able to go back to sleep because my mind is racing. I won last night, now what? I still know that I don't want to paint as a career. I would enjoy painting for myself or painting a loved one a gift if I had any. However, I don't want to get paid to paint, at least not at this point in my life. I roll out of bed, pull on my bear claw slippers, and shuffle over to my desk. I need to think about what I will do with my life, and what better way to do that than to jot down all my options? I grab my journal and a pen. I have always been able to think and collect my thoughts best outside, so I will sit by the giant oak tree in the backyard. There are no neighbors behind us, so it's nice knowing no one blocks your view of the mountains that rise behind the Stent's home.

I quietly open my bedroom door and tiptoe down the stairs, trying not to make any noise. I don't know if whoever is in the bedroom is still fuming, but I don't want to be on the receiving end of that. A smile spreads across my face when I get to the back door. I can see the scenery behind the house through the glass back door. I skip over to the tree and sit down, leaning against its trunk. I look up at its branches and leaves.

"Hey, buddy! I'm sorry I have not been out in some time. Life has been quite hectic with school, work, and the exhibit. I won, though! I won the exhibit," I speak softly to the tree, wishing it could hear me. The trees feel like they are my only friends outside of Dani. Talking to them always seems to be so easy and comforting.

"School is almost over... only three more days left. Then what? What am I supposed to do? Where am I supposed to go? I have no clue, and it is eating me inside." A silent tear runs down my face. I feel overwhelmed by the little time left and have no real direction in my life. Deep in my bones is a feeling I'm meant for so much more, but I'm sure everyone feels that way. The tree begins swaying in the soft breeze as if acknowledging my pain and confusion, letting me know I'm not alone.

"How I wish you trees could talk," I whisper upwards. I close my eyes and try to bring myself back to my task. I need to brainstorm and figure out what I'm going to do. I open my eyes and sit up straight, opening my notebook. I begin by heading the page with the word "LIFE." I chuckle, imagining myself deciding my life based on the game MASH. Wouldn't that be hilarious? What did I want to do with my life? Was there something that I would equate to greatness? What is greatness? I don't know. I write down some possibilities of what I can do. A painter? Work at Dani's, maybe one day take over the cafe for her? Move to the big city and find an office job?

I didn't overly want to pursue the painting route. I love painting, yet not in that way. I would be okay with working at the cafe for the rest of my life. It is a quiet and simple job. Yet, would I find that fulfilling enough? I could move to the big city and find an office job. Wear business casual every day, pencil skirts, and button-up shirts. I laugh deeply at that. I don't think I can imagine myself doing that. I can't picture myself in business attire, alone behind a desk and computer all day. I would feel so disconnected since there isn't much nature in the big city.

I don't know what life would be like if I chose that route. Nature is essential to my life, and cutting that out might be detrimental. I cross that one off of my list. I look up again at the branches of the aging tree.

"What if I became an art teacher? Not the ones in the school but an outside class, teaching kids how to paint?" Hope fills my chest. The tree sways as if in approval. That could be a great option. I can work with Dani until I get this all going. Maybe I can mentor only a few students so I'm not overwhelmed and can still help Dani. I jot that down on my paper and circle that several times. My hairs stand up on the back of my neck and my arms. A sense of someone watching me falls upon me. I close my journal and look around. I can't see anyone. I look out at the mountains and the scattered trees along the mountainside. Someone may be hiding behind something, but I don't know. I stand up, dust off the back of my pants, and continue to look around. The feeling persists, yet I can't see anyone anywhere. The feeling leaves me uneasy, so I decide to go back inside. I don't want to end up on the next episode of 48 Hours by staying out here.

"Goodbye for now, my dear friend," I whisper, leaning my forehead on its trunk. I turn and make my way back inside of the house. The feeling disappears when I get inside, and I sigh with relief. That was strange. I rummage through the fridge to find something quick to eat. There is not much; there never usually is. I grab a banana and milk out of the refrigerator. Placing them on the counter, I grab a bowl and the box of Cheerios. I pour the cheerios and milk, then cut the banana and add it to the bowl.

"Breakfast for champs!" I giggle. I chow down my cereal in the kitchen. I hate eating alone. I have done plenty of that in the last two and a half years. I speed through my food and wash my bowl as soon as I finish. I dry the bowl, place it back where I got it, grab my journal, and head back upstairs. I'll need to start getting ready soon to go to work. As I climb up the stairs as quietly as a mouse, I hear the sobbing coming from the Stent's room. Hillary is in there. I'm so torn on what I should do. I want to check on her to see if she's okay; however, I fear it will worsen things. I stand before my door and stare down the hall, debating. I quickly enter my room and set my journal on my desk. I turn and make my way back to the hallway. I try to walk as quietly as possible. Once I reach the Stent's door, I take a deep breath and knock.

"Leave me the hell alone, Tim!" she yells at the door, venom lacing her words.

"Mrs. Stent, it's me, Adilyn," I almost whisper, afraid of what will happen next.

"Oh! What do you need, Adilyn?" The venom has subdued in her voice.

"I just wanted to see if you need anything and to let you know I will be heading to work soon," I say, crossing my fingers that she does not open that door and throw something at me.

"I'm good, thank you—just a little upset, you know, the usual. Have fun at work and be safe!" she calls through the door, and I hear her sobbing. I'm in shock. She has never told me to have fun at work and be safe. That was the first time. I don't know how to feel, scared, worried. Warm that she maybe even cared?

"Okay. I'm sorry that you are upset. I hope you feel better," I say back through the door, tears forming in my eyes. I can feel her sorrow and frustration. It is so overwhelming. I wait momentarily, wanting to make sure she doesn't respond. Then, I walk back down the hallway. I can hear Hillary sniffling as I walk back toward my room. She may be a very closed person, but I do care that she's okay. I care about the people around me, whether we are friends, enemies, or whatever. It pains me when I can feel that someone is in pain and suffering on the inside. I close my door behind me and lean against my door, blowing out the breath I feel like I held in through that whole conversation. Gosh, what a morning, for sure. I hope the rest of my day is not this eventful. I decide it would be best to get ready now and leave for work early. I don't want to be here if Tim comes back fuming.

"The fight was pretty heated!" I tell Dani. I tell Dani everything. She is my best friend other than the trees. As soon as I got to work, I caught her up on how my morning had gone. She shook her head and rolled her eyes when I told her about the fight between the Stents and then Hillary in her room.

"That couple is not good for each other. He is pure toxic, and I don't know how Hillary can stand him," she huffs out, shaking her head in disapproval. I nod at her comment. At least I was not the only person who thought their relationship was not the greatest.

"I'm proud that you took the time to try and figure out your life. You would be a great art teacher who helps others find their artistic talent. You have always been great with kids; in reality, you are great with everyone. Most people do not give you the chance. You play a big game of being an introvert, but I would bet my life on it being the other way around."

I shake my head and huff out a breath with an exasperated roll of my eyes. Yet, I think deep down she may be right. "You are right, Dani. I wish I was accepted by more people than you and the trees," I say, with an overwhelming sense of loneliness.

"Well, of course, I'm right, honey. I'm always right. And yes, you do need more than just me and trees. Don't get me wrong, I'm more than enough and then some, but you do need friends. I'm sure that you will find that circle of friends soon," she says, with warmth in her voice, her eyes sparkling.

"I adore you, Dani," I bark out a laugh and wrap my arms around her, squeezing her as hard as I can. She wraps her arms around me and squeezes me right back. We stand there for a moment, enjoying each other's embrace.

"Alright now, stop trying to make me tear up, girl, and get back to work!" she exclaims and pushes me away jokingly, pretending that she will hit me with the towel in her hand.

"Alright, alright!" I laugh with my hands in the air. I turn on the espresso machine and get everything ready for today.

I should've knocked three times on wood when I hoped work would be uneventful. It was chaotic. I have never seen the cafe so full, ever. Many of the attendees of the exhibit last night came in. As soon as they saw me, they recognized who I was.

"Adilyn!! Oh my gosh! You are that amazing artist from last night!" they squealed. I'm taken aback by their excitement to see me. No one that has ever come into the cafe has squealed when they saw me.

The cafe was buzzing with life and conversation all around. I was constantly making latte after mocha after cappuccino. I was supposed to get off at 2; however, it was so busy that I couldn't bear to leave Dani to handle everything alone, so I stayed until closing.

"Oh dear, it is over!" I gasp, slumping into a chair.

"Yes, it is over, and we survived!" she says, gleaming at me back in the kitchen. I don't know how she isn't exhausted like I am. Then again, since she has done this for so long, she has accumulated more stamina than I have. I lean back, resting my head on the back of the chair, closing my eyes. I need just a moment of rest before I can think about moving. Only a few moments pass when the bell above the door rings. Someone comes through the door. Without opening my eyes, I yell, "We are closed. You can come back tomorrow when we're open!"

"I'm not here to buy anything. I'm here to see Dani," a deep, commanding voice says.

My eyes shoot open as I jump out of my chair and turn towards the stranger. "You?" I say in confusion. He is the guy I saw standing before my painting last night; I think he is. I didn't see his face then, but his build looks precisely like it. I look him up and down. Then my eyes lock with his. The corner of his mouth curls upwards.

"Me," he responds, tilting his head. My mouth drops open, and words evade my mind. This man standing in front of me is something else, almost godly. He stands tall and strong, wearing similar clothing to the night before. Simple black trousers with a black button-up shirt, sleeves folded up halfway, but boy, this simple clothing didn't hide his muscular frame; it accentuated it even more. His chiseled face frames his intense, steely eyes that seem to smolder with determination. He takes my breath away. Gods, he's stunning and staring right at me. A warm tingle runs through my body, covering every inch of me just like last night. It must be because of him, but why?

"Am I to your liking, dear one?" he says, with a coolness in his voice. His smirk is mesmerizing.

"Yes, you are," I say, without even thinking. My eyes widen, and my hands cover my mouth. "I'm so sorry. I didn't mean to say that." Trying to salvage my dignity the best I can.

"Are you sure you didn't mean to say that?" He raises an eyebrow.

"No, I didn't," I quickly say.

"It sounded to me like you spoke the truth."

"No, I didn't. Don't flatter yourself, buddy." Irritation starts churning inside of me. I want more than anything to get off of this subject.

"I don't have to flatter myself when you do it for me already." He says in the cockiest way that makes me want to punch him right in his beautiful face.

"You know what......" Dani cuts me off right before I can tell him to keep dreaming.

"Ash! My dear friend, how are you? I am glad you were able to swing by!" Dani calls out to the man. She strolls from the kitchen to where he is standing and embraces him. I look at her and then back at him.

"Adilyn, this is my friend Asher. Asher, this is Adilyn, the one I have told you so much about!"

He nods his head towards me, his eyes locked with mine. My fists open and close behind my back, trying to ease the irritation that Asher has caused.

"Nice to meet you, Asher," I say flatly, not genuinely meaning it.

"I will take care of the rest of the closing so you can head home. I am sure you are exhausted. You have worked so hard today. I appreciate you staying to help me," she dismisses me. Shock runs through me, along with the warm tingle that has yet to subside. She is dismissing me! I nod my head in response, not knowing what else to say. I've always stayed until close and talked to Dani after. It was our routine. I turn to put my apron up and grab my bag from the office.

"Have a good evening, Adilyn," Asher says with a dark smile. I turn to look at him. His eyes seem to shimmer with something.

"You... too," I clench my jaw and nod. Why did I feel so incapable of doing anything intelligent around this man? I do not know what has come over me, but I undoubtedly embarrassed myself tonight. I reach the office and close the door behind me. I lean against the door and cover my face with my hands, trying to collect myself from what happened. I can't believe what I have said to him. What was I thinking? "What is wrong with me? I have spoken to men before so why am I now having an issue?" I whisper. I grab my bag and head towards the front door. I can hear Dani and this stranger chatting in the kitchen. I swear that lady lived there in that kitchen! Yet some of the most fantastic food creations come out of that kitchen.

"Good night, Dani!" I yell out to her.

"Good night, Ad! Be safe! I love you!" she yells back. I smile, thinking about our conversation earlier. I have always had a weird issue with saying the 'L' word around people because of fear that they won't stay. I feel like people don't stick around because I never genuinely deserve love. I have always thought that I would never truly be wanted. I'm sure some of that stems from being abandoned as an infant. Some of it is the loneliness that I constantly feel. But tonight, I told Dani I love her, and she told me she loves me back. Tears form in my eyes. I still do not feel worthy, but I will accept the love that she gives me. I must have been lost in my thoughts because I slam right into something solid. My eyes dart up to see what I slammed into, and horror fills me. I just walked right into Asher. How the hell did I not realize that he was standing right there?

My mouth falls open. "Oh my gosh! I'm so sorry I didn't see you there. Are you hurt?" I'm shaken at what I just did. Did I hurt him?

Asher smiles widely. "I'm fine. You did step on my toe, and I'm sure I will feel the effects for days. But otherwise, I couldn't be better!"

What a complete prick! My eyes dart to his feet. There is no way that I could cause that much damage to someone like Asher! His taunting eats at the edges of my nerves.

"I didn't mean to do that! And your foot will be just fine." I blurt out, still jarred from our conversation minutes ago.

"I'm fine. Do not worry about it." He smiles at me, taunting me.

"Why are you standing in my way?" I want him to move out of my way and let me go along my happy way.

"I was simply trying to open the door for you as a gentleman should until you ran right into me. Do you not pay attention to where you are going?"

"Oh, well, thank you for the gesture. And I do pay attention to where I walk, most of the time." Embarrassment is flushing my cheeks. I almost always pay attention to where I am walking. I don't just walk into everyone and everything. I can't believe I was so distracted and careless that I didn't see him there. I usually can feel someone's presence when they are in the same room as me. What is wrong with me?

"Well, this must be the exception unless you just wanted a reason to touch me." He raises his eyebrow and licks his lip like I'm his next meal. Horror washes the embarrassment right away, replacing it. What a pompous jerk. I wanted a reason to touch him. He is so full of himself; I can't believe it.

"Oh my gosh, no, that is not even close to the reason! I was simply in a hurry!" I bite back, averting my eyes, and fidget with my fingers. This whole situation is starting to become extremely uncomfortable, and I am beyond over it.

"I see." Then silence. I look up at him. He is still standing in my way, not moving. Our eyes lock. I will not allow him to bully me around. He will be the one who moves first, not me. Determination fuels my need to be the last one standing in this face-off. Seconds tick by, or is it minutes? I don't know. Asher moves; he reaches behind himself and pushes the door open. I look out the open door, feeling triumphant that he moved first. I look back at him. I want to rub it in his face that I won the face-off just now, to show that I am better than him, yet decide that I am over this bickering with him for tonight. So, I shut my mouth tight and glare right at him.

"Good night, Adilyn." He leans over and whispers in my ear. I can feel his lips brushing the tip of my ear. Electricity shoots through my entire body. I suck in a breath, trying to mask the response that he causes me. He is so close to me that I can smell him. Cedar, cypress, and amber with a hint of lavender floods my nose. He smells like a magical forest. Despite his calming smell, my heart is pounding so hard. It feels like it is going to bounce right out of my chest. What the hell am I supposed to do? He sucks in a deep breath. Is he smelling me? What a creep! I need to get out of here right now. I take a small step back and look up at him, ensuring he will not step back in my way. I quickly say,

"Good night, Asher." Then I rush out the door. I don't want to be stuck there for a moment longer than I already had to suffer.

The night air is cool and crisp. I allow it to seep into my bones, calming my nerves. I inhale and exhale deeply a few times, trying to center myself. I cannot believe I let him have that kind of effect on me. The town is quiet. The sun has disappeared. I enjoy my walk home in silence, embracing what Dani has said to me and sorting through my experience just now with Asher. A mixture of emotions is flowing through me. I try to sort through the feelings Asher brought on, yet the thought of what Dani said comes back to my mind. She truly loves me, and that warms me. The sense of love washes over me and smothers the embarrassment I felt because of Asher. I walk the rest of the way home smiling.

Chapter Nine

Asher

Dani asked me to come by the cafe tonight to discuss the next steps. I wait outside, leaning against one of the tall oaks across the street from the cafe. Adilyn is inside speaking to the customers. She is radiant! Her smile is infectious. I can tell that she is blushing. Whatever the other person is saying to her is causing her to be a little uncomfortable; however, she doesn't cower from their conversation.

She is not the same beauty humans have, but a beauty that is out of this world. I watch her as she moves about inside the cafe. Her hair is in a bun on her head with stray strands framing her face. She gracefully holds herself, almost floating from place to place. Adilyn reminds me a lot of Iridessa. Her demeanor mirrors hers in the same way she carries herself and the sparkle in her eyes when she experiences genuine happiness.

The physical appearances are similar yet different in some ways. Adilyn's beauty surpasses that of Iridessa. Her eyes are a deep emerald green that can pierce one's soul if they aren't careful, and her hair is as light as the shimmering moon with streaks of silver throughout. Her sharp features are stunning. It is hard to look away from her face.

When I saw her last night, out of the corner of my eyes, I could sense the loneliness inside of her, the sorrow. I guess that is what her life up until now has caused her to feel. Feelings that she should not have to feel. I can relate, though. I lost my parents, and my life has not been the same. For the past seventeen years, my life has revolved around training and preparing myself for what is yet to come. Sometimes, I long for life to be simple, but unfortunately, that is not what I am called to do. I wonder what her life will be like in the future. Will that loneliness go away? Will my loneliness go away? Who knows.

The last few customers trickle out of the cafe in time for closing. I want to watch her for a moment longer in the shadows. She walks over to a table and slumps in the chair, leaning her head back. I chuckle at the sight of her. Shaking my head, I push off the oak tree and saunter to the door. I push the door open, and before I can get any words out of my mouth, Adilyn yells with slight annoyance, "We're closed! You can come back tomorrow when we are open."

I bite back the urge to laugh aloud as if that act will only annoy her even more. This woman is so fierce, and she doesn't even know it yet.

We banter back and forth. I know that I am getting on her last nerves. She snaps at me, and I try to conceal my smirk, knowing I have failed. Her gaze is upon me. Her mouth falls open as if she is stunned. Her eyes wander all over my body. I can see her irises widening as she takes me in. Enjoying this moment, I do not say anything. I swear it seems like she will try to devour me with her eyes, the heat simmering in them. I could stay here all night just staring at her; however, I had business to discuss with Dani.

"Am I to your liking, dear one?" I ask her.

"Yes, you are," flies out of her mouth before she can stop the response. Her cheeks turn red, and she tries to hide her embarrassment from me. I wanted to draw this moment with her out as long as possible to see what else she "accidentally" says.

"Ash! My dear friend, how are you?" Dani calls out and makes her way toward me, sparing Adilyn from more embarrassment. Dani strolls to my side and gives me a quick embrace. My gaze returns to Adilyn.

Dani dismisses her for the evening. I can see a hint of sadness mixed in with embarrassment in Adilyn's eyes. I know I got under her skin, and she is currently not my biggest fan. Then, getting dismissed by someone you consider family because of someone you don't like is not easy to swallow. I know how she feels right now; I, too, have been dismissed many times. I offer her a gentle, apologetic smile, aware that I cannot make things right.

We wish each other good night and she turns away. I watch her as she walks towards the back of the cafe. I stand in silence for a moment longer. The warmth that had filled my chest with her presence is now draining with her departure.

I sigh, disappointed, and turn towards Dani, "Do you need any help before we talk?"

"No, Ash. Adilyn pretty much got everything done. I will run to the kitchen and get us some tea, and then we can talk in the office." She smiles up at me and strolls back towards the kitchen.

I look around the cafe. I have been here a few times before; however, I've never looked around. It was a quaint little place. Its simplicity reminded me of Dani's Cafe from long ago. Dani was a big part of my life. I spent so much time in her kitchen while my parents were busy in meetings and doing who knows what else. The feeling of home rushes back to me. I used to get the same feeling when I visited Dani as a child.

She would always make me a tea that was so delicious and sneak me some of her famous muffins. How my parents would get so mad when they would find out that I was eating more sweets than they allowed me.

I haven't thought about memories of her and my parents in a long time. I continued to look around the cafe, and the more I saw, the more I became positive that she had ensured this place resembled the old one. She loved that cafe so much. I see stacks of books and chuckle to myself. She has always been a bookworm and has had books all around her, so it is unsurprising that she has books stacked on tables here. Dani has always said, "Something magical happens when you sit and read a book." She was convinced that reading would take you to worlds you would have never imagined. She believes that reading is an escape.

I was looking around at the different titles that scattered the tables when I heard the office door open. I stiffen. Adilyn had gone into the office and had finally emerged. I watch her as she makes her way as fast as possible to the front door with her head down. She certainly is still feeling a hint of embarrassment. Warmth creeps into my chest just as it had minutes ago, and a buzzing feeling runs under my skin. Something about her is calling to me, whether it be what lives inside her or her as a whole, I don't know.

"Good night, Dani!" Adilyn yells towards the kitchen.

"Good night, Ad! Walk safe! I love you!"

"I will, I promise. Love you too." A smile creeps on her face. The breath is knocked right out of me, and my heart stops. The sight of her genuine smile is so beautiful. If I could make her smile like that, over and over again, I would do whatever it takes. This woman is truly breathtaking. I move to stand in front of the door, blocking her exit. She must not have noticed me standing there because she slams into me. She looks up at me; horror fills her face as she gasps, covering her mouth.

"Oh my gosh! I'm so sorry I did not see you there. Are you hurt?" Her voice is shaking.

I smile at the fact that she thinks she hurt me. Her concern is genuine. Yet, when I taunt her, her fiery spirit comes back to life.

"Well, this must be the exception unless you just wanted a reason to touch me." I raise one eyebrow and lick my bottom lip. My imagination runs wild.

"Oh my gosh, no, that is not even close to the reason! I was simply in a hurry!" She looks down and starts to fidget with her fingers.

"I see," I reply. She looks up at me, and our eyes lock. We both stand silently, waiting for the other to move or say something. She furrows her eyebrows together, frustration filling her features. She is a stubborn one, for sure. She refuses to back down. I like that. I don't like women who are timid and back down easily.

A moment passes, and then I reach behind me and push the door open. Her eyes drift to the open door and then back to mine, closing her mouth and pressing her lips into a thin line. I can tell she wants to say something but chooses not to.

I lean over and whisper into her ear. "Good night, Adilyn." My lips brush the tip of her ear. She sucks a breath in and then holds it. Her scent is so intoxicating as I breathe her in. She smells like the oak woods from my homeland with a hint of vanilla and smoke.

She smells like home.

I can sense her heart racing wildly out of control. I take one more deep breath, memorizing her scent, and then step out of her way. She blinks several times and then releases her breath. She looks out the door and then back at me with wide eyes. She is frozen in place for a moment before it sets in that I have moved out of her way.

"Um, good night, Asher." She is panting as she rushes out the door and jogs down the road.

I raise a brow at her reaction. She certainly is in a hurry to get home. I chuckle. She is very intriguing, and I want to get to know her better. However, the ugly realization hits me, reminding me that there is no place for that, not now, not when so much is riding on this.

"Follow me, Ash," Dani calls out as she makes her way to the office with a tray of hot tea and cookies. I turn to look outside after Adilyn, a void forming in my chest along with the longing. My shoulders slump, and I close the door and follow Dani into the office.

"So, what's the plan?" Dani asks, blowing on the steaming tea in her hands.

"Well.... we wait. There is not much time left until it will finally be time." I say, staring out the window towards the shining town lights, trying to go through every possible outcome. I have to be prepared for every outcome. I have worked and trained my entire life for this moment. I'm not willing to let things end up poorly. I have to see it through.

"I know there isn't much time left, but we must figure out how to break the news to her."

"Of course, Dani. We will be honest about the whole thing. Honesty is our best option, and it's our only option. We can't lie about anything nor leave anything out." I contemplate what exactly we will say. What is the best way? How will she react? There are many questions I can contemplate; however, I will not know the answer until we tell her.

"I hope that she is understanding. I can't imagine what she will feel once she finds out." Dani says with worry, straining her voice.

We sit, quietly sipping our tea, staring out the window, racking our brains with what the next few days will bring.

"Do you think she will be ready once the time comes?" Dani asks, looking out the window at the night-consumed world around us.

"I certainly hope so, but only time will tell. We will have a lot to cover before we can enter Eldermyst. We can't cross her until she controls what lies within her. I will not take that risk." I say firmly, wishing that everything will be as it should be. It has to be.

"Agreed. She has to learn to control it; otherwise, we will all be put in danger trying to protect her."

I nod in agreement.

"I hope she is not angry with me for what I had to do long ago. Leaving her like that at the door in the cold." Dani shudders.

There is nothing I can say to comfort her. I am just as lost as she is. We are both hoping for something that we are depending on. Who knows what the outcome will be? Silence fills the room once again. I can't sit here a moment longer, dwelling in this feeling of uncertainty. I can feel it in the air: uncertainty and sorrow, immense sorrow. Her feelings hit me like a crashing wave. Words of comfort evade me, so I down the remaining tea I have left and stand up.

Turning towards Dani, I said, "Let me know if anything else is needed from me. For now, we will sit, waiting until the time is right." I can see the worry swarming in her eyes. "I must be off. I need to meet with Elouan to find out what's happening on the other side."

CHAPTER TEN

Friends?

ADILYN

Tomorrow is the last day of school, and all teachers have given up on teaching. I shuffle through my day almost as usual with the occasional high-five and congratulations on winning the art exhibit. Henry, on the other hand, is basking in his newfound glory. "Yeah, I'm going to be the next big thing." Henry gloats to a crowd of people flocking around him. I watch him from my locker. He runs his hand through his strawberry blonde hair and grins at the girl beside him. I chuckle because almost no one knew who he was before the exhibit. They're only paying attention to him because he is vocal about the opportunity he claims to have in front of him.

"It's so cool. I have been asked to paint a collection for the Big Shot art gallery in New York." He says matter of factly.

"Oh my, that's such an amazing opportunity! You will be super famous after that, I'm sure." Cindy squeals, and the rest of the crowd murmurs in agreement with her.

I roll my eyes at them because they need to cling to the next big thing, hoping they will become his next best friend and get fame. They are a bunch of piranhas waiting for their next meal. I look over and see Stephanie standing next to Henry and Cindy. She is tall yet petite with fair skin, big green eyes with long lashes, plump lips, and long, wavy, brown hair that sways behind her back. She was beautiful in a striking way. Her laughter flows in my direction like a melody. Something familiar hits me when I look at her. I have seen her only a few times; however, there is a more profound recognition within. I shrug it off, and there is no time to sit contemplating what that feeling feels like.

Henry looks my way. "Hey, Adilyn. Come over here!" He motions for me to join him and the crowd.

I stand at my locker for a moment, debating what to do. Do I want to deal with this group right now? What Dani had told me the other night came into my mind. I knew that I needed to suck it up and power through the things that made me uncomfortable. I had to get over my fears and put myself out there. There is so much to life that I won't be able to experience if I continue the way I am going. So I straighten my back and lift my chin. I close my locker and turn towards the group. I walk through the hallway towards them, plastering the biggest smile that I could manage to fake on my face.

"Hey, Henry," I look at him, then turn to the rest of the crowd. "Hey, everyone." The group smiles and nods back in response.

"What is your plan, Adilyn? Anything big coming up since the art exhibit?" Henry smiles a toothy smile.

"Well, actually, I have decided to start teaching painting classes. I want people to love art like I do and tap into their creativity." I cannot believe I said that out loud to someone other than Dani, let alone to a group of classmates.

"Really? Oh my gosh, I'm so excited you decided to teach others to learn how to express colors in a fun and creative way! I want to be your first student." Stephanie steps towards me and grabs my hands, jumping in excitement.

"Of course, I would love that," I respond sheepishly. I'm not used to people responding to me with such excitement. It is shocking. Doubt creeps into my mind. I want to think her words are genuine, but I'm uncertain. It could be that she is simply trying to be nice.

Cindy coughs, masking her words, "Loser."

"How do I get a hold of you? Then you can let me know when we can start." Stephanie rolls her eyes at Cindy, then turns back to me. A smile spreads across her face from ear to ear.

"Oh... um.. well... I don't have a phone at the moment, but I'm planning on getting one soon. You can find me at the cafe right now. I will let you know more details later if you would like." I say with hesitation in my voice. Everyone in this town has cell phones, and even 10-year-olds do. So, it made things a little awkward when she asked for my number. The bell rang, alerting us that the next class was about to start. Thank goodness for rescuing me!

"Okay! I will come to see you later at the cafe! I am so excited! Then we can also discuss self-defense training," Stephanie leans in and hugs me. I stiffen under her embrace, not knowing what to do. She lets me go, giving me another wide grin, then skips off to class. I stand in the hallway, trying to gulp down what happened. Did I get my first student? I shriek on the inside, not wanting anyone to hear the excitement about getting my first student.

Where was I going to have this class? Oh my gosh, there is so much that I need to work on to get things sorted out and started. I walk to my math class with a genuine smile plastered to my face for real this time. Life just may be looking up for me!

I sit in math class in the back of the room. The teacher explains that this will be an easy week. I think about the conversation with Stephanie and her excitement for learning how to paint. Then my mind drifts to last night and Ash. That man irritates me, but I sure know how to embarrass myself in front of him. I lay my face in my hands, hoping my cheeks would not blush for everyone to see. I can see clearly in my mind when he whispered in my ear. When he leaned towards me, I swear he smelled like cypress, cedar, amber, and a hint of lavender. It took me off guard. Those were a mixture of smells I have never smelled on someone before, not that I go around smelling people. Most people smell like salt, body odor, or perfume. Yet, Asher was different. The smell seeped from every one of his pores. It encompassed me. For a moment, I did not want him to move away. I could feel his soft breath brushing my ear, sending a rippling heat through my body, down to my core. I didn't know what was happening to me. Then he opened the door. No one has ever done that for me; it made me feel both irritated and warm. I was speechless. Did he not feel the same way that I did? I stared at him a moment longer, then ripped my gaze from his to look out the front door. I could feel the awkwardness building between us.

"Good night, Ash," I said as quickly as possible, and then I almost ran out the front door.

I could sense his stare on my back as I jogged down the road, putting as much space between myself and him. Why did this man affect me so much? He is just so irritating with his inflated ego. Ugh. I shake the thoughts of him from my head. I will not allow him to live another moment in my mind rent-free. I have better things to concentrate on, like figuring out the whole class thing with Stephanie. I debate my different options for an art studio, and it hits me. Dani lives above the cafe in a cute apartment that has three bedrooms. I was hoping to talk to Dani about moving into one of the rooms once I turn 18. I wonder if I can use the other room for an art studio. I can pay her rent when I get paid.

I will have to sit down and talk to her about it all tonight. I am almost 100% positive that she will say yes. I know she loves me. She has always had an open-door policy with me. I don't want her to think I am taking her for granted. She has been a rock, and I don't want to mess up our relationship.

As usual, I trek to the forest before I go to the cafe. I don't have as much time to spend there today as I usually do. I got out of school late. They held an assembly with all the seniors to discuss graduation and hand out caps and gowns. The graduation will be held at noon on the last day of school. I will have to make sure to tell Dani so that she can be there. I want nothing more than to have her there.

I can see the giant trees up ahead. I can't contain the smile that spreads on my face and the joy that fills my heart. I run the rest of the way to the trees.

"Friends!" I give the biggest hug possible to one of the trees. "It feels as if it has been forever." My head leans against the trunk. I close my eyes. I want a moment to feel the life in the tree underneath its bark. I focus on the humming that radiates from its center. I don't know why I think I can feel the hum in trees. No one else can, which makes me question myself and my sanity.

I open my eyes and look up the trunk to the branches reaching towards the sky. I listen to the song of the animals and the rustling of leaves. There is such beauty here in the forest. This place right here is home to me. I am so fixated on listening to the natural music that fills the forest that I don't hear the leaves crunching behind me.

I feel a hand on my shoulder, and my heart jolts almost right out of my chest. I turn around, ready to fight whoever or whatever just touched me. My heart is racing, and my adrenaline is flowing. As soon as I see who is behind me, I'm relieved.

"Stephanie, you scared the life out of me!" I gasp.

"I thought you heard me walking up. All those crunching leaves made my presence kinda obvious." she smiles.

"I didn't hear. I must have been distracted." I half-heartedly laugh.

"Yeah. I thought you were about to die there for a moment. Your face went ghostly white. I thought you were about to hit me with how you spun around so fast," she chuckles nervously.

"Yeah," I clear my throat. "What can I do for you?"

"Nothing. I saw you walking into the forest and wanted to join you, so I followed you to catch up."

"Oh," I mumble, shuffling my feet.

"I never really got to know you before, and I feel terrible about that." I can hear the pain in her voice.

"Oh, no worries! It is not uncommon. Most people are too scared of me, so they ignore me. I am used to it." shrugging my shoulders,

Stephanie barks out a laugh at my response. "I mean, I guess. I don't see why they would think that you are scary."

"Yeah, who knows? You are new, right?" Curiosity to what her story is.

"Yes! I moved here almost a month ago, right before the school year ends." She smiles.

"That's odd. Moving schools when you are almost done with high school." I say, puzzled.

"I guess it is, but the move here was important. So here I am!" Silence falls between us as we slowly stroll through the forest. We brush our hands along the trunks of the trees. Having someone walk with me is strange, but it's nice to know someone is here.

"I love walking through the forest. I feel this connection to nature, so this is my favorite place." I blurt out, not knowing why I needed to tell her.

"I know what you mean. I love being surrounded by nature." She mutters as she looks up towards the reaching branches. We continue to walk silently through the forest until we arrive at the road. I didn't know how much I needed someone's presence beyond Dani's. It is warming to have someone who feels the same way about the forest as I do.

We stop at the road. I look down toward where the cafe is, shifting on my feet, kicking rocks around. Stephanie looks directly at me, her gaze never wavering.

"Well, I have to go to work." I look towards Stephanie, not entirely wanting to leave just yet. Something inside of me is pulling towards her. I don't know what it is. Maybe because I have no friends, and this may be my first real friend. Maybe.

"No worries! I will see you later then. That way, you can give me more details about the classes?" She questions, looking up at me from under her lashes.

"Yes! I will have more information for you later, for sure!" Excitement fills my voice.

"Awesome! I will see you later!" She skips down the road, calling back to me. I look at her one last time, smiling and shaking my head. Then I walk with a slight bounce in my step towards the cafe. Joy fills my heart at my interaction with Stephanie. I knew it was something that I needed, especially now.

It was another busy night at the cafe. Life has been buzzing in town with the event and school ending. Everyone's making their summer plans, where they are going, and what they are doing.

It was so wild I had no time to take a moment and breathe. I constantly moved around, made coffee, and cleaned tables; however, the night flew by quickly. The last few people just left the cafe, so I need to clean the tables. I grab my rag and walk around the counter towards the tables. The front doorbell rang as someone came in. I turn and, to my surprise, see Stephanie walking towards me with the biggest smile. She walks right up to me, embracing me. I stiffen. No one has ever hugged me, so I'm unsure what to do. I lift the one hand and embrace her back.

"Um, hi," I say, trying to hide the shock in my voice.

"Hi! I did not want to come when it was busy. So I waited until closer to closing time. I figured I could help you close, and then we can walk home together." She lets me go and smiles widely at me.

"Walk home together?" Unsure what she was thinking. She barely knows me.

"I live a block down from you, silly!" she pushes my shoulder playfully.

"Oh!!!" understanding floods me.

"Yeah, that would be great."

"I can clean the tables. Do you want to sweep?" She grabs the rag out of my hand and turns towards the tables.

"Um, sure." I scratch my head, dumbstruck. Do I have a choice since she is already cleaning the tables? She begins to wipe down the tables, then flips the chairs upside down on top of the table, giving me room to sweep underneath. I watch her as she cleans, debating in my mind what's happening. I'm stunned that she talked to me earlier, walked with me in the forest, and is now here helping me do my job. Confusion floats into the back of my mind. Why is she being so nice? I bite the bottom of my lip, contemplating all the possible reasons.

"Well? Are you going to go get the broom and start sweeping?" she peers over at me with her hand on her hip.

"Oh yes. Sorry. Can I ask you a question first?" I look down timidly.

"Sure. What's your question?" She stood up straight and left the rag on the table.

"Well, why are you being nice to me?" Hesitation in my voice, unsure if I genuinely want to hear her answer.

"You seem real, genuine, unlike the rest of the people at school. I like real people. I cannot stand those that pretend to be something they are not."

"Oh...." I pause. "Why are you friends with them then? Cindy and Stacy?"

"Well, they seemed to have latched onto me when I arrived, and I could never truly shake them. They always talk about how I can be an actress or model with my looks, so I half think they are pretending to be friends with me in hopes of that happening. So, they can claim they were there from the beginning." she waves her hand over her face and body, holding back a laugh.

"Oh! Got it." I smile sheepishly. "I am going to get that broom."

Stephanie giggles and returns to wiping the tables. We make our way through the cafe, wiping tables down and sweeping. Soon enough, everything was done much quicker than if I were cleaning alone. I can hear the clanking in the kitchen and see Dani walking out with a tray of tea and cookies.

"I brought you girls some tea and cookies! However, you will need to lower some chairs if we are going to sit down." Dani smiles at Stephanie and me.

"Got it!" Stephanie runs over to a table that will accommodate all three of us and pulls the chairs down from atop the table, setting them on the ground. I put the broom up and head to the table. I sit down and reach out for a cup of tea.

"Dani, this is Stephanie. Stephanie, this is Dani, the owner of the cafe and my best friend."

"You sure know how to make an old woman like me blush, Ad," Dani says, batting in my direction.

"Ad?" Stephanie asks.

"Yes. Adilyn's nickname to me is Ad." Dani smiles at the girl sitting to her left.

"I like that! I think I will use that if it is alright with you?" gleams Stephanie.

"It is alright by me, dear," Dani replies.

We all sit at the table, sipping our tea and chatting like old friends. I watch Dani and Stephanie laughing over funny moments they have lived. Laughing over funny jokes they have heard. Their laughter made my heart fill with joy and warmth. I smile, marking this moment in my mind. This is a moment that I'm going to remember for the rest of my life. I want more moments like this where I can relax and enjoy my time with friends. My life, at this moment, is perfect, and I would do anything to make more of this happen.

"Dani, do you think it would be okay if I stay in one of your rooms upstairs once I graduate and possibly use the spare room for painting lessons?" I say shyly, half worried that I am asking too much from her.

Dani pauses, and it looks like she is trying to think.

"I can pay you rent; I promise." I blurt out.

"Of course you can. I don't know why you would think that you can't. For now, don't worry about paying me anything. You already help me so much here in the cafe." She looks at me with warmth in her smile and her eyes twinkling.

I sigh a sigh of relief. I don't know why I was so worried about Dani rejecting me. I should've known that she would say yes. She had offered not that long ago for me to stay with her. Yet the nerves of asking and not wanting her to think I was taking her for granted still ate at the back of my mind. "It's time for this old lady to get to bed, girls. "Dani slowly stands up. "We have been yapping like old hens for the last hour and a half."

"It is getting late!" Stephaine stands.

"Wow! I didn't see the time." I say, looking over at the clock.

"Time sure passes by fast when you are having fun with people you like." Stephanie winks in my direction. I laugh because she is right about that.

"I'm going to get my bag from the office, and then I will be ready to go." I stand up, grab my teacup, and place it on the tray.

"I will clean it up. Do not worry about it." Dani smiles at me.

"I can help clean it too, Ad." Stephanie chimes, excited to use my nickname for the first time. I can't help but smile at her, shaking my head.

"Alright, I will be back then in just a moment." I turn and walk to the office to grab my bag.

As I return from the office, I hear Dani and Stephanie whispering. I pause and hide behind the wall, trying to eavesdrop.

"I'm going to start training her," Stephanie mutters.

"Good, she will need to learn how to defend herself." Dani looks around.

"Agreed. That is a must, for sure."

Is there something I am missing? I thought they had just met, but maybe I was wrong. This place is a cafe, and she talks to everyone who enters. Strange that they would whisper about me learning to defend myself. I shake my head, trying to rid myself of the feeling that there is something I'm missing. I walk around the corner, smiling like I didn't just eavesdrop on them.

"Ready?" I ask Stephanie as I return from the office, slinging my bag over my shoulder.

"Yes!" She stands up quickly, slightly startled. "It was nice to meet you, Dani! I hope to see you again soon!"

"You too, Stephanie. I am sure I will see you again soon! You two walk safe, you hear me?" Dani grabs the tray and walks towards the kitchen.

"Yes, ma'am!" We say in unison.

"Jinx, you owe me a coffee," I say quickly to Stephanie. She laughs out loud and shakes her head in agreement.

"Good night, Dani!" I yell.

"Good night, girls." She yells back as we make our way to the front door. We walk for a few minutes in silence.

"It is pretty nice out right now." Stephanie interrupts the silence as we walk.

"You are right! Nights like this are when I love to walk. Not too hot and not too cold." I look over at her. "So tell me something about you. You know more about me than I know about you." I smile sheepishly, slightly embarrassed at that fact.

Stephanie walks to the side of the road and sits on a large rock. I join her. She is silent for a moment, thinking of what to say. "Well, I want to learn how to paint. Painting involves a great deal of creativity and imagination; it's a form of release that someone experiences when they become completely absorbed in painting. I admire people, just like you, that can do that." She looks down the road then turns back to me. "I love training. I have spent most of my life learning how to fight. I have learned how to use a bow and a sword."

"As in old times fighting? Like knights and stuff?" my mouth drops open, surprised that people still use that weapon.

"Not just weapons, hand-to-hand combat as well. My parents had always wanted me to know how to defend myself in many different ways, so they put me through different trainings to prepare me." She says with a hint of sadness in her voice.

"Oh! That is so cool. I wish I knew how to defend myself; however, I do not. I am sure that if a zombie apocalypse ever happens, I will end up one of the first to go because I would not know where even to begin defending myself."

Stephanie laughs from deep in her belly. "Oh my gosh! You are so funny! Thankfully, you have me as your teacher. I teach you something I love, and you teach me something you love." She raises an eyebrow.

I think about it for a moment. I would love to be able to defend myself, but I did not know the first thing about teaching someone to paint. So,

I can kill two birds with one stone, right? "Yes, I love that!" I reach out my hand. She grabs mine and shakes.

"Start maybe tomorrow or the following day?"

"Deal." She grins.

We make the rest of the way home, talking and laughing the entire time. It's almost as if I have known her my whole life. Things flow so easily between us. A sense of familiarity still lingers, not just the friend kind but what I imagine family feels like. She embraces me, says good night, and then walks down the road. I sneak into the house, trying to make the slightest noise possible. I know it is late, and the last thing that I want to do is wake my foster parents. They had a nasty fight the other day, and I'm still unsure if they finally made it up or are still on bad terms. I creep up the stairs and down the hallway to my bedroom.

Once inside my room, I sit on my bed and put my bag in the chair. Stripping my shoes and socks off, I lay back in my bed, letting out a long sigh. Today was a weird and eventful day. I made a new friend and created memories I will never forget. I also gained a new student and agreed to learn how to fight.

"What a day," I whisper. I turn to the side and see the Fae Princess book on my nightstand. I grab the book and turn over to lay on my stomach. I still have energy, so I will read myself to sleep. I open the book and begin reading where I last left off. The words on the page drag me in, trapping my attention.

CHAPTER ELEVEN

School Ends

ADILYN

Exhaustion is on the verge of consuming me since I stayed up again reading last night. I read about half the book and then forced myself to go to bed; otherwise, I wouldn't have slept. The story is so intriguing. The tale unfolds of a young woman who discovers her royal lineage and embarks on a quest to reclaim her crown. Along the way, she delves into her ancestry and faces numerous challenges, learning to overcome them. I look over at the clock and realize that today is the last day of school! I hop out of bed with a sudden excitement to finally finish school! Don't get me wrong; I love learning. However, knowing that high school is over brings me a new chapter in the book of life. I hurry to get ready, eager to meet Stephanie for our walk together. Our last few days together have been amazing. I genuinely feel like I have known her for my whole life. It is wild to have just met someone yet know them so well.

"I hope she makes it to her kingdom and regains her throne." Remembering what I had read only hours ago. Sometimes, I wish my life was more like a magical fairytale, like the ones I read in stories, happy fairy tales, not the terrifying ones. Other times, I don't know what I would do with myself if my life were like those stories. I would rise to the challenge. I walk to the bathroom, rubbing my sleep-filled eyes. I splash cold water on my face to wake up and start getting ready.

"It's time to leave." I bounce over to my desk to grab my bag. I sneak out of my room in silence and creep down the stairs. I pop into the kitchen to grab a Poptart to eat along the way, then turn back towards the front door. I inch towards the front door on my tiptoes and quietly open the door.

"Have a good day at school," Hillary whispers from the stairs. I stand still and look up the stairs.

"Thank you. It's the last day, so I'm sure it will fly right by," I whisper back to her. I take a step out the door and close it behind me. I walk to the edge of the porch and stand at the top step, soaking in the fresh morning. The sun slowly rises in the distance, blessing us with its warm rays. I look up the road and see Stephanie walking on the sidewalk in my direction. I smile wide and wave at her with great enthusiasm. Today is going to be a grand day since it's the last day of school! I'm free, well as free as I can be for the moment.

"Hey!" I wave at her.

"Hey! Ready for the last day of class?" She giggles. I walk down the patio steps and embrace her, surprising myself with the act. She must be rubbing off on me, or I must need that kind of physical contact. We fall into stride together, linking our arms, and talk about how we will organize our schedules to allow painting and fighting lessons, especially since, in three more days, we will have much more time on our hands.

Soon enough, we arrive at school. The walk went by so fast. I wave goodbye to her for now since we do not have any classes in common.

"See you by the library after school?" She turns back towards me and yells.

"Yes!" I yell back at her. I turn and make my way to my first class with the biggest smile. I think this is a true friendship blossoming with Stephanie. Butterflies floating around in my stomach at the thought of me truly making a friend.

The school day is over, so I find my way to the library where Stephanie and I agreed to meet. I wait outside of the library doors, looking around for Stephanie. I don't know her last class, so I have no clue which direction she will be going in. I shift on my feet while I wait in the beating sun. It was strange for me to wait around on the school campus after school ended. I usually make my way straight to the forest. Then again, I never really had a reason to wait around at the school. I turn to the left and spot Stephanie in the distance, skipping towards the library.

"She is a nut for sure." I laugh, shaking my head. It's refreshing, though. I'm so reserved, and she's so bubbly and outgoing. She truly enjoys the small things in life, such as skipping. She inches closer and closer by the second. My smile broadens as I see her closer. I wave at her. She waves back.

"Hey!" Out of breath as she reaches me.

"I think you love skipping more than training to defend yourself." Trying to contain my laughter as she crosses her arms and glares at me.

"Well, so that you know, skipping is fun, and you should try it more. It may lighten your seriousness a little." She snarks, then sticks out her tongue. I burst out laughing, no longer able to contain it anymore. She howls with me. People walk by and look in our direction with raised eyebrows.

"I am pretty sure everyone probably thinks we are crazy right now." I huff out between laughs.

"Who cares if they think that? We all are a little crazy in one way or another. Are we not?" She laughs harder. The next few moments are consumed with trying to control ourselves enough to stand up straight. I don't think I have ever laughed so much or deeply. Panting, I sit against the library building and pull my water out of my bag. Stephanie sits beside me against the building, taking deep breaths and calming herself.

"Thank you," I say, looking at her.

"What for?" She questions, confusion written all over her face.

"For becoming my friend, for making my life interesting and exciting. For sharing a laughing fit with me. I've never laughed so hard as I did just now." I rest my head against the wall.

"No problem. It's my honor to be your friend and share these moments with you. We both know that I am just that amazing!" She smirks and winks at me. I roll my eyes at her ego. She leans her head against my shoulder. We sit in silence for a few minutes. Stephanie raises her head and turns towards me. "Ready to go see the trees?"

"Yes! Let's go!" I bounce up and sling my bag onto my back. We link arms and walk toward the forest, chatting the whole way.

The trees line the dirt road and then go beyond for miles. We step off of the road into the forest. Unlinking my arm with Stephanie's, I run my hand along one of the trunks, feeling the rough bark.

"These trees never cease to amaze me. All that they withstand, yet they are still standing strong." I say in awe.

I close my eyes and let my other senses absorb my surroundings. I hear birds chirping, a squirrel scampering on a branch directly above me, leaves rustling, the wind softly shushing, and bees humming about. I feel rough bark with patches of soft spongy moss, the wind ruffling my clothes and hair, the warmth of the sun peeking through the tree's canopy, and the gentle brush on my arm of a falling leaf. I smell the warm earth beneath me, fresh, crisp air, nearby floral blooms, and musk of fallen branches. I let my surroundings sink into me. I open my eyes slowly and see Stephanie staring at me with her head tilted to the side and a finger on her chin.

"You truly connect with nature, don't you?" She asks.

"You can say that. I like to be aware of my surroundings, especially in nature. So I close my eyes and connect my senses: sound, touch, and smell. I know it is strange but after I do that, I feel stronger, more centered." I chuckle awkwardly, hoping Stephanie does not think 'I'm a freak after this.

"I get it! Allowing your senses to open up is a great thing. Being self-aware and aware of your surroundings is important in defending yourself. So, you are one more step to graduating from self-defense class!" She exclaims.

My eyebrow raises. "Graduate?"

"Yes! If it is easier to think of it this way, think of karate. One goes from a white belt to a black belt. That is similar in this case. You go from novice to expert. I am sure you will be kicking ass in no time." She winks and then turns to walk further into the forest.

"Right, in no time," I state sarcastically with the most giant eye roll ever. I follow her further into the forest. We walk silently, admiring the trees as we walk. I spot my favorite oak in the middle of the trees and hustle towards it. I lay my hand on the trunk, looking up the trunk to the top, and then turn to sit against the tree. I look at the patch of bloodroots, the same patch that sprouted to life the other day. They are all in full bloom now. Only that one patch, though; the other patches were yet to bloom. I must have been lost in my thoughts because I didn't feel when Stephanie sat down next to me.

"What are you looking at?" she says.

"The patch of bloodroots over there," pointing where they are.

"It's strange because I could've sworn those flowers were closed, like the others, but it's like they popped open."

"Those are pretty. What do you mean they popped open?" A puzzled look is written all over her face.

"I don't know. It's strange. One moment, they were closed, and then I closed my eyes and imagined the blooms in my mind. When I opened my eyes, they were in full bloom. Crazy, I know. I must be losing it." I bring my hands to my face, covering myself from the shame.

"That is interesting. I wonder what could've happened," Stephanie gazes at the bloodroots.

"Yeah, sorry for that. Some things I should leave to myself. I don't want to scare you away." I laugh awkwardly. I don't know how to do the whole friend thing, and I do not want a reason for her to run away.

"Girl, you can't scare me away. True friends do not run away over things, especially things like that. We stick it out no matter what." Stephanie bumps her shoulder with mine and smiles widely.

My heart fills with such warmth. My cheeks redden as I look away from her to try to hide my blush. She said true friends, and I hope that she means it. I didn't realize how much I needed a true friend until now.

"I wish you could see the flowers from my hometown. You would love them!" She exclaims.

"Where did you grow up?" I ask.

"I grew up in a small town called Etheria." She leans her head against the oak's trunk and closes her eyes.

"I have never heard of that town before," digging through my memory of Emeria's states and cities.

"I'm not surprised. It's a small town and nowhere close to here." She smiles, her smile reaching to her eyes.

"Maybe one day you will take me to visit and see your hometown," I respond.

"One day, I will take you, and I'm sure you will love it there." She assures. Something sparks in her eyes. I lean my head back and close my eyes. I can feel Stephanie leaning her head on my shoulder. Releasing all the worry and stress of life and just allowing myself to be. I take in deep breaths and release them slowly. My life is starting to look up. This moment is perfect. Right here, right now. I could not have asked for anything better than this. A sense of rightness and a sense of belonging fell upon me.

I slowly open my eyes and scan the forest. I turn to face her. She opens her eyes and looks at me.

"I'm so thankful that you came into my life. I never realized I needed a friend just like you." I squeeze her arm. I can't tell her enough just how thankful I am for her and her friendship.

She smiles softly, "I'm thankful I get to be a part of your life." I can see the honesty of her words in her eyes, yet there was something behind it. Something lingers in the back, as if she needs to tell me something but doesn't share it. I shake it off. We have not known each other for too long, maybe that is all.

"What is your family like?" I ask, realizing I have never asked her about her family. I can feel and see the sadness tearing through her. Tears start to form in her eyes. I can feel her pain almost as if it were my own. Something that has always happened to me when I'm around people who feel strong emotions.

"My family was amazing. My parents loved me so much. They were truly amazing parents and people." A tear slides down her cheek. Hesitation consumes me. I have never been in this situation, so I'm uncertain what to do or say. I reach up and softly wipe her tears from her cheek.

"I'm so sorry," I say as I grab her hands. "I can't imagine the pain you feel."

"I miss them so much. Life is so difficult without them. They were my rocks. They always had answers for me and always guided me." She sniffles. "However, I know they would be proud of me now." She tries to smile, but it does not quite reach her eyes. She blinks the tears away and inhales deeply.

"This is a great time to start our training." She chimes. I can tell she wants to change the subject.

"Let's do it then." I jump up and clap my hands together. I have no clue what to expect with training. This will be my very first class. We were going to start tomorrow, but I understand her need to distract herself from the awful memories of losing her parents.

"Okay! Are you ready to learn how to become a Valkyrie?" She jumps up, excitement starting to fill her.

"A what?" confusion must have been written all over my face because Stephanie roars out laughing.

"A Valkyrie is a female warrior. They were almost unstoppable and some of the greatest warriors ever."

"Well.... I guess so; why not? We are training anyways, so we might as well train to be badass females, right?" I chuckle. I had never heard of Valkyrie before. I would love to see a badass female warrior on the battlefield. However, I am sure it is just one of those make-believe things you read in books.

"Today, we are going to focus on our cores. We need to strengthen our core and lower back. It is super crucial to our training. That and balance." She huffs out as she pats her stomach. She leads me in several stretches to warm our bodies up before getting into the "good part," as she says.

I roll my eyes at her comment, knowing I have never really been an athletic person or one who has worked out. So, this would be an exciting time. I followed her step by step with each exercise she had us do; lunges, high knees, torso twists, and squats. Each set is progressively getting harder and harder. I struggle to keep up, panting like I have never exercised a day in my life, which is kind of true. My skin starts to itch as sweat runs down my temples and neck. I push myself to continue despite my muscles silently screaming at the force of extra work they are undergoing. I can feel this will leave me sore for the next few days. I know I need to do this, so I will not give up; I will finish this training. Determination pounds through me, pushing me to continue. Something inside of me feels right training with Stephanie. It feels like this is meant to be; this is what we are supposed to do. So, I'm embracing this new change even if it kills me!

One more squat and hold, then I'm done. I can feel the searing pain in my thighs that is on the verge of making me yelp in pain. Deep breath in and exhale slowly. I let my mind wander to ignore the pain. What would life be like if I was still with my parents? I allow my mind to play out what I think it would be like. I close my eyes, and there they are, my mother and father. My mother looks just like me, and my father looks solid and noble. They stretch their hands towards me, ushering me to them for an embrace. I slowly walk towards them.

"Alright, that was our last exercise for today. You did great." Stephanie says, patting my shoulder. My eyes flutter open, and I stand up. My legs feel like Jello. I shake my legs a few times, then slowly lower myself. I slump against my favorite oak, grabbing my water from my bag. I gulp down the water and try to catch my breath. I look up at Stephanie and see she has barely broken a sweat. She isn't even panting as heavily as I am!

"Wow, that was a lot!" I gasp, trying to suck in as much air as possible. Stephanie stands next to me, stretching her arms in the air. Envy fills me because she is not winded at all like me. She is standing there, perfectly fine, not gasping for air, as if she had not just finished an exercise session.

"Yes, we have to work on your training. You seem like you have never done a day of PE in your life," she chuckles. I grab a small rock that is next to me on the ground and throw it at her head. She dodges out of the way, and the rock flies right by her. She bends down and grabs a handful of leaves off the ground, throwing them at me. I laugh hysterically as I cover my head with my hands to avoid the falling leaves. Moving or dodging was not an option for me at this point. She begins laughing with me and then plops down next to me. She leans her head against my shoulder. Both of us have goofy smiles plastered on our faces.

"Thank you. I need a lot more work, but that was fun." I glance down at her. She winks back at me,

"Any time, friend."

"Friend?" I raise one eyebrow at her. I have never been labeled as someone's friend before.

"Yes, friend." She drapes her arm over my shoulder, giving me a side hug.

I made plans to see Stephanie for another training session after work tomorrow. She said she had some things to get done this afternoon to prepare for graduation, so she didn't linger long in front of my home. She was skipping off to her house. I had to hurry and get myself ready for graduation. I was going to work today, but Dani insisted I relax this afternoon before graduation.

A sense of being watched crawls over my skin. I turn my head quickly and scan the neighborhood. It was a quiet day on this street, and I could not see a soul. Stephanie had already walked up the road and turned down the street she lives on, so I knew it could not be her watching me. Yet, I can not shake the feeling that someone is watching me. This is not the first time that I have felt this way recently. God, I hope I don't have a stalker of some sort that is going to kidnap me. I do not want to go out that way. I do not have time to wander out trying to find the cause of my discomfort. I need to get ready.

I turn and jolt inside. I run up the stairs, trying to put as much distance between me and whatever is outside. My mind is swarming with a thousand thoughts: that strange feeling, work, training with Stephaine, my birthday, moving. It was never-ending. I want to start moving some of my things over to Dani's ahead of time. That way, I don't have as much to move when the time comes. I will pack some of my things right now and take them home after work. Now, yes, I did not have much at all, but moving stuff with no car was a little tricky. So, trips I would make.

I walk into my room and sling my bag into my chair. I dramatically flop onto my bed and chuckle to myself. What a day. What a week. So many life changes in such a short period. There are so many strange feelings and strange things happening. I close my eyes briefly and then sit up. I must get going, so I rise from the bed and walk to the closet. I can take some clothes and some books today. I rummage through the closet for articles of clothing that I do not wear as often. They will not be missed for the next few days. I stop short. I turn 18 in five days. I will be an adult in less than a week. The thought hits me like a train. I'm going to be an adult soon. I know my birthday is coming up, and I need to move, but I guess I never let the moving from teenager to adult settle in—a new chapter in my life, a new page-turning. Excitement buzzes through my bones.

I continue snagging a few clothing items from my closet and place them in a bag. I then turn towards my desk and try to stuff as many books as possible in my bag without making it too heavy. I will have to carry this to work. I don't want my bag to snap while I'm holding it. Once I have secured a few of my beloved books into my bag, I stroll to the bathroom.

I let my hair fall down my back in soft waves and place my cap on my head. I look at myself in my cap and gown and smile. I have made it this far, so I can only Imagine how much farther I can make it in life. I straighten my gown and look down at my watch. It's almost 5:00 p.m., so I must get going. I rush out of my room and quietly go down the hallway, not hearing a sound in the house. This graduation tonight is the chapter closing to high school and a new chapter opening to something better. I'm ready for more.

I drag my feet up the stairs toward my room. The shadows dance across the walls as I slowly make the climb up. I walk in a daze, half daydreaming, and the other half of my brain truly exhausted from all the excitement today. Dani closed the cafe early to attend my graduation. I was nervous yet excited to walk across the stage and receive my diploma, graduating with honors. When I was handed my diploma, I spotted Hillary in the crowd. It melted my heart to know that she came to my graduation. She hadn't told me she would be there, nor did I know she even knew when it was. Then again, this is a small town, and it's not hard to find things out there. I reach my bedroom door, turn the handle, and push the door slowly open. I drop my cap in the chair as I close the door behind me, dragging my feet. I flop onto the bed and look up at the ceiling. School is finally over. The thought settles on me, and I can feel the tension releasing in my chest. I lay in my bed and drift off to sleep.

CHAPTER TWELVE

Growing Friendship

ADILYN

I sit on the front porch, watching the morning sun climb the sky. Mornings are always so peaceful because everything is barely waking up. I love to listen to the songs that nature sings and not the noise from cars and humans. I open my eyes and see Stephanie strolling towards the house. I grab my bag of things and jump down the stairs, wincing slightly; my muscles are still tender from the previous day's workout with Stephanie. I jog to Stephanie's side, giving her a quick hug.

"Still sore?" She smirks, raising her eyebrow. I can tell she is trying to bite back a laugh.

"You're not?" I ask. She shakes her head, and she can no longer contain her laughter. She barks out laughing, and it is so contagious that I can't help but laugh with her.

"Oh, shut up!" I softly push her shoulder. We start walking towards school.

"Ready to officially start a new chapter in your life?" She asks, looking at me as we walk.

"I can't wait!" I say sarcastically. Part of me is super excited, yet there is a part terrified of what will come. We walk the rest of the way in silence.

We walk straight to the forest before heading to work. It is a ritual for me to stop by the forest first, even if just briefly, and it is a ritual I'm happy to start including Stephanie in. As soon as we enter the forest, I drop my bag along the tree line. I didn't want it weighing me down as I did my thing walking amongst the trees. I want to focus and enjoy the nature around me and not have my mind on the weight of my heavy bag. Spring is slowly fading into summer, yet the temperature has not started to rise. The sun is shining through the oak branches, kissing my face, warming me up against the cool breeze. The birds chatter, and the small animals are scurrying for food. I make a beeline for my favorite oak. I need to be brief, but I did not want to go without saying hello. I stroll up the massive tree and place my palm on its trunk. I look up towards the canopy and smile.

"What beauty, scars and all," I whisper. I wrap my arms around it, quickly squeezing the ancient tree. I let go and look upward once again.

"It truly is! Amazing what these trees have faced, and yet they stand tall." Stephanie quietly moves to stand by my side.

"The whispers of the wind and the songs of the forest guide my soul. Always and forever, my dear friend." I head back to where I had discarded my bag, and Stephanie strides beside me. I reach the tree line, bend over to pick up my bag, and sling it onto my back. I grunt as the weight collides with my back.

" What do you have in that bag of yours?" Stephanie raises a brow as she looks at me.

"It is some of my personal belongings from the Stents. I'm moving them over to Dani's." I adjust the strap so the bag isn't cutting into my shoulder.

"To Dani's?" Stephanie pauses.

"Yep! I will move in with her tomorrow since tomorrow is the big day!" I stop and turn towards her.

" The big day that you turn 18?" She cups her elbow with one hand and places a finger on her lip, thinking.

I nod my head in response.

"Exciting! Let me carry that bag for you." She reaches over, grabbing the backpack strap, and I allow it to slide off my shoulder. "I can help you move your things, you know?"

"I can't have you suffering carrying bags back and forth like me." I begin walking again, relieved that I had rid myself of the weight for now.

"No, of course not, silly. I have a car!" She shakes her head and giggles, swatting in my direction.

"Then why are you always walking?"

"Because you walk."

" Oh. Well then, yes, I would love for you to help me."

"You got it! I will pick you up tomorrow, and we will move all your things."

We walk the rest of the way talking about painting. A few minutes pass, and the cafe is up ahead of us. We stop right outside, and I lean to hug Stephanie. She hugs me back, squeezing tightly. Stephanie slides the bag off her shoulder and hands it back to me. I grab it, throw it over my shoulder, and turn to the front door.

"See you later," Stephanie calls me as I open the door. I turn and wave goodbye to her. I walk into work and see a few people sitting at the tables scattered throughout the cafe. One of the clients catches my eye. I sigh and roll my eyes. Asher sits in the far corner, sipping tea and looking out the window. He looks over in my direction, and our eyes lock. I stand there momentarily, just staring back at him. Everything in the room slowly slips away from reality, and he is left. The doorbell rings as someone enters the cafe, snapping me back to reality. I squeeze my eyes shut and then open them again, glancing at Asher. He nods and smirks, almost as if he is taunting me. He has already made a fool of me once, and he seems to be a distraction, one I don't need now. I rush to the office to drop my bag off since the strap had begun to dig into my shoulder. I return to the front and get my apron and a rag to wipe down tables. I can see that Asher is watching my every movement, his eyes never leaving me. I'm at work, I can't be distracted by this man, but what does he want? I walk straight up to Asher, determined not to allow myself to look stupid again. The closer I get to the table, Asher's smirk grows.

"What are you doing here?" I groan, placing my hands on my hips. The last time I saw him, I embarrassed myself. He flustered me with his enormous ego, and I maybe allowed something to slip without thinking about what I was saying first.

"I'm drinking tea, dear one. Is one not permitted to drink tea here?" His eyes look me up and down, licking his lips. What am I? A piece of meat for him to examine? Anger bubbling inside of me. This man is frustrating.

"Yes, people can, but why come while I'm here? And don't call me dear one!" I demand. Part of me doesn't like to see him because of his cocky manner, but there is a small part of me deep inside that ogles when I see him.

"How is one to know when you will and will not be here if they are new to this town and establishment?" tilting his head to the side.

"Whatever." I roll my eyes at all his formalities.

"Why do I anger you so much? Or do you not want to accept that you enjoy seeing my stunning face?" He smirks.

"You don't find your ego to be a little too inflated?" I snap. Dammit, he got me right spot on. Of course, I want to see his stupidly gorgeous face, but that is beside the point. I mean, who wouldn't want to see it?

"Well, I remember clearly you stated that I'm to your liking. So, if I have an inflated ego, I have you to thank for that." He winks.

"You are truly obnoxious, aren't you." I shake my head. "I don't have time for this back and forth with you. I have work to do." I turn and walk to the counter to clean the espresso machine.

"I will be here a little longer for you to drool over." He calls to me. I shake my head. He is so full of himself. I busy myself around the cafe, trying so hard not to steal glances in his direction. However, my attempts are futile.

The time flies at work with nothing eventful other than Asher and his ego. I walk up the stairs to the Stents and quietly sneak in. My time here is ending, and that thought saddens a part of me. I shake my head, clearing any sad thoughts from my mind because it's never good to go to bed upset, especially since my birthday is tomorrow. I let my mind wander about what I had planned. The next few days will be so refreshing, no school and training with Stephanie. I smile, and my heart jumps in my chest. I have become fond of my time with Stephanie and training with her. I can feel myself growing stronger, and I love the make-believe goal we are striving for. Valkyries. I sneak into my room, cross the room, slump onto my bed, And close my eyes. My mind continues to wander on all the happy what-ifs, and my eyes begin to feel heavy.

CHAPTER THIRTEEN

Asher

I stand hidden in the shadows, watching Adilyn train. I have been following her all day. Well, I follow her most days. One never knows what can pop out from around a corner at any given time. I was not willing to take those chances. Today, I watched her and Stephanie as they walked home. I saw Stephanie bid farewell to Adilyn and then make her way down the street and around the corner.

She must have sensed that I was watching her. I could tell by how her head jerked around, and she searched her surroundings. I chuckled because she would never find me, no matter how hard she looked. I can say that her senses are pretty impressive if she could detect that someone was watching her. Then she stormed off into the house like a terrified yet angry girl.

She emerged shortly after hauling a loaded bag of what I guessed was her personal belongings. Her short stop in the forest spiked my interest in her even more. From my understanding, she stops in the forest often, or so I have seen. I watched her walk straight to a massive tree in the forest.

She lays her hand upon its trunk and quietly speaks to the tree. I inched closer to hear better.

Then, with the help of the wind, I heard her whisper, "The whispers of the wind and the songs of the woods guide my soul. Always and forever, my dear friend."

She may not know who she is, but deep down, she knows who she is. The matter at hand is telling her. Soon enough, she will find out the truth.

I knew her next stop would be to work, so I went to the cafe to get there before her. I needed to pick something up from Dani anyway, and I felt like getting under Adilyn's skin just a little. I had to make my day entertaining somehow. Sure enough, I managed to get under her skin, even though she tried so hard not to be affected by my pestering.

I am hiding in the shadows, watching the two girls. Adilyn and Stephanie are training, Valkyrie training, to be exact. I smirk because Adilyn thinks the Valkyrie are some mythical beings from stories. Little does she know. I can see that she struggles with the sets Stephanie is dictating. It makes sense, though, that if one is not accustomed to physical activity, it takes time to become accustomed to it. Despite that, she is still graceful and determined. It warms my cold heart to see that. I can feel the determination rolling off of her. I can feel her inner power slowly rising to the top. She needs to continue to push herself. As soon as she knows, I can fully step in and help.

She will become a warrior one day and even a great warrior at that. All I can do for now is hope that she will be ready when the time comes. Ready enough to be able to step up. It's good for her; she will have us to count on.

CHAPTER FOURTEEN

Emerald Heart

ADILYN

The day finally came when I went from a teenager to an adult. My foster parents had expected me to boot myself out today, so I made sure that I was prepared. I took some items to Dani's the day before. I didn't have a lot and needed to move anyway. I never really accumulated much over my life. I've never seen the purpose since I never felt like I belonged.

I was taking my clothes from the closet so I could fold them. They were the last thing I needed to pack up; I was done. There is a soft knock on my door.

"Yes?" I call out, unsure of who would be knocking on my door. It must be one of my foster parents; who else would be here?

"You have a visitor," Hillary says through the door.

"Okay, I will be right down," I call back, setting my clothes on my bed. I open my door, and Hillary still stands there before me. A little startled,

I figured she would have notified me and left. She looks at me with a long face.

"Is everything alright, Hillary?" I ask, worry creeping in that something must be wrong.

"Today is your birthday. I know I have not done much for you in your time here, but I wanted to give this to you before you leave." She held out a small box wrapped in a simple piece of paper and a small bow on top. I look at her, not knowing what to do. Shock must have been written all over my face because she chuckles softly.

"Take the box, Adilyn. Open it." She smiles softly, sensing my uncertainty. She held her hand higher, motioning for me to grab the box. I nod my head and grab the box slowly. What could this be? I hold the small box in my hand. Hesitation begins to flood inside of me. I never really received any gifts other than from Dani.

"Open it," Hillary said softly. "Hurry, you do not want to keep your guest waiting downstairs."

Remembering why I came out of my room in the first place, someone was here to see me; I hurried and pulled on the bow, untying it. I unwrap the box and slowly open it. Inside the box is a necklace. I gasp as soon as I see it.

"It is the most beautiful thing I have ever seen, Hillary. Thank you so much! This means the world to me." Trying to hold back tears, I throw my arms around her. I have never hugged Hillary, nor has she ever hugged me. She gently wraps her arms around me.

"You deserve it and so much more. I may not have been there for you much, but I'm proud of you. I have always rooted on your team and always will." she says, followed by a sniff. Tears collect in my eyes, threatening to tumble down my face. I slowly let go of Hillary and look back at the necklace. It is a small emerald stone in the shape of a heart. I pull it out, and my hands tremble, making it hard to unclasp the necklace.

"Let me help you." She smiles, holding out her hand. I place the necklace in her hand and then turn, collecting my hair from the back of my neck. She places the necklace on and clasps it. I drop my hair and then turn back towards her, looking down at the beautiful emerald heart hanging slightly below my collarbone.

"Emerald is my favorite color," I whisper.

"I know it is. I saw this necklace; it had your name written all over it, so I knew I had to get it for you. Now, get going! Don't leave your friend waiting for you forever." She pats my shoulder and turns towards her room. Standing in the hallway, I watch Hillary enter her room and shut the door. I could see a hint of sadness in her eyes behind the constant mask she always wears. I have never noticed it before today. A ping of pain hits my heart. I was never super close to Hillary or anything, nor did I ever believe that she ever really liked me. I thought she put up with me simply because she had to. I shrug it off. I don't have time right now to look into it any further. Someone was waiting for me downstairs, so I turn towards the stairs and climb down.

I turn the corner, and to my surprise, Stephanie is lounging on the couch. She has a handful of floating balloons in one hand and a bouquet of sunflowers and bloodroot flowers in her other. Her smile grows as soon as she sees me turn the corner.

"Happy Birthday!" She squeals and jumps up, greeting me with a hug.

"Thank you! I'm surprised to see you here, but I'm not." I laugh.

"Why do you say that?" She asks.

"Well, no one has ever visited me at the house. So, it is new to have someone here to see me, yet it is not surprising that you would be my first visit." I smile at her. I have known this girl for only days, yet I feel like I have known her my whole life.

"Lucky you then, I am your first!" She throws her head back and laughs in response. Her laugh is so infectious and causes me to laugh along with her.

"These are for you since it is your special day." She grins and hands me the flowers and the balloons.

"Awe, thank you so much!" I reach out and grab the flowers and balloons. Lifting the flowers to my nose, I inhale deeply. Sweet floral aromas brush my senses. The beauty of these flowers up close is extraordinary. Stephanie takes a seat on the couch. I sit down next to her and smile at the remark she just made.

"How are you doing?" Stephanie turns to face me.

"I'm good, I think. I was in shock just now because Hillary got me this necklace for my birthday." palming the necklace so Stephanie could see.

"That is so you! How sweet of her." She smiles, examining the necklace.

"It truly is perfect. I was just surprised that she even got me anything." I sigh.

"So, what are your plans for today?" Stephanie asks.

"I don't have any plans other than moving the rest of my things. I don't work today. Dani said that between moving and my birthday, I could take the day off."

"Awesome! I'm glad you didn't have anything planned because I made plans for us!" She exclaims, clapping her hands together.

"I will help you move, and then we will go!"

"Where are we going?" hesitation lacing my voice. No one has ever planned something for my birthday like this before.

"It is a surprise! I can't tell you! Now hurry up, get your things packed, and get ready," She shrieks. "I will return in an hour, and we can go." She leans over and hugs me, then stands up and leaves through the front door. I sit there momentarily, rummaging through what happened and how I feel.

The past few days have for sure been quite a roller coaster. I won the exhibit. I was in the spotlight and survived. I made a life choice. I gained a friend and a new art student. I started training with Stephanie. Today, I'm officially an adult, and I'm moving out. Hillary bought me a gift. All of these emotions swimming through my head and my heart. I'm filled with happiness yet sad, determined yet unsure, courageous yet timid. I need to relax and worry about all of these feelings later. Once I had a clearer mind and more time, I could fully sort through everything I felt. I shake my head and then stand up. I guess I have to start getting ready for tonight.

Rummaging through my already-packed bag of clothes, I was so unsure what to wear that I blew out a frustrated breath. She didn't tell me where we were going or what we would do, so how am I supposed to know what to wear? I roll my eyes. Typical of Stephanie. My eyes scan each item of clothing I tore out of the bag, debating. I land on a cute oversized overall with pockets, a tee outfit, and combat-style boots. This will do. I grab the two items, toss them onto the desk, and then stuff everything back into the bag. I stand up and stretch my legs from all that crouching. I grab my clothes from the desk and then stroll to the bathroom to change. I stare at myself in the mirror, debating what to do with my hair. I don't know how to style my hair other than with a bun on my head and the occasional braid. I wish I had a mother who could've taught me how to do my hair and makeup. A mom who taught me to take care of myself and to have those intimate conversations with one I could confide in. All the things I wish I had in life.

Tears swell up in my eyes, fighting to be set free. I wipe my eyes, ridding them of the tears, and close them. This is not the place or the time for this. Not right now. I inhale and then exhale, opening my eyes. I begin to braid my hair. I want to do something different with my hair than the usual bun. As I braid my hair, I realize I don't feel the fire running through my arm muscles. A grin spreads with the realization that my training has helped to improve and strengthen my muscles. I finish the braid swiftly and then smile at myself in the mirror. I apply minimal makeup and then go to my room.

I have 15 more minutes until Stephanie is supposed to arrive, so I grab my book from my nightstand and lay on my stomach in my bed. I'm about halfway through the book. This book has snatched my attention so far and has left me on the edge of my chair, wanting more. The plot is so intriguing. I hate having to set it down and go about my life. If I could read all day, then I totally would! I'm enthralled in my reading when I hear a quiet knock on my door. The door opens slowly, and Hillary stands there. I turn my head towards her and smile.

"Hi!" I say, closing my book.

"What are you reading?" She smiles back at me.

"This book I found at the cafe. It is called 'The Lost Princess, and it's terrific."

"You have always been the reader, at least what I have seen and know about you. What is this book about?" She smirks at me.

"It is about a lost princess who grows up in another land and then finds out her true identity. I am currently at the part where she is on her journey back to her kingdom." I tell her.

"That sounds interesting. I'm sorry to disturb you again, but your friend is downstairs waiting for you." She mutters. I sit up and place my book on the nightstand. I stand up and grab my purse from my desk chair. I sling my bag over my head and walk to Hillary. I lock eyes with her and then reach to hug her. She stiffens and releases a sigh, then wraps her arms around me.

"I appreciate you, Hillary. You have been supportive and kind to me in your way. You let me stay here when I had nowhere else to go despite already having so much going on in your life." I squeeze her.

"Thank you." She loosens her grip on me. "Now, off you go! Have an amazing birthday night! You deserve it and so much more." She smiles, then turns to walk out of my room. She walks past my bag of packed belongings. She stares at the bag momentarily, then turns back to me.

"Today is your last day here, isn't it?" Sadness fills her eyes.

"Well, I thought that was the deal." I'm unsure of what to say.

"Yes, I guess you are right. That was Tim's condition for fostering."

"Um, if you want, I can come tomorrow for breakfast. I can pick up some things from the store and come by and make you breakfast if you would like."

"I would love that, Adilyn. How about tomorrow at 8 a.m.? If that is not too early for you." A soft smile graces her face.

"That sounds perfect." I smile back at her. She nods, then turns back around and walks out of my room.

Today alone has for sure been a roller coaster of emotions. I can't seem to wrap my head around it right now. Hillary has been trying more and more recently to be a part of my life, or at least she has let me know she is there. I wonder what is going on with her. As long as I have known Hillary, I know she has struggled internally. I have never learned why or with what exactly, but I know she has struggled. Those struggles have caused her to be very isolated.

"Adilyn, where are you at?" Stephanie yells from downstairs.

I turn and look around my room. This is time. I lean out my bedroom door and yell for Stephanie to come up and help with my things. I turn back and start grabbing bags. I only have a few bags worth of belongings left here. Clothes, art supplies, and a few books are gone. I can hear Stephanie trudge up the stairs.

"I'm in here!" I shout out so she can find her way.

"Hey." She says as she peeks her head into the room.

"Ready?" She asks.

"Pretty much. Can you help me with this bag?" I point towards the bag of my clothing by my desk. She strolls into the room

"Of course I can." She exclaims. She picks up the bag and turns towards me. "Are you ready for tonight?" Excitement fills her voice.

"Um... I honestly don't know. I'm not sure what we're doing, so I can't say if I'm ready," I say with a smirk, biting my cheek. I have no clue what we're about to do, so am I ready? Who knows?

"Gesh, you are annoying." She huffs out, then smiles. "Embrace the unknown."

"Well, let's go!" She turns and walks towards the door. I pick up the remaining bags and follow her out. I turn back to look down the hallway once I reach the top of the stairs. Gazing towards Hillary's door, I hope that she is alright. I feel my heart break at the thought that I'm about to leave this house permanently. I sigh and turn back to the stairs, making my way down. Stephanie waits for me at the door and opens it once I reach her. I look at her and try to smile at her, but my attempts fail.

"It will be alright. I promise." She states. I hope her words ring true and that everything is indeed alright. My life is already so up in the air with everything. I don't need false hope that everything is going to be okay.

I try to force the biggest smile possible and respond, "I know."

Once we cross the doorway, I see a car outside the house.

"Is that your car?" I tilt my head. I didn't know she had a car until yesterday, and I have never seen it with us, always walking everywhere.

"For the moment, it is." She walks down the front steps towards the car. What does she mean by that, I wonder?

"Hurry up!" She yells back at me, swinging my bag of clothes into her back seat. I run towards the car and toss my remaining bags in the back. Hopping in the car, I put my seat belt on and turn towards her.

"So..." in hopes that she reveals something, anything, about what we're going to do. I was not up for trying anything crazy or overly weird.

"So, hold on tight!" She squeals, revving the car engine.

She drives out of town and makes several turns down dirt roads. We drive for some time. Next thing I know, 30 minutes has already flown right by. We spent that entire time chatting and laughing together. It feels like only several minutes have passed. I guess when you are having fun, time flies. We fall silent, and I look out the window. Stephanie takes a turn that leads us into the woods. The sun is setting, coloring the sky with pretty pinks, purples, and soft hints of red. Small clouds are dancing in the sky, contrasting the backdrop. A smile spreads across my face, and I cannot help myself. The beauty that I was taking in was magnificent. The sky and the assortment of trees in this part of the woods are mesmerizing. There are oak trees, ash trees, a few pine trees scattered around, elm trees, and several other kinds. It's unbelievable yet so stunning to see all of these distant types of trees settled in amongst each other. The woods in

Claywood are nothing like this. They are beautiful, yes, but not quite as much. Claywood was not even close in comparison to this place.

"I never imagined that so many different kinds of trees would be all in the same woods."

"Yeah, it is pretty cool, isn't it?" she grins at me. I spend the next few minutes soaking in everything my eyes can see. I want to paint this. Something catches my eye. I look up ahead and see something. It looks like stables up ahead. I turn towards Stephanie.

"Is that what I think it is?"

"I cannot read your mind, so I don't know what you think. However, those are horse stables."

"We are going to see horses?"

"Yep! I thought it would be fun to go horseback riding while the sun sets." The biggest grin ever spreads across her face.

"This may sound stupid, but I have never seen a horse. I have seen them on TV and read about them in books." Embarrassment creeps up at that realization. I have never seen a horse in real life. I don't know how that is even possible.

"No worries. Once again, I will be your first." She winks at me. I shake my head and roll my eyes, trying to bite back a laugh. I laugh so much with Stephanie. She brings me so much joy, a pleasure I have never experienced. I stare at her a moment longer and thank the gods again for bringing her into my life. She pulls the car to a stop and parks. Taking the keys out of the ignition, she turns towards me.

"You ready for this?" She asks, grinning.

"I'm ready for this." I smile back. I jump out of the car, excitement bussing through me. We walk hand in hand into the stable. I stop only a few steps in. The smell of hay, earth, musk, and horse fills the air. I look around and see two massive creatures standing in stalls. My mouth drops open at the sight of them. I never knew horses were that big in real life.

Stephanie pats my shoulder. "Let's go meet them." She says quietly. "Please try not to drool on them, though, because they may not appreciate that." She chuckles. I close my mouth immediately and walk towards the horse to the right. This black beauty caught my eye. It is about one and a half times my height, and who knows how much this horse weighs. It's a lot more than me, for sure. This horse is the biggest one out of the three that are here. This creature is breathtaking not only because of its size but also because of its physical beauty. Dark as midnight with a sparkle. The mane looks like a black waterfall flowing down its neck. Its gaze locks with mine. I have never seen a creature with eyes like this one, an icy blue that starkly contrasts the rest of its features. There is something there in its eyes, is that understanding? Acknowledgment?

"His name is Arion." Emerging from the shadows, a man wipes his hands with a rag. His sudden presence startles me, and I gasp, taking two steps back. When I first entered the stables, I didn't notice anyone else; I thought it was just Stephanie and me there.

"The name is Elouan, my lady."

"Um, my lady?" He nods, almost as if bowing slightly, and holds out his hand. I look down at it for a moment. Then it finally registers that he is holding his hand out to shake mine. My face begins to redden, and I reach to grab his hand quickly. He brings my hand to his lips, softly kissing the back of my hand, and I'm stunned. What do I do or say? I felt like an idiot right about now. Elouan has an accent that I cannot quite place. I wonder where he is from. He speaks with a formality that I'm certainly not used to hearing.

"Yes. That is the custom to call a woman where I come from."

I raise my eyebrow. Where does he come from?

"Her name is Adilyn." Stephanie snorts out a laugh and walks to my side. "Cat has her tongue right now. I'm hoping the cat gives it back so she can stop embarrassing me."

My mouth falls to the ground. She did not say that. "I have my tongue, thank you very much." I snark back at her.

"Oops, it looks like that cat gave it back." She giggles. "Thank you so much, Elouan, for allowing us to come."

"Yes, thank you!" I say quietly, trying to recover from the pure embarrassment of what I just did and Stephanie with her remarks.

"I was just caught off guard by Elouan's formality. My apologies if I was rude." I glance up at Elouan, hoping I didn't offend him.

"My pleasure, my ladies," he says as he nods. He steps towards Arion, reaching out, and strokes the horse's neck. The horse huffs and turns to face me. My eyes lock with Arion. I suck in a breath and hold it, maintaining as still as possible. I will stare this horse straight in the eyes as long as I need to. I don't know how horses react, as stupid as that sounds. I don't want to spook or anger him because he can trample me in a heartbeat.

"This horse is old yet very strong. He can be very temperamental and doesn't like very many people." I glance at the horse and chuckle nervously.

"Well, just great, this horse will be the end of me."

"On the contrary, he seems to like you," Elouan looks over to me.

"He likes me?" I frown, confused about how this horse would like me, considering we just had a stare-down contest.

"Normally, he charges people he does not like to scare them. However, he hasn't done that to you." Elouan smiles, and Arion bobs his head up and down. I laugh nervously. This whole thing is ridiculous.

"Reach out your hand so Arion can smell you, and then you can pet him." Stephanie nudges me with her elbow. I lift my hand in the air, trying my best not to tremble. Do horses smell fear? Well, I hope that they can't. Arion takes a step towards me, and I hold my breath. Anxiety and fear crawl their way up my throat, grasping tightly. Then Arion extends his head towards my hand and sniffs in the air. He lets out a loud breath and then nudges my hand with his head. Everything freezes at that moment. The fear is on the verge of knocking me out, yet the adrenaline and excitement that this horse hasn't trampled me keeps me upright. I stand frozen, holding my breath, waiting for the horse to change his mind.

He nudges my hand once again, and his eyes connect with mine. There is a zap of energy between us. Arion nods. I blink my eyes because something strange happened. What was that? I look around to see if Stephanie or Elouan felt that zap of energy, but their faces don't give anything away. I turn back to face Arion with a newfound understanding. I knew Arion accepted me and would keep me safe. I have no clue how I know that, but that zap of energy made it click in my mind. I release my breath and look over at Stephanie.

Stephanie is standing by the other horse, whispering to the horse. I turn back and take a small step towards him. I turn and look at Arion. I nod once and take a small step towards him. He huffs out another breath in what seems to be boredom. I smile because there is this fantastic creature in front of me. I did not for once think that I would ever see a horse in real life. Before, horses were just creatures I read about in books. But now, standing before this majestic horse, I'm in awe of him.

He has a black coat as dark as the midnight sky. His mane is long and flows down his face and neck. There are braids and beads throughout his mane. He is stunning. I take one more step towards him and reach my hand out again. He nods at me, and I slowly touch between his eyes. He is soft to the touch. I move my hand to the side of his face and stroke softly. My eyes locked with his, and we had a mutual understanding. Then, out of nowhere, I lean towards Arion and place my forehead against his out of habit, just as I do with the trees so often. I close my eyes.

Then it hits me like lightning has just shot through me. I stumble back and gasp, forcing myself to sit down because I doubt the ability of my legs to hold me any longer. Stephanie and Elouan rush to me. They are speaking to me, but I can't hear the ringing in my ears. I lean forward, placing my head in my hands and leaning into my lap. I gulp in as much air as possible, yet I feel like someone is holding me around my neck. I can feel Stephanie rubbing my back slowly, trying to ease whatever is happening with me. I can't speak yet, so I can only imagine how terrified she is. I slowly raise my head and look up at her with tears streaming down my face. The pain and ringing slowly start to reside. She has a soft smile, and her eyes are filled with worry. I try my best to smile back at her when I feel a nudge at my back. I turn slowly afraid sudden movements will make me sick.

Arion stands there behind me, looking down at me. I hope I didn't scare him. Here I am, leaning my face towards his, then I fall back. He probably has no clue what is going on. He leans his head down and nudges my face. I reach up and place my hand on his neck. This massive horse is trying to comfort me. Tears begin streaming down my face in a consistent flow now. I close my eyes, inhale deeply, and place my forehead on the horse's face. Then, like that, it disappears. The pain, the ringing in my ears, all of it disappears. I sit there stunned.

I turn towards Stephanie, and so much confusion swarms around in my head.

"Are you okay?" concern fills her words.

"Yes, I am. I don't know what that was. I don't know what happened." I mutter.

"If I had a guess, my lady, the excitement of seeing Arion simply overwhelmed you," Elouan says.

"I guess," swallowing a lump in my throat.

"Yeah, you are probably overwhelmed with never having seen a horse before." Stephanie shrugs.

"I'm surprised he let you touch him. He must have a soft spot for you." Elouan grins. "It has been many years since he has taken a liking to someone. The last person he was fond of was his previous owner."

"What happened to them?"

"Well, she passed away. I believe that broke Arion's heart. He sure was attached to her. He has not been the same since; he is stubborn and temperamental." Elouan stares down at his hands.

"Oh," I whisper. I have always imagined that animals have similar feelings to ours, so I can imagine the heartbreak of losing a loved one. Elouan must have known Arion's previous owner. I can feel the sadness emanating from him. What is one supposed to say in moments like this?

Stephanie clears her throat. "Since you are feeling better and I'm not super excited about dwelling on sad things on your birthday, let's go on a ride!" Stephanie says, grabbing my hand.

"Um, Steph, I don't know how to ride a horse," I whisper, looking at the ground and feeling my ears heat up. Stephanie bites down on her lip, trying hard to stifle her laugh. However, I can tell it's on the verge of erupting. I glare at her. If she was anyone else, I think I would be upset with her laughing at me, but she is like family. I know she is not mocking me, so I push her shoulder, causing her to fall over easily since she was balancing crouched on her heels. The moment she hits the ground, laughter bursts from her, echoing through the small stable. She rolls back and forth on the ground, dying of laughter. Seeing her like that makes it impossible not to laugh with her. My laugh bubbles up from deep in my core, and by the time we finally catch our breath, we are both shedding tears.

"I love you. You are like family." Breathing sharply, trying to regain my breath.

"I love you too, Ad!! You are like the sister I never had!" She grins so big that it reaches her eyes.

"Now, let's go ride!" She shrieks.

"Let's do this!" I say with confidence; between her and Arion, I feel safe.

The night ended up being amazing! I learned how to ride a horse. I have never felt as free as I did while I was on Arion's back. It was pure bliss riding him. The wind blew through my hair, caressing my face. Despite being stubborn and wanting to lead the entire time, he let me lead him at the very end. When I jumped off his back, he leaned his forehead toward mine. When our foreheads touched, we looked into each other's eyes. I could see the understanding and respect in his eyes. This massive creature respected me, which blew my mind. Yet I share that same respect towards him as well. He may have been quite a pushy horse while I rode him, but he ensured I didn't fall off.

Stephanie had packed a light dinner for us to eat, picnic style. She laid out a blanket, and we sat on it, digging through the basket filled with food. She brought finger Italian sandwiches, veggie salad, and some fresh fruit. The feeling of true happiness settles on me right at this moment.

I'm so thankful that Stephanie planned all of this for me. She is a fantastic person; I'm lucky to call her a friend.

"Elouan said I can come again anytime to see Arion. He even said that Arion probably expects me to return to see him soon." I say, full of energy. I laugh at the thought of his comment. Arion was happier to get me off his back than anything else. Now, maybe I had no clue what I was doing, so he had to assist me, but he could have at least pretended that I was leading. A warmth runs through my veins. Life is genuinely starting to look up. I lay on the blanket, looking up at the stars with Stephanie. It is such a beautiful night.

"I can lay here all night looking at the night sky, counting the stars." I turn to look at Stephanie.

"Me, too," she smiles, not peeling her eyes off the night sky. We lay on the blanket, looking up at the night sky for what felt like forever.

"Unfortunately, it's time for me to get you home. You are going to Dani's tonight, right?" She turns to look at me.

"Yes, tonight will be my first night at Dani's. I'm going to go have breakfast with Hillary tomorrow morning."

"Hmm, that is interesting," she mutters.

"Yeah, it is so strange with her. We have never really had a great relationship or much of a relationship at all. She has, in my perspective, struggled as long as I have been there with some inner demons. Maybe she has struggled longer than that." I shrug.

"Who knows."

"Yeah, who knows? Life can be so complicated at times. One never truly knows what another person is going through, especially the battles they are having in their minds." I contemplate what Hillary's life must have been like all these years. What things has she gone through that shaped her into the person she is now?

"Agreed. You never know what one is going through, so I always try to be kind to everyone." She smiles softly at me. Understanding fills her features.

"You're right. I'm curious to see how breakfast will go."

"I'm curious, too, how it will go, so you will have to let me know! What will you do afterward?" She stretches her arms and sits up.

"Well, I'm going to work in the afternoon, but other than that, there's nothing." I sit up.

"Do you want to train tomorrow?"

"Train to be a badass female warrior? Hell yeah! We can start your painting class as well!" I bump my shoulder with hers.

"Oh my gosh, yes! That would be amazing! I would love to train and then paint." she squeals.

"It is a plan, then!" I say beaming. For the first time, I have a friend with whom I can make plans, someone I can experience life with. I'm no longer walking through this life completely alone.

Chapter Fifteen

New Beginnings

Adilyn

I woke up early to go to the small farmer's market this morning to pick up some things for breakfast. I have not come to the farmers market in some time. Life has become so busy with finishing school, work, and the art exhibit. I almost forgot how comforting the market was. I stroll through the small stands lining the local church parking lot.

The local farmers come to the church every Saturday morning and set up stands. They bring the recent crops that they have just picked. There are some other small local businesses as well. People that make things for a living. You can find many things here, from fresh produce to natural soap to clothing items and accessories. There is a gal that crochets items such as scarves and hats, cute purses, and farm animal amigurumi. Another lady sews things such as purses, skirts, and book sleeves, amongst other things. I walk through the market, admiring the local crafters' talent. Their talent is just as unique as the talent of local artists. The time, effort, and love go into each thing they make. I spot a stand of a crafter who makes simple yet beautiful jewelry. I head towards that stand before I head to get some fresh produce for breakfast.

I stroll to the table and smile at the lady setting a few bracelets on the table.

"Good morning."

"Good morning, darling." she looks up at me. Her smile is genuine. "How can I help you?"

"I wanted to take a look at your bracelets. I would love to get one for my best friend and me."

Stephanie is my best friend. How crazy is it to consider someone your best friend so quickly? A warmth fills my core, and a smile spreads on my face. She planned the most incredible birthday of my life, and I wanted to thank her for caring.

"There are some lovely matching bracelets over here on this side, darling." she points towards the right side of the table.

I look through all the bracelets and eye two bracelets. They are braided with a deep green, soft lavender string and a leaf charm. They are perfect for us both.

"I want to get these two! They are perfect." I pick them up and hand the two bracelets to her.

"They sure are nice! That will be $10." She grabs the bracelets and places them in a small, clear bag.

I pull some money out of my bag and hand her $10.

"Thank you so much! Have a great day." I grab the bracelets from her, stuffing them into my bag so I don't lose them. She nods at me and grins.

I turn towards the direction of the fresh produce stands. I wander toward the produce stands when I see the stand of a local blacksmith. He has several things on his table: small knives, hand axes, hammers, nails, and other tools. However, something glints in the light towards the back of his stand. It spikes my curiosity, and I want to see what it is. I am only a few feet from the stand and see a sword leaning against the backing. It has a pommel with intricate details. At the end of the pommel, there is an emerald stone. The sword is breathtaking.

"Howdy, ma'am. The sword has caught your eye, I see." a man chuckles.

I turn to look at him. He is an older, rugged-looking, hard-around-the-edges kind of guy who is kind and gentle. I nod at him and look back towards the sword. He walks over to the sword, picks it up, and then walks back towards me.

"It sure is a beauty." he tilts the sword so I can get a better view of it—the stone sparkles in the sunlight. The details on the pommel are fine. There is a mixture of lines and circles mixed with what I believe must be a language or runes.

"Did you make that?" I cannot peel my eyes off of the sword.

"I wish, ma'am, but I found this sword as surprising as it sounds. Would you like to hold it?" he lifts the sword towards me.

"I would love to hold it." I reach for the sword, grab the pommel, and lay the blade on my open, flat palm. I feel a zap where the sword touches my skin. I shrug at the feeling because weird things have been happening so often lately. I tilt the blade back and forth to see it better in the lighting. It is just breathtaking. I'm curious as to where he found it. Who misplaced this beautiful weapon? It seems to puzzle me.

"I found it one day while I went out fishing. I was walking from my house to the lake and found it in the forest. I tried looking around for the owner, but I did not see anyone at all. There was no trace of someone having been there either. It pained me to leave such a beauty out in the forest to rust over, so I brought it home. I don't need it much. Swords are not very commonly used nowadays."

"Are you selling it?" I look up at the man, crossing my fingers that he would say yes. This sword is beautiful in so many ways. The emerald stone in the pommel glistens in the sun, yet there is something more to it. Something old and magical.

"I was not planning on it, ma'am, but I'm in a good mood today. I see that your necklace is very similar to that stone there in the pommel of the sword." He nods towards the necklace hanging around my neck.

"Oh, this? Yes, emerald is my favorite." I forgot that it was there. My hand reaches up to clasp the emerald heart.

"Well, ma'am, the sword is yours then. Like I said, I do not need it, so it's yours. I ask that you take good care of it. It is very well made, and it would pain me for work as amazing as this to go down the drain." the man smiles at me.

"How much do you want for it?"

"Nothing, ma'am; as I said, I am in a good mood today, and this sword is now yours." he winks at me.

Another customer comes up beside me and starts looking at the hand axes on the table. He picks one up and turns it around, examining it.

"Well, thank you so much. I promise I will take good care of it." I give him the biggest smile ever. I am so thankful for this man's kindness when he does not know me.

He nods at me, smiles, and then turns to the man with the hand axe. I looked at my watch and saw it was 7:35. Darn it, I must hurry! I spent more time than I was expecting here in this market. I rush to the fresh produce stands to get something for breakfast with Hillary.

I pick eggs, tomatoes, potatoes, zucchini, onions, garlic, and broccoli. I am in the mood for a veggie scramble and some hash browns. I awkwardly jog to my foster parents' home, trying to carry my bag, a sword, eggs, and produce.

I arrive at the house and tread up the patio stairs. I open the front door and call out to Hillary so that she knows I have arrived.

"Hey Hillary. I am here!" standing by the front door.

"Hey, Adilyn. I'm in the bathroom, but I will be right down. I made coffee." she calls down from the upstairs bathroom.

I head to the kitchen to start preparing breakfast. The smell of ground coffee beans and freshly brewed medium-roast coffee floods my senses. I inhale deeply. I love the smell of coffee and its taste even more. I set my bag and the sword down in the corner. Gods know what Hilary will say about me bringing a sword into her house. I don't want to find out how she will react. I want things to go smoothly today. I grab a coffee cup from the cabinet and pour myself a cup first. Add the cream and honey, stir, then enjoy that first sip of liquid heaven. Setting my cup down, I turn to the kitchen sink and do quick work of rinsing the vegetables and cutting them up. Hillary strolls into the kitchen as I place the pans on the stove.

"Hey, how are you?" I turn to greet her.

"Good. Thanks for asking. You? How did the rest of your birthday go?" she grabs a cup from the cabinet and pours herself some coffee.

"It was amazing. I learned how to ride a massive horse at that!" I squeal at the thought that I rode a real horse.

"That must have been amazing! I'm so happy that you had a great birthday. You deserve it and so much more. Do you need any help with breakfast?" she sips her coffee.

"I think I have breakfast handled. You sit down." I turn to the stove and toss the diced potatoes and other vegetables into the pan. I quickly crack the eggs and mix them in a bowl. Once the vegetables are soft, I add the mixed eggs into the pan, continuously stirring until they are fully cooked.

We both sit down at the table and begin to eat. Things at first are awkward—the silence in the kitchen and not much to say. I can hear the birds chattering outside, the dog barking down the street, and the rustling leaves in the wind. I rocked in my chair, trying to think of anything to say. It is so hard because I have never honestly had much of a relationship with Hillary. She has been there, yes, but not indeed been there. After a few minutes, the silence starts to eat at me. I can't stand it for a moment longer.

"How are things going? How is Tim?" trying to find anything to talk about.

"Things have been better, but they have also been worse. Tim has left for good."

"Oh. I'm sorry to hear that." I mutter, uncertain what to say next. I know that she is more than likely better off without him. He always seemed like one who dragged others down from when I knew him.

"Oh, no need to be sorry, honey. I think it is for the best. He made a huge impact on my mental health, and not in the best of ways. He always told me I needed him to make it and that I couldn't live without him. For so long, I thought he was right and couldn't do it without him. That's why I stuck with him for so long." she says sheepishly, looking down at her plate.

"What changed things?" I'm curious as to what caused her to change her mind.

"Well...." she sighs, trying to collect her thoughts, "Several days ago, I had a dream. In this dream, there was a lady, and she told me that I need to shake off all the baggage weighing me down because I would be needed. She said you would need me." tears filling her eyes, she looks up at me quickly then back down at her plate. "Silly me for getting all emotional over here., I'm sorry."

"Oh no, please do not apologize." I reach to grab her hand and squeeze it softly.

"I guess I didn't realize the impact I made on your life by being so absent, and I'm so sorry. I guess you can say that I was not in the right place mentally, and I struggled with many things, yet that is still not an excuse. I should have tried harder." tears slip down her cheek one by one.

"I understand. Sometimes, the mental battles are the hardest to fight, especially on your own. It can be hard to explain the war going on in your head. I'm here, though, if you ever need to talk. I am sure Dani would lend a listening ear as well. She has much more life experience than I do."

I understand the mental battle and the cost it can have on a person. I also know that it is a battle that is hard to fight on your own. It breaks my heart to know that Hillary has been going through this alone. I may not have the greatest or closest relationship with her, but I do not want to see her suffer.

"Thank you, Adilyn. That means a lot to me. I may take you up on that offer. I also want you to know that the rule of you moving out was not my rule; it was Tim's."

I chuckle, "Not surprising."

"I'm here if you need me. I don't know if my dream will come true, but I'm here for you at any time for anything. You can count on me no matter what." she looks me in the eyes to convey her words' validity.

"Thank you, Hillary. That means a lot to me. I can never have too many mother figures in my life." I squeeze her hand once again.

"I never had kids. I guess it was never in the books for me, but I would be honored to try and be a mother figure for you. Now, I must confess that I don't know the first thing about being a mom so that I may fail terribly at times, but I will try." She smiles widely.

I smile back at her and feel the pressure lift from both of us. Things feel much lighter between us. I cannot explain my happiness about coming to this breakfast and talking with her. I needed to understand her point of view and see why she did things the way she did. By understanding now, I think that has taken that strain off our relationship.

We sit there finishing our breakfast, and the conversation starts flowing. The next minute, we are laughing until we are just about crying. This is such a different experience with Hillary. It is almost as if she has woken from her haze. That dream shook her to her core. I like this version of her. She is fun and bubbly.

We clean up and I tell Hillary that I have to leave. I have my training with Stephanie, then her art class, and I work afterward. I walk to the front door, and Hillary follows me. I turn to her to say goodbye, and she embraces me. Stunned, I am frozen for a moment. She is hugging me. I slowly regain my senses and raise my hands to hug her back. We stand in each other's embrace for a minute, soaking in this new change between us. She lets me go and smiles broadly.

"Thank you, Adilyn, for coming to make and eat breakfast with me."

"Thank you for allowing me. I'm delighted that we were able to talk. I feel much better knowing you will be in my life. I thank you for being someone I can count on." tears begin welling up in my eyes. It is a hard pill to swallow; knowing that she was suffering and that hearing I would need her made her jump to this change. The emotions are bubbling at the surface.

"Off you go before we both become puddling messes." she opens the front door and pats my shoulder.

I turn to walk out the front door and down the stairs. At the road, I turn and wave goodbye to her.

"Don't be a stranger now, okay?" she calls out.

"I won't! I will come by for dinner in two days." I shout back.

"Sounds perfect." she turns and walks back into the house, closing the door behind her.

I walk to my favorite place in the world, the forest. Stephanie agreed to meet me there for our training. I reach the border of the forest and smile. Peace begins to flutter inside of me. I place my hands on the oaks individually as I walk past them. Every time I come, these trees never cease to amaze me. I don't think that will ever change. The beauty that lurks amongst the trees is not for everyone, but it's for me. I spot Stephanie up ahead, standing by my favorite oak. She is sitting there and looks to be meditating. Crazy girl, I shake my head.

Her eyes shoot open, and she looks directly at me. Gesh, I thought I was being quiet. The goal was to sneak up on her, scare her, or at least try. However, with my bag and me trying to maneuver, hiding the sword behind my back probably made me a very noisy intruder.

"Hey, bestie." her face beams with joy.

"Hey! I have something for you and something to show you."

"Is that sword something for me or something to show me? I will not complain if it is something for me." she winks at me.

"No, that is not for you. I thought you already had some of your own. I saw this at the market this morning and had to get it. The sword called my name, not yours, sorry but not sorry." I smirk.

She rolls her eyes. "I guess, but you have to let me borrow it sometime. Let me see it already."

"Gods, you are annoying and impatient." I stick my tongue out at her. She laughs deeply. I pull the sword from behind my back and hand it to her. Her eyes widen, and her mouth drops open.

"This is beautiful and well made. The craftsmanship on this is spot on." Her eyes scan the sword.

"Right? I know nothing about swords, but I know about art, and this is like a piece of art. I can tell the person who made this prides themselves in their work." looking down at the sword.

"This is you, though. You're right when you said it called your name. I can feel that it belongs to you. The stone here on the pommel and the one around your neck are almost identical in color. Truly stunning! I will have to teach you how to use and clean it." She hands the sword back to me.

I lean the sword against the oak and sit beside Stephanie on the ground. She clears her throat.

"What?" I look at her.

"So what about that thing you said you had for me?" she raises one eyebrow.

"Yes, right. Hold on one moment." I grab my bag, place it in my lap, and rummage through it to find the bracelets I bought this morning.

"I got us matching friend bracelets," I mutter, hoping that isn't too childish of a thing to get someone. I pull them out of my bag and lay them in my palm for her to see.

"How pretty! I love it." She grabs one and motions for me to help her tie it around her wrist. I hold out my wrist so she can tie mine around my wrist. We both hold our wrists to see the bracelets on and side by side.

"They are perfect for us!" she exclaims.

"Yes, they are!" I agree.

"So........ how did it go?"

"It went strange yet really well." I knew what she was asking about. She knew I was planning on going to eat with Hillary this morning.

"Yeah?"

"Yeah. We had a heart-to-heart. She said that she and Tim are over and that she has struggled with mental health for quite some time. The most interesting part of our conversation was that she said she had a dream where someone told her I would need her one day."

"Hmm, that is very interesting." Stephanie lifts her hand to her face, contemplating what the dream must mean.

"Right? That is what I thought. Overall, it was a great time. I am going to go to her place for dinner in two days. Do you want to tag along?"

"Yes! I would love that! Are you ready to begin our training for the day?" She claps her hands together.

"Yes! Let's do it!" I jump up and begin stretching to start our training.

CHAPTER SIXTEEN

Art Lesson

ADILYN

"Oh my god, I'm all sweaty!" I wipe my forehead as we walk to the cafe after our training. "I will need to hop into the shower before we start your painting class if that's okay with you."

"Yeah, that's fine as long as I can shower after. I'm all sweaty, too," Stephanie says.

"Um, excuse me, you barely even broke a sweat!" I tease her.

She laughs and pushes my shoulder, "Someone has to be number one."

"You're obnoxious." I retort sarcastically, rolling my eyes.

"Obnoxious but amazing." She laughs harder.

I twist my hair into a bun on my head, waiting for Stephanie to get out of the shower. The spare room is all set up as a painting studio in Dani's apartment. I have all my painting supplies organized neatly on the desk. This will be my very first art class with someone. I have no clue what to expect. I don't know what the first thing about teaching someone is but thank goodness my first student is Stephanie. Trial and error, right?

"Hey!" Stephanie walks into the room, scrunching her wet hair with a towel.

"All set?" I look up at her.

"Yes! I'm so excited for this. I don't expect to be a great artist or anything. I'm just happy to learn something new."

"I completely understand. Painting is a good outlet for someone's feelings." I motion for her to sit beside me in front of an easel. She strides over and sits down next to me, turning towards me.

"So, where do we begin?" She sits straight in the chair.

"Great question. Let's do something I think both of us will highly enjoy. Let's paint the forest."

"We will both enjoy that! How should it look?"

"Well..." I think, "Paint it the way you see the forest, through your eyes. I will paint it the way I see it through my eyes, and we will see where it takes us both. Let the image come to your mind, and then let it take you as you paint. I find that is the greatest way to paint. You get lost in your painting, and it is a great release to anything you are holding on to that you may need to let go." I smile at her. I drag the small table between us and begin to squirt paint onto the paint tray.

I want us to paint something simple since this is her first time painting, and I wanted to see what I'm working with. I also want this to be an enjoyable experience for her and myself. I will need to learn how to teach others. Stephanie is an easy first student to my luck. She is not interested in painting as a profession or in making money off of her art pieces. Stephanie wants to learn for the fun of it. She mentioned that she had been informed painting is quite calming and assists in alleviating pent-up tension. That is her ultimate goal, to paint as an outlet. Due to those reasons, I will not go into all the special painting techniques and make this class more complicated than needed.

We sit side by side, painting an image we have spent much time in recently: the forest.

"So, I have a question for you. Valkyries are something that I am not very familiar with. I know they are in some stories, but can you tell me more about them? Considering we are training to be one." I ask as I continue painting.

"Yeah! I can. The Valkyries are badass women who trained extremely hard to become some of the greatest warriors ever. Their training is extensive. They must be able to pass numerous tests to become Valkyries. The tests that are laid before them to pass are not easy. Some of them are tests that can cost them their life. Others are tests that measure their skill and grace. Their stamina, agility, and precision must be spot on. Their skills were phenomenal once they trained and passed all of the required tests. They have won many battles and overthrown some of the worst evil ever. They truly are badass warriors. I have wanted to be a Valkyrie since I was a little girl. So, I started training young, and I worked hard every day so one day I could carry the title " Valkyrie."

"Wow, and we are training to become a Valkyrie. So that will take years for us to gain their skill level." I'm slightly intimidated by how awesome these women sound. I cannot imagine ever being that skilled to become one, but I am willing to go through the motions of training. I know the exercise and the training will be great for my health.

"Yeah, it may take time, but I have confidence both you and I will call ourselves Valkyries one day. As time passes, we will train to pass the tests they had to take to make that final step of mastery." her face beaming with excitement and determination.

"How did you hear about the Valkyrie? Read about them in a book?" I'm curious about what got her on this path of mastery and determination.

"Where did I learn of Valkyries?" hesitation on her face. "Well, um... my parents used to tell me stories about them when I was little. They were my bedtime stories as silly as that sounds. My dad always wanted me to know I could do and be whatever I wanted. My parents were very supportive of my dream to hold that title." Her smile fades at the talk of her parents.

I can't imagine what it would be like to lose a parent. I never knew my parents, so I never felt that desperation and loss. I never lived through that kind of grief that Stephanie went through and is still going through. That pain, that loss, does not simply fade over time. It lingers for the rest of your life; it haunts your waking hours and sleep.

Wiping away a tear that began to form, "I know we will do it, though. I know this will be something we achieve. Something we will be proud of, my parents as well. I can feel it and am so thankful you are on this journey of mastery with me. I'm so lucky to have you walking by my side."

Despite my disagreement, I admire her determination and confidence in our abilities. I'm sure I will be able to learn how to master our training, but not to the point of being a badass female warrior like the Valkyrie. I smile at her and turn back to the painting because I don't know how to comfort her loss and that empty feeling she has inside of her. There are no words to erase her pain, but I hope I can help lessen that hole and help her heal through painting.

We spend the remainder of the time painting in silence. It is peaceful. I enjoy spending time with Stephanie, even if we are silent. It is not this uncomfortable, awkward silence between us that hangs in the air. It is soothing just knowing the other person is right there. I feel like I have known her for my entire life. She feels like home to me, just like Dani. I can't explain why that is, but they genuinely feel like home, or at least that's what I think home would feel like. They make me feel like I matter and that I belong. They make sure I know I'm loved and make me feel loved. I'm so thankful I have these two and now Hillary.

Hillary has undoubtedly become a fascinating topic of thought, especially after breakfast. Although she wasn't always present during my time with them, her presence was not entirely lacking either. I never really noticed all the time that she was there and present. I only focused on the times that she was not there. Her situation was not the most manageable in the world. I only acknowledge bits and pieces of her struggles. I never looked at her situation as a whole. I tried to stay as quiet and out of the way as possible. Tim was sometimes temperamental, and who would not want to avoid that? I never really thought about what Hillary was going through under the surface. Mental health is something that I know is swept under the rug and not spoken about. That needs to be changed. However, I am also realistic, and I know I could not have known everything unless she told me. I feel terrible not being there more for her, but I cannot put all that weight on my shoulders. The internal battle is raging inside of my head. I was so lost in thought that I did not hear the door opening.

"You girls want some tea or coffee?" Dani peeked her head in the room. My head shoots up in her direction.

"Coffee sounds delightful." Stephanie chimes with a wide grin.

"Coffee sounds wonderful, Dani. Thank you. We're nearly finished here and will be down in a few minutes." I set down my paintbrush. My painting is officially complete.

"I will get some coffee made so that it is ready for when you two come downstairs." she smiles and returns to the cafe, closing the door behind her.

"How is it going over there?" I glance over at Stephanie.

"I think I'm done! Want to take a look?" excitement bubbling out of her.

I rise from my chair and stand behind her. I want to see the whole piece. Surprise flourishes inside of me. Her painting is stunning. The blend of colors she utilized melds seamlessly, with each hue enhancing the other. The trees could benefit from an improved technique; however, they are stunning and brimming with life. I can sense the peace in her painting. The forest I'm looking at in this painting is almost identical to the forest I envisioned.

"Well? Don't just stand there and not say a damn word." Stephanie says nervously.

"I'm impressed, Stephanie. I truly have no other words to say right now than I am impressed. I was not expecting to be impressed." I turn to her and smile.

She shifts her gaze, her cheeks blushing a soft pink. "Thank you. You advised me to let the image transport me, and that's exactly what I did. I envisioned the forest as it is when we train—serene and full of life. The image and feelings I felt when I envisioned it guided me through this painting. Now, I'm eager to see yours. I want to see how you view the forest!"

I gesture towards my painting, inviting her to view it.

"Holy gods, Adilyn, you are talented," she says, her mouth dropping open. "I believe we share a very similar view of the forest!" she exclaims.

I nod my head in agreement. We do indeed have very similar views of the woods. The lack of surprise didn't affect me as much as I expected. We have many similarities, almost as if we are family. We stand there looking at both of the paintings, admiring them. After a moment, I extend my arm, inviting her to intertwine her arm with mine. She graciously accepts, and together we turn towards the door.

"Let's go get our coffee." I smile at her.

"Let's go!" she smiles back.

Stephanie and I head downstairs to the cafe. I start my shift in 10 minutes, giving me just enough time to drink a coffee and rummage through the scattered books. Stephanie follows me as I weave through the tables, heading to the counter. I see Dani standing behind the counter, talking to a client. Dani is talking and laughing. The client hangs on her every word as though it were magic. She possesses that effect on people; they are always eager to hear what she has to say. I shake my head at her, smiling. Sometimes, I wish I had the same charisma that she possesses. I'm sure that would have led me down a different path, but at this moment, I'm pretty pleased with the path I'm on.

She looks at me and smiles widely.

"Hi! How did your class go?"

"It went great! Adilyn is a great teacher." Stephanie chimes behind me.

"I wouldn't claim to be a great teacher, but it went surprisingly well. Stephanie also turns out to not be that bad of a painter." I turn back to Stephanie, offering her a smile.

Stephanie looks straight at me with her mouth wide open. She reaches out and shoves me jokingly. "How dare you! I am an excellent painter, for your information." she shrieks.

"That is the greatest thing I've heard all day," I exclaim, my laughter booming from deep within. I double over to ensure I wouldn't topple over from the intensity of my laugh. Stephanie and Dani were quick to join in. The joy of this moment right here, right now, is priceless. All three of us laughing together and having a great time. The client coughs, causing us to stop laughing abruptly.

"My apologies, Darlene. These girls certainly know how to make me laugh. Laughing indeed keeps the soul young, wouldn't you agree?" Her eyes sparkle at the client.

"You are correct, Dani. I'm sure we all need to laugh more often. I must be off. I will stop by tomorrow for another great cup of coffee and talk." she looks at me, gives me a strained smile, then turns and walks towards the door.

I roll my eyes. Gesh, some clients can't be made happy by anyone but Dani. When I first started, I struggled so much with that. I wanted to make everyone happy, yet it was impossible. Some people will not like you even if their lives depend on it. I learned how to let it roll off my shoulders. Trying to please everyone was not healthy. I walk behind the counter and grab the two coffee cups that Dani is holding out.

"Here's your coffee, ladies." she winks at me.

"Thank you, Dani." Stephanie and I say in unison.

We weave through the tables carefully, sipping on our coffee and attempting to avoid spilling. I browse slowly through the titles of the books on the tabletops. Nothing too crazy that snags my attention. I sigh. I got lucky once, and I guess only once. We settle into the table in the back of the cafe and quietly sip our coffee, looking out the window. The day is bright, not too hot, and yet not too cold. Today is a perfect day outside.

"If only every day can be like today. Not only the weather but the memories as well." I smile softly, holding my cup in my two hands. I sip from my cup.

"Yes, today is a great day." she looks at me smiling.

I finish my cup of coffee and stand up. "I have to start my shift. I can take your cup if it is done," she nods, and I reach out for it.

"I'm going to run some errands. I'll be back later, okay?" I nod, and Stephanie rises to her feet and proceeds to the front door, quietly slipping out. I carry the two cups to the sink to wash them. After placing the cups in the sink, I grab an apron and prepare for my shift. A few clients are scattered throughout the cafe, sipping coffee and reading. I walk from table to table to see if they need anything, smiling along the way.

I glance out the window and spot Stephanie standing, talking to someone. I sneak up to the window to spy on her. I know I shouldn't spy, but curiosity killed the cat, right? And I'm curious. I peek out the window and see her talking to Asher. She glances around, ensuring no one can see her talking to him. What? From its appearance, it looks like they know each other. It isn't a stranger talking to another stranger conversation. Why is she talking to him? What is she hiding? Questions flood my mind. I had no clue she knew him, but I don't know who she talks to. Something feels off; I'm not sure what, though.

"Excuse me, ma'am. I want to order a coffee." a voice rings behind me. I spin on my heels,

"I'm sorry. On my way." I walk briskly to the counter to take the order.

Chapter Seventeen

Truth Unveiled

ADILYN

I wake with a sense of unease. Today, I have this feeling that something is going to happen. A strange buzzing deep within my bones leaves me restless. It brings uncertainty, and I don't know what will unfold. The last time I experienced this was with my previous foster parents; that same unsettling buzz forewarned me of the day they revealed their inability to continue caring for me.

Please don't let any bad things happen, especially since life is starting to go great. Let it be good for now. I hope God will hear my thoughts and listen to me for once. Savory and sweet aromas float into my room. Dani must be making breakfast. I jump out of bed and hurry to the kitchen. I didn't want to miss the chance to eat with Dani. I enjoy eating with someone. I had gotten so used to eating alone that I didn't realize just how much I craved the company of another.

"Good morning. Is there anything I can help you with?" I ask, side-hugging her since she was stirring eggs in the pan.

"I think I have most of it already done. I'm just waiting for the eggs to cook in the next minute. If you want to pour us some orange juice, that would be lovely." She looks at me and smiles gently.

I nod. I open the refrigerator, grabbing the pitcher of freshly squeezed orange juice. I place the pitcher on her small dining table and fetch some cups from the top cabinet. I poured the juice into the cups and set them on the table in our spots. She arranges the eggs, French toast, bacon, and hash browns beautifully on the plates as if they were breakfast from right out of the world's best breakfast restaurant. She brings the plated food to the table, setting it down, and we take our seats.

"How did you sleep?" She asks as she scoops some eggs up with her fork.

"Great! Thank you! I appreciate you allowing me to stay here with you, Dani. I hope you know that. I'm especially thankful for all you have done for me." I cannot tell her enough just how grateful I am for everything she has done and is doing for me.

"I know. Eat up before your breakfast gets cold." She scolds me, pointing towards my plate. I pick up my fork and look down at my plate. I close my eyes and inhale the scent of the food on my plate.

"You act like you have never eaten a real breakfast before." Dani chuckles, looking over at me.

"This breakfast is amazing, from the presentation to the taste!! For sure, my number 1 breakfast of all time." I stay silent for a moment, thinking through my words. "It has been years since I ate a breakfast like this."

"Well, I'm glad I can be a part of this with you, eating breakfast together. You will have to get used to it!" she smiles. "What is your plan today?" Dani asks, then gulps down the last of her orange juice before pouring herself some more.

"Well, today I have training with Stephanie. She is doing an amazing job at teaching me how to defend myself. Then, after that, she's going to come over. I will be in the cafe to help you around 11 if that's okay?"

"Of course, it's okay with me! I'm glad you are learning how to defend yourself Because you never know when that training will come in hand." She reaches to grab my plate and stacks it on hers. She pushes out of her chair and takes the plates to the sink.

"I can wash the dishes since you made breakfast." I stand up and grab the two cups on the table.

"That would be appreciated. Then I can go and get ready for my day." She pats my back and walks towards her room.

I fill the sink with warm, soapy water and grab the pans on the stove. I was trying to hurry to get ready before Stephanie arrives. I wash the dishes, thinking about my life, and a smile spreads. Happiness is what I feel Right at this moment. It's so wild just how much life can change in only a matter of a few days. One day, Stephanie came into my life, and we became best friends quickly; then, I moved in with Dani. My life went from mediocre to actually pretty good. Things were starting to make more sense, mostly. However, I knew in the back of my mind that something was missing, yet I couldn't tell what it was or even a hint of what it could be.

It was a calm day at the cafe, which is a nice change with it being so busy recently. The eerie feeling in my bones has continued to stick with me the entire day. My head is throbbing with the unease starting to weigh on me. Something is up, and I have no clue what it is. I begin working on my closing checklist and crawl into my bed upstairs. I slowly grab a towel to wipe down tables, trying not to make sudden movements and irritate my headache even more. I reach the farthest table, pausing to rub my temples, trying to relieve some pressure.

"I need to take a Tylenol or something else. Otherwise, this headache will get nasty." I sigh and begin wiping the table off, organizing the stack of books on it.

I hear the bell ring at the front door and turn to see who it is. Ready to yell at them that we are closed for the night and to go away. I see Asher standing in the doorway, as solid as a statue, not moving. Everything ceases to move around me, frozen in time, just like him. Something doesn't feel right, so I hold my breath, waiting for him to move or say something. My nerves are running rampant like a stampede of terrified wildebeests. The eerie buzzing in my bones intensifies, sending a shiver down my spine. Beads of sweat start to form on my forehead. I can sense something wrong, swirling in the air. Asher stares at me, frightening me, and this unsettledness lingers in his eyes. It feels like an impending doom Is about to arrive. This must be what I was sensing all day. This is the moment.

"Can I help you?" My voice trembles. Is he going to deliver terrible news? Did someone die? Is he going to kill me? Is this where my life ends? Panic starts to set in as bile starts to rise in my throat. My mind races a thousand miles a minute with the numerous horrible outcomes that could happen. My throat slowly closes, making my breathing ragged. I struggle to gulp down the air.

"We need to talk." He replies. I blink at his response and tone; his voice is so calm. Does he not feel the tension floating in the air? Does he not feel the impending doom hanging right above us? Maybe he is unaffected by it, so he seems so calm.

"I don't know you, so what is there to talk about?" Confusion and panic fill my thoughts. Something catches my eye, and a glimmer comes off of Asher when he moves slightly to the left. I finally look Asher over, really look him over. I notice his clothing. He is wearing all black, as usual; however, this time, it seems he is wearing something over his clothing. I squint to try to make out precisely what it is. Is that armor? Oh, he is wearing armor. The realization slaps me in the face. My eyes widen. Armor was worn a long time ago or in make-believe worlds, not in this day and age unless the person was into cosplay. Unfortunately, Asher did not seem like that kind of person. So why else would he be wearing it?

The armor is black and blends in with his black clothing, so I could not see it at first. From where I am standing, I can barely make out the intricate designs on the armor, but they are there, swirls and lines. It looks like runes are present almost everywhere. One of the designs catches my eye. There's an emerald stone in the middle of what looks like a rune in the middle of his chest. I have seen that rune before, or it looks pretty familiar. I unexpectedly take a step towards him. My body moves without the consent of my brain. What the hell am I doing? I should be stepping away from him, not towards him, but something is softly tugging me. There is a battle raging in my mind. I can feel something dark dancing all around, yet the design on his armor feels like they are calling to me. I want to see it clearly and examine it up close.

Asher coughs and my eyes dart back up toward his face. A grin spreads across his face, like a predator that found his prey. I freeze in place, stunned by his smile. It's so beautiful, yet the look in his eyes is so predatory.

"Hi, Ad!" Stephanie says in a cheery voice as she strolls up to me. She gives me a brief hug and then stands by Asher's side.

"Adilyn, Stephanie, and Asher, there you all are. Just the people I needed to see." I hear Dani say behind me, clapping her hands together. Excitement rings in her voice.

"Talk to all three of us?" I scratch the back of my neck. Why would she need to talk to all three of us? I can feel my chest tightening. The eerie feeling from earlier intensifies even more, causing my head to spin. Something isn't right, and I can feel it.

"Yes, we need to talk to you." Stephanie turns me towards her, a gentle smile on her face as if she can sense my anxiety building.

"What the actual heck is going on here?" I snap. What could all three of them need to talk to me about? I take a step back and bump into a chair behind me.

"Take a seat. We should all take a seat." Asher motions towards the table next to me. My knees buckle under me, and I slump into the chair, confused. Everyone else sits down around the table and stares at me quietly.

"There is something we need to tell you, Adilyn, about who you truly are and where you come from," Dani says softly, looking me straight in the eyes. I straighten in my chair, glancing at the three sitting around the table. What does who I am have to do with these three?

"I would like to start with who I am first," Asher says. "My name is Asher Thornheart. I'm the Captain of the Royal Guard of the Emerald Court. My family has been the Royal Guards for the Emerald Court for many generations." His eyes soften slightly. His eyes look like smoke is moving around behind his pupil. Captivating. I shake myself from the distraction and refocus on the conversation.

"What does any of that have to do with me? I don't even know where the Emerald Court is across the sea?" I shrug and tilt my head. That doesn't ring a bell, and I know I paid attention in Geography class.

Asher smiles. "The Emerald Court is a kingdom in Eldermyst, in the fae land, along with...."

"The fae land?" I cut him off, throwing my hands in the air. "Now, you have got to be kidding me! Alright, cameras, you can come out now. Candid Camera, you got me, that's enough!" I shout, turning my head, looking for the camerapeople to come out. However, there is nothing, just pure silence. My eyes widen, and I turn back to Asher. "I don't understand. Fae are from myths, fairy tales."

"That is what humans like to believe; however, we exist, not just in stories." Stephanie chimes in.

I turn to look at her, and then it happens. It's as if a mask is pulled right off her face, or maybe off mine. My mouth drops open as I take in her pointed ears and features that seem more prominent and beautiful. She is glowing with something from within. Her skin is a shade lighter, and her hair becomes this long, vibrant brown flowing down her back.

"How did I not see this before, at least the pointed ears?" Trying my best to hide my shock. I turn to look at Asher and Dani. They, too, have changed, just like Stephanie. My mind is swimming, and I am starting to feel clammy. Sweat begins to pour down my face, and I feel like I'm not getting enough air. I shake my head, hoping this was all just a dream. I look at them one second, then the next, everything goes dark.

I open my eyes and feel the pulse still lingering in my temples. I look around and find myself in my bed. It's dark out, so I must have been out for a little while. I sit straight up and look around, trying to recollect what happened. I remember being in the cafe cleaning, and then I remember

Asher, Dani, and Stephanie talking to me about fae and some court. Their features changed! I shake my head. That has to be just a dream, a bizarre dream. I throw my feet off the bed and stretch before standing up. I need to get some coffee and take a Tylenol to eliminate this headache that won't seem to go away.

"I don't remember coming to bed," I say softly.

"That is because I carried you up to bed. You passed out." Asher says.

I jump and look around to find him sitting in the chair in the corner of my room.

"What are you doing in my room?" I say sheepishly. I have never had a man in my room before.

"I wanted to ensure you were okay when you woke up." He says softly.

"I'm fine, thank you. I must have forgotten to drink enough water and eat a little more. I'm sure that caused me to pass out; then there is that weird dream." My mind is trying to sort through what is real and what is not. "I'm going to get coffee if you don't mind."

He nods and stands, waiting for me to pass. I walk past him and out to the kitchen, where Dani and Stephanie sit at the dining table sipping coffee. I picture them with pointed ears, just like in my dream. I rub my eyes, hoping to rub the dream right out of them. Dani reaches to pull a chair out and pats it, motioning for me to sit down. Stephanie stands up and walks to the cabinet. She grabs a coffee cup and pours coffee, then returns to the table and sets the coffee down in the empty spot for me. I wobble my way over to the empty chair at the table. I drop into the chair and reach for the honey and creamer, adding some of both. I stir my coffee and then take a sip of the delicious beverage. Silence hangs in the air, making things uncomfortable. I rock from side to side before speaking.

"So I passed out?" I half state, yet half question, looking for their reactions.

"Yes, you did. You passed out for a few minutes," Dani assured, nodding. She places her hand on mine and squeezes. I scan her face and see her reassuring smile. The realization dawns on me that whatever they said was no lie. I have known Dani my entire life, and she wouldn't lie to me like this. I inhale deeply before speaking again.

"What happened? Why did I pass out?"

"We were explaining who you are and what we are. You got overwhelmed and blacked out.

"Who am I, and who are all of you?" My voice cracks. Fear begins to rise in my throat, and I bite my cheek. It wasn't a crazy dream then. I have wanted to know who I am and where I belong my entire life, and now I'm finally going to find out, yet I'm afraid.

Asher cleared his throat. "As I told you earlier, I'm the Royal Guard to the Emerald Court. My duty is to protect the royal family, just as my family has for many generations."

Confusion floods me. "What does that have to do with me?" I blurt out.

"I need to give you a little backstory before we continue." Dani squeezes my hand once again, then withdraws her hand from mine. "Many years ago, the Elwoods reigned in the Emerald Court. Corian and Iridessa were fair and kind rulers. Like a King and Queen, they were the High Lord and High Lady of the Emerald Court. Their court was peaceful and happy under their reign. Many of the other courts looked to them for help and guidance. The Emerald Court was the largest Court of Eldermyst. One day, this dark force entered Eldermyst. They called themselves the Dark Orians, and they brought destruction and terror with them. They aimed to rule over Eldermyst completely, having all six courts bow to them. The Dark Orians knew that to take over Eldermyst, they had to seize control of the Emerald Court first, and then the rest would fall shortly after. They spent years trying to take control of the Emerald Court; however, Corian and Iridessa prevailed." Dani sighs, and pure sadness and despair fall upon her face. "They fought against the Dark Orians, trying to protect not only their court but all of Eldermyst and its people. They cared deeply for their country." Tears begin to well up in Dani's eyes.

"Then, one day, Iridessa found out she was expecting. The two were so happy for this miracle! They had not been able to conceive for centuries. Unfortunately, happiness was not all they felt; sadness filled them, too. They didn't want their child growing up in a world where they would be at risk with the Dark Orians. So, they made a difficult decision that broke their hearts. They decided to send their baby away once she was born until they could rid the country of the Dark Orians." The tears began to spill down Dani's cheek. She brings her hands up to her face, unable to stop the tears from coming.

I reach my hand out to rub her shoulder. My heart breaks for her because I can tell this is something t I have never witnessed Dani crying. I stand up and go to the living room to grab the Kleenex box and bring it back to the table, handing it to Dani.

"What happened after that?" I ask.

"Well, Corina and Iridessa fought as hard as they could until the Dark Orians tapped into a temporary power and destroyed them, along with their Royal Guards and others who were on their counsel," Asher responds, sadness swirling in his smokey eyes.

I couldn't prevent the gasp that came out of my mouth. "What about the baby? What happened to the baby?"

I look at everyone, and the room falls silent as if everyone is holding their breath. I can hear the birds chirping outside and the wind pushing the branches against the roof.

"She sits before us," Stephanie utters softly, looking at me with a weak smile.

I shake my head, "That isn't possible." Shock rattles me to my core, seeping into my bones. There is no way that is possible in all the gods' names. I am just a simple orphan girl that grew up in a damn forsaken small town. There is absolutely nothing special about me, let alone royalty.

"It is possible." Stephanie insists.

I can't breathe. This cannot be happening. There is no way in all the gods hell can this be happening. My head starts to spin. I cannot seem to grasp reality. This has to be a dream or nightmare.

"That makes no sense. I'm only human!" I argue, shaking my head persistently.

"No, you are not human. You are the lost Princess of the Emerald Court." Asher orders.

"Ad, Queen Iridessa's magic was connected to nature. Why do you think you have such a connection with nature yourself?" Stephanie questions.

"Then who are you?" I ask, glancing at each of them.

"As I said, Adilyn, I'm the Royal Guard to the Emerald Court, meaning my duty is to protect you," Asher states.

"Great!" I groan, rolling my eyes. Why must some overbearing asshole be the "one who is supposed to protect me" if I am going to believe this crap story? I shake my head in utter disbelief; Dani lays her hand on my shoulder, squeezing it softly, then places it back in her lap. She begins talking, so I turn to look at her.

"I started working in the kitchen long ago in the Emerald Court. Over time, Iridessa got to know me and became my best friend. We would discuss anything and everything. Go to each other for advice, and laugh together. Then, one day, she came to me and said she wanted to make me the Queen's counsel. I was in shock. I couldn't believe the High Lady would want me, a nobody, a cook, as her counsel." Dani chuckled softly and shook her head. "She had crazy ideas sometimes in her head, but she was dead set on me being her counsel. I have served her faithfully as her counsel ever since. I still do to this day." Dani glances up at me, smiling at me, then returns her gaze to her hands.

"Iridessa and Corian came to me when they found out about you. They were thrilled and loved you even before you were born. Their priority was to make sure that you were safe. They had a plan in place for any situation, any outcome." She sniffles.

"What do you mean, Dani?" Confusion laces my question. My parents loved me so much that they did all this to protect me.

"They told me that if something were to happen to them, I had to make sure you made it to the human realm and grew up safe. They told me to make you a special tea to stifle your powers until you were 18. They left me with a letter and a box for you in case something happened to them. I have held on to that letter and box this whole time, waiting for this day to come. I watched you grow up and gave you the required tea so that you could live a somewhat normal life here in this world. It pained me your entire life not being able to tell you the truth about who you are and where you came from. However, I obeyed the orders given to me for your safety."

"Why would they want to stifle my powers though?"

"They were afraid that if they couldn't defeat the Dark Orians and if they found out about you before your dropping, then you would never be able to take back the crown and save our people, our court, and Eldermyst. They feared for your life, and every measure they had in place was for your protection."

"Dropping? What does that mean?" That is something I don't recall ever reading in any books, so I'm not sure of the meaning,

"Yep. The dropping happens when a fae turns 18. It is the point in time when they come into their full powers and their aging starts to slow significantly." Stephanie states.

"So I will have to go through this dropping?"

"Yes, you will. However, you won't be able to until you are in Eldermyst. There isn't enough magic in the human realm to handle a fae drop." Stephanie leans forward, searching my face for understanding.

The room goes silent, except for the roaring in my head. I lean forward and rub my temples, trying to reduce the throbbing pain that has picked back up more intensely. So much information has been placed on my plate, and I'm doing my best to sort through it.

"This is a lot. I don't know if I can handle this because I'm not made to be royalty. That is not who I am, and it never has been." I mutter.

"Adilyn, it is who you are and who you have always been. You just have not been in the right place or had the right knowledge. You were born to rule. You are Alona Elwoods, High Lady of the Emerald Court, and we are with you." Stephanie says firmly. My eyes shot to hers.

"I'm who?" disbelief ran through me at the name she called me. I never once imagined that I had a name given to me by my parents, who loved me so much.

"Your true name is Alona Elwoods," Dani says, reaching out and grabbing both of my hands, looking me straight in the eyes. "Since your mother and father, the King and Queen, were murdered and you are officially 18, you are now the High Lady of the Emerald Court."

"I need a moment." My head is spinning. I push my chair out and stand, legs shaking. I need air, and I need to breathe. This is overwhelming. I step back and sway slightly, and the world starts spinning. Stephanie jumps out of her chair and runs around to me, grasping my elbow tightly before my knees buckle. I have always been taught that fae isn't real, and magic isn't real. None of what they are saying is supposed to be accurate, but it is.

"Let me lead you outside so you can sit, let everything sink in, and process it." Her eyes sparkle, and her smile is soft. I nod at her, words unable to form in my mind. She turns me towards the door and leads me down the stairs. Once outside, we carefully walk towards the forest. My mind is racing, trying to process the information I just received.

I didn't realize how we got to the forest so quickly until she helped me to sit down against my favorite tree. Stephanie sits down beside me, and we sit there in silence. I lean back on the massive trunk and close my eyes, inhaling, trying to calm the chaos in my mind.

I don't know what to think. So many thoughts are running through my mind, and I'm trying to sort them out. However, despite not knowing what to think, I know what they said is true. I feel it in my bones, and that is what scares me. I can't seem to fully grasp the story that Dani told me about my parents. I had parents who loved me so much. They protected me even after they had left this world. Part of me feels like this is some messed up nightmare that I am living in, but the other part of me knows this is reality

CHAPTER EIGHTEEN

Life Changing

ADILYN

I open my eyes and look around me, adjusting my eyes to the dark. I must have dozed off for a moment. I look at the intricate detail on the trunk. The age of this tree shows through its height and weathered scars lining the trunk. I raise my head and survey the forest. It is quiet, except for the chirping birds, bees humming, and rustling leaves. I turn to face Stephanie. She sits next to me in silence, her hand entwined in mine. Our eyes locked, and I had many questions for her, but I didn't know where to begin. There are so many emotions crashing into me. Yet, one emotion is currently eating at my insides: fear. Fear that our friendship was fake.

"Why are you tearing up?" She asks, lifting her hand to brush the strand of hair out of my eyes.

"Did you become my friend just because of what you guys claim I am? Was our friendship ever real? Was it all just fake?" I choke out, trying to push down the sob that was about to surface.

Her eyes soften, "I had been watching you for the past few years, in the shadows, Asher, as well. I got to know you that way. It started as my duty, yes, but as time went on, I truly wanted to be your friend. Finally, meeting you in person cemented my desire to be your friend. You are remarkably kind and talented, and it's evident that you seldom reveal your true self because others rarely take the time to get to know you. Despite being overlooked numerous times, you consistently overcome adversity. Your kindness and thoughtfulness shine through; you never consider yourself superior to others. You've never complained about the hand you were given in life; instead, you've faced it head-on. From the beginning, you've shown me nothing but kindness, which is why I adore you so much," she replies. "You are genuine and never pretend to be someone you're not. You always care for others even when they don't care for you. People can be hateful to you sometimes, and you do not let that break you or retaliate. You are such a strong person, and I thank god for letting me be your friend. I'm truly blessed." She squeezes my hand, trying to hold back tears in her eyes. "Besties, remember? I don't say that lightly, either. I have never had a best friend, Alona, and I am truly honored that you are that first for me."

This time, I'm unable to suppress my sobs. I cover my face and surrender to the overwhelming emotions built inside me. Tears stream from my eyes as if the floodgates have burst open, allowing all my worries to pour out with them. I can't understand why the revelation of the truth, my truth, made me so concerned about the authenticity of our friendship. I didn't want our friendship to be insincere or circumstantial, yet here she is, consoling me and affirming our friendship was genuine. It was motivated not just by obligation but mainly by genuine desire. A wave of relief engulfs me, and I can't hold back the tears any longer. She's here, providing me solace. She rests her forehead against my shoulder and remains there beside me.

I'm unaware of how much time goes by while I weep. I take a deep breath, the last tear rolling down my cheek. I think I have cried all that I needed to cry.

"Are you okay?" she asks, rubbing my arm.

"I feel much better. I guess I just really needed to cry. It is wild because the part that hit me the most about this whole truth was the thought that you were pretending to be my friend. I have never had a true friend, so I didn't want that to happen. "I whisper, shrugging my shoulders. "This whole situation, in general, is just so overwhelming. I didn't know how to handle it."

"I understand and am sorry you had to have those thoughts. That is very hard, but I truly want you to know I'm here for you." She reaches and grabs my hands, clasping them between hers. "So, I never got to tell you who I am." She smiles widely.

"Oh? Who are you?" I question, raising one eyebrow.

"I am Stephanie Elwoods. My uncle was King Corian." she pauses, waiting for it to click in my head.

"Wait? Wait...." shock floods me, and I throw my hands up. Is this real?

"I'm your cousin, Alona. My mother was your father's sister. My parents died alongside your parents, battling to protect us and our people." Her smile is tainted with sorrow, her eyes dull.

"Wait, so you are telling me that we are family? Like family, family? Like blood family?" I shriek. This news is going to make my heart explode with excitement! This is the best part of everything they have told me in the past day—the best life-altering news!

"Why are you laughing, weirdo?" Stephanie barks out! I knew she felt like home. I knew she felt like family. Now, it all makes sense. Joy swells up in my chest alongside sadness. Sadness because she lost her parents just like me. Sadness because she knew who they were. I lost mine, but I didn't think they even existed. However, I feel so much excitement about finally having a family. I reach over with shaky hands and pull my cousin in for a hug, laughing into her shoulder.

"This is the best news from the dump load you guys have unloaded on me." I laugh even harder. Stephanie laughs with me.

Everything feels so surreal. I have always wanted to know my family and where I came from. It has all started happening. This truth that has been revealed to me is terrifying. I don't know the first thing about being a royalty or anyone in power. I have so far to go and so much to learn. I understand this will take time to process, but I want to try. I want to know more about my family, who they were, and what they were like. I want to see pictures of them. I want to know everything there is to know, step by step. Thoughts swarming my mind of all the questions that I have.

I inhale deeply. "Let me do my tree thing, and then we can return. I have a lot of questions." I slowly start to stand.

Stephanie holds back a laugh and nods her head. "So, we can call it your tree thing now?"

I roll my eyes, "I didn't know what to call it, gosh." Shaking my head at her, I turn to face the giant oak that held me up. I look at it and trace my hand along the weathered scars along its trunk. I lean my forehead to the trunk and close my eyes, allowing my other senses to kick in. I breathe in the smell of the woods and feel the sun and wind all around me. I listen to the creatures roaming through the wood floor and branches above. I center myself, soaking in the strength of this ancient oak tree. After a moment passes, I open my eyes and stand straight.

I turn towards Stephanie and see her tracing the trunk of another oak a few feet away. She looks at me.

"Ready," I say. She nods in response, holding out her hand. I walk towards her and grab her hand, entwining my fingers with hers. I look at her. Stephanie is my family, my actual blood family. The smile broadens on my face. We walk together back towards the cafe.

I turn back at the border of the woods and whisper, "The whispers of the wind and the songs of the woods guide my soul." My head snaps towards Stephanie. She whispered the same thing as me. Shock runs through my body. She looks at me and smiles.

"We are family, remember? That is a family saying. We say that because the trees have always been our allies. Our lineage has always had some form of nature magic, especially with trees." She winks. "Look, they are waving." She whispers, nodding towards the trees. I slowly turn my head in the direction she is nodding. My eyes widen. I see it; I see the swaying of the trees and their branches, but that can't be true.

"The wind is just blowing, causing them to sway." Trying to brush off the reality of what is happening.

"No. The breeze is almost nonexistent right now, and that's not why they are moving. The trees are waving on their own." She smirks. I look at the trees in awe and realize what she is saying is true. I can feel my heart pounding in my chest and the ringing in my ears. This almost seems like too much. My world has been turned upside down in a matter of one day. Everything I thought I knew once before was thrown in the trash; it was all a lie. There is a world out there that I only dreamed of and read on the pages of a book.

"Wow!" I murmur. I have no other words to explain what I'm feeling.

Stephanie turns to me and smiles. She side-hugs me as we stand there in awe of the waving trees. They come to a stop gracefully, and I sigh;

my heart misses a beat. What an incredible sight. This is something that I think I have secretly known deep down inside. I have always wondered what if the trees could hear me. Now I know that they heard me all this time.

"I am ready to return to the cafe, so let's go. I have so many questions." I look at her. She entwines her hand in mine, and we silently walk back to the cafe.

The cafe's front door sign says, "Closed for the remainder of today due to family emergency." I raise my eyebrows.

"Family emergency? Is everything okay?" fear turns its ugly head inside of me. I have never heard of Dani's family, so what is this family emergency? This is not how I want to meet them.

"Don't worry. She thought it would be best to close for the rest of the day so she could sit down with you and answer all of your questions. Asher and I agree with her that it would be best." She squeezes my hand. "There is so much that we must discuss."

Relief falls upon me like a blanket. I push the door open and see Dani serving some coffee. She looks up at me and gives me a warm yet weary smile. I hate worrying her. She has been a crucial part of my life. I hate that I worried her. I walk straight to her and embrace her. She freezes for a moment and then wraps her arms around me.

"I'm sorry, Dani, for worrying you," I whisper.

"Oh, honey, there is no need to apologize. I understand how difficult this all is. Your life has been turned upside down. I'm sorry I had to hide it from you." she sniffles. "Well, I'm sure you have plenty of questions. So, let's go."

She hands me a cup of coffee and directs me upstairs. I grab the cup and follow behind her. Stephanie trailing behind me up the stairs. We walk through the front door of Dani's apartment and stroll into the kitchen. Asher is leaning against the wall, looking out the kitchen window. Asher turns his head, and his eyes lock with mine. He nods in understanding. He knows how wild this situation has been—Dani motions for us to sit around the kitchen table.

"So," Dani says. "Do you have any specific questions for us?"

"So many questions are floating in my head; I don't know where to begin." Dani nods her head in understanding.

"Well, we can start with your parents if you would like. Then go from there."

"That sounds perfect to me." I set my coffee cup down, trying to hide my trembling hands. Stephanie reaches over, grabs my hand in hers, and nods her head at me, letting me know that she is right there with me.

The next thing I remember is birds chirping outside of my bedroom window

CHAPTER NINETEEN

Monsters, Oh my!

ALONA

Yesterday was a long and overwhelming day. I discovered so many truths, things I never imagined could be possible. I wanted to work today to help distract my racing mind. Work was a little busy, but nothing too crazy. We had clients come in most of the morning, with everyone preparing to head out for their summer vacations. Stephanie stopped by this morning to tell me we will train after work. I tossed my apron into the washer downstairs by the office and trod up the stairs to get changed. I walk into my room and sit on my bed. I look over and see the Fae Princess book and laugh out loud. When I started reading that book, I wished my life were like a princess's. What irony that it turned out to be just like it. I shake my head at the thought of the events that have unfolded in the past few days. I had so much that I needed to learn about the culture of my people and my new role. I have a dinner planned with Hillary tomorrow evening. I need to train even harder than I thought before. Who knows if I will have to face the Dark Orians? I am unsure what even to expect when it comes to them. I make a mental note to ask about them so I am somewhat prepared in case I encounter them in the future,

I look over at the sword that I have leaning against the dresser. I pick it up and look at it. Strangely, I found this sword when I did, almost like it was meant to see me. Well, I might as well take this with me to train. I will need to practice using it. I grab the sheath that Stephanie gave me and strap it to my back. After sheathing the blade, I am ready to meet Stephanie downstairs.

I walk down the stairs, and Stephanie sits at one of the tables, waiting for me. Asher is seated to her left. I pause in my tracks.

"Ugh. What is he doing here?" Annoyance spreads through me. I'm exhausted from all the recent news that has dropped on me, and I don't feel in the mood to deal with his taunting today.

"I'm here to help you train." he cocks his head and smirks.

"You didn't tell me our training was going to change! It is perfectly fine just the way it is." I plead with Stephanie.

"I'm sorry. I am, but this is for the best. Asher is one of the best fighters in our land. He has trained his whole life. You need someone like him to help you and me train right now." She shrugs with an apologetic look on her face.

"There are things you need to be prepared to fight against. You are currently a liability to the team if you do not get proper training. We cannot afford to have you killed off because you refused to train under me. We need you to reclaim the throne. Our people depend on it." Asher says sharply.

My mouth drops open. Was his cold tone necessary? Even though he is correct, there is no need to be a jerk. I sigh and shrug my shoulders. "Yeah, I guess you are right." It pains me to have to say that he is right.

"Alright, let's go then." He stands and strolls out the door.

I narrow my eyes and glare at Stephanie, willing for all my annoyance to be written all over my face so she knows how I feel. I turn abruptly and storm out the door, following the jerk to train. Stephanie runs after me, catching up to me.

"Hey. I know you are not happy with me, but I promise you that it is important that you get as much help as possible in training. The things that we will face will not be pretty. They are deadly, and I do not think I can bear losing you." She grabs my hand, willing for me to understand her reasoning.

"I know I need all the help I can get training. I'm sure Asher is also the best to train me; I don't want to tell him that. The man doesn't need another ego inflation." I look at her and lower my voice.

"He does have quite the ego," she whispers back.

"I need to train hard because the path I need to take is not going to be easy, will it?" I glance at Stephanie, trying to read her face.

"It won't be." She frowns.

"I need to understand what I will face on our journey through Eldermyst."

"You will face monsters that you would think are only found in your worst nightmares. You will face things that will make you question your sanity. The Dark Orians have done things to creatures, causing them to mutate into something horrible." Asher stands in front of me, eyes vacant of all warmth. I shudder. I have never encountered anything I would consider a monster here in Claywood other than some cruel girls in my class.

"In the human world, creatures known as butterflies exist. I'm positive that you are familiar with them. These beings also exist in our world but are far from tranquil; however, their appearance may deceive you. They appear harmless until they reveal their true nature and ferociously attack, easily severing heads. They are comparable to the size of a cat. They bear a hideous skull on their body that always seems to be hungry for more. They are called Keasi. We will encounter beasts capable of devouring a person wholly without a second thought. They are indifferent to one's identity," He sighs, stopping himself from saying more, and continues to stalk towards the woods.

"We will face some things that will chill us to our bones and haunt our dreams. We don't know every monster that creeps in the shadows, especially with the Dark Orians creating new monsters as they please. There will be things you see, Alona, that you can never unsee. I wish that wasn't the case for you, but it is the only way for you." Stephanie glances at the ground.

"If I don't regain the throne, what will happen?"

"The Emerald Court will fall for good. Then Eldermyst will fall as well. I never thought I would see the day that was possible." She frowns, the light disappearing from her eyes. She bites down on her lip, and her eyes avert to the ground. "Only one thing is standing in the way of the Dark Orians from completely taking over."

"What is that?"

"You."

"Me?"

Stephanie nods. "Yep. Your parents cast a spell, you can say, on the Emerald Court with the help of my parents and Asher's parents. This spell prevents the Dark Orians from taking over just yet."

"How so?"

"They can't take over until the rightful High Lady has returned; only then can they try to strip the Court from her." She must have sensed my next question. "When they cast this spell, Iridessa relinquished her title as High Lady and passed it on to you. Then the Court would be safe until you could return and banish the Dark Orians. She knew that she was not going to make it out of the war they were fighting, so Iridessa did the only thing she knew was left to protect her people and her daughter."

"Oh..." I can feel the sadness rolling off of her, the heaviness in the air around us. She is heartbroken at the loss of her parents, and she is heartbroken over the fall of the Emerald Court. She loves her people, her Court, and her country. I want so badly to wipe away every piece of sadness that is consuming her. This woman is one of the strongest people I have ever known, and she cares so much for others. She is constantly placing the needs of others above her own. I wonder if anyone has sat down and asked her how she truly feels, allowing her to expel her emotions before things turn ugly. I can see the guilt she carries around like a cape. I sense the unworthiness that she feels, it's suffocating. I have been in her shoes, feeling so lost and lonely, as if the world's weight is on her shoulders. I don't know how to relieve her pain, so I do all I know. I grab her hand and squeeze softly. Her gaze looks up at me, and I smile at her. Her faint smile, in return, lets me know she needs some time.

We walk in silence the rest of the way. I am trying to wrap my mind around what I will encounter in this new land. Will I be able to beat them?

"I need to train my powers. How do we know what they are?"

"Well, most of the time, a child will gain powers similar to their parents'. If I remember correctly, Aunt Iridessa could command nature to move and grow along with communication with nature. Uncle Corian could move things with his mind and sense the feelings of others."

"My father could sense people's emotions?" A sudden jolt of disbelief shoots through me.

Stephanie nods in response.

"I think I have that ability too. I have always been more connected to the emotions of others. I always thought it was just me going crazy, but I could always tell what someone was feeling. It has been getting more intense each day since I found out. "

"I am sure you inherited Uncle Corian's abilities then. Sometimes it was a pain in the ass, though. I would try to lie about how I felt, and he always knew when I was." A faint grin at the memory spreads on her face, not completely erasing the pain from earlier.

"So, wait, did you know my parents?" I'm confused because she is the same age as me. If my parents died when I was little, then she had to have been a child as well.

"Yes, I knew them. They were amazing people and always so loving." She continues. "Time is different in our world. It does not fly by like it does in the human world. The fae have long lives. Some have been around for millennia."

"Wait, so you are saying that there are fae that are not only hundreds of years old but thousands?" I have so many questions flowing through my mind.

"Yeah, pretty much."

"Holy shit. How old are you?" I hold my breath, waiting for her to return with some wildly stupid response that she is thousands of years old.

"I am 50 years old. So quite young for a fae."

My mouth must have hit the ground because Stephanie gave a low chuckle. "I'm having a hard time thinking you are that old."

"I'm not really that old, at least for our people. I know it may be difficult to wrap your mind around right now, but I promise things will start to make sense soon enough."

"Are we going to spend all day gossiping, or will we train?" Asher barks out sharply, crossing his arms over his chest.

We come to a halt at the edge of the woods. I narrow my eyes at Asher and cross my arms, mimicking his movements.

"Just because I agreed to train with you does not mean that you can be a complete asshole all the time, Asher." I tilt my head and stare at him.

His eyes turn a dark shade of steel, and the corners of his lips curl up into a smirk. "Is that so?"

We both stand there, staring at each other. I'm not going to look away, and I'm not going to break first. This asshole will not be the one coming out on the top. I don't know what it is about him that makes my skin crawl, but he does it with such ease. All he has to do is be himself, and my skin crawls.

Stephanie clears her throat. I swear, how often will this happen between us, needing someone to step in and save the day or spare us from each other?

"So.... Are we practicing our stamina in our staring contest?" She snorts out. Both of us turn our gazes to her.

"Really?" I blurt out, irritation building up. I lower my head and look up at her from my lashes. I hope she can feel all the wrath I wish to unleash on her, but I won't because she is my best friend.

"Sorry," she shrugs, holding her hands up in surrender.

"What is that behind you?" Asher tilts his head to see what is peeking out behind my shoulder.

"This?" I reach back and grab the sword, unsheathing it.

He takes a few steps toward me and holds his hands out as if asking permission to examine the sword. I hand it to him carefully, trying not to cut one of his fingers off. He grabs the sword. He holds it up and turns the sword at different angles.

"Where did you get this?" he asks.

"From the local farmers market. There was a blacksmith there and he had it."

"Where did he get it from?" his eyes dart to mine.

"Um.... okay. You just scolded me for, as you said, 'gossiping,' and now you are doing the same thing?" I huff out a laugh. What a hypocrite.

"Where did he get this sword from?" He bites out, and his voice has more force this time.

"Calm down," I raise my hands, "The blacksmith said that he found it in the woods. He was out hunting, and he saw it leaning against a tree. He searched for the person it belonged to but did not find anyone. He said it would have pained him to have left it there, so he took it."

Asher shook his head but said nothing.

"Everything okay, Asher?" Stephanie asks.

"You don't recognize this sword, Stephanie?" He held it up for her to see.

"It looks familiar, but I do not know from where." she shrugs.

"Where did it come from?" I ask Asher because, with all of the seriousness, I am intrigued.

"Emerald Shadow used to be the sword of the first High Lord to exist. The sword was passed down through his lineage for thousands of years until it disappeared one day. The Oracles said it would reappear once the chosen one was of age. No one ever really understood who that was or when that would happen, but here it is." His eyes lift from the sword and scan my face.

"Okay..." I say looking between him and Stephanie.

"It's true, Al. It was written in the fates, as the Oracles said. This legend has been passed down from generation to generation so it wouldn't get lost. I thought that it was never going to come true."

"How long has it been missing for?" I am unsure that I want to hear the answer.

"It has been missing for almost one thousand five hundred years." I was stunned, silent. It had been missing for that long? That was many, many, many of my lifetimes.

"There must be a mistake. How do you even know this is the sword?" my eyes fall on Asher's face.

"My parents made sure that I knew everything there was to know about it. Our parents all believed that the sword would return soon, which is why the Dark Orians rose."

My mouth dries, every last drop of saliva evaporating. This is just what I needed: to have the thing that the bad guys want. "So, they are after it as well?" I groan.

"I think you are missing the most important part of it. Our parents knew that the sword was going to reappear. I think that High Lady Iridessa knew that it would return because of you. That it would return to you." Asher says firmly.

"Yes. You're a crucial part of this war. You will be the turning point." Stephanie places her hand on my shoulder.

"Hold on. You said that the sword's name was Emerald Shadow, correct?" Something clicks in my mind, my mind running at full speed. Asher nods his head in response.

"So which court did the very first High Lord belong?"

"The Emerald Court."

"Does that mean...."

"That you are part of his bloodline? Yes, you are one of his descendants." I can feel the color draining from my face. I came from the very first bloodline of fae that ever existed. Sweat begins to collect on the back of my neck. I feel myself rocking on my heels. My world begins to spin, and my vision starts to blur. I slowly bring myself to sit down so I don't injure myself by falling.

"Alona, Alona, are you okay?" Concern plasters Asher's face, and I see him rush towards me before I close my eyes.

Inhale... one, two, three, four.

Hold... one, two, three, four.

Exhale... one, two, three, four.

I feel a dull throbbing in my temples, but the spinning subsides, so I slowly open my eyes.

"I'm good," I say softly, lifting my hands to rub my throbbing temples.

"Are you sure you're okay?" Asher asks. I look over to see him kneeling on the ground next to me with one hand stroking my back. He makes me feel at ease, and the warm tingle begins climbing throughout my body, like at other times. The thought of this formidable fae warrior comforting me makes my stomach do flip-flops. I turn and see Stephanie on the other side of me.

"I'm so sorry, Alona. I know this is so much to handle. It is overwhelming to find out so much so quickly, especially life-altering information like you have found out."

"It is okay. I'm sure there will be a time when I will know every little secret hiding in the dark, and I won't feel so overwhelmed anymore."

Asher chuckles, "No, there will be new things that will come up and overwhelm you. That is life. You need to connect to your powers, using them in these situations, and then things won't be as intense anymore."

"What do you mean?"

"Well, when you access your powers, releasing a little power will help to center you. Whenever your mother faced challenging situations, she would grow a flower to ease the tension and remind herself of her true self. That was her way of centering herself and also calming herself." His eyes are gazing into mine.

I sense concern humming from him, yet he has a face as cold as stone. This man is a walking headache! I let his words settle into me. They make sense; sometimes, a release is needed. When I thought I was simply a human, I always used painting as an outlet when I felt overwhelmed. So, this is the same thing. I never had issues with passing out or super intense feelings when I felt overwhelmed, but that is because I was drinking Dani's tea to stifle my powers for so long.

"So, not only do I get worked up, but also the magic inside me?" I want to make clear sense of it for the future.

"Pretty much. The magic inside of you is a part of you. It thrives off of your emotions, so when your emotions are high, they build up, causing you to feel faint if you do not release them."

"Got it." I look down at the sword lying on the ground.

"So, what do we do about that?" I nod toward the sword and then look at Asher. If anyone knows what to do, it will be him.

"Well, we train with it. You learn to wield it as a sword and master its powers with yours."

I smile, ready for the challenge. "Let's get started."

Asher's eyebrows shoot to his hairline, surprised at my willingness. "Let's get started."

I sit down against my favorite oak tree, gasping for air. I thought training with Stephanie was hard. I was so wrong. Asher drilled us until I could no longer stand. Stephanie sat beside me and handed me a bottle of water.

"Thanks," I pant.

"No problem." she smiles at me and then looks at Asher leaning against the tree next to ours. Annoyance builds inside me because he is not even winded and stands there smirking at me, taunting me for the fact that I barely made it through. I roll my eyes and look away, sipping from the bottle Stephanie handed me.

"We need to determine your abilities and begin to sharpen them," Asher says.

"How do we go about finding out what they are?" I turn to look at him.

"Well, I'm going to guess they will be similar to the powers your parents wielded. So, we will start by trying to connect to the natural elements and see where it takes us. There's lots of work that must be done in limited time."

"Asher is correct. We should begin our journey to the Emerald Court soon. My informants have indicated that the situation in Eldermyst is deteriorating rapidly. If we wait too long, we risk finding neither a court to return to nor a country remaining. However, we must train you some before we can enter Eldermyst." Sorrow blankets her features. I nod my head. She is right. If these Dark Orians are as bad as they sound, then I need to get on my training and prepare myself quickly. Otherwise, nothing from my parents' Court will be left to return to. I inhale deeply and hold my head high.

"When do we start?"

"We start tonight," he replies.

"Tonight, after my dinner with Hillary it is. Meet back here at 8 pm?" He nods his head at me and then turns and walks away.

CHAPTER TWENTY

Bond

ALONA

Stephanie thought seeing Arion would be a good idea now that I knew the truth behind everything, along with the stressful day. She can tell that he brings me a sense of peace. I could not agree with her more. We only have two hours to spare, but it is still worth it.

I sit in the passenger seat, gazing at all the trees and hills as we drive by.

Stephanie clears her throat, breaking the silence. "So, there is something that I have meant to tell you; it has to do with Arion."

"Oh, for the love of god, I swear if something happened to him, I would probably die from being overwhelmed." My throat slowly clamps down, restricting the airflow into my lungs. The anxiety is starting to rise.

"No, no! Nothing like that. Well, there are two things I wanted to tell you. One regarding the pain you felt the other day when you met him and where he came from."

"Oh.... okay! I think I can handle that."

"So, that pain you felt wasn't because you were overwhelmed. It was a bond snapping into place between you and him."

"A what?"

"A bond.... Certain creatures can choose to bond with the fae in the fae realm. When they bond, the creature thinks the fae they chose is worthy."

"What is the bond for?"

"It is kind of like a soulmate, just not in a romantic way. You are one with that creature. They become an extension of you. Bonds between a fae and creature make them almost unstoppable together."

"Oh wow. I guess that is something else I will need to get used to. What about where he came from? Was he bonded with his previous owner?"

"Arion belonged to your family at one point in time." Her eyes glance at me, then back to the road. I sit in the seat next to Stephanie, mulling through what she just said, when the realization hits me like a brick wall.

"Wait, Elouan said that his previous owner died. Does that mean his previous owner was one of my parents?" my eyes widened with the realization.

"Yes. Arion used to be your mother's horse. She adored him, and he adored her. They were quite the pair, the giant and the beauty." She chuckles, reminiscing on old memories.

"Wow," I turn to look outside. I need a moment to collect myself and my thoughts before I say anything else. I am sure that Arion knew precisely who I was. My mother and I share similar characteristics.

"Was he bonded with my mother?"

"Yes, he was. When she died, he went through a very rough patch. We almost thought he would not make it because he was so heartbroken."

"Did he choose me because of my mother?" I hesitate.

"I'm sure that may be part of it, considering he was with your mother for so long. I'm sure that he can sense your mother in you. However, I must say that he would not have chosen to bond with you if he did not think you were worthy." She reaches out and pats my back softly. "You will become great. I know you will."

"I have a question. So, as you refer to them, fae possess powers. Do horses from Eldermyst have them as well?" my curiosity overwhelms me.

"A long time ago, most of them did. There are two kinds of horse bloodlines in our lands: power-wielding bloodline and nonpower-wielding. Unfortunately, with the Dark Orians polluting our lands, they killed most of the horses that possessed powers, so only a few are left from the power-wielding bloodline. "Sorrow consumes me whole.

These Dark Orians have caused so much pain and suffering to this land. They have to be stopped. Determination mixes in with my sorrow. I will be the one to stop them, even if it takes my life. I do not stand for bullies, precisely what they are." They must be stopped, Stephanie. I will stop them." I hold my head up high.

"I know you will. I believe in you, and so do your parents. You should know that Arion is one of the last standing power-wielding bloodlines along with Aoife. Arion and Aoife are mates. Arion, however, has been around the longest and is the most powerful of his kind ever lived." Stephanie smiles at me.

"Whoa, the most powerful?" I was stunned at the thought that the most powerful horse picked me. Stephanie nods her head.

"The non-power-wielding horses are called horses, but the horses that wield power are called Pterippi. So, Arion is one. He won't take lightly to you calling him a horse. He is very headstrong, if you haven't noticed." She giggles.

I roll my eyes because I know little about Arion; he is a headstrong creature.

"I have read about the Pegasus in books. Are they the same as what I have read, wings and all?" I recall the mythologies I have read with the Pegasus in them.

"Yes, they have wings which they can make vanish at will and reappear as desired. They wield powers that are often linked to natural elements." I rise from my seat and stroll over to the massive creature. I reach my hands out, stroking the side of his face, and lean my forehead against his. "Hey, big guy!"

He shakes his head, neighing in disapproval of the name I called him. I huff out a laugh. He is undoubtedly one hardheaded horse. I stroke his face and then move along to his side. After today, this massive grumpy creature has earned my respect and loyalty. He belonged to my mother, a strong warrior, and he chose me, someone who is far from being a strong warrior. He could have picked Asher, and even Dani would have been a better choice, but no, he chose me. I will cherish and serve him just as my mother did.

I look at Stephanie and ask, "Are we going on a ride?"

Her eyes gleam as she nods at me and strides over to Aoife. We both mount the horses, and off we go. The afternoon breeze blows my braid behind me and caresses my face. The smell of dirt, leaves, and moss floods my senses. I inhale deeply. Arion trots for a while, then takes off in a run. I grab onto the reigns and lean forward like I have been practicing. Each time I ride, it gets easier. Each time, he runs faster and faster. Each day, I feel more and more confident in my ability to take back my court.

The two hours flew by quickly, and I didn't want to leave. I could stay here all day riding and brushing Arion, but I had dinner plans that I knew I could not miss. After returning Arion and Aoife to the stable, Stephanie and I pile in the car. Smiles plastering both of our faces.

CHAPTER TWENTY-ONE

Asher

I sit on the bench outside Stella's, looking at the starry night sky. I know I must enter and speak with Dani here shortly. However, I need a brief moment to compose myself before entering. Numerous thoughts cloud my mind. The pressure in my temples is immense, especially considering Alona's ability to progress in her training. I wonder about possibly accomplishing all of Alona's extensive training and readiness. Time is slipping away from us, so we must make do with whatever training is possible. I must train her rigorously in physical, mental, and power aspects. Our journey to our court will be challenging, and there is no doubt about that. I hope she gains enough ability and strength both physically and mentally to endure the long journey.

When we told her the truth, it sucked the life out of her. She went into shock, and I was momentarily worried that we could not get her out of it. Stephanie took her to the one place where she could truly clear her mind and think through the forest. How is that not surprising to me? Her mother had a deep connection to nature. Alona must have a similar connection as well. When she returned, she was willing to listen to what we had to say and the plan.

Today, I was taken back by the sight of the Emerald Shadow strapped to her back. I used to think it was a myth. However, my parents, along with Alona's and Stephanie's parents, were confident it was returning. My parents made sure I knew as much as possible about that sword. They had the inkling that it would return to Alona, that she was the one it sought. When she handed it to me to examine, I could feel the vibrating power humming from it. I don't think that she sensed it, at least not yet. It was right in front of me; I was holding it. All this time, I thought my parents were crazy for believing a sword lost so long ago would reappear now, and here it was. So, we trained. I could see the determination in her eyes when she raised her head and agreed to train with me. At first, I thought she would refuse to train today, but she realized what was best for her and our people. I may have come off as cold, but holding her hand through training would not prepare her for what she was about to face. She needs to harden some of that gentle nature if she is going to survive.

I made sure to train her as hard as she could handle. Sure enough, she kept up with every move that I commanded her and Stephanie to do. Stephanie has trained for the majority of her life. Her parents were great warriors, so it is not surprising that she inherited those abilities and has that stamina. Alona will need more work; however, she slowly gets stronger each day. We will need to start teaching her how to wield her powers. Hopefully, she catches on quickly.

After speaking with Dani, I need to get with my informants to see the current location of the Dark Orians. I need to get us as prepared as possible before we leave and begin our journey.

I massage my temples, willing the pain away, then drop my hands to my side. I stretch my legs out before standing up. This human world dulls everything. Our magic is limited here, and I cannot seem to rid myself of my pounding headache. I stretch my neck from side to side. I can't wait to return home. I turn towards the door and enter the cafe. Dani is in the kitchen as usual. Cooking is her life; it always has been. She peeks her head out of the kitchen door and waves at me. In return, I nod and sit at one of the tables. I lean back in my chair, stretch my legs, and close my eyes. I hear footsteps approaching me, and I immediately know it is Dani. The smell of freshly baked bread blesses my nostrils. I inhale deeply; the scent of banana, cinnamon, and walnuts swirls through the air around us. I open my eyes as she takes a seat next to me.

"You know I love your banana bread." I grin at her.

"I know you do." she winks at me and serves a piece on a plate, handing it to me. Memories of when I was a child and all the times she would sneak me treats, like this banana bread, wash into my mind. I take the plate from her and bite into the bread. We sit there momentarily before I set the plate down and turn to her.

"So, how is she doing?" Dani asks, wiping her hands on her pant legs.

I can see the concern in her eyes. Dani is worried that Alona won't have enough time to train. She is concerned she won't be able to handle the journey. We share so many concerns.

"She is doing just fine. She will make it if we continue at the rate we are going. Once we cross into Eldermyst we will continue her training. She seems determined, and that's what will carry her, her determination and hope."

"Her need for revenge is also strong. I know she is angry over her parents despite never getting to know them."

I nod my head in agreement. "This will be a long journey, but I will not let my court fall. So, if that means pushing her harder, then I will. Our people will not die at the hands of those monsters."

She nods her head, then lowers it, thinking. I grab my plate to finish the slice of banana bread, take a bite, and savor the last bite as if it were my last. I set the plate down and rise from the chair.

"I must go. I need to contact the informants and find out where they are." Dani looks up at me; all light drained from her eyes, and she nods. She knows who I'm referring to. I stroll to the door to leave. When I reach the door, I turn back to face Dani, remembering what I wanted to tell her.

"Dani, it found her. The Emerald Shadow found her."

"Are you sure?" Her eyes widen.

"I'm positive. I saw it with my own eyes. I could feel the power radiating from it. We both know no other sword holds power."

Dani gasps, throwing her hands over her mouth. "Just as they thought. They knew it would come back. I thought they were crazy." She sits down so her feet don't give out under her.

I nod in agreement. Both Alona's and my parents knew the sword was going to return. They did what they had to protect the one person they thought it would return to. They sacrificed their lives for hers so that she could bring peace back to our people.

"I can't believe it. I thought that sword was a myth." She says in disbelief, running her hand through her hair.

I nod, "Part of me did as well."

" What now?" She questions.

"We train much harder. She will be the one who brings peace back to our land, and she must be ready. She needs to train in fighting, her power, and now with this sword."

"Do we know enough about the Emerald Shadow to know how to use it?" She asks.

"My parents taught me some, but it has been a while, so I must review all the texts and refresh my memory." Dani nods her head; I can tell words have escaped her.

"We will talk later." I turn back to the door and leave. I have so many things to do, and I don't have enough time to do them all simultaneously. First things first, I need to find out where those bastards are.

Chapter Twenty-Two

Dinner Plans

ALONA

I walk down the stairs to the cafe. Stephanie is waiting for me, sipping a coffee as usual. I smile and shake my head at her. Her friendship has been a blessing, and I honestly don't know what I would do without her. I wave at her and then turn towards the kitchen. I peek into the kitchen and see Dani pulling something out of the oven.

"Hey, Alona!" she chirps.

Alona. That is my real name. My parents gave me the name. It is so strange to hear Dani calling me that. I guess I will have to start getting used to it.

"Dani, what does Alona mean?"

"The meaning of Alona is 'oak tree'. Not too surprising, is it?" she smiles.

I laugh because it suits me quite well. "My favorite tree is the oak tree, which is perfect for me. They must have known that the oak tree would be my favorite."

"Well, Iridessa's favorite tree was the oak tree. She always said the oak trees were some of her most incredible natural friends. Not to mention, they are one of the most common trees in the Emerald Court. She could count on the oak trees for anything and everything. They are the ones that helped me sneak you out of Eldermyst. Corian and Iridessa made sure I was hidden the whole way here."

"Really? What is it like there?"

"It is stunning there. There are so many trees and abundant wildlife; the greenery is lush. It's teeming with life and beauty. The sunsets are incredibly colorful and breathtaking. It is like nothing you have ever seen. There are no words to describe the Emerald Court and Eldermyst."

"I can't wait to see it in person."

"I can't wait either! I made you roasted chicken and potatoes to take with you for dinner." She sets a pan down and reaches for some Tupperware.

"What?"

"I wanted to make you all dinner! I know you have training afterward with Asher, so I wanted to do something for you." her smile is heartwarming.

"Why, thank you so much, Dani. I truly appreciate it so much!"

She dishes the food into Tupperware, places it in a tote bag, and hands it to me. I grab the tote and hug her. I walk back out to the cafe and hold the tote in the air, motioning to Stephanie. She looks up and sets down her coffee mug.

"What is that?" she questions.

"Dani made us dinner for tonight, chicken and potatoes. Ready to go?"

"I'm down for that any day! Dani's cooking is magical, I swear!" She jumps out of her chair and walks towards the front door, holding it open for me. She skips to the car, opens the passenger door for me, then skips around to the driver's side. I get in, gently setting the food down so nothing spills.

The drive to Hillary's takes only six minutes. Stephanie parks in the driveway and we get out of the car. I walk up the porch stairs and knock lightly on the front door. A moment later, Hillary opens the door with a warm smile. She looks much better than before. Maybe getting rid of Tim was good for her. Life is flowing back into her, and it looks good on her. She has color in her cheeks and a slight sparkle in her eyes. Pleasure floods my chest; I'm happy for her. I hold up the tote and smile widely.

"Dinner is served," I say.

"We come bearing chicken and potatoes, thanks to Dani." Stephanie nods her head and smiles. Hillary opens the screen door and ushers us into the house.

"I don't think I have had the proper pleasure of meeting you," Hillary states, extending her hand to shake Stephanie's.

"My name is Stephanie, ma'am. It is nice to meet you officially." She grasps Hillary's hand in hers. Hillary nods her head and smiles. She gestures for us to follow her into the kitchen. She motions for me to set the food down on the counter as she pulls out some plates and utensils. I grab the plates and begin to serve the food. The aroma of roasted chicken and potatoes fills the kitchen. I inhale deeply, and my mouth waters. Stephanie rummages through the cabinets for glasses. After finding them, she gathers napkins and utensils and takes them to the table. She arranges the table and fills glasses with water for everyone. I carry the plates with food to the table, setting them down. We all take our seats and begin to eat quietly. Hillary clears her throat and starts conversing with Stephanie, inquiring about her life. The conversation flows smoothly.

"Yeah, Adilyn is teaching me how to paint," Stephanie chirps.

"Right, I'm teaching you," I say, using air quotes to emphasize my sarcasm and roll my eyes. Hillary's laughter fills the room at our playful banter. Being an only child and having no children of her own, I'm sure she finds our interactions quite amusing. Joy fills the air, and we laugh and chat for the rest of dinner.

The pressure rises in my temples as I struggle to decide whether to tell Hillary the truth. I'm uncertain why I feel compelled to tell her, yet the urge is there. Perhaps it's because of the dream she had where a woman told her I would need her—could it be a message from my mother indicating Hillary's significance in my future? The connection to what lies ahead is unclear, but I'm driven to uncover it. I glance at Stephanie, hoping she can read my mind, but she is too busy scarfing down her food. She sure does love Dani's food. I chuckle softly.

After we finish dinner, I clear the table and stack the plates in the sink. Hillary then rises to serve a cake she's prepared. It's German chocolate, a personal favorite of mine. With the first bite, my eyes close in delight. Stephanie and I, in unison, express our joy over the cake with a moan. I slowly eat the cake, savoring every single bite. I finish my cake and am disappointed that it is gone. I am half debating getting up and grabbing another slice of heaven. I set my fork down, turning my body to face Hillary. I need to tell her, and I need to while I have gathered the courage.

"So, Hillary, I have something to tell you, and I don't know how you will react." I peer up at her. Stephanie sets her fork down on her plate and straightens in her chair. She glances at me nervously. I know this is ridiculous, but I feel this is right.

Hillary glances at me, "What is it?"

I clear my throat, trying to build the nerve to tell her. "My name is not Adilyn. My real name is Alona."

"Oh! Did you find your parents? I'm so happy for you!" She claps her hands together.

"Not exactly," I say quietly.

"Oh?" Her eyebrows furrow together.

"I hope you don't think I am crazy after what I'm about to tell you, but I feel like I need to tell you this." Worry climbs up my throat.

"Oh, honey, I won't think you're crazy. You can tell me. I have heard it all." She smiles softly.

"Yeah, well, you have not heard this." I swallow.

She dabs her mouth with the napkin and places it on the table, leaning forward with her elbows resting on the table's surface. "Tell me, honey, what is bothering you?" Concern fills her features.

"Well...." I hesitate. Can I do this? I have to, so I sit up straight. "My name is not Adilyn; it is Alona Elwoods. I'm the lost princess of the fae court, the Emerald Court. My parents were King Corian and Queen Iridessa. They died protecting their people and me. I must return to my rightful place and take back my parent's court from the Dark Orians, the ones who killed my parents and have been poisoning the land, slowly killing the citizens of Eldermyst." I say quickly, trying to get it all out before I regret my decision. I hold my breath as silence settles in the room. We are all frozen in our chairs. Fear begins to consume me, and bile creeps up my throat. Did I make a mistake? Hillary is not saying anything; she is just sitting there frozen in horror at the bomb I just unloaded on her kitchen table. My eyes dart to Stephanie's. She shrugs at me, unsure of what to do. I can see the worry on her face.

"Hillary..." I whisper.

"Stop. Give me a moment, please. What you are saying is wild," She stutters and throws her hands in the air. She stands up abruptly and walks to the kitchen sink. She throws cold water on her face and leans against the sink, momentarily hanging her head down. I can hear her taking in deep breaths and blowing them out. Fear is consuming me. Stephanie's eyes glance at mine, worry swimming behind her pupils. I can tell she is holding her breath, just like me. We are frozen, waiting for what she will do or say. She slowly begins to stand up straight and turns towards me. My senses are all on high alert at the uncertainty of what will happen. She looks at me, and I can't tell what is going through her mind. Usually, I'm good at predicting what someone is thinking, but right now, I can't. She opens her mouth to speak, and I brace myself in my chair. I'm just waiting for the onslaught of hateful words. She shuts her mouth and shakes her head. What was she going to say just now? She bends at her waist, placing her hands on her knees. Tension is growing thick in the air.

"I need a moment to myself." She turns and walks out of the kitchen.

"Now what?" Stephanie whispers.

"I have no clue." I shrug, and terror begins to escalate inside of me. My hands start trembling uncontrollably. How is she genuinely going to react? Will she call the authorities, and then someone will haul me away to perform science experiments on me? We sit there in silence; the only sound is the clock ticking on the wall. It starts to eat at my insides.

Tick...

Tock...

Tick...

Tock...

I begin to rock back and forth in my chair, anxiety coming to an all-time high. Then Hillary slowly strolls into the kitchen and sits down. She brings her shaky hand up to rub her face.

"So let me get this straight. You are telling me that you are from a land I have never even heard of and the daughter of royals?"

I nod my head.

"What the hell is a fae?"

"Well, the fae are similar to humans. However, they live much longer and have magic abilities," Stephanie answers, trying to help me face this.

"So, you are saying that there are people that have magic?" Hillary laughs an unhinged laugh, making me shift in my seat, and then stands up. "There is no magic, and there never has been. So how am I supposed to take you at your word?" She paces in the kitchen.

I suck in a deep breath, knowing what I have to do. I glance towards Stephanie; she nods her head at me in agreement.

"I can show you." My voice trembles. I hold out my hand and envision a Bloodroot flower blooming in my hand. Just as I had envisioned it, it appears. Hillary gasps and sits back in her chair. She squeezes her eyes shut and then opens them again, staring at my hand. She sits there in silence, staring at my hand and the bloom. She shakes her head,

"I don't know what to say." She chokes out.

"I know it is a lot to process, but magic is real... Fae are real." Stephanie bites her bottom lip.

"This is a big pill to swallow..." Hillary lowers her head and takes several deep breaths. "We were taught our entire lives that magic was only in fairytales and never real. Of course, I'm surprised, but it all finally makes sense. All the flowers that randomly showed up all around our house; it was you this entire time." She moves slowly, brushing her hand through her hair. "You are different from the rest of us here in Claywood; you always have been. So is Stephanie. You both don't belong here in this world. I think a part of me always knew that." A gentleness fills her eyes.

Shock courses through me, and I inhale a short breath. What did she say? Did I hear her wrong? I never knew she noticed the flowers. I rub my arms absentmindedly. Stephanie let out the breath that she had been holding in. I stare at Hillary, dumbfounded. She slowly returns to the table and pulls her chair close to mine. She sits down, leans over, and grabs my hand. Her head hangs down, and her shoulders slump forward. The silence is unsettling. Finally, she carefully lifts her head, and her gaze locks with mine.

"I need to tell you something that I never told you before. I had a dream years ago; in this dream, a woman who looked a lot like you said the day would come when something would be revealed that would change my life forever. I thought it was a crazy dream then, but now I see it wasn't as unbelievable as I thought. I'm not going to let a new world scare me. You need me, and I, in all reality, need you, too. So, you tell me what you need me to do and where you need me to go, and I'm there."

I can't believe what I'm hearing. A silent tear slips down my cheek. She reaches out and brushes it off. I thought this would go so much differently and not in a good way. I was expecting the worst.

"Anyways, I am a middle-aged angry woman that just left her asshole husband that had treated her like crap the entire marriage. What do I have to lose? Need me to kick someone's ass? You got it. I am ready and angry enough." A smile slowly unfurls across her face.

I can't help but let a laugh escape my lips. Stephanie's eyes widened, and then she joined in laughing. I lean over and throw my arms around Hillary. "Thank you so much for being there for me."

"Anytime, honey." She embraces me back. We stay in each other's embrace momentarily and finally let go.

"So, what happens next?" Hillary turns to Stephanie.

"Well, I guess what happens next is really up to you. You can stay here or go with us to Eldermyst." Hillary pauses for a moment, thinking through her options. She looks at me momentarily, then turns back to

Stephanie. "I'm coming with you guys. What do I need to learn or to do to prepare?"

"Well, Alona needs to learn the customs of our people, so you might as well learn with her. You can train with us if you would like. You need to be prepared to fight because it will come to that at some point."

"Girl, I used to be the dart champion and I'm pretty good with an axe." She winks at Stephanie.

Stephanie bursts out laughing, "Well, that is great. You are off to a better start than Alona over here." I roll my eyes and stick out my tongue at her. How was I supposed to know that one day I would need to know to fight to kill some gruesome beast?

"It is decided. I will begin learning the customs of your people, and perhaps I could train alongside Dani. One middle-aged won to another would make an excellent pairing." She grabs my hand and squeezes it.

"Hillary, that means so much to me; it truly does."

"What time shall I arrive tomorrow to begin?"

"Well, we can tell Dani to expect you at 7 am. Will that work for you?"

"You bet! I will be there at 7 am." We spent the next 30 minutes laughing and sharing stories, then bid Hillary farewell, promising we would see her tomorrow morning. Stephanie and I get into the car and sit there for a moment in silence.

"Wow, I thought that was going to turn sour quickly. Especially when she stood up and walked to the sink."

I nod in agreement. It could have gone wrong, yet the gods were on my side, or maybe my parents were on my side. I exhale deeply and stretch my neck from side to side. I lean back in the seat and turn to look at Stephanie.

"Yeah, that could have gone bad. Thankfully, she took it better than either of us expected. I think it's because she has been stuck in this town and stuck with Tim for a long time. She never really had much adventure in her life."

"Maybe it is her time for adventure."

"Yes, that and that dream of hers. I want to hope that my mother went to her in her dreams. Maybe Dani has a picture of my parents? It would be nice to know for sure it was my mother."

"Oh, I am positive that Dani has a picture. Aunt Iridessa was her best friend."

CHAPTER TWENTY-THREE

Hillary

I watch Stephanie and Alona leave and walk into the living room. I plop down on the couch and let out a long breath. I rub my face to collect my thoughts about tonight's event. I had always known that Alona was different; I never knew how different she was. It almost still feels unreal. When she told me, it felt like my world was closing in. My throat closed, and I struggled to breathe. I had to move, and I had to do something. It was too much to process. I felt overwhelmed and needed to pause to process what had been said, yet my analytical side required proof.

Magic existed only in fairytales, never in reality. That is what we have been taught our entire lives. I needed to see it with my own eyes to accept it. There she sat and grew a flower in her palm. Magic is real. I had to believe her after that. She had given me proof. So many thoughts were crowding in my mind. A dull throb grows behind my eyes from too much thinking. I lean forward, placing my elbows on my knees and then my face in my palms. I didn't think much about the dream I had years ago until tonight.

Tonight, it all came together and finally made sense. Disbelief consumes me. Magic is real. Fae are real. Magical lands are real. A place called Eldermyst exists. I tell myself over and over, allowing the realization of this newfound truth to wash over me. "Eldermyst," I mutter, letting the thought sink in. I will be going to that magical realm soon. I'm going with them to Eldermyst. My breath catches. I straighten my back and stand. I need to get things in order if I leave, such as the house and work.

I walk up the stairs to my room to grab my phone. Unlocking the screen, I go to my texts

Hillary - Tim, I will be moving within the next few weeks. You might as well keep the house. I will prepare all the paperwork.

Tim - Where do you think you are going?

Hillary - It's none of your business.

Tim - So I can come back to the house now.

Hillary - God, no. I will tell you when. I have no desire to see you or deal with you.

Tim - Whatever.

Locking my screen, I shake my head in disbelief at his ingratitude. It's a mystery how I've tolerated him for so long. A yawn escapes from my lips, and it has been a long day. Crawling into bed, I let the thoughts of Eldermyst carry me gently into sleep.

CHAPTER TWENTY-FOUR

Mental Wall

ALONA

The night air is refreshing on my skin. I slowly meander to the woods where Asher and I agreed upon meeting earlier today. Thoughts consume me of everything that has been dumped on me. At first, I thought it had to be a joke, but after thinking about everything, it finally made sense. Things in my head finally started clicking. All of the dreams I have had of magical places were all Eldermyst. I wonder if the people I have seen were also from Eldermyst.

I shake my head at the thought that Eldermyst has been with me my entire life.

I step into the lining of the woods and instantly feel at ease.

"You're late," Asher says dryly.

"It's 8:01." I lift my wrist and look at my watch. "I got here as soon as I could."

"Like I said, you are late." He frowns.

"I'm sorry, okay? I'm trying." I bite the inside of my cheek.

"I expect better from you." he raises his voice.

I shake my head, half tempted to turn around and return to the cafe. If this is how the night will go, I don't think I am up for dealing with his saltiness.

"Is this how you are going to act tonight?" I cross my arms, eyes narrowing to a pinprick.

"Act like what? Responsible? Disciplined?" He snaps, clenching his jaw.

"No, act like a jerk." I stomp to stand before him, glaring up at him with my hands on my hips. I hope he can feel the anger rolling off of me. He glares down at me, fists to his side. I can feel every muscle in my body tensing up.

One moment, I'm furious, and the next, I feel like I'm drowning in an overwhelming amount of anger, sorrow, and impatience. It hits me so hard that I stumble back, gasping for air. I drop to my knees, grasp my chest and lean forward, trying to suck in as much air as my constricted lungs will allow. Sweat starts beading on my forehead.

"Alona, are you okay?" Asher lowers his voice. He kneels beside me, placing his hand on my shoulder.

"I feel too much." My lips tremble as I choke out the words.

"Okay, take a deep breath." His strong hand rubs my back, soothing me. "The first thing we will need to do is to train you how to build a mental wall to block out the emotions of others."

As he continues to rub my back, the tension in my chest slowly loosens. His presence gives me a feeling of safety. My lungs expand, and I fill them with air. Then the air around me fills with concern, his concern.

"What are you talking about?" I mutter, finally being able to get words out.

"You are, even in the human realm and having drunk magic-stifling tea, sensitive to the emotions of others. Now that you haven't drank any tea, your abilities are surfacing. So, we will need to work on how to control that power. To open the door to feel the emotions of others when you want and block them out when you don't."

My eyes widen as a rush of adrenaline runs through me. It makes perfect sense. I have always had a keen sense of how others feel. I thought I was more empathetic than others, but this entire time was magic.

"Is this what it will feel like all the time?" I gaze at Asher, waiting for his response, hoping it won't always be this bad.

"Not exactly. People don't always have strong emotions so they can vary. Sometimes, it will be overwhelming, and other times, it will be manageable." His touch slows, yet his hand doesn't leave my back.

"If I put up a wall, will it block out the emotions completely?" I lean into his touch.

"Correct, you can block them out completely. Your father could maintain his mental wall while still experiencing feelings to a certain extent. He cared for others so much that he chose not to completely shut people's emotions out. Over time, you will figure out what works best for you."

"So how do I do that... put up a mental wall?" Wonder fills my tone. Will I be building a wall? Will I be drawing a wall? Questions flooding my mind.

"Well, you have to envision yourself mentally building the wall. At first, it will be hard until you master it. Then it will be second nature."

"That makes sense. So, I close my eyes and mentally build whatever wall I can think of?"

"Well, most people build walls in places they are most comfortable. My wall is the castle of the Emerald Court. I build up a wall of the castle, stone by stone."

"So, your comfort place is the Emerald Court castle?" I peer up at him. He nods, not saying anything. I look away, towards the trees, and imagine what the castle must look like. I want to know more, but it must be something he doesn't want to talk about, and I understand. So, I leave the subject alone.

"Okay, so I just close my eyes and picture myself where I feel safe?" My brows furrow as I try to piece everything together.

"Correct." He responds.

"Then I start to build a wall?" I ask.

"Correct, again." He nods.

"Okay." I take a steady breath, allowing myself to relax. I lean forward with my hands on my knees. I close my eyes and let my mind wander, taking me to where I feel safe: the woods. Of course, they are not woods from here. I'm positive now they are the woods from the Emerald Court. I walk through the woods and admire the giant trees all around me. There are various kinds of trees here: oaks, cedars, pines, redwoods, and more. I continue my trek and brush my hand along the trees as I walk, out of habit. The aged bark is covered in patches of soft, spongy moss. I smile and inhale; cedar, oak, moss, and lavender fill my nostrils. This is the smell of home. Lying in a pile-up ahead of me are stones. This is where I am supposed to build my wall; I can feel it. I pause, looking around once more at all the trees. I think the gentle, caressing breeze calms my soul and encourages me. I take a few more steps towards the stones, positioning myself next to them.

I lean over and pick one up. It is smooth and surprisingly light. I look at the stone and see that it looks like a white marble with touches of deep emerald swirling throughout it. I lean back down, placing the stone on the ground. I continue the same motion, stone by stone. It feels like time has flown by, and I'm almost done with my wall. I look over at the last stone lying on the ground, then back up at my wall. I examine the wall I built and realize I will need to practice building this wall. It looks sturdy. However, there are holes here and there where one can see through. I sigh and turn back to the stone on the ground, picking it up. I lift it above my head to put it in the last open place. I push it into place and clap my hands together. I did it! I built the wall! Then everything goes quiet, and the restlessness in my chest disappears. I closed off the emotions, well, most of them. I need to tell Asher.

My eyes fly open. He is sitting beside me, staring towards the trees in the distance. My breath catches. He is breathtaking.

He turns slowly, and his eyes meet mine, "So? How did it go?"

"Well..." I pause, feeling around. I can feel the concern deep in his core, but now it's not nearly as intense as it was earlier. It is now a faint buzz: "I did it, but I know my wall-building skills need work."

He throws his head back and laughs. He let out a laugh from deep within, a laugh I never imagined he could produce. A weight settles in my chest. I blink slowly, stunned in place, as the world fades away around me. He is the only thing left here with me.

"What are you staring at?" His eyes meet mine, and a soft smile still paints his face.

I stare into his eyes, unable to say anything. He tilts his head and raises an eyebrow, questioning my motives.

"Nothing." I stand quickly as the world around me returns and dust off my pants. I glance at him as he rises. "It has been a long day, so I should be off. I need to rest because we have a long day tomorrow."

"Oh," He runs his hand through his wavy hair. "Okay."

"I will practice my mental wall. Thank you." I nod, spinning on my heels, and briskly walk back to the cafe.

"Alona, are you busy?" Dani knocks on my bedroom door.

"You can come in. I'm not busy." I look up at Dani as she enters with a box. She pauses and looks at me, then back at the box.

"I told you the other day that your parents left you a box and an envelope. Now that you know the truth, I can give Them to you," She takes a few steps toward me and lays the box down on my bed. My gaze follows the box. "Well, I will leave you alone for this." She turns and quietly makes her way out of the room.

I stare at the box for several moments before mustering the courage to open it. My hands tremble as I pick the box up and place it in my lap. I slowly grasp the lid and pull it off, setting it on the bed beside me. I look at the box and see an envelope on the top. I take a sharp breath and reach in to grab the envelope. I pull it out of the envelope with trembling hands. I turn the envelope over and slowly open it. I pull out the piece of paper carefully saved inside.

Our beloved Alona,

If you are reading this, that means we did not make it. We have loved you so much ever since we learned that we were expecting you, and we are so sorry that we aren't there for you now. It breaks our hearts to know that we don't get to be there to watch you grow up, take your first steps, say your first words, learn your powers, and grow into a fantastic woman and High Lady. You are the light of our world, and we are so proud of the person you will become. We wanted you to know that we are always with you; you have to look inside you, and you will find us.

Just look within,

Mother and Father

My chest constricts, and I lay the letter next to me, looking into the box. Inside the box is a black velvet bag with a gold drawstring. I carefully pull it out of the box and move the box over, placing the velvet bag in my lap. What is inside of it? I take a deep breath and pull open the drawstring. I slowly reach my hand in and feel my hand brush against metal. My hand jerks out of the bag, slightly spooked. I don't know what is inside this bag, and I guess I'm just on edge. I inhale deeply, close my eyes, and force my hand back into the velvet bag. I grab the metal and pull it out before I overthink it. I lay the item on my lap and open my eyes. Upon my lap is an intricate gold crown with sparkling emerald gems adorned on it. I lift it and examine the details of it.

The emerald crystals are in a tower form and look almost like tree trunks rising high. There are emerald towers upon the crown, and gold leaves and flowers are woven throughout, with a moon in the front. The crown is magical. This must be the crown of the High Lady of the Emerald Court. I slowly rise from the bed and walk to the mirror perched on the dresser. I look at myself in the mirror and bring the crown up, placing it on my head. I fix my gaze on myself in the mirror, entranced by my new reality. This was my mother's crown. She wore this as she ruled her Court for many, many years. I may feel like I can't do this, but as soon as I put the crown on, I knew I would bring peace back to my land. I stare at my reflection a moment longer before a yawn escapes from my lips. I carefully pull the crown off my head and place it back into the black velvet bag. I put the bag back in the box and set it on my dresser. I will have to take it with me to Eldermyst.

I lay in my bed staring up at the ceiling, trying to process the box and letter left by my parents. I'm exhausted from the past two days, full of chaos and change. So many new and complicated things surfacing in my life. I'm a lost princess of a fae land. My parents were the High Lord and Lady of the Emerald Court. A group of bad guys killed them, and they were called the Dark Orians. I have special powers that have been suppressed my whole life. The powers more than likely have something to do with nature; however, it is uncertain since they have not been able to surface. The tea Dani would make me suppresses my powers. I was not supposed to find out about it until I was 18. My parents wanted me to grow up and have a somewhat everyday life. Stephanie is my cousin. Hillary is leaving everything behind to go with me to Eldermyst. Now that my parents are gone and I'm eighteen, I go from being the lost princess to the High Lady of the Emerald Court.

A tear forms in the corner of my eye, and I wipe it away. I have been emotional lately with all this going on, all the bombs dropping with secrets. I must remain strong. There is so much at stake right now and in the future. We discussed last night the necessary actions I must take. My training to hone my combat skills is a must. They warned that the journey to reclaim the throne would be difficult. I will encounter numerous challenges, some of which may be lethal. I need to learn the customs of our people and what's expected of me.

The very thought of becoming a High Lady is daunting. The idea of life in the public eye was never something I envisioned for myself; I have always avoided that. However, in this instance, my feelings differ. Despite the anxiety it brings, perhaps this is my destiny. I have always wanted to do something that changed lives. This is my chance to impact people's lives. Determination builds in me to learn about my family, reclaim what belongs to them, and avenge their deaths. I didn't know them, but hearing everything my parents put in place to keep me safe lets me know their dying love for me. I will destroy the person responsible for stripping them away from me.

Sleep begins to settle upon me, consuming me. My eyes slowly drift shut until I fall into a deep sleep.

I'm walking through a forest, much like the forest in Claywood, which is vibrant and full of trees. There are different kinds of trees with oaks scattered throughout. Oaks are reaching the heavens, old and full of life. I walk to a large oak and place my hand on its trunk. I feel a spark of energy run through me. I can sense emotions. I look around, wondering where these emotions I think are coming from.

Then, a whisper caresses my ear, "We have always been here." Realization registers in me; I can feel the tree's emotions. Astonished, I look back at the large tree, and a smile spreads across my face. A leaf crunches behind me, and I turn immediately to see what is coming. I freeze, expecting an animal, a bear, or something to run out. However, it isn't an animal coming at me; no, two people are weaving through the trees. They reach the opening where I stand, and they pause. Before me stand two individuals adorned with crowns and clothed in rich emerald hues. Their clothing consists of deep emerald tunics and chocolate brown trousers with elaborate detailing across the fabric. The man is tall and muscular and has a light olive skin. He has sharp features and light brown hair. His eyes are a deep brown color that shimmers behind the pupil. His smile is captivating and comforting. The woman has fair skin and almost white hair. Her eyes are a deep emerald color, just like mine. A smile spreads on the woman's face. Her smile is even more captivating than the man's. She is so beautiful. I carefully examine the crown on her head, and my eyes widen. I know that crown; it was the one inside of the box. I look them over again, and shock rolls through me as I realize who is standing before me: my parents. Their letter told me to look inside, and I would find them. I didn't think I would be able to see them.

"How is this possible?" I cover my mouth.

"We have always been with you, our dearest Alona. You simply couldn't reach us since you couldn't remember who we were." the man says with such love.

The woman approaches me and halts, waiting for me to approve her advance. I nod and close the remaining distance between us. She wraps me in an embrace, and I embrace her back, burying my head in her shoulder as tears cascade down my cheeks. These are my parents. Their presence here baffles me, and whether this is their actual appearance remains uncertain in this dreamlike state.

Nevertheless, I will savor every moment I spend here with them. My father closes the space between us and embraces my mother and me. Tears flow from each of us. I can stay here in this moment with them for the rest of my life, soaking in all the lost time.

"We are so proud of you and the woman you have become," My mother pulls back, wiping the tears from her eyes. No words came to me to describe what her words meant to me.

"We will always be proud of you," my father rubs my arm.

"Alona, a challenging journey lies before you. Nevertheless, your father and I have faith in you. We are confident that you will persevere. We trust your ability to make wise decisions and carve out your path."

"We wanted to ensure your safety and allow you to experience a normal life before being thrust into this chaos. We wished that we could be by your side. Our hearts ache for being taken away from you when we were before ever having time with you to watch you grow. This has placed a heavy burden on you. I deeply regret that we could not be there for you, my dear child. We will strive to support you as much as possible, though our hands are bound at times."

"I know I never had the chance to know you both, but I am so thankful for the opportunity you both gave me, for the unconditional and never-failing love you had for me to ensure that my life would be okay. I hope that I can fill your shoes. I don't know the first thing about being a queen, let alone about our people. I hope that I can make you and them proud."

"We will always love you. We have ever since we found out that you were growing in my stomach. Remember, we will always be with you in here and here," my mother smiles, reaching to touch my temple and then my heart.

Sorrow fills me with the thought of everything I have missed out on with these two people standing before me. A silent tear falls down my cheek. Corian reaches out and brushes it off of my cheek.

"You must train your powers and master them. Prepare yourself," she says." I don't even know what powers I have."

"My guess, my dear child, is that you have inherited both of our powers. Mine is the ability to connect to nature and command it. Your father can command the wind along with feel people's emotions."

They both smile at me, embracing me once more.

CHAPTER TWENTY-FIVE

Emerald Court Customs

ALONA

I woke up early, went out for a run, and then got ready for my day. I am sipping some coffee at one of the tables in the cafe. It is 6:50 am. How much my life has changed over the past few weeks is unbelievable. I went from having no friends, unsure of my future, to having friends, a support system, and a throne to reclaim. My life has changed for the better. I am lost in my world, thinking about everything that has happened, when I hear a tap on the front door. I look up, and I see Hillary waving through the window. I am surprised that she came. I don't know why I am amazed, but I am. I figured that she would have thought I lost my damn mind last night and decided against coming.

I stand up from the table and yell, "Hey Dani! Hillary is here."

I jog to the front door and open it. "Good morning!"

"Good morning, Adilyn... I mean Alona. I promise I will get it one of these days." she smiles sheepishly.

"Oh, no worries! I have to get used to it myself! Come in!" I step aside, giving her room to enter. "Would you like a cup of coffee?"

"Yes, that sounds wonderful."

"Okay! Coming right up! Take a seat over there at the table I was at." I gesture towards where I had been sitting. "Dani will be out in just a moment."

I go behind the counter to make Hillary a vanilla latte. I have seen her drink that on occasion. Dani comes whisking out of the kitchen, as always. She is carrying a tray full of food. I smile at her. She loves cooking and always says that a good conversation comes from a decent meal.

"Oh, good morning, Hillary! It is so lovely to see you!" she chirps.

I do not know how anyone can be that happy this early in the morning.

"Good morning, Dani. Thank you for having me here this morning. I brought what I thought I would need: notebook and pencil." She leans over to pull the notebook and pencil from her bag.

"Oh no, darling. We will not be starting with that. First, you must eat up. I cannot have you here on an empty stomach in my cafe." She sets down the tray and hands Hillary a plate full of food: scrambled eggs, French toast, bacon, and hashbrowns. She sets the remaining four plates down on the table. Four plates? Dani, Stephanie, me. Who else?

The front door opens, and Asher walks in. The gods must not favor me at all this morning. He has been very tough on me with training recently, pushing me to my limits each day. I swear he does not know how to smile, let alone how to be kind. I don't think he has one nice bone in his body! He looks in my direction, smirks, and winks at me. I roll my eyes as dramatically as I possibly can so that he sees the annoyance I feel. I cannot stand this man, but unfortunately, I must put up with him.

I finish making Hillary's coffee. I carry the latte and freshly brewed coffee to the table. I sit on the opposite side of Asher; the farther away, the better. Stephanie waltzes in and takes a seat next to me. A grin plasters her face at the sight of the breakfast laid out for us. We all sit there in silence for a moment.

"Well, what are you all waiting for? The food is going to get cold. Eat up!" Dani demands.

"Thank you for the latte, Alona. Vanilla latte is my favorite. I did not know you knew that." Hillary blushes.

"I have seen you drink that a couple of times. By the way, you drink coffee the rest of the time. I figured that a vanilla latte was your specialty coffee drink." I grin at her, and she nods approvingly as she sips from her latte.

"We are here to learn the customs of the Emerald Court." Dani looks at Hillary and me, and we nod at her.

"Some things will only apply to Hillary since she is human."

Hillary shifts in her seat. The realization that I am not human is unsettling. I have always considered myself human. Stephanie said I would not see my true form until I entered Eldermyst. Something about the human world dims the powers of the fae. There is so much for me to learn.

"Hillary, if a fae you do not know offers you food and you eat it, they can get the truth out of you. It acts as a truth serum for 10 minutes. Not every fae you encounter will want to do that, but some will want the truth about the heir so they can harm her. Fae cannot lie, but they can omit parts of the truth. Please do not drink the fae wine, as it can cause a human to enter into madness. Do not accept or make any deals with a fae, especially one you do not know well. Everything comes at a cost and will not end well for you."

Hillary inhales deeply and finishes writing each rule. I admire her. She is taking this very seriously and very well. My life was turned upside down, but so was hers.

"Okay, got it. Pretty much ask you guys beforehand before eating anything." She winks at Dani.

"Yes. We will need to make sure that you can defend yourself at times. We will do our best to protect you at all times, but there may be a time when we will need you to protect yourself. Some things you come up against won't be easy enemies to kill either." Dani says dryly.

"I can do it. I was with a verbally abusive man, so I have a lot of pent-up anger that I can unleash on any monster coming at me. I will do my best not to be a liability for you all." she glances at each of us.

"Alright. You can train with me then, Hillary. Us old women need to stick together." Dani grins brightly at Hillary.

Gratitude flows through me, warming my chest. This scene warms my heart because my blood and created family are all coming together as a team. This is precisely what I have been longing for my entire life. A smile spreads across my face.

"What's making you smile so broadly over there?" Stephanie tilts her head and raises an eyebrow, questioning me.

"Oh, nothing. I am just happy, that is all. My family is all coming together." I say shyly.

I glance around the table at everyone, smiles spreading across the room. My eyes land on Asher, and his face is expressionless and cold. Yet, there is a small light glittering in his eyes. What is he thinking? Does he even want to be here? I doubt it. He is constantly being a jerk and barking out demands whenever he gets the chance. This man makes my blood boil, and he knows it. My now-consuming anger toward Asher burns out the joy that had built up in my chest. I huff out a loud sigh and turn back to Dani. I need to breathe and keep my composure. I will not let this man ruin my good day anymore.

"For you, Alona. You will enter Eldermyst, and your true self will surface. The full force of your powers, your pointed ears, and your features will all come to the surface. You are the heir to the throne of the Emerald Court. Some will love and protect you in the other courts; however, not everyone will. It would be best if you were prepared for that. We do not know who has been turned by the Dark Orians with promises of power. So, we will have to tread lightly. We will need to seek out allies. You will need to present yourself as a High Lady. In the way you move, speak, and fight. If you do not, then hope is lost for allies."

"As a what?"

"Queens in your world are called High Ladies in our world," Stephanie responds.

"Oh... They are the same thing, though, correct?" I ask.

"Yes, the only difference is queens are human and have no magic. Those who are High Ladies can only come from the royal bloodline. High Lords and Ladies are mighty fae." Dani responds with a smile.

I nervously laugh. "Right, very powerful; I am just beaming with power," I say sarcastically, waving my hands.

"That is because you have no experience in our world, Alona. However, you will be expected to become a High Lady, commanding the respect of all. They will hold you to the same standards as your mother." Asher bites.

Silence falls upon me and the others. What he is saying is accurate, and I know it. Yet, it is also so terrifying. How am I, Adilyn, supposed to command respect? Will I fail my mother and her people? I bring my knees to my chest and wrap my arms around my legs. A heaviness settling on my chest, the pressure of living up to an expectation I am uncertain about, and the loss of people I should have known. I sit in the chair, hugging my legs for a moment longer. No one moves or says a word. I can see Hillary out of my eye with her head in her hands. This is a lot for her, Stephanie, and Dani. I am not alone in this feeling of pressure and overwhelm. I am not alone in this battle. I suck in a deep breath, and I set my feet back on the floor. I sit up straight in my chair, not allowing sorrow and anxiety to consume another moment of my life.

"What do you mean by how I present myself?" trying to grasp everything I need to accomplish.

"You must be a High Lady, Alona. Command respect and cherish the people of Eldermyst. High Ladies are both gentle and fierce, graceful yet lethal when necessary. They uphold what is right and never retreat." Asher says this time with a gentler tone.

I suck in a breath. Can I be these things? What will happen if I can't, will the Emerald Court fall for good? These people here have dedicated their lives to my return. I cannot let my Court fall. I cannot let that happen.

"Hey, you've got this! It's not as difficult as it seems. Stay true to yourself always, and you will be more than enough. It might sound silly to say this, but your mother remained true to herself throughout her entire reign. She was kind, fearless, and a force to be reckoned with. She stood for justice for all and sought out that everyone was cared for. She truly cared for her people and showed it. She was out in the towns, often tending to the needs of her people and just being with them. She was not a High Lady who ignored her people. She laughed, joked, and fiercely loved her family, friends, and people. She was always willing to lay her life down for the good of her people." she says softly, sorrow lingering as she speaks of my mother.

"Being a High Lady isn't about wearing frilly dresses, Alona. It's about caring for your people and acting in their best interests. It involves fighting for and earning their respect, just as you respect them. There is no specific language you must speak or education you must have. You possess all you need to be a High Lady. Be yourself and always consider what's best for your people. You already care for others around you. You have always been made for greater things, and you know that." Stephanie says, nodding at me. Everyone nods in agreement.

"You've always been special. You have always been kind even when others have not been kind to you. You have always thought of others' well-being. You will make an amazing queen or High Lady, whatever they are called." Hillary leans over and pats the top of my hand before leaning back in her chair.

"Will I have to marry someone to be High Lady?" I'm curious if the rules are the same there as they are here.

Asher's face drains of color, and Dani laughs, clapping her hand on her leg. "No, honey, you do not. The fae do not believe in that nonsense. We believe that High Ladies and Lords can rule on their own. There is no expectation for them to marry just to rule. At some point in time, if you desire to marry, then I am sure you will have a line of suitors waiting." Dani glances at Asher, who chokes on his water.

I glare at him, narrowing my eyes. He glares right back at me. We sit there glaring at each other until I hear someone clearing their throat. I turn and see Hillary is the one behind it.

"Sorry, it was getting awkward with you two having a staring contest. I wanted to save the rest of us here from that."

My mouth drops open, almost hitting the floor, so it felt. "I was not having a staring contest with this asshole."

Hillary chuckles, "No, darling, you were not. Bad of me to assume you were."

I glare at Dani and Stephanie. They are in their seats, heads down, and choking on their laughs.

"I am going to the bathroom." I toss my napkin on the table and storm out of the room. Once I enter the bathroom, I lean against the door. Should I have reacted that way? I drop my head into my hands. I am sure High Ladies don't let stupid comments get to them. I push off the door and stroll to the sink to splash cold water on my face. I look up at the mirror and see myself. My parents said they believed in me. Hillary, Dani, Stephanie, and even Asher believe in me. I cannot let them down. I will push forward and take back what is rightfully mine. I will not let a title, a monster, some bad guys, or an asshole deter me from taking back my court.

I stand straight, hold my chin high, and return to the table.

"Yes, if that is what you desire, you can pledge her your life." Dani nods at Hillary.

"What are you talking about?" I missed the first part of this conversation. Who is offering who's life up?

"Oh, we were talking about possibilities for the future. A High Lord or Lady can have those who decide to offer their life in service to them. This means the one offering will be bound to the High Lord or Lady, and the High Lord or Lady is responsible for protecting the one offering their life. We can discuss it later. I am curious as to how it is going with the Emerald-shadow." Dani perks up in her chair, waiting for my words.

"Well, we trained with it yesterday, and I believe we will be there later today."

"You did not feel anything?" Her eyebrows furrow together.

"Um.. what do you mean?" Lost as to what she is talking about.

"Never mind, honey. I think you will know what I mean when it happens." She winks at me. "So Hillary, what are your plans? Do you plan to go with us permanently? For a short period? What is your plan with your house?"

Dani bombards Hillary with questions. Hillary shifts in her seat and sets down her coffee. She pauses for a moment, thinking about her answer.

"Well... I thought about this all last night; I could not sleep."

My heart pains knowing that she did not sleep. She struggles so much with sleeping without adding more to her plate.

"I have decided that I will be going with you permanently. As for my house, I will be giving it to Tim unless our money here is of any use there."

Dani smiles widely, her smile reaching her eyes. She leans over and grabs Hillary's hand. "The money here is useless, and we will happily have you permanently. I already know you will enjoy our realm much more than here."

Hillary smiles back at Dani and pats the top of her hand. We spend the next hour discussing what will be done with all of our belongings that we cannot take on the journey. We can only bring what we carry, as Asher says. I brought up the thought of donating it to those in need. I can give my painting supplies to Everett and my clothing to the women's shelter. Asher said we must ensure we have clothes for all kinds of weather. We will be making the journey and crossing into several of the courts. We must bring clothes guy for warm, hot, and cold weather.

Curiously, each court is different in weather and terrain, changing starting at their border. Asher said the Obsidian Court is next to the Ivory Court, so it goes from dark and gloomy to icy and cold. I can't wait to see it and experience it for myself.

CHAPTER TWENTY-SIX

Training

ALONA

I look at the clock—5:00 am. I jump out of bed and get my running clothes and shoes on. This marks another morning I've woken up early by choice. I've started my days with a run through the forest, running through the uneven terrain to build stamina. I can sense my muscles gradually strengthening, which is a great sign. Afterward, I train with Asher, strengthening my powers along with perfecting my fighting skills. This is starting to become a habit that I immensely enjoy. I love feeling my body getting stronger. I have quite a bit more energy during my days as well. I cherish the solitude in the forest, though—that sunrise in the distance, painting the sky with beautiful colors of orange and pink. The view of it from the forest always makes my heart skip a beat.

With my newfound knowledge of my connection to nature, I always make sure to spend a few minutes talking with the trees, knowing they hear me. It baffles me that I secretly knew deep down inside that they could hear to me. It was soul-stirring to know the trees were alive. Little by little, I'm beginning to feel their emotions. Asher said that I would understand what they wanted to tell me one day, once I enter Eldermyst and my full power, was released. I am excited for that day to come. Soon enough.

I quietly descend the stairs and head for the front door. I open the door and slip out like a thief in the night. I close the door quietly behind me and run right into a wall. I first thought it was a wall until I looked up. It is Asher. Asher has been waiting for me outside the cafe as I emerge this morning.

"Can I help you?" I say dryly.

"I have decided to join you while you run, my lady."

"Um.... no, thank you. I'm good. I wouldn't want to inconvenience you." I begin jogging, hoping he gets the hint that I don't need a chaperone.

He jogs up alongside me, keeping pace. "I run in the mornings about this time, so it only makes sense that we run together." He smiles wickedly. I almost trip over my foot, hoping to catch myself before he notices. That smile—what was that besides absolutely breathtaking?

"Whatever, you do as you please anyways."

"Do I though, my lady?" his eye churning with something dark.

"Conversation over before it ends poorly for both of us. Just shut up and run since you won't leave." I roll my eyes. He is just so damn cocky. What does he think he is going to do? Sweep me off my feet? Right, not today, asshole, not today. I chuckle to myself.

Asher jerks his head in my direction and raises one eyebrow. "Should I be concerned for my safety, my lady? Should I prepare myself for you to attack me?"

"SHUT UP! For the love of all the gods that exist, shut up." Frustration flutters through me and I narrow my eyes. This man is intolerable.

We continue to run the rest of the way in silence. He not once left my side, keeping pace the entire time, yet I could sense that was difficult for him. He has trained his whole life, so running alongside me must have been like running alongside a turtle for him. I stop and slowly make my way towards my favorite large oak. Asher must have known I needed space, so he strolls a few feet in the opposite direction.

"Hello, my dear friend," I say as I lay my hands on the trunk. Closing my eyes, I focus solely on the tree before me. Within seconds, energy courses between the tree and me. I sense the life within the tree and its joy. Ever since I discovered my ability to connect with them, all I have felt from these trees is happiness and peace.

"I wonder if the trees in Eldermyst feel the same..." A thought spoke out loud.

"I don't think they do. We say our people are being poisoned; all the trees and life in Eldermyst are our people, too. They are being poisoned as well, cut down, and discarded like they are nothing. I'm sure the trees are crying for help there." Asher murmurs, lowering his head, and a few strands of his dark hair fall into his face.

"That's horrible. I have to save them." My chest tightens at the thought of all the suffering happening in Eldermyst at the hands of the Dark Orians. I must put an end to it.

"I hope you do," he says softly.

"Do you think I can?" I begin to fiddle with my fingers, afraid of his response.

"I think you can and will." He looks me in the eye and nods softly.

"Thank you," I whisper.

"Let's get to learning how to kick ass." I try to change the mood.

Asher and I rarely talk about anything besides training, so a real conversation with him is refreshing. I assumed he believed in me, or why else would he be here? Hearing that he thinks I can do it is reassuring.

We spend the next two hours training, working on building my mental wall faster and more efficiently. Stone by stone, the wall goes up and comes back down. Fewer holes scatter my wall with each try. I can feel the emotions fading to a dull feeling in the back of my mind when I place that last stone in its place. We also train with my powers, diving into my well of power and bringing up power without thinking twice about it.

"Okay, this time, I want you to make something grow. We must master the simple things to move on to bigger things." Asher instructs.

I close my eyes and jump down into the well deep inside of me, grabbing as much power as I can and bringing it back up. I can feel my body warming, and a tingle runs through my veins. My magic is filling me, consuming me. I imagine blood roots sprouting all around me, filling the ground. I focus solely on the flowers with everything I have. I open my hands and allow the warmth to enter my fingertips and flow out.

A floral fragrance hits me, and my eyes flutter open. My jaw drops at the beauty around me. My hand darts to my mouth, and I slowly spin and see blood roots blooming in a circle around me. There has to be at least one hundred of them. My stomach flutters with butterflies swarming inside of me. I start jumping up and down joyously like a child who just got told yes to eating a cookie. I spin, and eye Asher, who is leaning against a tree with his arms crossed, watching me. I stop jumping and smile. I hold my hands so he can see all the flowers surrounding me now.

"Can you believe it?" I can't stop myself from smiling. "I did this!"

The corners of his lips curl up, and he places his hand on his chest, nodding, "My lady, I'm impressed with how quickly you are catching on. I wouldn't expect any less from you."

My chest tightens, and I can feel color flushing my cheeks. "Thank you."

Each day, I can feel that I'm getting better. I'm learning how to grasp more and more power from my well. I made huge progress with bringing forth my powers. Today, I made so many flowers pop up! I felt like a little girl who found treasure when it happened. I squealed and jumped for joy. They were so beautiful. I could not believe what I created. It is incredible to feel when my powers manifest in my body, running through my veins. Once I enter Eldermyst, I will manifest my full powers. I can't even begin to understand how that will feel.

Asher and I quietly stroll back to the cafe. My body is slightly sore, but not nearly as sore as when I first started training. The crisp air dries the sweat that beads on my forehead. I look over to Asher, who always has a cold, distant face. however, he seems to be lost in thought.

"Can I ask you some questions?" I pause and turn towards him.

Asher stops, crossing his arms, "What?"

"The more I practice using my magic, the faster it will be?"

"Yes, you will get to a point where you won't need to close your eyes and mentally dive into your well. It will just come to you with a simple thought."

"What are the Dark Orians like?" I need to know what I'm going to face. I must prepare myself for the battles I will fight.

He sighs and is quiet, trying to collect his thoughts. "They were a group of fae who were unhappy with their powers and wanted more. They wanted to be the most powerful and rule over all of Eldermyst and the surrounding fae islands. One day, they went to the Dark Under Lord and sold their souls in exchange for power. They became corrupted. They then set out to destroy everything and everyone that stood in their path. Our parents couldn't just sit on the sidelines like the other Courts. They knew that they had to do something to try and stop them from slaughtering the people and life of Eldermyst." Asher's gaze lowers, and he drops his arms to his side. His fists clench at his sides, trying to control his sadness and anger. I can feel both emotions rolling off of him. The feelings are so strong I feel like they will knock me right off my feet, bile rising in my throat, and my breathing is labored. These emotions feel overwhelming and consuming. If this is how he feels, my heart breaks for him. I build up my mental wall to block out his feelings so I can be present for this conversation. I need questions answered, and I can't tap out mentally now. Stone by stone, my wall is in place.

"But how did they know who the Dark Orians were?"

"When you see them, you will know exactly who they are. They have pale white skin and black lifeless eyes. The skin around their eyes is stained black from the evil that consumes them. Their mouths are stained red from all the blood they drink. They are fast and powerful because they drain life and magic from the fae they kill."

"That sounds scary. They drink blood?" Nausea rolls through my stomach at the thought of someone drinking blood.

"Yes, that is how they gain the magic from the fae they slaughter." He shakes his head and frowns.

"They are the ones that killed your parents?"

He nods once and grasps the back of his neck. His gaze turns to the ground, hiding the pain in his eyes, and he begins to walk. The waves crash up against what feels like my glass wall. The emotions are consuming. I double-check my wall and see that it is in place. His pain must be overwhelming since I can still feel it through my wall.

I reach out my hand and gently place it on his shoulder, trying to comfort him. He stiffens, halting in his tracks. "Hey, I'm sorry for your loss. My words might not mean much right now, but I'm sorry."

"I don't need your pity. My parents died just like yours. They died as heroes. All that matters now is to finish what they started." He shrugs my hand off his shoulder and then walks away.

I am left here on the side of the road, speechless. Do I run after him? Do I let him go? I know he is an asshole, but he doesn't deserve to feel that pain alone. I watch as he gets farther away. My feet won't move, and maybe that is for the best. I'm the last person he wants to talk to. I slump my shoulders, look at the ground, and slowly walk back to the cafe.

I walk through the front door and see Dani wiping tables down. Hillary looks to be studying in the far corner. They both look up at me and smile. I try to smile back but can't seem to force myself to. I can't seem to shake the emotions I felt from Asher. Dani sets down her rag and comes to my side.

"Is everything okay, Alona?" Hillary is by my other side a moment later. Worry is written over both of their faces.

"I don't feel so well."

"What happened?"

"I asked Asher a question about the Dark Orians, and when his answer touched on the subject of our parents, I could feel his emotions. They were so overwhelming because I still could feel them through my wall.

If I wouldn't have had my wall up, his emotions would have planted my butt on the ground." I half smile, not wanting to worry them too much.

"Will she be alright?" Hillary glances at Dani while she strokes my arm, ensuring I don't fall backward.

Dani nods and steers me towards an open seat. We all sit around the table, and my face drops to my hands. "Asher took the loss of his parents very hard. They were everything to him, and then, one day, they were stripped away. I think that loss hardened his heart. He never truly grieved their loss, so he has so much emotion pent up inside of him just waiting to break free."

I glance at Dani, knowing that her words ring true. I had my wall up, yet his emotions were still strong.

"So, you can feel strong emotions?" Hillary's brow furrows.

I nod.

"Has it started to surface more without the tea?" Dani leans forward, placing her arms on the table.

"Yes, I have started to feel emotions more recently. The other day, Asher's emotions knocked me to the ground; they were overpowering. Asher walked me through putting up a mental wall after that to help ease the discomfort."

Hillary rubs my back. "Well, I'm sure it's difficult to maneuver your emotions and the emotions of another. Mastering that wall seems to be your best option, then darling."

I sit up. "I hear that still feeling someone's emotions to an extent is a benefit. Sometimes I agree, and other times I can't entirely agree."

"Sensing someone's emotions can be life-altering at times. Let's say you meet someone one day and are unsure if they're being genuine toward you. You can tell if they approach you with hatred or any other emotion. So, sensing someone's emotions could save your life or the lives of others."

"I didn't think of it that way." I'm contemplating what situations I will encounter where it may be useful.

"Your mother possessed a deep connection with nature and a unique talent for influencing natural elements. She could communicate with trees, plants, and animals, perceiving their feelings and interpreting their communications. Your father was blessed with the ability to feel the emotions of humans and fae. He also had a connection with the wind."

"Whoa, that is kind of scary yet amazing at the same time. My human mind has a hard time understanding that magic is real." Hillary sits back in her chair, extending her legs in front of her.

"Right?" I agree with Hillary. My father had a connection with the wind. I wonder if I happen to have the same as well. I don't know how magic or lineage works in Eldermyst, but I will explore it. Curiosity blooms in my chest. Would controlling it be the same as when I control nature by simply jumping into the well and focusing my thoughts on the wind?

"It will be okay. We will get through this. We will all get through this." Dani squeezes my hand, bringing me back to the present with them. A smile flourishes on my face. Her confidence in my abilities and the abilities of all of us to make it through helps to settle the unease in my chest.

"Thank you, Dani. It is ridiculous to think that literally, not even a month ago, I was living what I thought was a normal life. Then I found out I wasn't even human."

"I know! It was a shocker that I had a magical being living under my roof for a handful of years." Hillary blurts out.

We all look at each other, and laughter erupts, lifting the mood among us by a mile. Stephanie walks into the cafe and stands in the doorway with her hands on her hips. A smile plasters her face. "What in the world has gotten into the three of you?"

"We were just discussing how I'm no longer a human." A tear slips from my eye from laughing so hard.

Stephanie rolls her eyes and shakes her head. "You bunch are crazy." I bite my bottom lip to prevent myself from laughing more, but Hillary breaks first, and a laugh erupts from her, followed by the rest of us, including Stephanie. She makes her way towards us and leans down to hug me. I half hug her back and stand up.

"Group hug everyone!!" I shout. We stand there, embracing each other.

"I love you ladies so much," I whisper, wanting to let them know how I feel for each of them. They each play a huge role in my life, and I would be crushed if I lost any of them. Part of me desires everything to stay like this with no battles, no bad guys, no issues. However, I can feel deep down inside that my life is not supposed to end that way. I am meant for so much more.

CHAPTER TWENTY-SEVEN

Arion

ALONA

S tephanie thinks it would be an excellent idea for me to see Arion
again. I agree, but I want to see him in his true form, wings and all.
Based on what the others have told me, this world masks our authentic
appearance and will only surface briefly if it is willed or in Eldermyst.
Magic is stifled here, and only a fraction of a fae's power works here.

Only in Eldermyst and the surrounding fae land will I be able to see
him with his wings. It makes sense, though; this land has no magic of
its' own. Who knows how humans would handle seeing 'make-believe'
creatures and things that we have only ever read about in books,

We discussed that strengthening the bond between Arion and myself
would benefit me. He will be with me every step of the way in Eldermyst.

Stephanie and I drive to the stables to see Arion and Aoife. Butterflies
begin to take off in my stomach, that feeling you get when you're a young
teen when you get excited. I have always dreamed about unicorns and

flying horses. My dream has become a reality. I can't wait for the day to see Arion in his true glory.

"So you said Arion and Aoife are mates, correct?" I look over at Stephanie.

She steals a glance in my direction before turning back to the road. "Yes, they have been for centuries."

"What exactly does that mean?"

"Mating bonds can occur in both animals and fae. While there are slight variations, the similarities are quite significant. When an individual finds their mate, they experience a unique connection, like an invisible string pulling them towards each other. Once the mates recognize this bond, it solidifies into place. The mating bonds cause an overwhelming desire and need for the other that overcomes any other feeling. This bond, once solidified, creates a strong and loving relationship between the pair."

"Oh, wow. So, this mating bond you speak of is similar to what humans call soulmates?"

"Yes and no. Soulmates are the same: one person is the other half of your soul. However, soul mates do not have the same connections as mates. Mates have a deep spiritual connection other than the physical connection. A mate can feel the other person's emotions almost like theirs. When one of them gets injured, the other also gets injured. They are pretty much two sides to one coin. Also, it is said that mates can speak to each other's minds."

"Wait, so have a mental conversation with each other." The thought of that seems wild to me. I read once in a book years ago where the two main characters became mates. It never went into depth about the mating bond, so this is all new to me.

"Yes, they can hold mental conversations. It's weird watching because you can tell they are talking to each other by their body movements, but you have no clue what they are saying. My parents did that all the time....., and so did yours." She steals a glance at me, reaching out her hand and grasping mine.

"I wish I could have seen that." Sorrow overwhelms me. I will never have that chance to see my parents do those things. I need to clear my mind about this. I don't want to upset Arion since he can sense my emotions. "So how does one know they are mated and when it snaps into place?"

"Well... it is said that everything clicks into place and you just know then desire takes over. The need to be with the other becomes consuming." Stephanie chuckles awkwardly.

"Wow, that sounds pretty intense. Have you found your mate?"

"Not yet. I spent most of my life training to prepare for you to return. I never considered that a possibility, at least for now. I hope that one day I will find my mate."

It pains me to know that she has put her life on the back burner because of me. I'm uneasy that people have lived their lives preparing for me to return to the Emerald Court, and I had no clue that any of it existed. Here, I was living a somewhat everyday and carefree life while they were dealing with devastation in my country.

"I'm sorry," is all I can manage to say. I look down at my hands and begin fiddling with my fingers. I'm sorry—all those years that she lost due to me. How can I ever give her that time back? My throat begins to constrict. I take slow, deep breaths, trying to calm my anxiety. The only thing I can do now is train hard and defeat these dark bastards who have stripped so many people of their loved ones.

"Don't be! I chose to train and prepare for you. I knew you would come back and take the Court back."

I smile meekly at her, trying to believe her words.

"One thing about mates I have not told you yet is that they have this weird thing where they can't be apart for many days. I think the longest one can be separated from their mate is twelve days. However, they are strongest when they are together. Their magic blends and can make them a powerful duo."

"That's interesting. I wonder why that is."

Stephanie shrugs her shoulders and pulls the car to a stop. We arrive at the stable, and sure enough, Arion is standing right outside the stable entrance waiting. He almost looks annoyed. I chuckle softly and shake my head—crazy horse. Aoife strides to Arion's side and shakes her head towards us as if waving. I smile widely. These two are quite opposites. Arion is stubborn and grumpy most of the time and Aoife appears to be a cheerful horse. We get out of the car and walk to the horses.

Stephanie holds out her hand as she gets closer. Aoife walks towards her, nudging her head in Stephanie's hand as soon as they are close enough. Arion stays put, making me close the distance between us. I roll my eyes at the stubborn horse. Of course, this one would be the one that picks me. I reach out as soon as I am a few feet from him. He lowers his head, and I wait for his permission to touch him. I stand still a foot in front of him, waiting. He hasn't moved, and I don't want to try my luck today and end up trampled by a horse. After a moment that felt like an eternity, he nods, permitting me to stroke his face. I reach slowly and lay my hand on his forehead. He is such a beauty. I stroke his face and slowly step to the side of him. He gazes at me. There is so much wisdom and experience in his eyes.

"How are you today, Arion?" I ask softly.

He nods his head, and I smile. I stand beside him for several minutes longer, soaking in as much of his peaceful side as possible. I wonder if this was also what it was like for my mother. Was he also grumpy with her? Elouan strides out of the stable, wiping his hands.

"Good afternoon, my lady." he bows at the waist.

Did he bow? Heat creeps into my cheeks, and I shuffle back and forth on my feet. "Good afternoon, Elouan."

I never thought people would ever be bowing to me! I'm not worthy enough for that. Stephanie senses my uneasiness and strolls over to stand by my side.

"It's a lot, I know, Alona. It will become less uncomfortable with time, but you must accept people bowing to you. You are the heir to the throne, the High Lady, so that everyone will bow, but to clarify, I'm not bowing to you." she winks and says sarcastically.

I burst out laughing because she knows how to make the situation lighter. Elouan chuckles softly.

"The previous time you were here, my lady, Arion chose you. However, what needs to happen is you need to choose him now."

"Huh?" I blurt out.

"Similar to what we were talking about in the car. It is a similar bond of mates, yet it is not mates in that sense. The Pterippi chooses a rider they feel is worthy of them, and then the rider is to accept the bond."

"What happens after that?"

"Well, after that, the rider and Pterippi become one, similar to the mating bond. You can tap into the powers of the Pterippi. You ride in unison and fight in unison. You become a part of each other." Elouan states.

"Oh.... well.... er... what do I do then? How do I accept it?" I pray to the gods it is nothing crazy like drinking his blood or something super painful.

"To accept the bond, you must first cut your palm, rub your blood on Arion's forehead, and then apply it to your forehead. After that, you must touch your forehead to his and close your eyes. Besides the pain from cutting your palm, you will feel an electric shock through both yourself and Arion. Once the bond has been completed, you will know." Stephanie says.

"How will I know?" I raise an eyebrow.

"Trust me, you will know." She smiles at me and pulls a dagger under her pant leg.

"You carry weapons around?" I was dumbfounded that I never realized she carried weapons around.

"Yes. I always have several daggers on me at all times. You never know when you will need them." She hands me the dagger.

I grab it and hold it in my hand. Am I going to go through with this? Is it even worth it? Doubt floods my mind with all the bad endings that can happen with this bonding. Stephanie reaches out and grabs my shoulder.

"You have nothing to worry about, Alona. The short-term pain is worth the lifetime bond that you gain. Aoife and I are bonded, and I would not think twice about changing that. She has saved my life and will continue to do so many times."

Elouan nods in assurance.

I stare down at the dagger. I'm going to do this. Arion was bonded to my mother, and I want to follow in her footsteps. I lift the dagger above my palm and my hand trembles. I inhale deeply, slowly lowering the blade onto my palm and dragging it across. Prickles of pain follow the blade, and beads of blood form along the slice. I hand the dagger back to Stephanie, then look at the blood slowly puddling in my palm. I look up at Stephanie, and she nods her head. I turn to face Arion. I dip my finger into the puddle of blood and bring my trembling finger up to Arion's forehead. I hesitate momentarily, glancing at Stephanie and see her smiling at me. I look back at Arion and press my finger to his forehead, then drag my bloody finger across. I dip my finger back into my bloody palm and then trace a line on my forehead. I look at Arion for approval. He nods, and then I touch my forehead to his, closing my eyes.

Light bursts behind my eyelids. A white-hot pain sears through me, and it takes everything in me not to scream out. It feels like the pain is not going to end. I can feel my trembling hands grasping the side of Arion's face. Tears pour from my eyes like a waterfall. My world starts to tilt, and I swear I will pass out because it is so overwhelming. Then it stops, and the pain disappears, leaving me feeling raw.

"The bond has been completed, little Emerald." a deep voice echoes in my ears. I open my eyes and look around to see who said that. I can't see anyone other than Stephanie and Elouan. My eyes dart from one place to the next, searching for the culprit. Stephanie reaches out and places her hand on my back.

"It's okay. Alona."

"Who said that?"

"Said what?"

"That the bond is completed."

"I did!" the deep voice laced with annoyance rings in my head.

My eyes slowly turn to Arion. Horror falls on me. I begin shaking my head.

"There is no freaking way this is happening!" The voice is in my head, and it is coming from Arion. I stumble back a few steps, trying to regain my composure. I dart straight for the nearest tree and heave up all the contents of my stomach. Stephanie runs over and soothes me by rubbing my back.

"Maybe I should have told you so you knew what to expect. That is my fault." She says apologetically.

Still hunched over, "I think I would have still got sick." I inhale deeply and then exhale, allowing the nausea to pass. "Between the pain from a moment ago and now someone talking in my head, my stomach is on a roller coaster ride."

"Are you done feeling ill, or must I wait longer."

My eyes dart to Arion. I can tell by his tone of voice and looking at him that he is annoyed with my weak stomach.

"How do I do it? How do I talk to him?" I stand up straight and look at Stephanie.

"You simply think whatever you want to say to him. Your mind already knows who the message is for, so it will connect your mind to his."

"Our minds are connected?"

Stephanie nods her head. I slowly walk towards Arion, hands trembling. I stand in front of him, and my gaze locks with his.

"I didn't pick a weak fae, so don't disappoint me. You will need to learn to master that stomach of yours."

"I'm sorry. I wasn't expecting you to be in my mind."

"This will be the one time I allow it to slide. The next time, you will not hear the end of it. Understood?"

I shake my head, still trying to understand what is happening. I knew the fae had special powers but didn't think a bond could do this.

"We must train to ride hard and fast, little Emerald. There is a time coming when we will need to fight. Once we cross back into our land, you must train to ride me while I fly."

"Wait, what? What did you say? Fly? Me, ride you while you fly?" pointing at him in shock. I can see it now, falling off midair. There goes all that hard work and training.

"Yes, soar, little Emerald. Fear not, for I will let no harm come to you. There will be moments when we must ascend for a clearer perspective to relay it to the others. And sometimes, flying simply surpasses walking."

"You knew my mother...." I don't know why that came to my mind, but it did.

"Yes, I knew your mother. She was my bonded rider for many years." his head lowered.

I can tell the pain echoing in his voice. I didn't want to question him further, at least not now. I cannot imagine what it was like for him to lose her, maybe as painful as it was for Dani.

Chapter Twenty-Eight

Truce

Alona

I lay in bed staring up at the ceiling. It is 4:00 am and I can't sleep for the life of me. In only a few days, we will leave Claywood, which I have called home for eighteen years. I will embark on a journey into the unknown. A heaviness of all the responsibilities that I will face settles on my chest. I have so many lives depending on me now. Not only the lives of my friends but also the lives of my parents' court, my court, and the lives of an entire country. A country I had no clue about, a country filled with fae and magic, one that I never believed existed. Magic was only supposed to be in fairytales and fantasy books.

I lay in bed thinking about things I have read in books—books that have transported me to magical worlds filled with magic, adventure, love, and fae. Will it be the same? Will there be sprites, dragons, ogres, sirens, and unicorns? Or is all of that simply human make-believe? I won't know until I arrive, but I will see and experience it myself. However, there is some truth in them. Pterippi, magical lands, and fae all do exist. Excitement bubbles in my chest, thinking of what else I will find.

I dreamt of going on adventures in magical lands, falling in love with a handsome warrior that would sweep me off my feet, and manifesting magical powers that I used to save lives. I dreamed big and dreamed of things I thought were impossible. I smile, knowing that dream is going to come true in a matter of a few days. Well, part of it.

I sit up slowly and throw my legs off the bed. It is time to get ready and go out for my daily run. For the past two days, Asher has accompanied me running. Part of me hates his overbearing, mother-hen presence. However, the other part of me is okay with having him there. Having someone who won't pry into how you feel or bombard you with questions is nice—someone who is just there. Sometimes, I need to be silent and think through things. Sometimes, I must let my mind go and not think about the impending future.

I rise from the bed and mindlessly wander to my dresser, grabbing my running clothes, black leggings, and an emerald green tank top. I stand there for a moment. What do the people of Eldermyst wear? I have not thought of that until just now. I chuckle softly at the silly questions that come to my mind. I change quickly and put my running shoes on. Then I tiptoe down the stairs. I can tell Dani is already awake, but I have grown so accustomed to being quiet early in the morning that I do it out of habit. I reach the bottom of the stairs, and a delicious aroma swirls in the air: brown sugar, cinnamon, apples, and butter. I inhale deeply, and my mouth begins to water.

"Whatever you are making smells delightful, Dani," I call out. I walk towards the kitchen to see what she is making that smells so delicious. I peek in and find Hillary standing in the kitchen with Dani. They both are wearing aprons covered in flour. I smile at the two whisking the mix in the bowls, chatting away like they have been best friends their whole lives. Friendship is what Hillary needed desperately, and a part of me thinks this is what Dani needed as well after losing my mother.

"I'm surprised to see both of you in the kitchen so early." I cross my arms and lean against the doorway.

They both look up, and their smiles beam. My heart melts a little at the joy I see sparkling in their eyes.

"Good morning, honey! I'm teaching Hillary to make one of the Emerald Court's favorite pastries, Stella's Muffins."

My eyebrow raises, "Wait? Stella's?"

Dani chuckles, "Stella was my mother. Stella's Muffins was her secret recipe. I had a small cafe in the castle called Stella's. It was a lot like this one."

"I cannot wait to try them!!"

"Maybe we will save you one! I'm afraid I may eat them all with how they smell." Hillary laughs.

"My first decree as the High Lady of the Emerald Court is to insist that you save one of the muffins for me." Laughter bubbles out, joined by Dani and Hillary.

"Your wish is our command, my lady." Dani curtsies, bowing her head.

I roll my eyes and shake my head. "I'm going to go running. I hope you both don't inhale all of the muffins before I get back."

I smile at them both before turning and heading for the front door. I open the front door, and sure enough, Asher is waiting outside on the bench by the front door. He looks up at the sky, clouds slowly rolling in and the stars fading away.

"They are making Stella's Muffins?" He asks, keeping his eyes on the sky.

"How did you know?" I tilt my head, curious.

He turns to look at me and softly grins, a hint of sadness in his eyes, "I love Stella's Muffins. As a child, my parents only allowed me to have one per week. They thought they were too sugary for me. However, Dani used to sneak me some while my parents weren't looking. They were my favorite thing to eat as a child."

"They must be amazing then." I smile softly.

I stand there, gazing at him. He has just shared a cherished childhood memory with me. It's a memory I'm confident he holds close to his heart. A time in his life when his parents were still alive. I could hear the hollowness in his voice, and I could feel the heaviness in the air. I know losing a loved one is crushing and almost impossible to overcome. I can tell that he has not allowed himself to grieve the loss of his parents fully. He avoids it by putting it in the back of his mind and throwing himself into his duty. I can feel his grief lingering deep under the surface, screaming to be let out. I find myself at a loss for words. I'm sure he will not want to talk about it, nor do I want to force him. At some point in time, he will have to grieve; otherwise, he will be lost forever.

He clears his throat and clears the memory from his mind. "Let's go. There is no time to stand around." He returns to his cold facade. He turns and begins to jog away. I'm left there, the warmth stripped from me with that sudden change in his behavior. I could feel the love and pain emanating from him because of that memory. Then I could feel him slamming the door shut on those memories, ridding himself of his emotions. I run to catch up to him. We run the rest of the way in silence.

"I made it farther this time!" I exclaim, out of breath. I flop down by my favorite tree. I close my eyes and inhale deeply, trying to catch my breath. I ran five miles this morning, a new record for me, and I feel winded.

"Yeah, you could run even farther if you tried harder." Asher leans against the tree across from me. He pulls out a blade and flips it between his fingers.

I roll my eyes. Always more. This man is never happy. It can never be enough. I grab my water and take a big gulp.

I stand, "Time to train?"

Asher pauses and glances at me. "We will train with your powers today for a little while. Later today, you must go and train to ride Arion in case there is a battle."

"Ride Arion in a battle?"

He nods, "He will greatly help cut down your enemies in a battle, but you must ensure you do not fall off him in the process."

I bite my lip and look down, swaying leaves back and forth with my hand. I knew I was going to face enemies and fight. I never considered riding Arion in a battle, but it makes sense. I can cover more ground that way, and he can fly. The only thing that makes me uneasy is that I have only ridden Arion four times and I have only ever ridden him. Then add flying on top of that. This will be entertaining for the group to watch, at least.

"Makes sense, but shouldn't I know what power I have? When will we know? Shouldn't I just be able to feel it already or something? We know some of my power relates to nature, but is that it? How will I be ready if we can't figure it out?" Desperation seeps into me.

I feel like time is crashing down, and I won't be fully ready. My desperation is going to drown me.

Then I hear it, a swoosh in the air. I jerk my head up to see what is causing the sound and see that Asher has thrown his dagger at my head! I throw my hands in the air to cover my face from being hit and close my eyes. Please don't hit me, please don't hit me, please don't hit me, I chant in my head. The adrenaline in my body is on high alert. Is this how I am going to die? A dagger to the head?

Clapping comes from Asher's direction. I peel one eye open slowly and then the other and slowly lower my hands. The dagger has halted midair and seems to be frozen. How is this possible? I look around and see that nothing is holding it there. Shock rolls through my entire body, along with fury.

"Why the hell would you do that? You tried to kill me!" I shout at Asher; anger floods my senses. I grab the dagger with my trembling hand out from midair and throw it at the ground by his feet. I stumble to my feet and stalk towards him. I can feel my whole body shaking with anger.

He smirks darkly at me, "I just wanted to see if you had your father's abilities. Seems to me like you do."

"You threw a dagger at my head in hopes that I had my father's ability. What would you have done if I did not? Let me die, you asshole?" I fist my hands to hide my trembling. I'm enraged. I feel like if I don't gain control of my emotions quickly, I will explode.

"I would have stopped it before it hit you. You don't need to worry about that. I will never intentionally harm you, my lady." He lowers his head, half ashamed of what he just did. I sure hope he is ashamed of what he did. His actions are careless and reckless.

"You are a piece of work. I hope you know that!" I shout at him, pushing his chest. I'm fuming, so I know what is best right now is for me to leave. So, I storm off towards the cafe. I'm done training for today. I will not allow myself to make irrational decisions. I need to hold myself to a higher standard if I am going to become the High Lady of the Emerald Court.

The walk back to the cafe is a quick one. I'm so focused on my anger rather than on my surroundings. I storm into the cafe, furious, and slam the door shut. Dani is standing in the middle of the cafe. She narrows her eyes and glares at me.

"What in the world did my door ever do to you?" She says firmly, crossing her arms.

"I'm sorry, Dani. I didn't mean to slam the door. I hope you saved one of those muffins for me. I need it right about now." I freeze in place as embarrassment falls on me for my behavior. There could have been a customer inside the cafe, and here I am, storming in and slamming doors.

"Let me get you something to help calm yourself. Take a seat and cool down," Dani nods towards a chair. Dani turns and walks towards the kitchen.

I slowly make my way over to the chair and slump down in it. I drop my face into my hands, trying to collect myself, and let my anger fizzle. I take a controlled breath in, then exhale slowly. Hillary comes out of the bathroom and walks towards me. She sits down in the chair beside me. I can't look her in the eyes because she heard the scandal I created out here. She reaches over and rubs my back. She does not say anything for a few minutes. She lets me feel what I need to and pass the feelings I need to pass.

"Are you okay?" she questions quietly, her hand brushing my shoulder.

I take a deep breath before answering. "Asher makes me so mad with his stupid tactics."

"Tactics for what?" Concern fills her voice.

I slowly raise my face out of my hands and look over at her, "Seeing if I have certain abilities. Asher threw a dagger at my head to see if I had the same powers as my father. Thank the gods I did, but still."

"That sounds scary. Do you think he would ever truly harm you, though?" she tilts.

"No," I murmur. I know he would never truly harm me, and part of me is mad at myself for getting so upset over this.

"Okay, and do you think he has your best interest at heart?"

"Yes." I sigh.

Dani strolls out of the kitchen with a plate in her hand. The plate is filled with delicious-tasting muffins. My mouth begins to water, and I have to swallow my saliva.

"Well, honey, we may disagree with his tactics, but I doubt he would have allowed anything to happen to you. I understand your frustration, and I would feel the same way. However, I know he is just trying to prepare you quickly. He wants what is best for his people and for you." Dani says as she sets the plate down on the table.

"Yeah. I think you are right." I look up at her, our eyes looking.

"Just be open with him. He has grown up training to be a warrior his whole life. He never really learned how to treat a woman. He needs a little guidance. He needs someone to teach him. Maybe he needs someone to push back and test him."

"I don't even think he knows how to be someone's friend!" I chuckle, tension releasing from my chest. "You must be as amazing as me even to tolerate you." I mimic Asher the best that I can.

Laughter spills out from all three of us.

"Your impression of him was perfect, and I don't even know him that well." Hillary giggles.

"I love you ladies! You know how to brighten my spirits." I embrace Dani and Hillary at the same time. "Okay, I'm going to go back. I must train and master these powers even if Asher is frustrating."

"Don't forget to eat your muffin first. I can't promise you there will be anything left after this." Dani nods towards the plate and chuckles.

"Oh yes!" I snatch one off of the plate and stuff it into my mouth. I moan as I chew. "This is amazing," I say with a mouth full of muffins. My eyes close, and I chew it slowly. This is so much better than what it smells. I see why they are so loved!

"If this happens to be the only thing I can eat for the rest of my life, then I'm fine with that!" I chirp, grabbing another muffin from the plate and devouring it.

I walk towards the door and exit. Asher and I collide as I turn the corner.

"Ouch." I begin to fall back. Asher reaches out quickly, grasping my waist to prevent me from falling. We both stand there, with his hand around my waist, staring at each other. My breath hitches as warmth spreads through my body, and I feel a tingle in my skin where our bodies are touching.

"Um, you can let me go now." I cough, clearly shaken at how being this close to him makes me feel.

"Oh, my apologies, my lady." He lets go quickly. The warmth evaporates immediately.

I clear my throat. "I was on my way back out to apologize to you. I should not have allowed myself to get that upset over your actions, as scary as they are. I understand that we are losing precious time by the minute, and I need to be ready or at least know what I need to learn once we get to Eldermyst. If I have no idea what magic lives in me, then you have no idea how to help train me. So, I'm sorry for storming off. However, I'm not sorry for overreacting, though."

The look in his eyes is a look of pure surprise. He lifts a hand and scratches the top of his head. "Oh, um, I was coming to apologize too."

I cross my arms, "Continue." This will be good.

"I should not have thrown something at your head."

"A dagger, you mean. You should not have thrown a weapon that could kill me at my head?"

"Yeah, that. I'm sorry about that. This time crunch is overwhelming, and like you said, we don't have much time. This is not a fight we can afford to lose either, for the sake of our people and land." His eyes shift away from me. He rocks back and forth on his feet, placing his hands in his pocket.

I truly understand where he is coming from. This is not just about me; it is so much bigger than that. It seems like he has taken on the weight of all of Eldermyst. He is taking on a burden that is too big to carry alone. An overwhelming sense to help him rushes over me. I want to share the burden with him; I don't want him to face this by himself.

I extend my hand toward him. "Truce. We are a team. You will not carry this burden alone." My voice shakes, and tears fill my eyes. The emotions of releasing this anger toward him and calling a truce are overpowering.

His eyes shoot up to mine, shock is written on his face briefly, and then the facade comes back into place. He looks down at my extended hand and back up to my face. A soft smile creeps onto his face, and he reaches out and grabs my hand. We stand there shaking hands and staring into each other's eyes. Warmth creeps down my spine, tingling the nerves. I snap out of my daze and pull my hand back.

"Let's try this again." I begin to take off, walking back to the woods. I stop and turn back. "I want you to know that I still think you are an asshole." I smile widely and continue walking.

"Can we call it a day?" I pant, bending over. My eyes look up towards Asher's. I grin widely at the sight of him sweating. He finally broke a sweat!

"Yes, we can call it a day." He inhales sharply.

I flop down on the ground and lean against a tree. "Oh, thank goodness." I lean my head back and close my eyes. I need to catch my breath before I can do anything else.

We just spent the last four hours training. I made a small tree pop out of the ground and caused the tree to move a few feet. I'm getting a better handle on grasping my power from deep within. I don't have to think about it as much. Asher says, it is like my power is buried in the ground, and I have to dig until I can reach it. Once I have dug deep enough, I will not have to dig again. After that, we moved on to fighting. I blocked quite a few of Asher's strikes in hand-to-hand combat. I even struck him a couple of times. I think I caught him off guard, and he was pleasantly surprised that I hit him.

After hand-to-hand combat, we worked with the sword, learning how to swing it and where to strike my enemies. The sword feels light in my hand like I'm holding a feather. It fits perfectly in my grips like it is meant for me.

"You're a fast learner," Asher says.

"I must have a decent teacher then." I laugh.

Asher's laughter rings out, and I'm as enchanted as the first time I heard it. The sound is enchanting, and I find myself wanting to hear more. Gradually, his laughter fades away.

"Why don't you laugh much?" My eyebrows furrow, and I'm curious why he is always so serious.

"Um.... My life has been about training and waiting for your return. I never really had the time or reason to laugh. After my parents died, all happiness was sucked out of my life." His head drops.

His words cut like a knife. It pains me to know that so many people have been preparing for my return, and I was living carefree. It hurts even more to hear that his parents died, and it stripped him of all his joy. I can't imagine a loss like that, losing both parents. My chest constricts at the realization of what my people have suffered. As I inhale deeply, a newfound determination flourishes in my chest. I want better for my people, especially for Asher.

"You should laugh more." I place a hand on his shoulder.

"Why?" he asks, his head still hanging low.

"One, because it is good for you, and two, because I say so. Lastly, I would love to hear your laugh more often," I say, my stomach drops. What on earth did I say?

Asher gazes at me, motionless and silent. He is taken aback momentarily by my response, then his demeanor changes. His eyes darken to a steely shade, with smoke curling beneath his irises. "Is there anything else you require of me, my High Lady?" he asks, smirking. My cheeks begin to flush at the sound of his sultry voice.

He has always referred to me as "my lady," but now, for the first time, he calls me "High Lady." A part of me likes the title, yet another part fills with dread at the weight that the title brings. And why must he say it in that manner? I need to leave immediately because a sense of unease overwhelms me. I stumble to my feet quickly.

"That's it, just laugh more. I'm heading back to the cafe," I say as I jog away, attempting to escape the awkward situation I've found myself in.

CHAPTER TWENTY-NINE

Asher

I sit on the small bench outside the cafe, waiting for Alona to emerge for our run. I have accompanied her on her runs the last few mornings. I enjoy not running alone. She is not overbearing and doesn't need to fill the space with meaningless words as we run. I look up at the morning sky, and the smell floats right to me. I inhale deeply, knowing right away what Dani is making inside. She's making the one thing I loved so much as a child. I haven't had one of those muffins since my parents died.

A wave of pain crashes into me at the thought of them being gone. My parents were killed right in front of my eyes. I rub my face, trying to rid the memories from my mind. The front door swings open, and the smell hits me full blast: brown sugar, cinnamon, apples, and butter. Alona steps outside and sees me. I stare at the sky, trying to wrangle in my memory; however, the overwhelming feeling of sharing it with her overcomes me.

"They are making Stella's Muffins?"

"How did you know?" Surprise rings in her voice.

I chuckle on the inside at her reaction. Does she think I don't enjoy sweets? I slowly take my eyes away from the sky and look at her, feeling a soft smile creep on my face.

"I love Stella's Muffins. As a child, my parents only allowed me to have one per week. They thought they were too sugary for me. However, Dani used to sneak me some while my parents weren't looking. They were my favorite thing to eat as a child." I feel my voice a little shaky as the memory spills from me.

She looks at me, really looks at me, and smiles softly.

"They must be amazing then." She replies

One moment, I was staring at the sky, and then the next moment, my memory was slipping from my lips. I confide in Alona a childhood memory that I try to ignore. I don't know what possessed me to share that with her. I don't particularly like talking about my parents. It is too painful for me. I don't wish to be reminded of their horrific death. Disappointment in myself leaks into my soul; there is no time for being weak.

Once I regain my senses, I clear my throat, "Let's go. There is no time to stand around." Slamming my mask back in place, I realize I can't be open with her. She doesn't care, and it's not her problem anyway. I turn and jog off, leaving her behind.

As I'm jogging, I try hard to slam out the memories of my parents. The less I think about them, the better. There is no room for emotion, no room for grieving.

Alona catches up to me, running. She runs alongside me the rest of the way in silence. She knows I don't want to speak about it, so she doesn't push it. I respect and understand that. I feel miserable with the way that I treated her. I know she doesn't deserve to be dumped on and then kicked.

We run for longer than we have ever run. She follows me without a word. I push myself more and more to forget what happened and what I dug up from the past.

I can hear her panting, and I know her limit is close. I could have pushed her more but decided against it. I turn down the road leading us to the forest path. The exact path that we take every day.

I wonder what her reaction will be once we get to Eldermyst. I wonder how she will react to the Emerald Court. She loves this forest so much. However, this forest is nothing compared to the ones in the Emerald Court. The forest there has so many varieties of trees that live in unison. They are massive, and it almost seems like they are touching the heavens when you look up from the ground. You can feel them alive, humming. As you walk through the forest in the Emerald Court, you can hear the creaking of the trees swaying back and forth, talking to each other. The colors are not only of the trees but also of everything, which is so much more profound and rich. This human realm is so muted and bleak. Sometimes, I feel like life is slowly fading here when I think of Eldermyst in comparison. There is no comparison at all. Eldermyst is more stunning and alive in every single way and then more.

Arriving in the forest, she slumps down on the ground, panting. Alona opens her eyes and exclaims that she has run farther. Her excitement about running farther this time makes something bloom in my chest. Pride in her accomplishments looks good on her. I need to stay focused, so I taunt her to get her to start training.

"Yeah, you can run even farther if you try harder." My words came a little harsher than I had planned. I can see a flash of pain in the depths of her eyes, and then it quickly fades.

She stands up. "Time to train?" She says flatly.

"We will train with your powers today for a little while. Later today, you must go and train to ride Arion in case there is a battle." Tallying everything in my mind that we need to work on.

"Ride Arion in a battle?" Surprise is written all over her features.

"He will greatly help cut down your enemies in a battle, but you must ensure you do not fall off him."

Did she think he would not be with her for a battle? She must not fully understand their bond then, at least not yet. Once we cross into Eldermyst, everything will snap into place, and she will fully understand. She is bonded to him, and he is to her. They will never be apart, and the bond will not allow it for too long. The only thing that will separate them will be death.

I listen to her, questioning how she would know what powers she will have. I understand her desperation. She wants to learn just as much as I do. We need to know how to train her. I see her internal conflict written all over her face. Her eyes begin to well up, and she slams them shut.

I don't know how to help her. If I were training one of my soldiers and they reacted like this, then I would throw something at them. I take my dagger and throw it without thinking. She has the same powers as her mother. Why wouldn't she have the same or similar powers as her father? The council, the High Lord, and the Lady of the Emerald Court all believed that Alona was the key. They thought that she would save the world. They suspected that she would be powerful. So, there is something inside of her that can stop my dagger from hitting her. If not, then I will have to stop it.

The moment the dagger left my hand, her head jerked up. Horror fills her deep emerald green eyes. She throws her hands up in reaction, and then the dagger stops. It floats inches from her arms that are blocking her face. I can feel the wind whipping around the dagger, so she must be in command of the wind. She did it, though! Now we know what other power we need to train.

I clap my hands, letting her know that she stopped the dagger. She snaps to look at me, rage simmering beneath her eyes.

"Why the hell would you do that? You tried to kill me." She shouts.

"I just wanted to see if you had your father's abilities. It seems to me you do," I respond, pleased to have uncovered more information about her abilities.

"You threw a dagger at my head in hopes that I had my father's ability. What would you have done if I did not? Let me die, you asshole?" I can see the slight tremor in her hand as she fists them close. She is distraught and has every right to be. I don't want her to think I would have allowed the dagger to kill her; no, that is not a part of my duty. I take my duty very seriously.

Unfortunately, sometimes, that is how soldiers train, putting their lives on the line to learn. I grew up like that, and brute force is used to train your magic. It was how most warriors trained. It helped prepare us for battle as well. However, I grew up with magic and fae, and she did not. I can only imagine how complicated things must be in her mind trying to navigate a new world that you are yet to see, simply having to go based on the words of others.

"I would have stopped it before it hit you. You don't need to worry about that. I will never intentionally harm you, my Lady." I try to smooth over what I did. Am I proud of myself? Hell no, I'm not. I look away from Alona, unable to look at her in the eyes. She is now agitated, and I don't know how to fix it.

"You are a piece of work. I hope you know that!" Anger laces every single word that lashes out at me. Her strike with her words hit their mark right on my chest. I reach up to grab my chest, tension building inside. I was wrong, and we both knew I was wrong. She storms off towards the cafe, I guess.

I want to follow up to apologize, but if I do, I may not live to see tomorrow. I slump against the tree, taking deep breaths, trying to calm the tension in my chest. This can't be the one thing that takes me out of this world. I would be highly disappointed.

I know that throwing a dagger at her was not the smartest thing in the world, but I also knew I wouldn't allow it to hurt her. It was still careless.

I close my eyes and lean my head back. She left minutes ago. I wonder when this will pass. Will she be angry for the rest of the day? Rest of the week? Who knows, but I know I need to apologize to her. I slowly lean forward and rise to my feet. I drag my feet back to the cafe, trying to figure out what to say to her.

The night sky is beautiful, even for the human realm, with the sparkling stars. I needed to get out and try to relax a little. So, I decided to come to the meadow. I find a clear spot where I lay down and fold my hands under my head, gazing at the open sky. The flowers are casting dancing shadows in the moonlight. The breeze softly swaying them back and forth brings the floral scent straight to my nose. I soak in my surroundings, enjoying a bit of the human realm before leaving.

Today was a difficult day, for sure. First, you had me share a personal childhood memory with Alona. Then I threw a dagger at her head. I honestly do not know what came over me today. Her presence is intoxicating, and it makes me do irrational things. It makes me want to open up and tell her the dark skeletons hiding in my closet. I must be going crazy. I also know time is essential, and we are running out quickly. I need to get my shit straight and stop allowing her to affect me so much.

I exhale and shake my head. Seriously, what was I thinking? I don't know if I can forgive myself for it. I replay what happened today in my mind.

A smile creeps on my face as I think about what she said. "I want you to know that I still think you are an asshole." Her smile was radiant. If that smile were the last thing I would see in this lifetime, I would die happy. My heart skips a beat, and a small kernel of warmth grows. I bring my hand to rub my chest.

I have never had someone have such a significant impact on me as she does.

CHAPTER THIRTY

Roots

ALONA

The morning air is fresh. I can feel the sun kissing my face. We venture deeper into the forest this morning to train.

"Stand still and concentrate." Asher snaps.

"I'm standing still!" I narrow my eyes at him and shout back. Irritation begins to tighten in my chest.

"No, you're not. I can see you moving."

"Now you are being ridiculous," I mutter quietly.

"What did you say?"

"I'm doing my best; I don't need you breathing down my neck the entire time! Get lost somewhere over there for now." I gesture off in the distance. It's hard to concentrate around him for several reasons without having him dictate everything on top of it. He glares at me and turns to walk away. I sigh; maybe now I can practice.

When we first started training, I had no clue how to access my powers, let alone what my powers were. Then Asher told me one day to envision accessing it. I tried, and he was right, so I did just that. The thing that came to mind was a water well. One throws a bucket into a well to pull up water. Over the past few days, I've found that by envisioning jumping into the well, I bring up more power.

I relax my arms at my sides and close my eyes. I concentrate on diving into the well of power. I plunge into the hole and can feel myself falling. I fall until I hit a cushion and know that I landed on the surface of my power. I bend over, wrap my arms around as much as possible, and jump upward. As soon as my feet hit the ground outside the well, I feel the power humming inside me, tingling throughout my entire body. I let my mind empty completely, letting the power run through my veins. I inhale deeply and picture tree roots shooting out from the ground. I open my eyes and extend my hand, and what I envisioned happens before my eyes. The extensive root system juts from the ground, shooting high in the air. I see Asher, with his back facing me, so I will the root to reach out and graze his shoulder. The moment the root is feet away, he jumps out of the way and turns to face me.

The root races back to the hole it shot out from, and I lower the walls I have trained to have up. I focus on Asher and his emotions, zoning in on his feelings. They hit me like a brick wall, irritation, anxiety, pride, and desire. I focus on that last emotion, desire. It's intoxicating and inviting.

I lowered my wall to see if I could use his emotions to my advantage; however, it ended as a disadvantage. I'm so focused on his feelings that I don't see him run toward me and lunge. My brain snaps back to reality with Asher only feet away. My body is still humming with power, so I throw my hands up, creating a wall between Asher and myself. Asher comes to a halt inches from the wall of roots and leaves.

"Why did you get distracted?" He barks behind the wall.

"I didn't!" I throw my hands up and begin to stalk away. Some days, I feel like we are becoming friends, and others, like today, I feel like our relationship is taking ten steps back. He can be so over and harsh on me that it becomes hard to deal with. I'm trying my best, but he doesn't see that. I just learned that I had powers, and I'm trying to learn how to use them in a world that stifles magic.

"Allowing yourself to get distracted will kill you," Asher grunts.

Stephanie emerges from behind a tree, clapping. "That was truly amazing! You are getting the hang of your power!"

"Thank you! What's up?" I accidentally bite out a little too harshly.

"Well, you have been working so hard recently in training. I wanted to take you out for a picnic." She throws her hands up in surrender out of fear of me biting her head off.

"That sounds wonderful! I'm free now!" I throw a disgruntled look toward Asher, then look back to Stephanie.

"Let's go then!" She links her arm with mine and leads me back to the street. I take deep breaths, letting the anger flow out of me. This will be a good day, and I won't let him ruin it.

CHAPTER THIRTY-ONE

The Courts

ALONA

Stephanie found this meadow last week while she was on a run. When we arrived, I was speechless. It is a beautiful day out. The sun is just the perfect temperature, and the meadow is filled with wildflowers of all different colors. If heaven existed, this is what part of it would look like.

Stephanie and I lay a blanket down on the ground and then sit. The soft breeze brushes through my hair, carrying the scent of recently bloomed wildflowers. The sun kisses my uncovered arms, leaving a warmth on my skin. Today is perfect for a picnic and enjoying a little time off. We have been so busy with training and preparing for our trip. We have not had much time to relax. I extend my arms behind me and lean back, throwing my head back and allowing the sun to kiss my face. Stephanie unpacks chicken salad sandwiches, chips, Capri Suns, and chocolate chip cookies. We munch on our food between conversations.

"Thank you so much for suggesting we have a picnic." I smile.

"Your life would be boring without me." She teases.

"Whatever would I do without you," I remark sarcastically, rolling my eyes. She winks at me, and we continue munching on our lunch.

"Do they have these in Eldermyst?" I hold up a Capri Sun.

"Nope," she shakes her head with a smile.

"Aww darn! I love these things!"

"When I first saw them, I was so confused. Then I tried them, and yes, I agree with you—they are good!" Stephanie chirps.

"What is Eldermyst like?" I sit up, curious if it's similar to the human realm.

"Well, there are six courts."

"Only six?"

She takes a bite of her sandwich and nods her head. Once she chews her food and swallows it, she answers. "Yes. There is the Emerald Court, Ivory Court, Amethyst Court, Obsidian Court, Cerulean Court, and Solonia Court." She takes a sip from her Capri Sun.

"Is each court big?" trying to grasp the size of the country as a whole.

"Each Court varies. Most are about the size of four to five states. The Emerald Court, however, is the largest of them all. It equals about eight states."

"Oh wow! That is bigger than I thought! I thought each of them was the size of one human state. Are there cities or towns in each Court?"

"Yep!" She picks up a chip and pops it in her mouth, crunching it between her teeth.

"My mother went and oversaw each of those towns?" Amazement blankets me. If the Emerald Court were that big, she would still care so much about her people and spend all that time visiting each town.

"Yes, she did. She was one of the best High Ladies Eldermyst has ever had." a smile reaches her eyes.

"Those are big shoes that I will have to fill then." Anxiety starts to nibble at my chest.

"Yeah, but you came from the woman with those big shoes, so you will fit right into them," plopping another chip in her mouth. As I eat my sandwich, I look out at the meadow and the abundant wildflowers. How did I never know about this place before?

"What is each Court like?"

"The Ivory Court is always cold; a white blanket of freshly fallen snow nestles on top of everything. You can hear the soft crunch of snow as you walk through the Court. Icicles hang from the branches of trees and off roofs of homes; soft sunlight glistens through them, causing a light rainbow to dance on the ground. It is the perfect Christmas Wonderland, as humans call it. Oh, and the smell of fresh, damp pinecones." She inhales deeply and smiles. "It is beautiful, especially if you like the cold and snow. The castle there is not huge. It's made of ice and glass. Part of the structure is inside the mountain, the Ivorian Mountains. You would think that would make it feel like an icehouse. The funny part is, despite it being cold and icy, the castle is always pleasant and toasty. They make a delicious hot chocolate with cocoa, cinnamon, oatmeal, and honey. It's perfect for curling up under a blanket beside the fire and reading a book. "

"Okay, I have never really experienced snow, but I am all for cuddling up next to a fire to read a book!"

"Right? It's perfect for reading, and then add one of their amazing hot chocolates, and you're in heaven." Stephanie beams.

"What about the others? Are they similar?"

"The Obsidian Court is the opposite. There is always an overcast, causing the skies to be a muted gray color, vacant of the sunlight. It's warmer since it's close to the volcanos and lava. Some volcanos scatter throughout their lands. Some volcanos have been simmering there longer than I have been alive. While you are close to the volcanos, you can hear the hissing and bubbling sounds coming from inside. The sulfur smell is so strong that it singes my nostrils, and I can only handle it for so long. It is quite a sight to see, though, for a few minutes. Thankfully, the castle is not next to a volcano. The Obsidian Court is for sure a dark and gloomy court and can feel like it's going to suck the life out of you. Despite the harsh environment, the people there are not evil; on the contrary, they are very kind and full of life. They are accustomed to the gloominess of the Court; however, they don't let that drag them down. I have visited there a few times. The castle is quite a dark beauty. The walls and floors are made out of polished black marble. The High Lady of the Court sits on a white marble throne. Zara loves dramatic effects, so she insisted on the throne being white. Setting that aside, she is truly kind. If you walk through the castle, you will stumble upon the hidden garden inside. The High Lady spends a lot of time there tending to the garden. It is magnificent and so lush. The flowers are dark, and you can't find them in other courts. I will have to take you there to see it."

"Oh, so it is the opposite of the Ivory Court!" I picture what it looks like in my mind. I have only ever seen volcanoes in books and movies. I can imagine the heat that emanates from them. The mental image feels so real I can feel sweat beading on the back of my neck as if I were there. "I hope the other are not the same."

"Not at all. The Solonia Court starkly contrasts the Ivory and the Obsidian Courts. It is always so bright and sunny. I don't think it ever gets truly dark there, just overcast when it is nighttime. It reminds me of a summer day here, warm and vibrant. The skies are bright blue, with clouds dancing around. There are fields and fields of sunflowers outside of the castle and surrounding town. It is so beautifully green with pops of colors from the flowers that fill the air with wonderful scents. It can get a little hot, but it is the perfect weather for swimming in the cool springs throughout the Court. The castle sits atop a hill, a beacon for all to see, surrounded by a busy town. There are houses, shops, schools, and so much more. The Solonia Court has some of the greatest artist galleries, though. There are many colors, and I'm sure they use them as inspiration. Along the border of the Solonia Court, there is a beautiful forest, and you may feel like you have to enter, but it is highly recommended that you stay clear of it."

"Why?"

"If you want to keep your life, you will stay out. There are wild animals that roam that forest. The Solonia Court has bargained with them: no one will enter the forest and bother them and their ways of living, and they will not terrorize the Court. "

"Oh! Has anyone entered?"

"I know of a few that have, but they never came back out." I swallow my saliva. "That does not sound like a place I will be entering."

Stephanie laughs and shakes her head very dramatically. "The Cerulean Court is beautiful. It's surrounded by ocean. The castle sits on a cliff overlooking the endless, clear blue water, the beach, and the nearby town. It is truly breathtaking. The scents of sea salt and seaweed consume the air. It is peaceful there, watching the waves gently crawl up the shore. It is a great getaway, especially if you need to unwind. Long walks on the beach will leave you so refreshed, you will come back a new person." Stephanie laughs. "You can stand on the edge of the balcony in the castle, and it almost feels like you are flying because it hangs over the water."

"Wait, so the balcony is just hanging off the cliff?"

"Yes!! The balcony floor is made of glass, so you see the waves crashing into the cliff when you look down. It's terrifying yet exhilarating at the same time."

"Is that even safe to stand on?" my jaw drops.

Stephanie throws her head back and laughs. "Yes, it never breaks. There is magic that keeps it in one piece."

"Um... okay. I imagine it's a spectacular view, though."

"It is truly breathtaking."

"Are there any towns close by?"

"The town close by is a quaint little town. There is nothing overly amazing about it, but it has a homey feeling. The people are so welcoming. When we go, they will all want you to try their food, and I promise you that you will try the most amazing seafood you've ever tried there."

"I have never seen the ocean, so I will want to visit there!"

"We will have to take a vacation there once life has returned to how it is meant to be." Her smile doesn't reach her eyes, and I know she is referring to me being able to regain the Emerald Court. My chest tightens at the thought of the journey that lies ahead. It's daunting, but I will make it to the end. I will tell myself that every single day until it becomes true.

Silence lingers between us for a moment before I clear my throat. "Yeah. What about the other courts?"

"Right, the other courts. Well, there's the Amethyst Court. It's a court of endless meadows blooming with wildflowers. The colors of all the flowers are boundless. The scent of blossoms, water, and moss drifts along the breeze. You can see rolling hills as far as the eye can see. The climate remains warm all year. Gentle rivers that meander through the Court are perfect for dipping one's feet and relaxing. This is the Court where new life is born. The castle is covered in vines and roses, creating a spectacular sight. Many of the people that live in this Court will be found barefoot. They love the feel of the ground there, the soft dirt and grass between their toes. The wildlife there is small, also like birds and squirrels here. They will approach you if they are not afraid of you."

As Stephanie speaks, I nibble at my sandwich, trying to imagine the Court she's describing. A place that I have seen in my dreams. Thinking about it, I believe I have seen glimpses of each of them in my dreams over the years. The realization hits me like a semitruck. Eldermyst is woven into me. You may take me out of my country, but you can't take my country out of me.

"What about the Emerald Court?" I turn to face her.

"The Emerald Court is by far the greatest of them all. I may be a bit biased, but it is. The weather reminds me of the weather here in the fall time. It is perfectly in between, not too hot nor too cold. There are miles and miles of flowers and trees of all different kinds. You can walk for hours and find a new place every single day. The wildlife is abundant, and you can hear birds singing and insects humming. You will see deer and bears running through the forest. They are different there than here, though. Here, the animals are afraid of humans; there, the animals respect the fae and are not afraid. All life is accepted and respected in the Emerald Court. The small towns are tucked away inside the forest. The people are so happy and full of life. People there are quick to help and slow to point a finger at someone else. Life truly is amazing, and a big part of that is because of your mother. She loved her people fiercely, and they learned to love fiercely, too. Oh, and I can't forget about the castle; it is stunning. It's made out of white and green marble. Vines crawl up so many walls, and trees grow inside the castle in different areas. It's hard to explain; you must see it with your eyes."

I pull my knees up to my chest and wrap my arms around them, setting my chin on my knees. The Emerald Court sounds fantastic, and it is a place I would love to live in. I have dreamed of belonging and living amongst the trees my whole life. I smile now, realizing that I have simply been dreaming of returning to my true home.

"I think I have seen some of these places in my dreams," I say, looking over at her.

"I'm sure you have; they are a part of you. They always have been, even though you did not know. You may be able to take the fae out of their land, but you cannot take the land out of the fae." She smiles widely at her mockery of the human saying. A laugh explodes from deep within my chest.

"I love you," spills from my lips. I bring my hand up to cover my mouth.

"I love you too," she grins, looking back at me. The laughter subdues, and we both sit there staring out at the meadow full of flowers.

"What is your favorite color?" I'm curious to know more things about her. I know so many profound things about her, but not so many mundane things like colors.

"My favorite color? Well, my favorite color is purple. It is more of a deep purple, like plum. I would ask you yours, but I already know it is emerald green." Guilt rides through me. She knows those trivial things about me, yet I don't know that about her.

"What is your favorite food?"

"Hmm... I have to say that my favorite food is Stella's Muffins."

"I had never heard of them until the other day. I don't think there is something similar to them in the human realm."

"I guess it's just a thing from home, but boy, they are to die for, literally. I need to tell Dani to make some more!"

"Deal." I grin at my best friend. I honestly don't know what I would have done without her. She has been a strong rock for me during such chaos and change; she has not hesitated to be there or help.

"What is your favorite holiday?"

"Hmm..." she raises a hand to her chin. She takes a moment to think about the answer to the question. "It would have to be the Autumnal Solstice."

"What is that?"

"Humans know it as Autumn Equinox. It is the time that we thank the land for the abundance she has provided to us over the year. Everyone gets dressed up in their finest, and the people come together. There is a big festival where we sing and dance. Oh, you cannot forget about the food! Oh, there is so much food!"

"That sounds like so much fun!"

"It truly is! We dance and laugh the night away with friends and family. I can't wait until you can be a part of it! We will have so much fun, and the people of the Emerald Court will love for you to be there. You will bring them hope."

"That sounds amazing!" I pause and think about the future that I will have—the people who will be a part of my life and the new responsibilities I will take on. I want to be a part of it. I want to dance the night away with the people of Emerald Court. I want to be a part of their lives. I want to follow in my parents' footsteps.

"Do you have any siblings?"

Stephanie shakes her head no. So, she is an only child.

"What do you want to do with your life?"

She contemplates the answer and then glances at me. "I want to be a Valkyrie and one of the Emerald Court's advisors. "

"Oh?" I tilt my head and look at her.

"I want to be able to make a difference for the best in the lives of my people. I want to make sure that there aren't people like the Dark Orians tormenting the people of Eldermyst. I want to stand for those who can't stand up for themselves. I want to do something that truly matters. I want to live a life that will honor my parents and make them proud." A faint smile forms on her face.

"I completely understand what you mean. You have such a beautiful heart for serving your people, Stephanie. I will be super lucky to have you as one of my counsels. Together, we will live a life that will make our parents proud." My voice shakes slightly. An overwhelming emotion falls upon me. I can't tell if it is her emotions or mine; maybe it is both of ours. The overwhelming need to live a life that will make others proud feels like I can drown in the emotion itself. It is so strong, and that tells me that we are determined enough to make it happen. Stephanie straightens, pretending to bow. I smile at her, gulping down a deep breath, building that mental wall, willing myself to calm the emotions.

"I will be honored." She smiles, eyes sparkling in the light.

"I will need loads of help with this whole court and politics thing."

"As you already know, I will be right by your side." She nods her head in acknowledgment.

"Thank you! That means so much to me to know that I have people like you on my side."

We sit there for a few minutes munching on our remaining lunch, enjoying the beautiful day out.

"Have you ever dated anyone?" I'm curious to see if she's like me with no experience.

"I did for a short period when I was younger. We were young, and I had just lost my parents, and he was there for me."

My eyes widened, and my hand came to cover my mouth. "Oh... my.... Gosh. Was it Asher?"

"Oh, gods no! It was someone you have not met." She laughs.

"Oh, thank the gods!" Relief washes over me.

"Why do you say that? Asher is not a bad choice."

"Have you spoken to him before? The man has a stick permanently up his rear end. He is either cold or thinks too highly of himself. He can be a flat-out jerk."

Stephanie lays back with the force of her laugh that erupts from her. Confusion fills me as to why she is laughing so hard. I didn't say anything funny.

"What is wrong with you?" I bark.

"You are so funny. Asher is not truly as bad as you think he is. He is a nice guy."

I roll my eyes. "You must be confused with who I'm talking about. Asher, the asshole that trains us, that Asher. There is not a single nice bone in his body."

"So, you don't like him? Not even the looks of him?" She raises her eyebrows a few times.

"I will admit that the man is pretty good-looking, but that is all he has going for him. He is so dull when he is not being mean or egotistical. He is always so serious. I don't know why he doesn't smile or laugh more. He is like a stubborn statue with no humor."

"Whatever you say."

I pick up a chip and toss it at her. "Shut up. I swear you're annoying." Shaking my hands in the air.

"I love you too!" She blows a kiss at me. I shake my head in disapproval. I want nothing more than to move on from the topic of Asher.

She looks at me, "But seriously, Asher isn't that bad. When his parents died, he devoted himself to training. He had to become the greatest warrior that ever existed. I think he was avoiding processing the loss of his parents."

I look down at my hands, and a heaviness falls on my chest. That pains me to think of him in pain. I take a few minutes to absorb that information. I inhale deeply, grab my plate of food, and eat.

"What is your favorite song?" I ask, swallowing the chip.

"My favorite song is an Emerald lullaby that has been around for a long time. My mother used to sing it to me when I was a child."

"Can you sing it for me?"

She pauses for a moment, clears her throat, and then nods her head. Pain flashes in her eyes. She straightens and closes her eyes as if trying to recall the song.

"In the Emerald Court,
where the magic thrives,
Love whispers, and the trees come alive,
Hush now, little Emerald,
to sleep, you'll be led,
Through the magical lands, you will tread,
Where the emerald glow paints the starry sky,
Gazing up in a magical meadow, you'll lie,
Magic dancing all around as the night unfolds,
Story of love and beauty in the sky being told,
Sleep, little Emerald, in the Emerald's grace,
Dreams will guide and protect you in this magical place.
Sleep, little Emerald soon, you will see,
Just how magical your life can be."

Her small, quiet voice carries such a powerful song. It's a beautiful lullaby engrained in the Emerald Court's history. Her voice was so delicate, yet there was a hint of sorrow. A sense of sadness mixed with joy slams into me. She sings with so much emotion in her voice. It is a fantastic glimpse into the childhood of all those who call the Emerald Court their home. A song parents sing to their little ones as they are preparing for bed. I'm sure it reminds her of her parents and her people. She has been stripped of her parents and has been away from her people. Silence falls upon us as her singing comes to an end. Stephanie sniffles and raises her hand to rub the tears beginning to form in her eyes. Then, realization dawns on me.

"That is the song Dani hums!" My eyes search hers.

"It is! It's a reminder of home since she has been away for so long."

"It's beautiful," I reach over and grab her hand.

I lay on my bed after a great yet sad afternoon. I loved having the chance to get to know Stephanie more. Yet, some things broke my heart about her past. Dani knocks at the door and peeks her head into my room.

"Hey, how are you?" She says with such cheer in her voice. I sit up,

"Come in." I pat a spot on the bed next to me. Dani comes in and takes a seat next to me. She turns and smiles at me.

"We will be having a dinner tonight. All of us. We must talk."

"Oh?" I say, raising my brows. "Is everything alright?"

"Yes honey, everything is alright. We have some things to discuss about the journey."

"Oh, okay! I will be there then!"

"Okay." Dani smiles and stands up. "Dinner will be ready at 6 pm."

"Do you need help with anything?" I look up at her.

"Honey, you already know my answer. I got it all handled. Just make sure that you are out there at the table at 6 pm. You have 43 minutes." She walks towards the door and exits the room. I lay back down, wanting to rest a little more before the dinner. However, the uncertainty of what we will discuss is eating at the corners of my mind. I'm sure it is about the big journey ahead of us.

CHAPTER THIRTY-TWO

Oath Talk

ALONA

I stroll out of the room at 5:58 pm and walk to the kitchen table. An aroma fills the room of seasoned meat, potatoes, and carrots. My mouth begins to water. Dani is at the counter serving food on the plates. I look over to see if I can help; however, Hillary is just finishing up with the table. She set up five spots: Stephanie, Dani, Hillary, me, and.

"Hello, Alona." A calm, sultry voice rings behind me. Asher. Of course, he would be here. He is a part of this group and tolerable often, but the man knows how to get under my skin.

"Hey," I respond flatly, sighing out loud, hoping he notices my annoyance with his presence.

He nods and strolls to the table with his hands in his pockets. He looks so typical like that, with his hands in his pockets. He usually has his hands in a fist, is ready to fight, or messes around with a dagger. He takes a seat at the table. The front door swings open, and I turn to see who it is. Stephanie comes through the front door with a bright smile on her face. She skips joyfully to the table. She pauses once she gets to my side, giving me a quick hug, then continues to the table and sits down. I follow behind her, taking a seat between Stephanie and Hillary. Dani places plates full of yummy-looking food down on the table. I stare at my plate and inhale the smell of seasoned roast beef, mashed potatoes, and steamed broccoli and carrots.

Dani is the last one to take a seat. Once she sits down, we all start to dig into our food, unable to resist much longer. The moans begin to escape everyone's lips shortly after.

"God, this is amazing, Dani," Hillary moans as her eyes roll. "I second that," I say in agreement, stuffing another fork into my mouth. Dani chuckles and continues eating. Everyone eats in silence because of how good the food is. We are so focused on enjoying our dinner rather than talking. That will come later. I fork my last bite into my mouth and set down my fork in disappointment. I bring my napkin up to my face and wipe it off quickly.

I finally look around the table to see everyone else finishing their dinner. I push my chair out and stand up. Since Dani made this fantastic dinner, the least I can do is pick up the dirty plates from the table. I walk around the table, collect all the plates, and walk to the sink. I place them in the sink and begin to wash them.

"Alright, Alona, if you can sit back down," Dani calls me. I quickly turn and grab a dish towel to dry my hands before returning to the table. I take my seat next to Stephanie. I lean forward, crossing my arms on the table.

"We will be leaving in three days," Dani says and looks around at each of us. "Yes, in three days, we return to Eldermyst."

"How do we get there?" I ask. It has been dancing in my mind recently.

"Well, not far from where the stables are, there is this door, you may call it. It is not visible to the human eye but only to the fae eye. It's about 10 feet wide and 10 feet tall. That is where the two worlds meet. Once we cross it, we will have entered Eldermyst."

"Is it painful to cross the door?" my voice shakes.

"Well, honey, it will give you a good zapping, that's for sure." Dani chuckles. "But it isn't anything that you can't handle."

"I guess." I laugh nervously.

"We will travel through a hidden path back to the Emerald Court. We want to avoid encountering anything unexpected or the Dark Orians. Since we are taking the hidden path, reaching the Emerald Court will take us a little longer. We will have to cross through most of the courts." Asher declares.

"That is fine though. As we pass each court, we will try to gain allies." Stephanie responds.

"You will need to train along the way. It will be much different for you there. You will gain full access to your powers, so you must train how to control them. Without mastering that, you can't expect other courts to aid you." Asher bites, ignoring Stephanie's comment. He glares at me. I know he is getting anxious as each day gets closer, wanting me to discover and master my powers.

"Have I not been doing that already?" I snap back, annoyance rising in my chest.

"Yes, but on a much smaller level. The training here will greatly help you, but you will have much more power to control there. We want you to be as prepared and as protected as possible. Arion will gain his full powers as well. The bond between you two will fully snap into place as soon as we cross that line." Stephanie chimes in, trying to ease the tension in the room.

"Also, once we cross into Eldermyst, those who chose to pledge their service to you can do so," Dani says, clearing her throat and trying to change the subject altogether.

"Wait, what?" I stutter.

"We may have briefly mentioned this before, but those who want to pledge their lives to serve you can do so. Most of the time, this will be those close to you, such as personal guards, court counselors, etc. I pledged my service to your mother." Dani smiles at me.

"What do they have to do? What happens after?" I question.

"To pledge themselves, they must slice their hand; you slice yours, and the blood must intertwine. That seals the oath, and then your wish is their command. They are bound to obey and protect you." Stephanie responds.

"What is the oath?" Hillary says for the first time in several minutes. I know she has a lot she is trying to take in, just like me. I nod in agreement with her question, wanting to learn as well. Asher leans forward in his chair, resting his elbows on his knees.

Closing his eyes, he declares, "I vow to honor and protect the High Lady of the Emerald Court, to uphold her well-being even at the cost of my life. I will serve her loyally and honorably for all the days of my life. To my High Lady of the Emerald Court, I pledge my oath to be upheld until death takes me from this world."

The room falls silent. I'm processing the Oath that Asher just said. They will protect and honor me with their life, even if that means death. My chest tightens, and it is hard to breathe.

"I'm unsure how I feel about this: the oath and all. I don't want to restrict people from living their own lives. I don't want anyone chained to me." I lower my face into my hands, trying to regain control over my breathing. People will gladly take the oath, but I want them free. I don't want to pin them down and stick to me. A war is going on in my mind, and I don't know which side is winning. I would love to have them in my circle, but I don't want them to lose their life over me.

"It's not as you think. As I've said, I pledged my life to your mother, and I didn't lose my own life and identity. Pledging one's life doesn't mean giving up living for yourself. It signifies a promise not to harm and to offer protection when summoned. It's not solely for your benefit; it also benefits the one who gave the oath. Those who pledge themselves to the High Lady or Lord are 'enchanted,' as we call it. They become tougher to kill, their powers intensify, and they heal quicker than usual." Dani soothes, a gentleness in her eyes.

I nod my head, trying to piece everything together in my head.

"Do any of you plan on taking this oath?" I look around at each of them, scanning their faces for any hesitation or doubt. They all nod their heads, including Hillary. What if I am not enough for them? I bounce my leg on the floor, trying to stop myself from letting anxiety consume me.

"It's our choice to take the oath, and it is your choice to accept it. Before you say no, I think you should hear us out." Stephanie assures.

"Okay." I nod.

Hillary turns towards me to speak first. "I think I should be the first one to respond. You know I have nothing special, no spectacular magic or fighting skills, at least not like the rest. However, this has been something Dani and I have discussed in great detail recently. I wanted to know all there was to know regarding what my life would be like once I crossed into Eldermyst and how it would change. I know that part of me thinks this is all still some sick joke someone is playing. It is hard to wrap my mind around all of this. But the other part of me is at peace. I'm at peace with my decision on this journey. I also think that I was made for this.

Something in my bones calls me to you and everyone in this room. I may be a simple human without magical powers, but I should be there for you. So, I would like to make that step by taking the oath once I can."

"I want to take the oath as well, cousin." Stephanie nods her head. "My mother and father served your parents for most of their lives. The bond that was there between them was so complex yet so beautiful. I know you will fill your mother's shoes and do even more than she did. I want to be a part of that, a part of your growth. I want to be in your life always." A smile spreads across her face, her pearly whites shining.

"You know I will also be taking the oath. I served your mother, and it is only right that I serve you," Dani says.

"My High Lady, I would be honored to serve you. I want to take the oath and serve you until my last breath as your Captain of the Royal Guards. My father served as the Captain of the Royal Guards under your parents. I want to follow in his footsteps," Asher offers, something like hope flickers in his eyes. My heart begins pounding fiercely in my chest.

I take a sharp breath and sit straight, holding my chin high. "I would be honored if you all were sworn to me. I promise to do everything I can to protect and bring peace back to the Emerald Court." I feel every word that comes out of my mouth deep in my soul. Silence fills the room as the words exchanged between all of us settle.

"So how will it be done? All at once?" I ask. Dani glances around the room, her eyes landing on Asher.

He clears his throat, "I was hoping I could take my oath now."

"Now? Here?"

"Asher is the strongest, and his magic can bond outside Eldermyst." Dani gazes at Asher. I look at him. I shift in my seat and roll my neck, trying to release a fraction of my tension.

"Okay," my voice shakes.

He stands up and kneels in front of me. His eyes lock with mine. He pulls a dagger from his sheath, his eyes never leaving mine. He opens his palm and drags the dagger across.

"I vow to honor and protect the High Lady of the Emerald Court, to uphold her well-being even at the cost of my life. I will serve her loyally and honorably for all the days of my life. To my High Lady of the Emerald Court, I pledge my oath to be upheld until death takes me from this world and away from her." My chest tightens. Something is lingering in those last few words, something left unspoken.

He reaches for my hand, and I hold it out for him. He nods for reassurance before dragging the dagger across my palm. I nod in return, fighting to keep my hand from shaking. He slowly cuts across my palm, and I wince at the pain that follows the blade. I look down and see bubbles of blood sprouting from the cut. Slowly, more blood begins to collect in my hand. My hand trembles more as he lifts his bloody hand to grasp mine.

His eyes search mine for any regret or change in decision, but he won't find it. I'm honored to have this group pledge an oath to me whether I feel worthy. Our hands intertwine, and the air knocks right out of me. A warm sensation builds in our hands and begins to climb up my arm. I look at our hands and see a light exploding from between our clasped hands. The warmth creeps up, reaching my heart and climbing up my neck. My heart pounds furiously in my chest, and I grasp my chest with my free hand. I breathe slow and deep, trying to center myself. Then, the warmth reaches my head, and it feels like an explosion goes off. My ears start ringing, and I feel dizzy. I look at Asher and see his head bowed and eyes closed. Worry flutters in my chest. Is he alright? I reach my hand out and cup his cheek. His eyes dart to mine, and then everything stops. Time freezes, and it's just me and him. His eyes are glowing, and

I have never seen anything more beautiful. The pain fizzles away, and I can see now. I feel the tension releasing, and I drop my shoulders. I know I should say something, but the words can't seem to form in my mind.

A smirk forms on Asher's face, "High Lady, now I'm yours."

"Um, okay." Something in his voice tells me that he isn't simply referring to the oath, but what does he mean? I draw my hand from his face and place it on my chest. I sway back in my chair. His eyes go dark, and his smirk fades, his face going back to stone. He drops my other hand, and the warmth evaporates right out of me. My skin begins to tingle uncomfortably at the severance of our contact. He rises and walks back to his chair. I blink several times and look around.

Everyone is staring at me.

"Are you okay?" The concern is written all over Hillary's face as she hands me a rag to clean my hand.

"Yes, I'm good. Thank you, Hillary." I smile at her. I glance at Asher, and his face is emotionless. Did I upset him? Who knows, especially since he is grumpy most of the time anyway. I look around at the others,

"Then what will each of you become? Asher took the oath as Captain of the Royal Guard, but what about the rest of you?"

"Well, that is up to you. You decide what our roles are if we even have a role. However, I must say you know me, and you know I would prefer to stay where I love, in the kitchen." Dani smiles.

"So, like Executive Chef?" I'm not surprised that Dani wants to be in the kitchen. It is her place of peace and comfort.

"Yes," she grins.

"Alright, Executive Chef, it is." I wink at her.

"We can discuss the different court roles if you would like," Dani comments.

I think about all the fantasy books I have read with courts, and something comes to mind. "There are advisors, correct?" I ask Dani.

She nods.

"Then Stephanie, I want you to be my right-hand top advisor. Hillary, I would like for you to be an advisor as well. I know this is a different realm and will take time to learn, but I think you would be a great advisor."

"Oh honey, Eldermyst may be a different realm, but it's similar to Claywood. People are people. And I agree with you that Hillary would make a great advisor. She is filled with so much knowledge and understanding, even if she doesn't let people see that side of her." Dani looks at Hillary as she speaks, truly conveying Hillary's importance and value to us. We all know Hillary thinks less of herself and hasn't allowed her authentic self to shine. Hillary blushes and looks down.

"Would you be okay with that?" I ask her softly. Her gaze meets mine, and she nods. I turn towards Stephanie to hear her response.

"I would be honored, cousin, to be your top advisor. You need me and my knowledge of politics as well." She teases. I rest my elbow on the armrest and place my head in my hand. I smile because everything is slowly coming together.

CHAPTER THIRTY-THREE

Wind

ALONA

I came out to the forest to practice on my own. I don't hate practicing with Stephanie and Asher, but sometimes, I need time to just be alone. I want to sort through my powers and see where they take me. I know that I have a connection to nature—I have a decent enough grasp on that. I also know I inherited my father's magic, which is something I need to explore more.

I stand among the trees, closing my eyes and inhaling deeply, centering myself to see if I can feel it. I jump into the well of power in my mind, plummeting down farther—farther than I have ever gone. I land at the surface, grasp as much power as possible, and bring it back up. Each time I plummet, the rise becomes more accessible and effortless.

I allow my power to surface and consume me, heat coursing through my veins. I empty my mind, trying to sense what more is hiding in the dark. At first, nothing happens. I peel my eyes open, and still nothing comes out. Disappointment settles in my chest. This can't be that hard, considering I did it when I stopped the dagger from hitting my face. I blow out a puff of air and close my eyes once again. Center myself and let my surroundings sink in. The soft creaking of branches above me, the soft breeze caressing my face, leaves scattering on the ground, the soft buzzing as the bees fly by, the smell of moss and damp wood. I slowly let everything sink in, mentally noting each thing I hear, feel, or smell.

I will focus on one thing which may help this work. I run through the image of my surroundings in my mind. Leaves, I am going to have a leaf rise.

"Leaf, I command you to my side," I forcefully say.

A soft breeze caresses my face, blowing my loose strands around. Okay! Maybe this is a start! Perhaps I'm moving something, but the fear prevents me from opening my eyes. I concentrate again, focusing on a leaf, willing it to rise. I can feel beads of sweat forming on the back of my neck. Then I hear it—a rustle of leaves. My eyes fly open, and I check that it is not an animal charging right at me.

"Wow," I mutter softly, taking in the sight before me. Leaves are dancing in the wind right in front of my eyes. The wind rises and brushes across my cheek.

"Thank you for listening," I whisper into the air. The sight of the wind responding to me expands my chest. I feel a jolt of energy and force my eyes shut to try again.

I jump into the well and bring up more power this time. I allow it to fill me, tingling every inch of my body. I inhale deeply and whisper, "Come to me, my friend." I hear the rustling of leaves and feel the brush of wind. I slowly open my eyes, and standing before me takes my breath away. There is a giant wolf created out of leaves. The wind swirls together to make this animal with leaves perfectly placed. If I were farther away and saw this, I would think it was an actual wolf, living and breathing. The wolf lowers its head as if it is bowing to me. I slowly extend my hand, curious by the sight before me. My hand reaches the wolf's face, and I inch it slightly closer. My hand enters the wolf's leafy form, and the wind dances across my wrist. My breath catches, and I grasp my chest. This is amazing! I never in my life thought I would be experiencing this. The wolf looks up at me. Then it hits me: I am moving the leaves with the wind. I am commanding the wind.

I reach the cafe and hurry inside.

"Dani!" I call out, excitement bouncing from one foot to the other.

"Is everything okay?" Dani hurries down the stairs, clutching the hem of her skirt in her fist. Once she reaches the bottom of the stairs, she looks up at me and sighs. "Oh, thank the gods. I thought something was wrong."

I giggle. "I'm sorry! I didn't mean to worry you. Something happened, and I'm so excited to share it with you."

Stephanie comes bolting down the stairs. "Oh, I can't miss this!" She squeals.

"So...."

"Speak, woman! You are going to drive me insane taking so long." Dani scoffs.

"I understand that you said my father's power was connected to the wind. Today, I managed to move something but used the wind to move it."

"Wait, what did you move? Spill the beans." Stephanie bounces back and forth.

"Well, I wanted to try and figure out my powers so that I can be somewhat prepared once we leave. So I decided to walk down to the forest...."

Stephanie interrupts with a cough. "As always," a smirk plasters her face.

Rolling my eyes, I continue telling my story. "So, as I was saying, I attempted to redo what I did the day Asher threw the dagger at my head. I shut my eyes, putting all my focus and energy into moving something. I sensed the wind caressing my hair, swaying it gently. I opened my eyes, and I noticed the leaves dancing in midair. I wanted to see if I could do more, so I concentrated again. Upon opening my eyes, I saw a wolf sculpted from leaves, held together by the swirling wind."

Dani's eyes go distant, trying to piece together what I just told her. Then, as if a lightbulb goes off, her eyes return to the present.

"The very first High Lord possessed powers similar to what you are speaking of."

"What do we know about the first High Lord?" I want to know more about him.

Stephanie pulls out a chair to sit down.

"Well, the first High Lord's name was Keijo. There are many rumors about how he got here, but no one knows exactly how. He has been the most powerful fae that has ever lived. His power was very similar to yours. He could communicate with nature and animals and control the wind. Similar to what you can do. He also had command over the water and could sense people's emotions."

"So just like me almost? I'm only missing water."

Dani nods her head.

"Wow. Do we know anything else about Keijo?" I ask, leaning forward in my chair.

"It was rumored that he had a dragon," Stephanie responds.

I can feel my eyebrows touching my hairline. "Oh?"

"Yes, but rumor has it that it isn't the kind of dragon you are thinking of. They say it was a dragon with butterfly wings." Dani leans back.

"What?" I have never heard or read of such a thing in stories. However, my heart begins pounding because I have seen one in my dreams. I have drawn dragons with butterfly wings before, and I thought then it was only in my imagination.

Stephanie nods.

"There is no record of anyone seeing it, but that was long ago. Those records could have been lost. However, they are called Asulaas. There is only talk of that one; no one has ever seen any since then. So, I consider that our myths." Dani places one hand on her hip.

"Asulaa..." I repeat.

"Mm-hmm, that is what Keijo called it."

"I wonder if it is real then, and if so, why have no others ever been seen since then?" So many thoughts cloud my head about this intriguing creature.

"Alright, I'm getting back to it. I am so proud of you, though, Alona. You are growing increasingly into the High Lady your parents would have been proud of." Dani pats my back and smiles gently.

She makes her way back to the kitchen. She has many ends to tie before we leave, mainly with the cafe. She will give the new owner the keys tomorrow since we will go in two days. I can't imagine how Dani feels. Claywood has been her home for the last eighteen years of her life. It has to be difficult for her as well. I sigh and lean back in my chair. I close my eyes and try to picture the Asulaa.

"I have a few ends to tie up as well. I have to find a new owner for my car." I hear the chair creak as Stephanie rises.

I peel one eye open and look at her. I smile and nod my head. I asked her where she got that car the other day, and all she did was laugh. It makes me think that maybe she stole it, but who am I to judge? I reaped the benefits of her having a car. Otherwise, I would not have done nearly as much as she and I have done together.

She leaves the front door, and someone comes in right after. I open my eyes and look over at the client.

"I will be right there!"

They nod at me. I stand up and make my way back behind the counter. Henry stands at the counter with a wide grin on his face.

"Henry, it's you?" I say flatly, plastering a fake smile on my face.

Henry was once a pretty decent person until he won with me in the art exhibit. After winning, he changed. He became more entitled, especially when big galleries reached out to him. Thankfully, I don't have a phone, so I never had big-timers reach out to me for my artwork.

"Adilyn, how's it going?" he asks.

"It's going we...." I begin to say.

"That's great! Can you believe that I'm finally leaving this place?" He cuts me off mid-sentence.

So, help him if he comes to gloat; I don't have time for this. I roll my neck, trying to ease some of the tension in my neck and shoulders.

"Oh, how exciting. I'm glad for you." I say.

"Yes. I will be moving out to Los Darthos in a few days."

"Oh, wow. That is a huge city, so much different than Claywood. I'm sure you will do amazing there." Los Darthos is the biggest city in the entire country. That is where all the rich and famous live or spend most of their time there. I'm happy for him, knowing this is a big step in his life and career. I know he will do much better than I would have in his position. Being a prominent artist is not for everyone. Just like being a High Lady is not for everyone.

"What can I get you?" I sigh, ready for him to order and leave.

"Well, I would love a salted caramel latte." He chimes.

"That will be $6.78," I say.

I'm curious about what Dani will do with all her belongings here, and I'm guessing she will leave them for the Grovers. We can't take any of it with us, nor can we take the money. If we can't carry it, it's not coming with us. Part of me wants to give out free coffee since the currency here will be useless in Eldermyst. However, I'm sure that offering free coffee would bring the entire town to the cafe's doorstep, and I'm not fond of the idea of a hectic afternoon. Dani said I don't need to work and could spend my time training, but I want some normalcy for now, especially since my life will never be this way again.

Henry hands me a $10 bill. I take it from him and give him his change.

"I will have your coffee out momentarily." I grab a cup and start grinding coffee beans. As I begin making his coffee, he starts droning on again about how amazing his life will be and what a disappointment I'm not following in his footsteps. I drown out his voice with the thoughts in my head. I'm from the lineage of Keijo, the very first fae. It is interesting how humans have myths of creatures that we do not have here in our world but that are in the world of the fae. There is a connection somewhere. However, I find the myth of Keijo's dragon even more enjoyable. There is no writing of this creature, and no one can for sure say that it ever existed. It makes me wonder what could have happened there. The dragon is etched in my mind. I can envision it. When it starts to slow down here at the cafe, I am going to try and sketch it

Making coffee is second nature. I steam the milk and pour it into the cup. I secure the lid and walk back to the register. At this point, he is still there blabbing on about who knows what. I will give it to him; the man certainly knows how to talk. I pull the corners of my lips up, forcing myself to smile and hand him his latte.

"Thanks, Adilyn. So, I heard that the Grovers are taking over this place for Dani?" He takes a sip of his latte and looks back up at me.

"Yes, they are. They will do amazing things here!" Cheer in my voice.

"Well, I hope everything is alright with Dani. I'm off. I must go pack my bags and prepare for the big move." He nods and raises his latte in the air.

"Well, I wish you all the success and happiness in the world, Henry. Safe travels." I call out to him.

I watch him as he walks out of the cafe. We are both preparing for big moves; however, my move is much more life-altering. I go back and grab a rag to begin wiping things down. I wipe down the espresso machine, glance at the clock, and see it is almost 7:00 pm. I will be closing up for good here shortly. I'm curious as to what the Grovers will do with the place. Will they keep it as a cafe? Will they renovate it? There are several different things that they can do. I would love for this place to stay just the same, but I understand this is a new page for this place and a new page for the Grover's. I wish them the best in their upcoming venture.

Most people ordered coffee to go today, so the tables don't need major cleaning. I quickly walk around to the tables to wipe them down. After I wipe off the last table, I head to the back to toss my rag in the washer. I come back up front with a pad of paper and a pencil. I sit at one of the tables and close my eyes. I allow the image of the Asulaa to fill my mind.

What color was it? Was it large or small? I slowly sort through all the questions. I can see a dragon with a body about twice the size of Arion, a deep emerald body, and deep emerald and navy-blue wings, as clear as day. The wings are massive and similar in size to those of Arion.

However, the Asulaa's wings were black with intricate dark navy blue and emerald green swirls. There's an iridescent glow radiating from the dragon's wings. The Asulaa's has horns perturbing from its head. Its body is covered in rough scales, and its back is lined with slated spikes, except for a tiny section between its wings. The color of its belly is a slightly lighter emerald green, giving the dragon a beautiful ombré effect.

I follow the image of the dragon from the top of its head down to its tail. My hand flows across the page with my pencil as my vision spills out. Once I finish drawing the Asulaa, I lay my pencil on the table and hold my page before me. What a stunning creature. If this is what the Asulaa looks like, how I wish I could see one in my lifetime.

It makes me wonder what the reason would be that only that one has ever been mentioned. Did the Asulaa possess a kind of power that the fae thought could be utilized as a weapon? Or were fae simply too greedy and want to get their hands on something so rare? Whatever the reasoning, whether they truly exist or are make-believe, I think they must have been some of the greatest-looking creatures, aside from Pterippi. I wish there were more information about them.

CHAPTER THIRTY-FOUR

Winning the Battle

ALONA

Asher accompanies me on the morning run, as usual. We stop at our routine practice place near the massive oak I admire. I have spent considerable time here, which has helped me feel more grounded and grow my abilities. Each day that passes, I'm getting stronger and stronger. The magic in my core is growing. I can feel it more, diving into my mental well and drawing it up. I'm also getting physically stronger. I run longer and farther.

Asher stands in front of me. We always begin our training by stretching.

"Isn't this kind of pointless to stretch before?"

"No, it's a must; we can't have our High Lady pulling a muscle, now, can we?" sarcasm dripping from every word that comes out of his mouth.

I roll my eyes. What a jerk. "So, I'm expected to pause a war so that I can stretch? Hey everyone, time out for just a moment. I need to stretch my hamstrings first, and then we can continue. I don't want to pull a muscle." Acting out as dramatically as possible, throwing my hands in the air, and making a T.

Despite my sarcasm, I'm trying to think of everything logically. I won't be able to pause and stretch in the middle of a fight. I need to prepare my body for what will happen. I need to know how to care for myself when I don't have the time to stretch. I know that stretching is essential, but I need a workaround; the lives of too many depend on it.

"Shut up and stretch." Asher barks out the order.

I shake my head, yet I follow his every move without saying another word. God forbid he is even more unhappy with me than he is already. Today, he is not in the greatest of moods, and I'm unsure why. He started our run like someone had peed in his Cheerios. I feel like I'm walking on glass around him. If he isn't being sarcastic, he is ripping off my head. I swear, sometimes this man has bipolar disorder.

Asher instructs me to begin working on my sword stance. He said I must master this with efficiency. I have to agree. If I can't stay on my own two feet and swing a sword, I will be a liability to everyone, possibly causing them to lose their lives. I stand in place, holding the sword tightly in my two hands. I bounce on my ankles, assuring my legs and knees will bear the upcoming impact. Asher stands next to me with slightly bent knees. He looks at me and nods his head, notifying me to begin. I work on my horizontal and vertical sword cuts. Starting slow and then progressing to a faster pace. I want to be able to do these moves without having to think. I want my sword-wielding to become second nature to me. I breathe in and out with each swing.

I count each swing in my head... one, two, reset, one, two. I do this for quite some time, ensuring each swing is precise before moving on to the next stance. Once I feel I'm doing pretty good, I work my upper body crosscut slices. Breathe in with one move and breathe out with the second. I allow the movement and the sword to take me, gracefully swinging the blade through the air. I glance at Asher. He stands beside me, his swings matching mine. However, his movements are executed with confidence, precision, and power. He appears to be in a lethal dance with his sword, which seems like a natural extension of his being.

"Is there something wrong with my face, High Lady?" he cocks his head and raises one brow.

"No, I'm simply in awe of your skill. You and the sword are one. I hope to master your level of skill with a sword. You make it look like an art." Momentarily forgetting what we were doing, I nod and return to training. Taking a deep breath, I firmly grasp my sword and start swinging.

Several minutes pass by of silence, and only the sound is the swooshing from our swords cutting through the air. Asher jumps in front of me and brings his sword down on me. I jump back, gripping my sword tightly and preparing myself for a fight. My heart is pounding so hard that I feel like it is going to pound right out of my chest. I swing back at him, just barely missing his arm. Damn it. We swing back and forth. I dodge his hits. He is slowly inching closer and closer to me. He swings, and his sword graces my left shoulder. I look down at my shoulder and the slice he just made through my clothing. I can see bubbles of blood starting to form on the fresh cut.

"Ouch!" I yelp, squeezing my eyes shut.

He swings again at me, taking me by surprise and knocking me to the ground. I hit the ground and scrambled for my sword. He kicks it away from me and holds his sword to my chest.

"Was that necessary? You just cut me, then knocked me down." I groan, anger fuming inside of me.

"Do you think the person you fight against will allow you to stop and inspect your injuries? No, they wouldn't; they would have taken that opportunity to kill you." He barks out. "Again."

"Gosh, no need to be so mean," I mumble. I stand up, taking my stance once again. He swings the sword at me again. I stumble back and gain my footing quickly.

"What are you mumbling?" He sneers.

I ignore his question, concentrating on retrieving my sword. He's standing right over it. To have any chance of getting it back, I need to make him move. Scanning my surroundings, I notice a large broken branch to his right. I must reach it to use it as a makeshift weapon until I can retrieve my sword. I dodge as he swings at me, inching closer to the branch with each step. He swings again, and I duck, rolling beside the branch. Grabbing it firmly, I rise to one knee and swing at the back of Asher's knees. The swing seems to unfold in slow motion. Just as I expect Asher to evade my swing, the branch connects, striking the back of his knees and snapping in two. Asher stumbles and falls forward, grunting in surprise and pain. The sound is music to my ears.

I fumble to my feet, rushing to my sword. I grab it, gripping it tight, and prepare to continue the fight. Asher jumps back onto his feet and begins to circle me.

"You think you were smooth with that strike, didn't you?" a smirk on his face, taunting me as he circles.

"I don't think I was smooth; I know I was. It was good enough to make you fall flat on your face." I bent my knees, stabilizing my stance. I would not go down again.

He circles me, swinging his sword, trying to make a hit. I block strike after strike. I can feel the sweat beginning to drench my shirt.

I let my determination settle in, determination to defeat Asher in this fight. He will not come out on top, I will. I scan to see what I can use to help me beat him. We are in the forest surrounded by trees. The lightbulb turns on in my mind. I'm not a human. I have powers deep down inside of me. I do not need to rely strictly on my brute force but also on my magic. I dove deep into my well of power, willing myself to bring it up. I can feel the magic climbing up higher and higher inside the well. My bones begin to hum with the building power inside of me. I continue watching and blocking Asher, scanning for the perfect opportunity. He circles me again, and his back is to my favorite oak. This is my shot to make my move. Using the sword as a channel, I will use my power to move towards the massive oak. The sword begins to hum in my arms, lighting up.

A shock flashes on Asher's face, and then his cold facade falls back into place. He lowers his head, eyes looking up at me from through his lashes.

"You are not winning this one, High Lady," a dark smirk falls upon his face.

"Are you sure about that?" I crouch and cannot stop the grin from spreading on my face. A second passes, and roots from the massive oak shoot out of the ground, reaching for Asher's legs. They wrap around his ankles and yank him down. More roots come to the surface, latching onto his wrists, pinning him. This is my opportunity to strike. I rush to him and place the tip of my sword under his chin, brushing softly on his neck.

"You lost." I pant.

He nods and smiles, "Well done."

I sheath my sword and will the roots to disappear. They unravel their grip on his wrists and ankles, slithering back into the ground. I reach my hand out to Asher. He looks at my open hand and then back to my face. He slowly reaches out and grabs my hand. I help to pull him up. He stands up, inches away from me, and our eyes lock. Our hands still grasped. I can feel the electricity swirling through my hand into his. I let go quickly, hoping that I did not just hurt him. I take a step back and look down at my hand.

"You did not do anything to me, don't worry." His tone was tender.

My eyes dart towards him. "What was that then? Did you feel that?"

"The electricity passing through our hands? That was just our magic connecting to each other's. It can happen at times."

"Why?" I pry, wanting to know more about this new world.

"Just because it does. Why do I need to give you an answer?" He snaps.

"What? Why would you not answer me if you knew the answer? You know, I know pretty much nothing about this new world. I only ask to learn." My brows furrow. I can feel the pulse slowly creeping into my temples.

He glares at me, not answering my questions. My hands begin to twitch with the built-up annoyance.

I place my hands on my hips, rolling my eyes. "It is impossible to have an actual conversation with you," I say sharply. I cannot deal with him anymore. I stalk towards the massive oak, needing to get away from Asher before my head starts to throb. I also need to thank the tree for helping me win this battle. I reach the tree and place my hands on the trunk, sucking in a shallow breath. I do not want to be angry while speaking to the oak. I exhaled a long breath, releasing all the tension that I felt. I lean my forehead against the trunk and close my eyes.

"Thank you, my dear friend," I whisper.

"We are at your command, High Lady." a soft echo in my mind.

The gratitude I feel for this oak fills my heart until it is about to burst. I smile softly, take a small step back, and bow my head. I want the trees to know how much I respect their willingness to accept me.

I lay my hand back on the tree and send a thought. "Thank you! I appreciate all of your support and am honored by it!"

I'm growing increasingly connected to nature every day, and it ceases to amaze me. This was something that I had wanted all my life, and here we are; it has come true. I feel so blessed to have the magic that I have, the connection to nature. At first, I could only sense their emotions, but now I can faintly hear them. As long as my forehead is pressed against their trunk, their voices become audible. By touching the trunk, I can feel their emotions. Each day, I make more and more progress.

I turn to leave and make the hike back to the cafe. I practiced the entire morning with Asher, and I still have much to do and learn. I need to take a shower and start studying the Courts of Eldermyst. I decided it would be best to learn as much as possible about this realm. I will research who all the High Lords and Ladies are, the history of each court, and what to expect from each.

I take a few steps back towards the road, and I feel someone grasp my wrist. I turn around in full alert mode. Asher is standing there with my wrist in his hand. I shake my arm hard enough for him to let go.

"What in the hell do you want?" I demand.

"Where are you going?"

"First of all, I do not need to answer you, and second of all, I have practiced all morning with you. I am so sweaty that I feel like I just got out of the shower. I also have other things to do!"

"I did not say you were done." He folds his arms across his chest.

"I said I was!" I sneer, turning and walking away. I swear to all the gods I would kill this man if I could. Unfortunately, I need him too much to do that right now. I storm off, huffing. I do not know why he gets under my skin as much as he does, but he does. He makes my blood boil.

I do not know what is with me these past few days and allowing Asher to get so under my skin that I wish I could peel my skin right off. He angers me so much with his cocky 'know it all' attitude. Asher is not all that, and then there are some, as he thinks. He is a raging pompous asshole that needs to get walloped once. Maybe then that would knock some sense into him. Until then, I do not know. I guess I will have to learn how to deal with him or bite my tongue until we finally get to the Emerald Court.

Then, a thought enters my mind. Maybe, just maybe, it is not necessarily Asher that is the one at fault, not wholly. Perhaps he is only part of the reason. Maybe the other part of the reason is my anxiety about what my life will become. Will I be enough? Will I be able to save everyone? Will I be accepted, considering I have been MIA for eighteen years? The thoughts swarm my head, and I can feel my anxiety coming.

The anxiety is dragging me down, grasping one of its nasty hands around my throat and squeezing tightly. My breaths begin to hallow as I fight to suck in air to fill my lungs. My heart begins slamming into my rib cage, feeling like it will burst right out of my chest at any moment. My head starts to wobble, and the world begins to spin. I know my anxiety is getting the best of me.

I inhale deeply and whisper to myself. "I am a rock. I am a fortress. I will not fall, not now, not ever." I repeat it to myself over and over until my breathing begins to come back to normal, and my heart eases up on its pounding. This is not the first time anxiety like this has taken hold of me.

I need to think about something else before I end up destroying something that I don't mean to destroy because my anger and anxiety are on high alert. I let my mind wander to the training I just had with Asher. I am replaying our practice fight, analyzing what I could have done differently. How could I have taken him down faster? What can I do next time not to be taken by surprise and lose my sword? The thought of what a real battle will look like crosses my mind. The end of each real battle with an enemy means that someone will lose their life. I also know that losing my sword in a fight will mean losing my life. That thought sends a shiver down my spine, an unease creeping into the back of my mind. I cannot imagine what it will be like to make my first kill. It is not something I would like to do; however, I know that the lives of many may depend on it. I am willing to sacrifice for the greater, even if it chips away a piece of my soul every time. I allow that thought to settle into my soul.

I stop abruptly in my tracks. I know what I need to do. I need to push myself to my limits until I have mastered fighting. I drop my shoulders and bring my hands to my face, breathing in deeply. I raise my head and turn slowly back towards the woods. I need to let my determination, anger, and anxiety push me to win every battle. I need to learn how to utilize those feelings so I can win. I take step after step back to the spot where we train. Asher is sitting on the ground, head dropping between his pulled-up knees.

"Instead of training, you are sitting. Wow, someone needs to work on their discipline." I taunt him, sheathing my sword and readying my stance.

His gaze jerks to mine, confusion seeping into his features.

"Let's go, big boy. This time, I will take you down without losing my sword." I narrow my eyes and smirk at him.

He slowly rises from where he was seated and draws his sword.

"Are you sure about that? Or do you actually want to see me lying down and you over me?" His eyes darken, tension building in the air.

"Awe, how adorable! You think I desire you in that way?" I laugh out loud. "More like laying in a grave as I stand on it." Then I launch at him.

We swing, strike, and dodge for what seems like an eternity, but I know it is only moments. He circles me, and I follow him step for step, strike for strike. He nicks my leg; I nick his shoulder. He swings his sword at me, and I spin, dodging it, and bring my elbow into his side. He trips forward and falls to the ground. I re-establish my stance and hold steadfast to the Emerald Shadow. He rolls onto his feet and stands. A wild grin spreads across his face. He throws himself forward, lunging at me with his sword. I barely dodged this time, and he hit my shoulder. The blade just barely graced my shoulder. This time, I do not pause to look. I spin to stand next to him, slamming my body into his back and kicking out his knees. He falls to the ground, hitting his shoulder on a rock. He groans in pain.

"Why don't you just stay down, big boy? You like to be on the ground."

"Why take the fun out of kicking your ass?" He grins.

As he stands back up, he swings out his leg, kicking my feet. I lose balance and fall to the ground. I yell out as my head hits the ground. Fury begins to bubble inside of me. I jump back up, and I start swinging one after another. He blocks each strike.

I swing, blocking him. He holds my sword there. He leans in and whispers, "Seems like someone has an anger problem." Then he pushes my sword back, "Let's make this interesting."

I raise an eyebrow. How can we make this fight more interesting? Then, a branch lifts off the ground and begins to come at me. I duck and hold my arms above my head. The branch crashes into the tree behind me. I look up and see a dark smirk on Asher's face. He can move things, telekinesis. My mouth falls open, and I take a step back.

"You can move things!" My voice shakes.

He nods his head.

"Why didn't you tell me?" I ask.

"You never asked." He smirks.

If this is how he will fight, then so be it. I grip my sword and bend my knees. I need to learn how to fight sword for sword and magic for magic. I charge at him. As he runs towards me, I call a root to the surface. It shoots out, trying to knock him off balance. He spots the root just in time and jumps over it. Another branch comes from my side and collides with my left shoulder. I stumble forward but quickly regain my balance. The branch begins to swing again; however, this time, I am faster, striking it and breaking it into two. The sweat is coating my forehead and dripping down my neck.

I focus back on Asher, willing for the wind to come to my aid. A gust of wind blows leaves right into his face, causing him to release one hand off the sword to swat at the leaves blowing around his face. As I watch him, a rock hits my right shoulder, and a branch hits the back of my legs, knocking me to the ground.

"Damn it!" I yelp.

I lose focus, and the leaves surrounding him drop to the ground. He regains his hold on his sword and charges for me. He is a step away from me and brings the sword down on me. Luckily, I roll out of the way just in time. Jumping back on my feet, I face him. This will not be an easy fight, so I must give it my all. I center myself and dive into my mental well, bringing my power to the surface. Once I feel it right at the top, I throw it at him.

Wind begins to swirl around him, creating a barrier that causes him to be stationed in place. He tries to break through the walls of the wind; however, he cannot break it. A root shoots out of the ground, wrapping around his leg and pulling him down. The moment he is on the ground, I lunge forward and hold the sword to his chest.

"I win again." Panting.

"I let you win again." He smiles, indeed smiles, and my heart feels lighter.

I sheath my sword and once again hold my hand out to him. He does not hesitate to take my hand this time, and I pull him up. He stands and is inches from me. Our eyes lock, and the world seems to fade away. His eyes are so beautiful. I have never really taken the time to look at them. They are a dark, steely grey, yet there are swirls of a light grey smoldering in them. They remind me of the smoke of a campfire, something comforting. His lips part, wanting to say something, and then he steps back. The distance between us leaves me feeling hollow. I suck in a breath and close my eyes, regaining my composure.

Opening my eyes, I look at him and smile. "Good fight."

He nods in agreement. "You are getting better and better by the day."

Chapter Thirty-Five

Asher

Elouan relayed a message this morning that the Dark Orians have invaded another town, destroying it and burning it to the ground. How many more people will they slaughter before someone stands up to them? I don't know how much more I can sit around and allow.

I met Alona for our routine run, hoping that would lighten the mood, but the dark cloud over me wouldn't go away. She silently ran alongside, sensing I needed space to sort through my thoughts. I'm grateful for her understanding.

Alona amazes me as each day passes. She is so intelligent and is grasping her new reality quickly. She has advanced so much, not only in her magic but also in her fighting.

I can see her out of the corner of my eye. She is so graceful in each movement. I smile as the thought of when she first started enters my mind. She was very clumsy with the sword. It slipped out of her hand multiple times. It's nice she caught on quickly and is starting to master the stance. Utilizing her sword will be a big part of her fighting. However,

I do need to prepare her with hand-on-hand combat. She will have to handle both situations once we leave this place.

I quickly decided to see how she would react if I caught her off guard. I go from being by her side to standing before her and swinging my sword down on her. She is dazed at first, but she makes up for it quickly by dodging my blow. She brings her sword up to meet mine. We go back and forth, swinging and blocking. I circled her, trying to see if I could get her to stumble. She follows stride for stride. I swing and. I swung towards her arm, and she was a second too slow. My blade scrapes the surface of her skin.

"Ouch!" She cries out.

She stops and stares at the wound. Blood begins to bubble from the wound. I suck in a sharp breath, feeling my heart skip a beat. I did not intentionally mean to cause her physical damage; however, I must keep going. What is done is done. Her focus is not where it should be. She must learn that you must never take your eyes off your enemy. Well, at least not until they are dead. I move and swing at her, knocking her to the ground. Her sword falls out of her hand, and I quickly kick it away.

Was that necessary? You just cut me, then knocked me down." Her eyes widen, anger flashing deep in her emerald eyes.

"Do you think the person you fight against will allow you to stop and inspect your injuries? No, they wouldn't; they would have taken that opportunity to kill you." I hiss. "Again."

She needs to learn what a fight will be like. You end up dead when things don't go your way in a fight. I can see the tension radiating as she rises from the ground. She mumbles something under her breath in anger. I can't make it out, but I know it is nothing good.

"What are you mumbling?" I sneer, trying to anger her more. Pushing to see what she is made of.

Her eyes scan our surroundings, trying to find a way to gain an advantage. She inches closer to me, and I know she is trying to figure out how to get to her sword. I will not make this easy for her. No opponent would. I swing my sword, aiming for her other arm. She dodges attempt after attempt. I take a step towards her and swing at her. She dodges by dropping to the ground and rolling. She rolls right next to me and grabs a broken branch lying on the ground. As I turn towards her, she makes an impact with the back of my knees and the broken branch. Pain shoots up my legs; I stumble forward and fall. Shock consumes me, and my muscles contract as I hit the ground. I blink several times, and I snap out of my momentary shock. I cock my head to the side as I jump to my feet, "You think you were smooth with that strike, didn't you?" I smirk and begin to circle her, grasping my sword firmly.

"I don't think I was smooth; I know I was. It was good enough to make you fall flat on your face." She mocks me.

"You are not winning this one, High Lady." Determined not to let her win this one, or at least not let her win easily. She will have to fight her way to the top of this fight.

Then she surprises me. She crouches down to the ground. "Are you sure about that?" A sinister smile spreads across her face as she places her hands on the ground.

I feel the ground begin to rumble one moment, and the next, roots are shooting out from the ground. They dart towards me, wrap around my ankles tightly, and yank me to the ground. I fall back. More roots pop out of the ground and wrap around my wrist. My eyes widen as she rushes up to me and holds her sword to my throat. She got me.

"You lost." She pants.

I smirk at her. "Well, done."

Warmth fills my chest at the fact that she took me to the ground. She utilized her determination to fuel her.

I must admit I was not expecting this from her. She surprised me. She took in her surroundings and used them to her benefit. That is all I hoped for her to get outside the box and be creative when fighting. One moment, I knocked her down; the next, she was striking me with a broken branch, and now she has me pinned down and sword to my throat. I wanted to see what she could do. I was not disappointed.

She sheaths her sword, and the roots retreat, freeing my limbs. She reaches out a hand to offer help. Curiosity runs through me. Why is she offering to help me up when she enjoyed every second of knocking me to the ground? I reach out and grab her hand, and then it happens. It feels like I have been struck by a lightning bolt, knocking all the air from me as she pulls me up. I didn't think I was going to be able to stand. I look up at her face and see worry written all over it. She was not nearly as affected by that as I was.

The next few moments pass in a blur. The pain is lingering and causing my mind to be hazy. Alona asks me a question, and I answer in a sarcastic tone. She wants to know what happened, but I cannot tell her. She cannot know, not now, not ever.

"Just because it does. Why do I need to give you an answer?" I snap, needing her to stop for just a moment so I can recover. I cannot let her know I am as affected as I am. I need her to stop questioning me. She storms off to the giant oak tree. I hear her soft words thanking the tree for helping her win against me. I scoff; I partially let her win. The pain subdues and slowly fizzles down.

She turns and starts making her trek towards the road. Where the hell does she think she is going? Irritation creeps into my mind. I approach her and reach out, grasping her wrist and stopping her.

What in the hell do you want?" She shouts.

"Where are you going?" I demand. We have more training left to complete.

"First of all, I don't need to answer you, and secondly, I have practiced all morning with you. I am so sweaty that I feel like I just got out of the shower. I also have other things to do!"

"I did not say you were done." I cross my arms, watching as the anger boils in her eyes.

"I said I was!" She turns and storms off.

I blow out a breath. Time is of the essence, and she is running away from practicing. Maybe that is for the best for right now. I need to collect myself. I carefully reach a tree and sit down, hanging my head between my knees. I need a moment to think about what just happened between us. This is not something she needs to know right now. Maybe she never needs to know this.

She had returned, and we fought again. This time, she was much more graceful. The shock ran right through her when I finally used my power. We fought blade to blade and magic to magic. She did excellently despite not having trained her whole life.

"Let's go. I hid a few muffins last night before they were all gone! I wanted to make sure that you at least could enjoy one." She chirps.

She did what? She hid muffins so that I could have one? There is a crack in my heart and a flood of warmth. I do not know what to do, and I do not understand what is happening. All I do is stare at her, speechless for the kindness that she is showing me. She blinks a few times at me, waiting for me to move. I don't, so she slowly walks to me, locking her arm with mine. She tugs on me softly, motioning for me to walk with her. I do one step after another. We walk back towards the cafe. Once we arrived at Stella's, she told me to wait. Then she runs behind the counter and rummages through where the coffee beans are stored.

"Here it is! See!" She holds up a Ziplock bag with two muffins inside. Her eyes are gleaming in the light pouring through the open windows.

She did save me one. I slowly smiled, feeling honored that she thought of me, especially since I had not been the kindest person to her. She grabs some napkins and then skips her way back to me.

This woman is stunning and kind, beautiful, intelligent, and talented. She is so many things.

"Earth to Asher." She waves a hand in front of my face. I must have been lost in my thoughts. I look at her, and she has a muffin perched on the palm of her hand. She lifted her hand and motioned for me to take it. I reach out and grab the muffin.

"I have not had one of these in almost eighteen years," I say quietly, then take a bite. I close my eyes and try to stifle the moan that slips from my lips.

Her grin only widens as she watches me devour my muffin. Once I am finished, she hands me hers, nodding for me to take it.

" You can have it. I had several yesterday, and who knows when Dani will be able to make more." She is so genuine. At that moment, my belief that she didn't care broke. She does care immensely, even if she isn't willing to acknowledge it. Maybe this will work out.

CHAPTER THIRTY-SIX

Goodbye

ALONA

Tomorrow is the day that my life changes for good. Tomorrow morning, we will leave Claywood and make our way to Eldermyst. My nerves have me by the throat. I have been told what the courts look like, what the people are like, and what I will face; however, it is still unknown.

There are several things that I need to get done. I have to pack my bag today. I will also need some good hiking shoes and combat boots. I have been told that the terrain will be rough in some parts.

Stephanie told me she would be by around 9 am to pick me up. We need to go to the next town over and get a few items since there aren't many decent stores in Claywood. I have a bag of clothing to take to the women's shelter. I can only take four days' worth of clothing, so all the rest must go. It is hard to think I'm leaving behind everything I have ever known. My whole life has been here.

I'm ready for the new chapter in my life to begin. I'm prepared for an adventure. I'm ready to take on my destiny just as it was foretold. I walk downstairs, and the Grovers are there. Everett's little face turns towards me, and he lights up. He runs towards me, and I bend to scoop him up in an embrace. I squeeze him and rub my nose on his neck. He giggles and squirms in my arms. I carefully set him back on his feet, and he grabbed my hand and led me to a table with his drawings. I wave at Deborah and Carl so I don't interrupt Dani while she talks.

"Here are the keys. Do whatever you wish to do at this cafe. I hope you will keep it the same, but it is your choice." When everything started getting put into motion with us returning to Eldermyst, Dani approached them about taking over the cafe. She said she wanted it to go to someone she knew needed it most. I'm sure Dani could sell the cafe quickly to someone, yet she still chose the Grovers. She knows the Grovers would benefit the most from it, and I couldn't agree more. They can live upstairs and won't have to worry about rent. Carl wouldn't need always to be away from his family working. He can still be there with them and provide for them. I'm sure they were shocked when Dani presented them with the offer. They were wary to accept at first because they were unsure if it was a joke. Carl thought there was a catch to the deal, something he had to do or give. He was stunned when Dani repeatedly told him that there wasn't. They deserve to take over the cafe. I have seen their struggles over the years and know it has had a toll on them. "Oh, Dani, why would we ever change it?" Deborah says shyly. Deborah is a frail woman with golden blonde hair. Her blue eyes have so much kindness in them. Wrinkles around her eyes paint her soft features. Exhaustion has consumed her beauty, but it is still there. "Well honey, it isn't everyone's cup of tea, and I want you to make it yours, add paintings, coloring pages, whatever you like." Her kindness fills the room. "One last thing, everything in here stays. I will not be taking anything at all. I want you guys to have it along with this." Dani hands over an envelope to Carl. Carl slowly extends his hand and takes the envelope. His eyes dart to Dani, then me, worrying about filling them. He is in his mid-30s, yet it looks like he is in his mid to late 40s. He has deep lines surrounding his eyes. The dark circles staining around his eye make it look like he has gone many days with little to no sleep. Life and its circumstances have aged him. He is wearing a blue baseball cap and has dark chocolate brown hair that reaches to the bottom of his ears. His eyes are gentle, contrasting with his rugged, long beard. His salt-and-pepper beard touches his chest. He opens the envelope and immediately tries handing it back to Dani, shaking his head, and takes a step back. Sorrow pings in my ribcage. What is going through his mind right now? Why would he deny the money in the envelope? It saddens me when people don't know their worth. Carl does not know his. Dani steps forward, grabs his hand, and pushes the envelope into it, forcing his fingers to close around it.

"No. I will not accept this, Dani. You must take it back, please." He pleads with her. Carl's hand begins to tremble. Deborah stills and glances between Carl and Dani. She slowly reaches for the envelope, pulling it from Carl's hand. Deborah peeks inside of it and falls silent. She shakes her head continuously.

"We cannot take this, Miss Dani; you are already doing too much for us." Deborah's voice shakes, and her eyes begin to water.

Dani's eyes find mine, and I nod in understanding. I stand up from the table where I was seated with Everett and walk to Dani. I stand next to Dani and look at Deborah. Our eyes lock, and she jerks her hand towards me with the envelope.

I lift my hands, "We will not accept this back. You must take this."

Dani and I had discussed what we would do with everything, where it would go, and who would get it. She wanted to leave everything since we could not take any of it. I planned to leave all of my earnings and savings to someone. There's no need to take money with me to a world that doesn't have a use for dollars. Dani and I agreed that everything would be left to the Grovers. It is fitting that they keep it all; we don't need it, and they are far more than deserving.

I'm donating my clothing but leaving the art supplies here. Leaving my art supplies here would be great for Everett since he loves art. I can picture it now; he is in my art room, painting away. I glance over to where Everett is sitting. He is perched on a chair, coloring in a dinosaur coloring book. Strands of his golden blonde hair fall into his face. A smile spreads on my face.

Tears well up in Deborah's eyes, and she fights to keep them contained. I take a step towards her. I slowly reach my hand out to grab her hands. I hold her hands and the envelope between mine. I inhale deeply.

"This is for you. You both have struggled for so long. You have been here in this town, and no one has helped you when you needed it most. The most painful thing is that you never reached out for help out of fear of what they would think about you two." I look from Deborah to Carl, then back again at Deborah. "You, Deborah, and you, Carl, are far more deserving of this blessing than you will ever realize. Your struggles and pain do not define you, but your character and constant kindness define you. This is a gift from us, and quite frankly, I would be upset if you refused the gift." I squeeze her hands. I want her to know how deserving she is because I can feel the worthlessness that she feels. Being alone and having no one to turn to for help has been hard for them. I want them to know they are seen and loved.

Carl bursts into tears, and Dani throws her hands around him, embracing him. I can feel his emotions hanging in the air. His emotions are a mixture of pain, disbelief, and joy, mainly joy. Their overwhelming emotions bombard my senses. I pause momentarily and build that mental wall quickly, trying not to let their emotions overwhelm me.

Deborah doesn't move; her body is stiff. She's still in shock. I slowly bring her into an embrace.

I whisper in her ear. "You are deserving no matter what you tell yourself."

She begins to sob into my shoulder, squeezing me tightly. "Thank you so much!" She whispers between sobs.

"Mommy, why are you crying?" Everett rushes over, pulling on Deborah's dress.

"They are happy tears, my sweetheart." She releases me and reaches down to pick Everett up. She nuzzles her nose against his neck, and he laughs. I can feel the joy spilling out of him. Heat radiates through my chest. This boy's laughter has just made my week.

I need a moment to myself, so I sneak out of the cafe while Dani and the Grovers finish talking. I told Dani I would return shortly, so she gave them a tour of the cafe and upstairs apartment. They will start their move-in tomorrow after we leave. I feel like a piece of my heart will be left here when we leave. I may not know Carl well, but I know Deborah and Everett. A small sob escapes from me at the thought of having to leave that sweet little boy. I didn't realize just how difficult this would be.

Walking down the road from the cafe, I have my hood drawn up and my hands tucked into my pockets to conceal their trembling. I'm eager to go on this journey; however, I'm filled with sorrow that I'm leaving. I have so much on my mind that I need to sort through. I must say goodbye to the forest that has been my sanctuary my entire life. They have been my lifeline. I'm leaving tomorrow, and I doubt I will be returning. I want to thank them for the years of comfort and peace they have given me.

I step off the road into the forest. My steps are slow and dragging. I feel heavier inside with each passing step. I make it to the massive oak that I always visit. I look up at its canopy, admiring the journey this tree has gone through. I slowly pull my hand out of my pocket and place it on the trunk. I close my eyes, fighting back tears at the sorrow radiating from the tree. They know I'm leaving. They know I more than likely won't be returning. I slowly lean my forehead to its trunk.

"Hello, my dear friend." My voice breaks.

"Hello, dear High Lady," the whisper leans into my mind. I don't know what words to say. I am so overwhelmed with my sorrow that it leaves me speechless.

"My High Lady, please don't be sad. We know your leaving is for the best of our brethren." The soft voices from all of the oaks whisper in unison. Tears pour down my cheeks like a waterfall. I turn and sit down, leaning my back against the massive oak. I pull my legs up and hug my arms around them, laying my head on my knees. I sob into my knees. The sorrow is so intense, and I know I need to release it. Release the pain I feel for leaving this place behind, leaving Everett behind. I allow the sorrow to release with each falling tear, cleansing my soul. The journey that lies ahead of me will be challenging. It's a journey I'm not 100% ready for, but I know I need to go. I let the sorrow roll through me and then out of me. The tree root slowly pops out of the ground to not startle me and brushes my hand. It is a soft gesture, but it means the world to me.

"Don't cry, loved one. You will always be with us in spirit." the soft voice echoes in my mind.

"As you will always be with me in spirit," I whisper.

I allow several more minutes to pass, giving myself a few more minutes. I stand up, feeling ready. I slowly wander back to the cafe. I feel much better yet terrible at the same time. I don't think the pain of leaving will fade just like that. However, the comfort the trees gave me made things easier. I know I have such a big responsibility, and I'm okay with that. I wipe the last tear from my eyes, and I slowly smile. I remember as if it was yesterday that I cringed away from anything to do with being in the spotlight, but now, here I am, and my life will primarily be in the spotlight. It just wasn't the proper spotlight, I guess. I didn't belong, and I knew it deep in my soul. I think that's why it wasn't so difficult to accept the truth. I see a rock on the side of the road, and I kick it the rest of the way back to the cafe. With each step that I take, I feel lighter and lighter.

I make the long climb up the stairs, exhaustion consuming. I wander into my room and look around, checking that I have everything I need for tomorrow. Everything looks in order, so I slowly walk to the bed and pull back the covers. I climb in and pull the covers back over me. I lay down, and sleep overtakes me. Tomorrow, my life will change.

I'm in the forest where there are many different kinds of trees. It is so beautiful. The vibrant colors of life here dance as the trees sway in the soft breeze.

"Hello, Alona." A soft voice behind me.

I stiffen. I know that voice. I have heard it once before in a dream. I slowly turn, and there my parents are. A smile breaks across my face. I stay still because I have no idea what I'm supposed to do. Do I rush to them to hug them? Do I bow? The lost time with them hits me in the chest like a semi-truck. I will never experience life with them outside of my dreams, and who knows how long that will last?

My mother walks towards me slowly, my father following behind her. I don't know if I will ever get used to seeing them, even if only in a dream. I meet them halfway, throwing my hands around my mother.

"My love, how are you?" My mother's soft voice rings.

"I'm good, excited, nervous, terrified, but good." I pull back and gaze at my mother's face. She is the definition of beauty. My mother has long, ash-blonde hair like mine in a long braid down her back. On her head sits a crown with such an intricate design it looks otherworldly. Her eyes are a soft hazel, and the world makes sense when I look at them. I lean forward into her embrace again, resting my head on her shoulder. My father comes up to my side and rubs my back.

"My darling, I'm so proud of you and how much you have grown in only a few days. You are taking after me!" My father says, his voice husky. I look at him and smile.

"It's hard. I went from believing that fae and magic were all make-believe to learning I have powers and need to save a kingdom I never knew existed." My voice shakes. I look at my mother and father. They radiate strength, wisdom, and power. I am nowhere close to being like them. Part of me is unsure if I will ever be.

My mother pushes my shoulders back so that she can see my face. "My love, you are so much more than you think. You are the one that has been foretold about over a thousand years ago. You will be the one that will save all of Eldermyst and bring peace back to it."

" It was foretold that a girl will rise out of the ashes from both the fae and the human land. "She will have the mark, silver strands running through her hair, just like Keijo. She will bring peace back to the land of

Eldermyst. She will be the most powerful fae that has ever existed." My father says, truth ringing in his voice.

" When I was pregnant with you, I knew that with the Dark Orians nearing, I didn't want you to be in danger, so I planned to send you to the human world, away from the Dark Orians, where you could live and grow. We had no idea that you were the one who was foretold. We had no idea of knowing until you were born. Then we saw the sign in your hair. There has never been anyone born with silver strands in their hair. We knew right away that what was foretold was indeed coming true." My mother recalls.

" I always thought it was supposed to be the child of a fae and human together. Never in a million years did I think that you, growing up in the human realm, would be what it meant." My father chuckles.

"So, my life was always destined to be this way?" I ask quietly, mulling through everything they have told me.

They nod their head in unison." No matter who you are, we love you very much and will always be right here with you." My mother places her hand on my heart. I can feel their love deep into my soul, and the realization of my truth washes over me.

"I accept," I say, closing my eyes and accepting what destiny has planned for me.

"I have been waiting for you." A deep voice echoes in my mind, not a voice I have ever heard, yet familiar at the same time.

I jolt awake. My eyes open, and I look around. I am in my bed, in my room. There is no one here.

CHAPTER THIRTY-SEVEN

Journey Begins

ALONA

We woke up early in the morning to begin our journey to Eldermyst. The sense of being on edge overwhelms me, causing me to be a little jumpy today. The unknown awaits. I'm stepping into a world where I belong, but it's still mysterious. We pile into the car that Stephanie had "borrowed" and drive towards the stables. Once we arrive, we all unload and grab our bags, throwing them on our backs. I look around at the stables, burning this place into my mind. So many good and happy memories happened here.

I can sense his impatience, and a smile grows on my face. Arion is such an impatient creature. I shake my head as I spot him huffing on the side of the stable.

"What are you smiling at?" Arion's deep voice rings in my head.

"You're the most impatient creature alive, aren't you?"

"Well, if you walk faster, maybe I wouldn't be so impatient."

I chuckle to myself. Hillary glances over at me and raises an eyebrow.

"Pterippi bond... I always get that grumpy old thing talking in my head." I nod towards Arion.

"I heard that," he grunts, pinning his ears. I suppress a smile so as not to offend Mr. Grumpy any further. I walk to his side; he nips at me, and I dodge him.

"I didn't mean it, you know that." I laugh in surrender. I reach my hand out to stroke his mane. I can feel his muscles tensing under my hand. The soft rumble of his magic shocks my senses. I know he is anxious to get back to his home. I stroke him softly, allowing his strength to seep deep into my bones. I will need it. After several moments, I glance at the others and Asher motions for us to gather.

"As you all know, we will be entering Eldermyst today. Hillary and Alona, this will be your first time in Eldermyst. Be on your guard at all times. We don't know what can be hiding in the dark shadows. Follow my orders, and we should make it to the Emerald Court in one piece."

"I understand, but boy was that a great pep talk. Thank you, Asher." Hillary teases, patting his shoulder. We all grin at her. She slowly eases into the group and comes out of her shell. It is a fantastic thing to see. He rolls his eyes and looks at me. I nod at him in understanding. I know what he is saying is true. I have no clue what to expect once we cross.

"Let's head out then." He nods back.

Asher leads the way, with Stephanie at my side and Dani, Hillary, and Elouan walking behind me. I follow him in a daze, not truly paying attention to my surroundings. I trust that, for now, Asher will make sure I am safe as we travel. This knot forms in my stomach, pulling tighter and tighter as each minute passes. Nausea rolls through me. I can feel my self-doubt on the verge of exploding inside my mind. Can I complete the journey to the Emerald Court? Am I capable enough to defeat the Dark Orians? Will my people accept me? Am I enough? A constant stream of questions overtakes my mind, and my head feels hazy. My breathing becomes shallow as I struggle to fill my lungs with air. I wish I could block out the battle going on in my mind. I know I should be aware of my surroundings, but I can't stop it. I need to sort through as much as I can before we enter into Eldermyst because there is no room for distraction in Eldermyst, as Asher has told me. One wrong move, one careless mistake, and it can cost lives.

As I finger the necklace Hillary gave me, I focus on placing one foot in front of the other. Right, left, right, left. I look over at Stephanie, and she smiles warmly. The knot in my stomach eases for a moment. I know that I am surrounded by people and creatures that will fight for me. I look back to the ground and feel weight slowly beginning to lift.

Asher stops in his tracks. I walk into his back, distracted. He whips around, "Doing this again, now are we?" He teases me.

"Sorry, I know I shouldn't be distracted." I lower my head, tucking a stray strand of hair behind my ear.

He reaches his hand out, lifting my chin to look me in the eyes. "Your life has been turned upside down, and things you thought were make-believe are real. You are being thrown into a world and a battle you know nothing about. Be easy on yourself, but remember, once we enter Eldermyst, I need you at your best."

My breath catches, and I slowly nod, not tearing my gaze from his. His hand slowly caresses the side of my face. A warm electricity sparks where his hand grazes my cheek. The more I gaze into his eyes, the more I see understanding and longing shimmering in them. I feel something there between us, like a string that pulls tighter each time moments like this happen.

"Alright, you two. We have a realm to pass into. This old lady wants to go home." Dani scolds, her hands on her hips.

Asher drops his hand, and I feel the absence of his warmth on my cheek. It feels as if the life has been sucked right out of me.

"Sorry, Dani. So Alona and Hillary, since you have never been to Eldermyst, the door is between those two large oaks." He gestures towards two massive oaks. They seem much larger than any other trees in this area. At first glance, I don't see anything there. I squeeze my eyes shut and open them, squinting in the direction where Asher gestured. Then, I saw a tiny shimmer between the two trees. It was almost as if the light had hit a drop of water right there. I slowly take one step at a time, inching towards the doorway. I can feel the energy vibrating off it, almost as a change in the atmosphere the closer I get to it.

Hillary squinted. "I don't see anything."

"Well, it is to be expected. You won't be able to see it now. Maybe you can eye it after you're surrounded by magic for some time." Stephanie places her hand on Hillary's shoulder. Hillary smiles softly. "Well, let's get this show on the road then," I say hesitantly, rubbing the back of my neck. This is happening. I am about to cross into a different realm in seconds. I swallow and wrap my arms around myself, embracing myself, trying to keep my heart from pounding right out of my chest. My gaze darts between Dani, Stephanie, Asher, and Elouan. Their smiling faces are full of excitement to return home. I envy them.

"Little Emerald, the Emerald Court is your home, too." Arion's voice is gentle in my mind.

"I know. I guess I am just worried I won't be enough. My mother left such big shoes to fill..." fear tears through my chest and wraps its hand around my throat.

"I would not have bonded with you if I believed you could not succeed. Now stop waiting around and take us home." he nudges my arm, propelling me to walk forward. I look at Asher; he quickly smiles and steps through the doorway. Then he is gone. My eyes widen, and I look around. He disappeared.

Stephanie steps up next, standing in front of the doorway. "See you on the other side." She looks back, her hair bouncing over her shoulder. Then she walks through, and she disappears as well. Arion and Aoife follow next.

I stand next to Hillary and watch each one disappear into thin air. Hillary looks at me with awe in her gaze. Dani walks up to Hillary's side, grabbing Hillary's hand. Humans cannot cross the barrier without a fae guiding them by the hand. This precaution prevents humans from accidentally entering and losing their lives. Hillary lifts a shaky hand, tucking a strand of hair behind her ear, and takes one step towards the doorway with Dani, then another, and another.

Hillary pauses and turns her head towards me, smiling. "This is where our adventure begins!" Then she steps into the doorway with Dani. They disappear like the others.

I inhale deeply and roll my shoulders. I can feel the tension building in them. I stare at the doorway, and as each moment passes, I notice it gets easier to see.

Elouan steps beside me, "My lady, it is time to go." His smile is genuine. I glance between him and the doorway, nodding.

I breathe and step through, immediately sensing the barrier's vibration. Then, there is a painful zap that runs through my entire body as if I were struck by lightning. The pain is almost unbearable, and it causes the hairs on my arms to rise. I stop, bending over, panting with the uneasy feeling rolling through me as if my stomach belly-flopped in the water. My temples are throbbing, but I'm too unsteady to lift my hand to ease the tension. I try to calm my breathing, trying to focus to get past the pain. Then I remember Hillary. My gaze darts to Hillary, leaning forward, hands on her knees, inhaling loudly. Dani said the effect of the crossing on humans is more intense than on a fae, so I can't imagine the pain she feels. I slowly stand upright so I can check on Hillary. Deep breath in, hold, then slow breath out. I sense the pressure in my temple disappearing along with the pain. My hand rises to my temples to soothe the lingering pain. I glance at Hillary, who is slowly standing up, and her eyes lock with mine.

Hillary gasps and covers her mouth. "Oh my gosh, Alona. You are stunning!"

"Um... thanks?" I shrug, lifting my hands. I glance at the others to see what suddenly made Hillary like this. My gaze catches on Stephanie, and my heart skips a beat. My jaw drops. She is breathtaking! Her long, dark hair is a rich brown that appears to shimmer in the sunlight. She radiates an ethereal glow as if it is coming from within her. The tips of her ears peek out from her hair. Her features are much more defined, yet they're mesmerizing and otherworldly. My eyes dart to Dani, with the same ethereal glow and pointed ears. She is stunning. Her hair looks even more fiery red. I lift my hands to my ears and feel the points peeking out of my hair. I have them, too!

I go to examine my hands and notice something on my left arm. There is an intricate design climbing up my arm. I turn my arm over to examine my entire arm. Starting at my pointer fingertip up to my shoulder, I see an intricate design of what looks like a tree and flowers. The tree extends up my arm. The design is so astonishing. I blink a few times, turning my arm back and forth to examine it. Why is this on my arm? I look up at Dani for answers, yet words don't seem to collect in my mouth.

She must have known what I would ask before I could get the words out of my mouth. "All High Lords and Ladies bear a mark of their court, distinguishing them from the rest and which court they belong to. The

Emerald Court mark consists of trees and flowers. That is what the High Lords and Ladies of the Emerald Court have had most association with regarding their powers."

"My parents had this mark as well? No one else has this?"

"Your parents had one very similar. And no, others won't have a mark to that extent. Someone who offers their life in service to their High Lord or Lady will receive a mark. Their mark, however, will not be as large or intricate." Dani smiles, placing her hand on my shoulder.

"What's the cause of the hold-up?" Asher calls from behind me.

I slowly turn to look at him. I'm frozen in place. This man was stunning before, but he's even more beautiful now. His eyes are dark and steely, like smoke is swirling behind his pupils. A subtle gold encircles his pupil, drawing me into his gaze. I scan the rest of him, seeing his high cheekbones, full lips, and even more muscular body than in the human realm. My mouth waters, and I swallow. I look right past him to see a pair of wings directly behind him.

Shock courses through me. "What are those behind you, Asher?" I point.

He smirks, "What are these?" He raises his hand to brush the edges of the wings.

I nod my head, still eyeing the massive wings resembling those of a bird. They are folded tightly against his back, yet I can still see the lush black feathers with golden tips shimmering in the sunlight.

"They are my wings."

"Your wings?" My brows furrow. "But only fairies and dragons have wings." My mind races a thousand miles an hour to remember what had wings in folklore or fantasy. Nowhere have I read that fae have wings.

He chuckles, shaking his head. "Are you calling me a fairy or a dragon?"

"No. No, I am not calling you that! I never knew fae could have wings, and your wings are so breathtaking," I gasp and cover my mouth. I need to shut up before I dig myself an even bigger grave.

Dani laughs loudly. "Well, some fae have wings. Faes that have wings are usually warriors."

"Some of the best warriors, I must add." Smirking, he cocks his head, examining me.

I hear Arion a few steps behind me, neigh with cheer. I quickly drop Asher's arm and spin on my heels to see what is causing the commotion. I can't believe my eyes at the sight. Arion and Aoife are glowing. The terror begins coursing through me. My heart pounds as I run towards Arion. I can sense something is happening to him, but I don't know what. I have to do something either way. Then, all of a sudden, the light grows so brightly that I must avert my gaze, throwing my arms to block my eyes, slamming my eyes shut. The next moment, I felt Arion's nose nudge my arm. I slowly peel my eyes open, worried the light might blind me, but the light has disappeared. I open my eyes completely. What I see is not what I was expecting to see at all. Shock rolls through me like waves. That is Arion, but it isn't Arion. He nudges me again, and I place my hand on his face. Hillary opens her eyes and gasps loudly.

"Yes, little emerald, it is me, and I'm okay. Your eyes are beholding my true form." I hear his voice in my mind, more ethereal now than before.

"This is you? Oh, my dear, you have wings!" My eyes venture up to his wings.

"Well, you were told I'm a Pterippi, and we have wings." His tone is filled with annoyance.

"You are beautiful. I have gotten used to seeing you as just a normal horse."

Arion huffs with irritation. "Excuse me, but I am no 'normal horse,' as you call it."

I smile, stepping back to take in his entire appearance. His black hair has an ethereal glow, and the breeze gently tousles his mane. His wings are massive. Their dark, deep, inky black feathery wisps catch the sunlight and shimmer as he stretches them out. Standing next to Arion is Aoife. Aoife is the exact opposite of Arion. She has a pearl white coat with an iridescent sheen. Though not as large as Arion's, her wings shimmer in pearly white, outlined with hints of purple. Aoife is overall slightly smaller than Arion.

I knew that things would appear different once I crossed into Eldermyst. I didn't expect it to be this shocking. Dani, Stephanie, Asher, Elouan, Arion, and Aoife are beautiful. I could stare at them all day. A song from the birds floats to my ear, much different than the songs from the birds in Claywood. I turn and scan my surroundings. The doorway to the other realm is nestled between two massive oaks, much larger than the ones on the other side. They are humming, full of life. I walk to the tree in front of me. My eyes scan the trunk, which seems to be going on forever. I place a hand on the trunk out of habit. The rough bark with soft moss patches brings me peace, leaking into my core. I close my eyes and, leaning forward, place my forehead on the trunk. Energy bursts through me like an explosion, and a dull hum rings in my mind.

"Welcome to Eldermyst High Lady." a soothing ancient voice rings in my mind. I know immediately it is the tree. Then all the trees whisper in unison, "Welcome, High Lady."

"Thank you," I mutter.

"You have a long road ahead of you, High Lady. However, you only need to call, and we will be at your service." The ancient voice says.

"You won't be able to travel with me on the journey."

"We may not be able to; however, I state that we are at your service for all trees."

"My lady, we must go," Stephanie says softly, aware I'm speaking to the trees.

"Go, High Lady. Be safe." I turn to face the group behind me.

"Okay, I'm ready." The ancient voice still ringing in my head.

"We must travel around through these mountains to remain unseen. We don't know who has sided with the Dark Orians, so we must be as precautious as possible." He nods towards the small path ahead of us. My eyes follow the path up a slope and see the sky far off. We are surrounded by massive trees that block the sky with their large canopies. It makes sense to travel along this path; nothing in the air can spot us under all the branches and leaves. Asher begins walking up a path, and I follow in step behind him, scanning my surroundings and trying to soak in as much as possible. Whispers of welcome flood my mind as we walk by the trees. The trees look more ancient and solid here, as if they have been around for thousands of years. The trunks are so broad that it would take several people to hug around them. The leaves scattered on the ground are the size of my hand.

I breathe in, and an earthy smell floods my lungs: oak, cedar, sage, moss, clove, and lavender. The smell makes my head hazy for a moment. I have never smelled anything like this. Everything is more intense here: color, smells, touch, everything. It's almost like everything is alive, including the scents. Asher told me that once. I can feel the hum in the air and know it is from the nature around us. I spot a bird perched upon a cedar branch ahead of me. It is bigger than in the human realm and is a deep navy-blue color. It ruffles its feathers and then turns to face me. The bird freezes, slowly cocking its head to the side. Its gaze is set on me.

I pause and stare back at the bird. It nods and then takes off weaving through the canopies.

"That is a linta." Elouan stands next to me, looking upwards.

"There is a lot that I need to learn." The realization falls on me that I have barely scratched this world's surface. He nods in response and begins walking up the path. My gaze follows him, and I can see the top of the mountain we have been climbing. We are almost at the top.

We reach the mountain's summit, and I stride directly to the cliff's edge. Gazing out, I behold Eldermyst. It's a breathtaking sight. I pause in my tracks, unable to move. Words fail to capture this realm's essence; it seems it has been lifted straight from my dreams. I slowly release a deep breath, and a smile flourishes.

I gaze out across the land. There are deep purple and white blooms with lavender intermingled among the flowers in a meadow that looks like it extends forever. In the distance, a river traces the meadow's edge. Birds glide overhead, and the scent of lavender caresses my nostrils. I can see small animals playfully running in the meadows. Farther off in the distance, I can see a small village. Vines intertwined with flowers look to be creeping up the walls of every building. This must be the Amethesyt Court. I'm here. I am actually in Eldermyst. I can't stop smiling at that thought.

Finally, my journey home begins.

Thank You!

Thank you so much for reading my debut novel! Please follow me on Instagram @haley.reads.34 and leave a review!

Follow Alona on her journey to Eldermyst; Book 2 will be coming in the Winter of 2024.

Made in the USA
Columbia, SC
03 July 2024